GOOD MORNING,

IRENE

Tor books by Carole Nelson Douglas

Good Night, Mr. Holmes

Probe
Counterprobe

SWORD & CIRCLET:

Keepers of Edanvant
Heir of Rengarth
Seven of Swords

GOOD MORNING,

IRENE

Carole Nelson Douglas

TOR®

A TOM DOHERTY ASSOCIATES BOOK

A Tor Book
Published by Tom Doherty Associates, Inc.
49 West 24th Street
New York, N.Y. 10010

Map illustrations by Darla Malone Tagrin
Maps by Carole Nelson Douglas

Printed in the United States of America

Library of Congress Cataloging-in-Publication Data

Douglas, Carole Nelson.
     Good morning, Irene / Carole Nelson Douglas.
       p.   cm.
     "A Tom Doherty Associates book."
     ISBN 0-312-93211-1
     I. Title.
PS3554.08237G59   1991   90-27490
813'.54—dc20   CIP

First edition: July 1991

0 9 8 7 6 5 4 3 2 1

For Harriet McDougal,
a tireless and passionate
editor and advocate

SEVEN PERCENT IS NO SOLUTION

Sherlock Holmes stood by the window staring down at Baker Street, his left shirt cuff undone. In the languid droop of his hand I could read the presence of cocaine in his veins.

To see a figure of such singular energy and dedication, one whom I had often witnessed pursuing an investigation with the eagerness of a hound on the track, to see such a man inducing lethargy into his bloodstream on the sharp silver prick of a needle was more than a friend and medical man could bear in silence.

"Holmes! Surely some suitably inspiring case is in the offing." I lowered my newspaper with a rustle. "Your retreat to a seven-percent solution seems due less to its usual spur—idleness—than to some morose turn of thought."

He turned slowly, his tall, narrow silhouette limned against the window's fog-filtered autumn daylight. "Is that a deduction, Watson, or an inquiry?"

"I would never presume to deduce your feelings, Holmes. The fact remains that despite a plenitude of cases, you cling to the hypodermic."

"Surely no crime." He fastened his cuff as he sank bonelessly into the velvet-lined armchair and regarded me with an irritatingly placid smile.

"No, not a crime," I admitted. "Any cognizant adult may purchase cocaine, morphine, opium, laudanum or other narcotic derivations at a chemist's shop; even some of my fellow physicians indulge in such substances. Yet I must object before a habit becomes an addiction."

"Oh, pooh, Watson!" He spoke without rancor. "You know that my mind requires exceptional stimulation and that true mysteries are as rare as dodoes these days."

"What of these atrocious murders of the Whitechapel streetwalkers?"

Holmes's eyelids flickered at my mention of the sensational killings that had galvanized all London that late summer and autumn.

"Mere butchery, Watson," he said, dismissing the Whitechapel Ripper, "with no more resemblance to a masterpiece of crime than your melodramatic renderings of my cases bear a likeness to Greek tragedy."

He stared toward the cluttered bookcase that housed memorabilia of his cases—or rather, toward a particular shelf upon which a certain photograph caught the tepid light. My diagnostic powers turned in a new direction.

"Is it possible, Holmes, that it is not the lack of formidable new cases but the irritant of an old one that discomfits you?"

"Speak plainly, Watson. I have merely indulged in a seven-percent solution of cocaine. I am not lost in an opium daze."

"Very well, then." I crisply folded my newspaper. "How can the trifling matter in which you untangled the King of Bohemia from the bewitching adventuress Irene Adler outrank the serial slaughter in Whitechapel?"

Holmes smiled. His eyes rested on the lovely likeness of the lady in question.

"A connoisseur of crime is no moralist, Watson. The simple misdirection of a letter, accomplished on a high enough level of government, could topple nations. The exquisite irony of identical Christmas geese could—and did—foil a daring jewel theft.* The slaughter of the geese was incidental to the problem and its solution. Mere butchery—on any scale—will never command my curiosity; it is all too common."

"Think what a man of your powers could do to rid society of such brutes, though! Certainly the police are helpless."

"The police are always helpless. But my mind will not work solely in the cause of right; it must be piqued, it must be coddled. It requires the proper problem. Often it requires the proper opponent."

"And you have lost a worthy adversary twice over," I said with a nod to the photograph. I was referring to the report of Irene Adler's death last spring, along with that of her new husband, Godfrey Norton, in an Alpine train accident.

Holmes remained silent, his hawklike profile sunk upon his chest. I was reminded of photographs of Abraham Lincoln, the melancholy American president who presided over that nation's bloody Civil War. When Holmes glanced up again, I was struck by the roguish twinkle in his eyes.

"Ignore my carping reservations about your literary efforts, Watson! Such a drama you concoct from the simple fact: Irene Adler flees England with the photograph of herself and the King of Bohemia still in hand.

"Your romantic soul assumes that her promised silence on his unprincely behavior cannot assuage that royal person's wounded heart at the loss of the woman he would have made his mistress but not his queen," Holmes declaimed derisively.

"Well, Watson, such a bittersweet resolution would satisfy Robert Louis Stevenson, but you do not stop there; no, you further propose that the world's only consulting detective has also fallen under the lady's spell and that he—myself—pines

---

*Holmes refers to "The Adventure of the Blue Carbuncle," in which he recovered the Countess of Morcar's fabulous gem.

at the fact of her absence and apparent death. Bravo, Watson;
it shall make a fine play. Perhaps you can title it *Heloise and
Holmes.*"

"Fine for you to jest, but surely you are not pleased to have
been outwitted by the lady."

"The King of Bohemia was right in one respect. She had a
soul of steel. I admit to relishing our duel and would deign to
say we fought to a draw. If she won, it was not by much,
Watson, not by much. And besides—"

Holmes's long, flexible fingers lifted from the side table a
heavy gold snuffbox of exquisite workmanship. "—His Maj-
esty was sufficiently satisfied with the results to send me a
handsome gift beyond the gold he paid for my services. No,
Watson, my attempts to escape ennui are not due to romantic
causes. It is obvious that your own mind leans in that
direction . . . were you not lurking at the window after the
recent visit of Miss Mary Morstan, hmm?"

"How could you surmise that, Holmes? You went out
immediately."

"Ah, but I looked up from the street, my friend." He spoke
on before I could muster any defense. "Besides, I lack no
cases. Observe my desk. It overflows with communications,
including some from François Le Villard of the French
detective service. I am lending him assistance in the vexing
matter of a will. He returns the courtesy by translating my
trifling monographs into French."

"Someone else is recording your cases?"

"Easy, Watson, dear fellow. No one else is recording my
investigations. You have sole, if inaccurate, jurisdiction over
that portion of my life and work. I have penned some pieces of
my own, however—monographs on matters that intrigue me:
the one hundred and forty varieties of tobacco ash; methods
of tracing footsteps; manufacture marks of leading hatters,
mad or otherwise; the trademarks of a secret international
society of master criminals; the arcane history of pocket
watches, whose commonplace faces can tell the astute inves-

tigator far more than the time . . . But I bore you, Watson. My ramblings no doubt arise from a state of lamentably altered consciousness, while I wallow in romantic mourning and such utter idleness that I can hardly choose which project to attack next."

"Enough, Holmes!" said I, taking up my newspaper again as a shield against this relentless pricking of my poor imaginative bubbles. I should have known better than to think that my detective friend could suffer such blows to the heart as mortal men feel.

Chapter One

LIFE AFTER DEATH AND
OTHER INCONVENIENCES

⁓❦⁓

The tragic and premature death of my friend Irene
Adler was perhaps the most difficult circumstance of her life.

Dying while still young held a certain romantic, even
operatic, appeal for a nature such as hers, with its keen sense
of the dramatic. She eagerly scanned the London, Vienna
and Prague newspapers, lapping up the homage of her
obituaries with unconcealed glee.

"Listen to this from the *Times*: 'possibly developing into
the age's supreme dramatic soprano . . . a voice as darkly
velvet as the finest Swiss chocolate, suited to the most
melting renditions of Lieder since these classic songs' compo-
sition. As Sarah Bernhardt's Divine Voice elevates the spoken
word, so the late Irene Adler's dusky soprano enthroned the
sung syllable.'

"Why could I not have garnered such perceptive reviews
when I was alive?" she demanded. "And I don't fancy that
'possibly.'"

Although the news of Irene's—and her bridegroom,
Godfrey Norton's—demise in an Alpine train wreck was as
greatly exaggerated as was Mr. Twain's adventure into pre-
sumptive quietus a decade later, at first it seemed the ideal
escape from an awkward situation. Now, in the summer of

1888, after the Great Adventure, it was proving merely inconvenient.

I had joined Irene and Godfrey at their villa in Neuilly, a charming village near Paris, to indulge in a period of self-congratulatory elation.

Numerous champagne flutes were lifted by the newlyweds; I myself frown on alcoholic beverages. (In France, I admit, it is hard to frown on anything, which is no doubt why that country has such a wicked reputation.)

We toasted their marriage; we saluted Irene's successful escape from London, and her continued possession of the photograph of herself with the King of Bohemia despite all attempts to wrest it away from her. Even I lifted glass and eyebrows in the hush that always followed mention of the name of our esteemed opponent, the consulting detective of 221B Baker Street.

We toasted, too, Irene's virtuoso hunt for Marie Antoinette's famed Zone of Diamonds, a floor-length girdle of knuckle-sized stones now absorbed into the workshops of Tiffany & Company. These were emerging anonymously one by one in brooches and dog collars adorning the world's wealthiest and loveliest bosoms and necks—some of the latter actually canine, such are the lavish ways of our day.

Irene's own souvenir of the long-lost bauble—a twenty-five-carat diamond in the old French cut that would serve as a ring or convert to a pendant—blazed gloriously at her throat on formal occasions.

Aye, there was the rub, as our Bard put it long ago in a different context. The diamond burned her throat like a fiery badge of mingled triumph and despair.

For she was mute to the world. The erroneously reported death—the Nortons had missed the fatal train, upon which they had reserved a compartment—had stilled Irene's singing career more effectively than had the king two springs before, when he had caused her summary dismissal from the Prague National Opera.

The magnificent gemstone, won by her own wit and no mere man's favor, could not be flaunted on the stage, where her performing sisterhood flashed the booty of their offstage labors in millionaires' boudoirs.

All the belated appreciation of her art rang hollow. Expeditions to the fitting rooms of Worth or Paquin could not console Irene for the loss of her work, her fame, her very identity. She bought gowns and boots and hats like a fiend in that first flush of escape, of triumph, of wealth that had been beyond supposing when she and I, the late Parson Huxleigh's impoverished daughter Penelope, had shared humble rooms in London's Saffron Hill district.

Yet none of these glorious gowns could appear on stage. When Irene faced French society, it was as "Madame Norton," the unknown wife of a transplanted English barrister, not as Irene Adler, the American-born opera singer whose beauty of voice and visage had brought her worldwide recognition and adulation. Indeed, should anyone have recognized Irene—and she took an actress's care with her coiffure and clothing that no one should—she would have denied herself so convincingly as to lay her past to rest even more deeply.

As for her more subtle reputation as a puzzle-solver, that was left as far behind as were Saffron Hill and Baker Street.

Irene Adler—my friend and former chamber-mate, retired opera singer, one-time amateur detective, erstwhile actress—had all to which a woman of thirty could aspire: a handsome and devoted husband, money enough to live comfortably for some time, undiminished beauty and a wardrobe with which to embellish it; in short, she had unlimited time on her pretty, piano-playing hands . . . and nothing whatsoever to do.

Even mock Death does have its sting.

Chapter Two

FALSE PRETENSES

❧

"**Irene, have** you gone mad?"

She was flinging shawls, shoes and bloomers from the deep drawers beneath her bedchamber wardrobe.

"Mad?" A flushed face lifted from her labors. "Of course I have gone mad. How could I have purchased so many things that I cannot find the only items I wish to locate?"

She recommenced pawing through a writhing mass of ribbons and corset laces with the frenzy of Lucifer—the black cat she had given me—worrying a rug into the proper tangle for a nap. That beast joined the fray even as my thoughts evoked him, his claws snagging snakes of flying laces.

"Irene, please. *Calmez-vous, s'il-vous-plaît.*" My use of French always caught her attention, perhaps because my accent was so dreadful.

"I do *not* please to be calm, and your French is not soothing, Penelope. If anything, it is inciting. Oh, where are the blasted things? Just when I need them so desperately!"

I joined her and the wretched cat on the Aubusson rug, on which sunlight splashed as if onto warming pond water, and tried to tidy the rejected articles of clothing.

"Oh, leave it! You are not a maid, Nell," Irene objected in a way foreign to her.

I quieted. "Perhaps if I were, I would have more to do."

"I'm sorry." Her hands clapped contritely to her face for a moment. When she eyed me again, peering over her fingertips as over the scalloped rim of a fan, rueful amber-brown eyes begged forgiveness. "I took lunch with Sarah Bernhardt today and—"

"Sarah Bernhardt!"

Irene smiled. "You pronounce that name as if it were 'Marquis de Sade.' She is only an actress."

"She is a scandal beyond her profession! How can you consort with such a woman, Irene? She has taken dozens of lovers . . . some of whom last but a day. She is beneath you!"

Irene's eyes flashed like molten gold, heated enough to incinerate the footlights had she been before them. "Sarah is a consummate performer. We have much in common. At lunch we compared notes, so to speak, on our vocal techniques. Sarah attacks words as I attack F sharps; she is a wonder."

"How did you meet this immoral creature?"

Irene's head shook impatiently. "I introduced myself. Then . . . we were fast friends."

"Introduced yourself! Surely not. You cannot reveal your identity."

"I identified myself as Madame Norton, an American who has sung in the States and who is an admirer of Mademoiselle Bernhardt. Don't pout, Nell; it is all true."

"All but your admiration of that awful woman, I hope! I cannot believe that you, who refused to use your profession as a royal road to men's beds, would deign to make her acquaintance."

"Bernhardt is an artist first; she chooses and refuses men as fancy takes her. She is the first actress from the Comédie Français to form her own company and tour internationally. She is a force unto herself; perhaps she finds the concentrated attentions of a single man debilitating to her career and shares herself among many in order to devote herself to none. There is much to be said for turning the tables on the male sex."

"Irene." I was speechless beyond intoning her name. Lucifer had settled in a swath of sunlight to observe us with the calm, approving gaze of a libertine, a role he doubtless played to the hilt on his nightly prowls. I shuddered for the genteel, unsuspecting female cats of Neuilly.

Irene patted my hand. "Don't fret. Godfrey need not worry. Ordinary, middle-class marriage can be enthralling with an exceptional man. But I judge Sarah Bernhardt by no standards save her own. What did the King of Bohemia say of me to Mr. Holmes? That I had a 'soul of steel.' So does Sarah, only hers is cut steel! That is why I wish to find my old walking boots. We have an assignation on the Boulevard tonight."

Irene sighed with satisfaction as her hands at last pulled the desired boots—and the dark serge shapes of her male "walking clothes"—from the abyss of the drawer.

"A bit somber for Gay Paree," she complained. "Perhaps Sarah can find me more-dandyish attire in the theater wardrobe—though not too effeminate. That would give the game away."

Irene held the musty old things to her bodice and smiled dewily, as if crushing velvet and damask to her bare skin.

"Irene, you are not . . . you and this woman are not walking out as men this evening? Surely?"

"Of course!" She snatched up a brush and began cleaning the frock coat until Lucifer blinked his green eyes in a whirlwind of dust motes and decamped. I sneezed.

"Oh, Nell, even your sneeze sounds disapproving. This will be a *petite* adventure, that is all. Sarah has never gone out 'en homme' in public; it is quite a necessary exercise for her acting. Besides, respectable women are not commonly welcome in the great cafés of Paris, and I am eager to see these boulevard wits in action."

What could I do? Irene was her own woman, to say the least. She left the cottage at four o'clock in the guise of a British gentleman, leaving a message for Godfrey that she would return by seven.

Her eyes danced as she tipped her glossy top hat and flourished her cane at the door. The coachman, having been summoned to the front gate, inquired where "Monsieur" wished to go.

"To the devil," I whispered as I watched Irene depart in the open landau, looking for all the world like a young gentleman about town.

Godfrey came home at six. As exquisite as was Irene's young-gentleman guise, the sight of Godfrey made one aware of the noble reality of the sex she aped.

He was tall, nearly six feet, raven-haired, and possessed of excellent manners as well as good sense. The regularity of his features and his impeccable dress often earned him the epithet of "dashing," but it was the acuity and kindness in his gray eyes that had won my undying admiration. At my parson father's death, I was left an orphan. Had I had a brother, I could not have wished a more ideal candidate than Godfrey.

He left his hat and stick in the hall, then glanced into the music room, where the antique grand piano lay open. Irene was wont to spend hours in this room, playing melancholy Grieg upon the worn ivory keys.

"How was your day?" I asked with sisterly duty.

"I made some acquaintances among the Académie Française. There appears to be need on this side of the Channel for an attorney with a knowledge of British law, especially in regard to the performing arts."

"With your mastery of French, you are ideal to set up such a practice, Godfrey."

"Would that I had a similar mastery of French law!" Godfrey laughed and rolled his eyes in a mock-Gallic way. "No wonder Molière satirized the profession; it is a labyrinth of ancient custom, of amendments enacted and rescinded by each new wave of revolution . . . and of outright self-interest."

He glanced around, his eyes resting first on the dreadful parrot, Casanova, cracking seeds in his foot in his window-side cage; on Lucifer, crouched beneath Casanova's abode with obvious hopes; on Sophie, our stout maid, who was delivering a late tray of tea, and lastly on me again.

"She has gone out," I said, handing him Irene's note.

"Oh? It can't be the dressmaker's at this hour."

"Nor the hairdresser's. It is the . . . costumier's, I fear."

"Irene planning to act again? She could, you know, under a pseudonym. Her French is exquisite, thanks to her operatic language studies."

He sounded so approving—and relieved—that I loathed to disabuse him of his innocent fantasy, but I did. "She is with Sarah Bernhardt," I blurted.

He showed no alarm. "An excellent associate for a rising foreign-born actress."

"They are strolling the Boulevard. In male dress. To-gether."

"Ah. Until seven, she says." Godfrey refolded the note and took the cup of tea I offered, although in my agitation I had forgotten to add his customary sugar.

"You are not shocked?"

"Why should I be? The second time I saw Irene, she was so appareled. The sight of her lifting the homburg to release those waves of chestnut hair remains one of my fondest moments."

"It was one of my most mortifying," I confessed. "Although you knew me as your typist, you had not known Irene then, save for the quarrel of your first encounter. You had no notion of her ability to alter her looks and dress so radically. I dreaded what you should think of her bold disguise, even though we owed to it our escape from Bohemia and from the king's agents."

He smiled with that older-brother air that annoys as much as reassures me. "My dear Nell, pardon me for not telling you exactly what I thought of Irene when she revealed herself to me in that carriage; some things are best kept between man and wife."

"I–indeed," I rushed on. "It is not for me to inquire into your private affairs, that is to say, into your domestic business . . . er, your intimate—" Everything I said treaded nearer to indelicacy.

Godfrey laughed and sipped his unsweetened tea. "Irene must have her adventures, Nell; marriage will not change that, nor will locale. I am glad that she is finally venturing into her new surroundings. It is nothing for me to start again in a foreign land; I was not known publicly in my own. I can practice law here, even visit London fairly anonymously. Irene—" he frowned and stirred a small silver spoon in his cup to better blend the absent sugar "—Irene has given up a great deal to marry me, to leave London: her career, her very identity."

"She would do it again, a thousand times!" said I, eager to reassure Godfrey that Irene's restlessness owed nothing to her domestic state. "If only—"

"Say it, Nell. You know that I rely upon you for the truth."

I blushed. "I am not convinced that performing is a proper avenue for Irene just yet. The Paris theater bristles with petty jealousies and corruption, even more so than ours at home. A respectable married woman—"

"I thought Irene had served notice that she would never be 'a respectable married woman'."

"Surely she did not warn you so also?"

"But she did, and I quite approve. Respectability often cloaks the ugliness of hypocrisy, Nell. If Irene is free to be herself, she will earn the respect of those whose opinions really matter."

"Then perhaps you will not find my next suggestion out of order."

"Which is?"

"That you keep an eye open among your new associations for some small assistance that Irene can give you, in her old way of . . . looking into . . . matters."

"You mean that I should find her work as an inquiry agent? Not a bad notion, Nell, although the kind of law that is practiced across borders and language barriers is tedious, unexciting stuff. Land and coin transactions, titles, inheritances. A missing heir is the tastiest bone I'm likely to turn up. Tame work, after Irene has unearthed an executed queen's diamond girdle and escaped a vengeful king."

"Still, it would not hurt to find something to occupy her."

"You amaze me, Nell." Godfrey finished his sugarless tea without complaint. "I thought you disapproved of Irene's investigative ways."

"There is much I disapprove of and cannot change," I replied. "I disapprove of idleness more, for therein lie the seeds of mischief."

"Perhaps Sarah Bernhardt will draw her into a tangle," he mused. "Irene is as curious as a cat; she cannot resist a locked door or a buried body."

I could not help glancing at Lucifer, whose cream-dotted whiskers were disappearing beneath the tea table.

Then Irene came in, boot-heels rapping the slate hall floor, cheeks pinked by the evening air. A small, dark cigarette was clasped between her pale lips. She cast herself into a chair, her trousered legs stretched to the fire that Sophie had lit earlier.

"What a frolic!" she began, regaling us with chapter and verse of her excursion with Sarah Bernhardt to the cafés. The recital took some minutes, only ending when Irene rose to mimic the needle-thin Sarah lounging among the dandies, and herself accosting an acerbic wit who had challenged her to a duel for the crime of topping his witticisms.

"A duel! That is going too far," I said weakly.

Irene flourished her cane like a sword. "What an experience for an actress! We women are never allowed to execute—" Irene lunged fiercely with her blade at the fireplace poker—"the adventurous parts, not even in operatic trouser roles. Sarah could be my second. Don't worry, Nell, these boulevard wits are great cowards; one cannot sit about and drink absinthe all day and cast *bon mots* into the air like seed to pigeons and still have any sang-froid left for duels."

Irene lounged again on the chair. "But duels are not my interest, and I fear that these boulevard wits shan't be for long, either—shallow, vain, foolish souls whose monocles magnify their own images rather than the world around them."

She crossed a leg to reveal pale spats. "Well, Godfrey, what did you do today?"

"I didn't see enough of you," he answered promptly.

Irene laughed and ran her fingers through her loosened waves of hair. Their eyes feasted on each other with such sudden intensity that I excused myself and retired to the music room.

At dinner an hour and a half later, Irene shone like a diva in one of her bare-shouldered Worth gowns. Her cheeks were flushed and her mood mellow, an effect I attributed less to her hours in the public company of Sarah Bernhardt and more to a private hour with Godfrey Norton, thank God.

Chapter Three

WHAT THE FISHERMEN FOUND

❧

I f a s showy a hothouse bloom as Irene Adler, now Madame Norton, suffered the pangs of transplantation, a shy violet such as myself underwent its own quiet attack of wilt.

I had not felt so displaced since I had become suddenly unemployed in London in 1881. The green girl whom Irene found faint from hunger and anxiety outside Wilson's Tea Room and swept under her brown faille wing had matured into an independent woman who had supported herself as a typist for the barristers of the Inner Temple—until now.

Although Irene insisted that the proceeds from selling Marie Antoinette's Zone of Diamonds to Charles Lewis Tiffany be divided three ways, Godfrey and I knew that all of the money was rightfully hers. Godfrey at least had a claim through his late, unlamented father's original possession of the jewels (John "Black Jack" Norton had been a scoundrel even his wife and son had disowned), if not by marriage to Irene, matters that neither of them would consider relevant.

I had no claim except Irene's generosity, and I was ever an ill recipient of charity. So I chafed at my idle state, but I could not soon repair it. Although I wrote and read French, I spoke far less Frenchily than the raucous Casanova, whose Parisian accent embellished scurrilous lines of Baudelaire.

A typist who requires a translator that she may function is no boon.

I felt as stranded in Ile-de-France as I had been on London's teeming streets seven years earlier, dazed by foreign sights and sounds, dreadfully afraid that I was somehow being found wanting again.

Friendship had bonded me to Irene—that, and the notion that I was of some use to her. Now I had a rival even in that role, a red-haired broomstick of an actress who cast her sinuous coils around admirers like one of the gigantic parlor snakes she kept in her exotic rooms on Boulevard Péreire.

I mentioned none of these fears to Irene or Godfrey. Spinsters grow used to feeling redundant, I suspect, and to saying nothing.

Yet I hoped that Irene's infatuation with Sarah Bernhardt would fade. They were too much alike; Madame Sarah's erratic flame would ever vie with Irene's steadier radiance.

"You have been quite as confined to quarters of late as Casanova," Irene observed one morning as we lingered over breakfast. Godfrey had left for the day.

"There's not much occasion for an outing in Neuilly," said I.

"But there is all Paris!" Irene's sweeping gesture threatened to overturn her teacup, filled with vile black coffee in the American fashion. Now that she had means, I had discovered that cigarettes were not Irene's only vice.

"Paris is a day's expedition, and I do not care to risk myself or my French in such a frenetic capital."

"Then we shall bring Casanova as translator." Irene rose to feed that devouring beak the last of her croissant.

"Gracious, no! Should a Frenchwoman overhear his vile doggerel—"

"She would recite it along with the bird. Paris is not the bland, boiled-shirtfront city that London is. Paris is fresh, inventive, sophisticated—"

"Dissolute," I finished.

"Daring," Irene said in reproval. Her eyes sparkled a challenge. "Where would *you* like to go in Paris? Name a destination and it is yours."

"Not Montmartre."

"Of course not. Much too . . . Bohemian."

"Indeed. Nor the Boulevard, not even in broad daylight."

"Naturally not. Much too . . . Baudelaire-ian."

"And I have seen Notre Dame—"

"Much too . . . Romanish."

"You know what I would really like to see, Irene?"

"What is left?" she murmured to the odious bird, blowing a kiss at its huge yellow beak.

"Pretty bird, pretty bird," the creature squawked.

"Bel oiseau, bel oiseau," Irene crooned until the parrot cocked its head and repeated the French phrase with irritating success.

"I should like to stroll the Left Bank," I plunged.

"The Left Bank! But, Nell, that is more Bohemian than Montmartre and the Boulevard put together."

"I've heard that booksellers set up shop on the riverbank near Notre Dame. I should very much like to look for antique volumes there."

"Bibles, no doubt."

"I do know that *bibliotheque* is the French word for 'library'. I wish to peruse this street-side library."

"Bibelot is the French for 'bauble'; perhaps we can finish with a stroll down the Rue de la Paix."

"Done!" said I, who had not expected to spend a dry two hours amongst musty volumes without trading Irene a jaunt into the glittering storefronts of the milliners and jewelers. So we set out.

Autumn was a distant thought on the horizon that August day. Paris lay tranquil under robin's-egg skies, most of its

denizens having gone to the country on holiday. The Seine
reflected Notre Dame's famous towers in a wriggling fashion
that resembled the work of those demented Impressionist
paint hurlers.

We ambled along the Left Bank, visiting dried-up antiquar-
ians who sold pieces of the past volume by volume. Their
customers seemed universally attired in long coats, misshapen
hats and too-short pants. Despite the unsavory company, I
plunged into the bookstalls. My eager fingers (far cleaner
than those of my fellow bibliophiles) soon were dusted with
gilt from rich old pages. I quite felt a child again, exploring
treasure boxes in the Shropshire parsonage lumber room.

Irene trailed me, playing the indulgent nanny and stopping
now and again to skim some elderly theatrical memoir. I was
quite aware that this outing was intended to humor me. After
deep immersion in a Douay Bible—much too Romanish
indeed; "blessed are the meek" had been rendered as "blessed
are the debonair"—I turned to tell Irene that she was free to
scamper directly over to the Avenue Filthy Lucre.

But Irene no longer followed me.

I turned again, feeling a mild thrill of panic. How would I
ask these shriveled book vendors, whose French was no doubt
whistled through toothless gums, where my companion had
gone?

"Oh, dear," I said, comforted by the sound of an English
voice, even my own.

I looked up and down the avenue. Below the wall, on the
walkway edging the river itself, the odd stroller was visible,
but none wore a red felt bonnet with an upstanding crimson
ostrich plume. Oh! how would I describe Irene's garb in my
crippled French? I was lost beyond *chapeau*. *La plume de ma
tante* did not seem to suffice for an ostrich plume.

I had removed my gloves before examining the dusty
volumes, for I hadn't wished to dirty the white kid. Now my

bare hands flew to my face, where icy fingers chilled my fevered cheeks. I turned again, ready to screech Irene's name publicly, like a fishmonger, if need be.

At last!—the very bonnet, bobbing along down by the river. I hastened to find stairs leading below. Irene stood on a stone embankment by the gentle, lapping Seine.

"Irene!" I called from above.

She turned with an expression of intense distraction, even satisfaction. I had not seen her so vibrant recently, save in Godfrey's company.

"Come down, Nell!" she commanded joyfully. "Watch your step! They've found something in the water."

I paused in my instant obedience. "A dead fish, likely."

Irene was craning her neck like a cockney gawker. "Oh, it looks a great deal bigger than that. Do hurry, Nell! I think it's a body. I don't want to miss it."

"Irene, come back! Irene . . . well, you shall certainly not approach those rude men unchaperoned."

Once I had committed to the stairs, my feet stuttered down the risers, rushing me as if eager toward a knot of rough-looking men crowding the embankment.

Nearer the water, the picturesque river's native stench reared its noxious head. I took one great breath and determined to inhale through my mouth thereafter. This resolve lent my voice the accents of an adenoidal child.

"I-reend. I-reend. Please wade, *wade!*"

She did not wait for me, and fortunately did not take my last instruction literally, but paused just before her black kid boots met the murky waves that licked the stone.

The men huddled over some object—seemingly a tangle of netting. I breathed easier, but not through my nose; apparently we were merely witnessing a submerged log being dragged ashore.

Then the men, wet to their knees, struggled back, and I

saw a fish-white human form rolled up onto the sopping pavement.

In a country parsonage it is not uncommon to view death at close quarters; certainly I have seen my share of village corpses arranged for burial. Funerals were as frequent among my father's flock as christenings, life and death maintaining a particularly noticeable balance in a small parish.

Yet something about death by water blends the most awful aspects of mortality with remembrances of the church's joyful, liquid welcome of each soul to the world. It seems a sacrilege, this fatal, final, unnatural baptism; at least so it has always struck me.

The men were grunting in particularly guttural French (for all French is guttural; so much for the language of "love"). A fellow in a navy blue jacket and fisherman's sweater straightened from studying the corpse to regard Irene and myself.

His gesture was as short and sharp as his words. He ordered us away. I gladly turned to comply, but Irene swept a fist to her hip, brushing aside a layer of gentility as another woman might lift her veil. Her voice dropped into throaty French. I had before me a soubrette from the Comédie Française, long familiar as a shockingly bold Paris type.

"Ah, Monsieur," she trilled. Rapid French followed—coaxing, bullying, flirting. The Fisherman of Rome, the Pope himself, could hardly have brought himself to deny this charming, cajoling *gamine* who had materialized beside me. Irene's hands spoke as quickly as her voice—pointing to the corpse and the opposite shore, lifting to the watered-silk heavens as she shrugged or laughed, clapping once when an answer pleased her.

The men might as well have tried to stand mute on Judgment Day. There was no mercy. Irene skinned them of their testimony as she might peel a grape at table.

In the end, two of them escorted us back up the path, their rough hands, redolent of cod-liver oil, at our elbows.

"*Merthi, Monthieurs,*" I murmured as our escorts left us on the upper path.

Irene inhaled happily and stroked her kid gloves smooth over her knuckles, wriggling long fingers as if anticipating a piano exercise. No such wholesome occupation was planned.

"I must go to the Paris morgue, Nell."

"The morgue! Is nod *one* corpsth a day suffithient, Irend?"

"You know, your French accent is much improved when you breathe through the mouth. I noticed that when you thanked the fishermen. You must exercise so, as a singer does. But first, how to storm the morgue? Parisian authorities are likely to be most uncooperative to English ladies wishing to view the remains of dead strangers."

"*You* are Americand," I said indignantly, forgetting to breathe normally. "*I* amb English, and I cerdainly do nod intend to visid the Parith morgue."

"Oh, but you must! You are crucial to the identification. I fear you stood too far back here to make a reliable witness."

"Idendification of what!? Widness to what? He was . . . is . . . a dead French fitherman."

"Oh, no. Not French. Decidedly not French. Dead, yes, but not French. And not a fisherman, I think, though his dress was crude."

"Irend. I wished a simble stroll along the book boodths. I did nod antidipade hurling to the riverbank to view a corpsth and then being dragged from Seine-thide to morgue!"

"But you did *not* view the corpse, Nell, or you would never question my need to examine it more fully. We have seen one like it before."

"We? Before? Whend? Irend, whend have we viewed a corpsth before?"

She gazed at the chestnut trees shading our path. Below us,

the men grappled with the body; behind us, pages of old books rustled like leaves of dry grass.

"London. Chelsea. September of eighteen eighty-two, I believe, although I shall have to consult your very useful diaries for the precise date. We saw the dead man, still dripping from immersion in the Thames, lying most docilely upon Bram Stoker's dining-room table."

Chapter Four

EXHUMED FROM THE DIARY OF A PARSON'S DAUGHTER

❧

Florence Stoker was accounted a beauty, but next to my friend Irene Adler, she was merely pretty.

Both women's faces radiated the assurance that beauty gives its possessors, but introspection, not intelligence, animated Florence Stoker's eyes. The delicate eyebrows sketched by such diverse artists as Edward Burne-Jones and Oscar Wilde seldom lifted or fell with vital emotion, not even when her young son hung bawling from her skirts, as he did at that moment—until a servant pried him loose and took him upstairs.

An odor of seawater and sewage mingled with the dim chamber's scents of beeswax and gaslight. I stood in the Stoker front parlor at 27 Cheyne Walk feeling as needful of clinging as young Noel, yet too irrevocably adult to admit the impulse. Instead, I studied the two lovely women so seldom in proximity—anything to avoid regarding the thing on the dining-room table.

Irene leaned over it, rapt, one hand pressing her scarlet bonnet ribbons to her breast so they would not impinge upon the corpse, ribbons that swayed in the evening gaslight like strands of dripping gore.

Yet only water beaded the waxed tabletop. And only water blotted the figured carpet with goutlets as black as blood.

"How interesting!" Irene mused, embarrassingly intent. "This man was so suicide-bent that he struggled with you in the water until you overpowered him? But he is old, spare . . . and *you*, my dear Bram—"

Happily, her words directed my attention to someone among the living. I regarded Bram Stoker with the same strange remoteness from which I viewed that scene so like a newspaper's lurid illustration.

Bram Stoker was at the prime of life: a mammoth man, nearly six foot six and as broad as a bear. He stood dripping on his wife's cherished carpet, looking so forlorn that each droplet might be a tear shed for the life he had been unable to preserve. Water had washed his features of all color and rusted his bright copper hair and beard to a dull, wet luster. He and the corpse that lay upon the table shared a pallor his wife's rice-powdered face could merely imply.

"Drowning panics many victims." He shook his soggy head. "The poor soul took me for some demonic pursuer. He fought me as if death were a salvation. His strength was phenomenal."

"Perhaps you should begin at the beginning." Irene bowed even deeper over the body to inspect its left hand as Bram Stoker, manager of the day's greatest actor, Henry Irving, told his dramatic tale.

"I was traveling this evening by steamboat to the Lyceum, as I do on theater nights. The hour was shortly after six o'clock, that fleeting time when twilight paints the clouds pastel and chars the trees and rooftops to silhouettes. I stood by the rail savoring the dusk. Then, to my amazement, a figure vaulted the barrier and plunged into the dark water. I threw off my coat and dived after him.

"I could see his white-haired head bobbing on the waves. By now the sunset had tipped the wave crests with points of pink St. Elmo's fire. How oddly beautiful it was, though the water was icy and the current vicious. I reached him quickly, but the fellow kept his face fastened to the water despite my attempts to propel him otherwise. He seemed some . . . mad dog, drinking down his own death."

We gazed at the still and sopping recumbent form. How difficult to imagine the frantic strength that had allowed this scrawny man to resist a Goliath such as Bram Stoker, bent on rescuing him.

"They tell me," Mr. Stoker went on, "that we struggled for five minutes before onlookers could haul us both back aboard the *Twilight.*"

"Ah," Irene murmured, acknowledging the dramatic irony of the steamer's name.

"Indeed." Stoker's theatrical instincts were as quick as hers. "A French doctor nearby examined him and pronounced him dead, but to me he seemed merely insensible, so I brought him here and sent for my physician brother in hopes—"

His wife muffled a cry. "Oh, Bram, anyone of sense would have known the wretch was already dead! Can you never accept the inevitable?"

A silence deeper than death lingered between the pair.

Irene, undisturbed, elevated the dead man's left hand on the point of her right forefinger. "The middle finger is missing. How odd."

"He is—was—a sailor, by the reefer jacket we removed," Stoker said. "Many lose fingers—and more—in a long life at sea."

"But the *middle* finger. Is that not . . . interesting?"

"Really, Miss Adler." Florence Stoker's voice drenched us like ice water. "You show as much appetite for the macabre as my husband. Perhaps that is why he insisted you view the remains."

Irene lowered the lifeless hand to the polished mahogany, a surface so glossy that a ghostly reflection seemed to reach up to take it.

"Perhaps we share an interest in the mysterious," she said

mildly. "The mysterious is often macabre and always theatrical. Dr. Stoker"—she turned to the tall quiet man who waited by the sideboard—"was the victim dead by the time he was brought here?"

The physician advanced with a soldier's firm step. "I assumed not and did my utmost to revive him. Drowning's an ambiguous death, Miss Adler. It submerges life subtly, unlike the cut-and-dried devastation of the battlefield. I did my best and failed."

"Poor man!" I couldn't help murmuring, although my sympathies lay more with the valiant brothers who had tried to save a life than the victim so sacrilegiously set upon destroying himself.

"Yes." Irene glanced at me. "He *was* poor, but he had great expectations."

"Indeed?" The doctor, polite but nonplussed by Irene's frank appraisal of the corpse, leaned closer.

"The watch fob is of far finer quality than the watch," she noted. "Either he had pawned a watch of equal value or he aspired to owning one in the future."

"Could he not have stolen the fob?"

"Of course, but hardly without the watch. And if he was vain enough to keep the fob, he would certainly have kept the timepiece. I do not wish to be indelicate, Doctor, but I see that you have loosened his shirt and singlet."

"A necessary step in my revival attempts. I apologize for subjecting ladies to the sight."

"Do not apologize! I would ask you to bare more."

"Irene!" I remonstrated. Mrs. Stoker clapped a hand over her mouth and left the room in a disapproving rustle of silk petticoats.

Irene continued, "It is only that I glimpse a rather intriguing insignia on the chest—a dark blot of some kind."

"Possibly a leech," Bram Stoker put in.

My hand flew to my mouth, but I remained. It would have

been odiously improper to leave Irene alone with three men, even though one of them was dead.

"Doctor?" she inquired.

His bushy red brows lifted at her commanding tone, but he bent to push aside the wet clothing even farther. Then he drew back, as if startled. "I say, it's a—"

I stiffened, expecting him to pluck a slick black leech from the dead man's sunken white chest.

"—a tattoo."

"So it is." Bram Stoker had joined in peering at the dead man's secrets.

Irene straightened and looked at me. "Nell, I believe you always keep a note pad and stenographic pencil upon your person. May I borrow them?"

"What . . . whatever for?"

"I must sketch this most unusual marking. It will take but a moment. Mr. Stoker, you are dripping on the subject matter of my sketch, I fear; pray step back. I shall be done in a thrice and long before the coroner's men come."

"And this is that very sketch?" Godfrey asked in our sunny, present-day parlor in Neuilly-sur-Seine.

He lifted a piece of yellowed loose-leaf from my diary, from which Irene had read to us with great effect, and looked at it.

"You are both as morbid as the brothers Stoker," said I.

"Of course, my dear Penelope!" Godfrey grinned at me, like an older brother who has just unearthed something disgusting from the herb garden. "Missing digits, arcane tattoos and a dedicated double suicide six years and several hundred miles apart would stir an archangel to morbidity."

"Today I saw only the missing middle finger on the man's

left hand," Irene said. "A tattoo, however tantalizing, is pure speculation, Godfrey. But it will not remain so, if you can introduce us into the Paris morgue to examine the body in full."

"Us?" I protested faintly.

"Come now, Nell," Irene said. "Your valuable observation skills will help determine whether these two dead men have more than their manner of death in common."

"What does it matter?" I returned. "Bram Stoker received a medal for his attempted rescue, but Irene Adler earned no reward from overseeing the sad scene at Cheyne Walk. Mrs. Stoker could never abide the house afterward, and I don't blame her."

Irene smiled. "My reward was seeing that preternaturally composed lady unravel a bit. And now, Nell, fate has thrown another mystery of the great rivers to my very feet."

"'O'," Godfrey pronounced, studying Irene's sketch of the first suicide's tattoo. "And a needlessly ornate one. Devil of a thing to have inked upon one's chest. What can it have to do with the seafaring life?"

"More important—" Irene produced an impish smile "—what can it have to do with two men's deaths?"

Chapter Five

LES INCONNUES DE LA SEINE

"**One would** think, Irene, that you were going to the opera rather than to the morgue," I remarked the next morning.

Drawing on champagne-colored kid gloves, she smiled with satisfaction, then spun in the front hall so that the tiered lace flounces of her skirt fluttered like linnets' wings. Irene's ensemble was a symphony in mauve and ecru, from pale kid boots to the lace parasol that tilted over her shoulder.

"Good cheer is always more welcome in a grim place than at a gypsy carnival," said she.

"Open umbrellas indoors are bad luck," I retorted.

"A parasol is nothing so serious as an umbrella, which is invariably large and black, like a beetle—not *petite*, dainty and quite harmless, as well as useless."

But she collapsed the contraption and rested its ivory ferrule on the hall stones, bracing it like a walking stick. From the front parlor, Casanova loosed an approving (I daresay) whistle.

"The daintiest thing under a Paris bonnet, I swear," said Godfrey, negotiating the narrow stairway at a gallop. He bowed to joust with the primroses on Irene's headgear for brief possession of her cheek.

"Then we are ready for La Morgue?"

I retained an expression of neutrality. Godfrey nodded briskly, donning his shiny beaver hat once we had preceded him outside into the late summer.

At the end of our meandering walkway, coach and coachman, called André, stood ready. Birds were trilling their tiny throats out, and bushes whispered in the breeze as the poplar tops along the main road heaved to and fro. It was all too, too utterly bucolic, to paraphrase a London acquaintance, from the thatch-roofed cottage at our back—I glanced at Casanova's window; the old beggar crowded to his cage bars, and the plump shadow of Lucifer switched its tail in the sunlight on the sill—to the vista before us of fields and sun-flushed sky.

"Really," I said. "Why forsake this idyllic retreat for a useless inquiry into the sordid death of an unknown sailor? Have you any notion of how many bodies are pulled from the Seine each year?"

"No, my dear," Irene admitted. "Have you?"

"Certainly not, but it must be . . . dozens."

"Probably hundreds," Godfrey put in as he saw us into our conveyance.

"And they are all probably still decomposing at the morgue, waiting to be claimed," I added.

"We will claim nothing but the truth," Irene promised as our carriage rattled down the rutted country lane. "We've merely an honest interest in one of these poor drowning victims. Are you sure, Nell, that you don't wish to claim a kinship? Think of the opportunity for thespian endeavor: the worried sister or cousin, brave but upon the brink of sobs!"

"Irene, please! I expect I shall be on the brink of quite a different and even more unseemly reaction." Godfrey gazed out of the coach window and whistled like a hedge lark.

But even I had to admit that Paris sat very prettily under a bonnie-blue bonnet of sky veiled in wispy clouds. The pristine spire of Sacre Coeur indicated the seedy environs of Montmartre, and Notre Dame's towers dominated the misty distance.

Cobblestones rang to our horse's hooves as our coach neared the great cathedral—a green-copper-capped, gray stone mountain rising at the prow of Ile de la Cité, the central boat-shaped island on which Old Paris had been founded. Bridges both old and new spanned the Seine's forked waters, acting as flying buttresses to the Ile de la Cité itself.

On the Left Bank, our horse clopped dutifully past booksellers' booths to the island's stern, where the grim Palais de Justice threw up its old and bloody bulwarks. The delicate spire of Sainte-Chapelle lifted from it like a pristine white plume from a rather soiled hat.

Sunlight sparkled from the stately new Hotel Dieu, its pottery chimney tops looming ahead of us like rusty lances. That same daylight did not favor the low, stone building before us. Despite its Greek pediment surmounted by gables and chimneys, La Morgue was a crude, anonymous structure hunkered on the banks of the Seine like a starving dog. From the mercurial river wafted the same fetid odor we had noted when the dead man was tugged ashore at the Ile's other end.

We all three pressed to the coach windows to gaze at this infamous structure for a sober moment.

"Not the original morgue building, of course," Godfrey said. He smiled reassuringly at me. "And certainly not where the victims of the Terror ever lay. That was the Grand-Chalet, demolished early in the century. Its function was soon moved to the Right Bank, nearer to the Louvre, and then—all too appropriately—to a vacated butcher shop on the Left Bank. This is the third location, from my reading of Paris history."

"I can quite see why nobody would want it," said I, frowning at the morgue's gruesome bulk.

"No body alive." Irene beamed upon the grim, smoke-singed pile as a miser might upon stacked gold louies. "Shall we join them?"

Ile de la Cité was thronged with seven-story buildings whose hunched mansard roofs cast us in constant shade. Irene twirled her gay parasol nevertheless. On our left, the Seine flowed by, crowded with flat barges and jaunty little "fly boats" crammed with passengers. The quayside was a low, broad road of stone, so to speak, reached by stairs from the tree-lined boulevards above. Along it people strolled, the odd idler lounged, and some poor women even scrubbed their washing, laying it to dry along the stair rail.

Near the morgue, no such homely activities thrived. Here only silence and shadow hovered over the dark water. A short, narrow bridge led to its gates. From the bridge one could glimpse an odd-looking, wide barge drawn up alongside the morgue, and men with stretchers bearing the dead to line the bottom of the boat.

"Hardly the watery way to Avalon," Irene commented. "Let us storm this unpleasant place and be done with it."

Godfrey, who had accompanied us with grave restraint thus far—a testimony to his impeccable manners—proved invaluable when we entered the building. The officious Frenchmen within were no match for his fluid mastery of the language and his even more adept command of the national love for debate and rivers of red tape.

Godfrey produced several thick papers bearing ribbons and sealing wax, the latter engraved with obscure symbols. He waved these and his hands with equal zest at the morgue-keepers we encountered—three of them, each with more numerous badges upon his person and a more pronounced sneer upon his features—until it seemed that Godfrey and his questioners were engaged in an endless, arcane duel of gestures.

At last we were led past a gate and through a series of vast, echoing chambers, each one as welcoming as a crypt. Godfrey turned to me, recognizing that unlike Irene, I stumbled rather than strode in the French language.

"I have established my connections with the French legal system and the nature of our query. Now our hosts must consult their records to determine where our particular corpse rests."

"How . . . delightful."

"Twelve corpses have been snatched from the Seine's watery arms in the past two days alone. We would not want to inspect the wrong one."

"Certainly not." I glanced at Irene, who had seemed remarkably meek during the long discussions.

She read my thought. "A fishwife on the bank may cow the Gallic fisherman; French officials are less susceptible. Observe the fate of the great French beauties during the Terror. Sometimes maidenly reticence has its uses."

My shrug concealed a shiver. This great stone pile was as cold as its silent residents.

The records chamber was a high-ceilinged horror. Our guide leafed through a massive ledger, looking as if he played St. Peter on Judgment Day. Rather than contemplate the depressing number who had died in Paris over the centuries from plague, guillotine and even, I suppose, old age, I studied the architecture.

My eyes came at last to the sole angelic image amid the empty elegance—a wall-hung plaster likeness of a young girl's face, her expression rapt, her eyes closed, yet seeming to see straight up to heaven.

Irene had spied the plaster head also. She was regarding it with an expression less uplifted than my own—rather, with a kind of disbelief, as if this innocent young visage were a marble medusa that chilled her blood.

She whispered something to Godfrey, who glanced at the bust and then froze as he imbibed its strange power. He directed our guide's attention to it.

A bored glance, a Gallic shrug, a sharp burst of French.

Godfrey looked again to the face, his features reflecting Irene's odd expression of distress.

"What is it, Godfrey?" I asked.

"She—it—is famous among *les inconnues de la Seine*. The unknowns of the Seine," he translated. "Drowning victims who are never identified."

"She drowned and was never identified? Then how can she be famous?" I demanded.

"Her fame is anonymous, but wide nevertheless," he replied. "She was found decades ago, with an expression so . . . hellishly . . . exalted that a death mask was taken from her unclaimed corpse. From that mask, thousands of plaster casts were made; everyone had to have one. She decorated cottages and drawing rooms; for a time women even used a whiter face powder in tribute to her. Then the fashion subsided, as all such enthusiasms do. The morgue still keeps her bust as a memorial."

"The expression is remarkable," I admitted. "Yet the French are shockingly bloodthirsty; I have heard that they took death masks of Louis the Sixteenth and Marie Antoinette fresh from the guillotine."

"Not only that," put in Irene, "but the same young woman who had sculpted the Bourbon royal family in pre-Revolution days was set to molding death masks of the severed heads. She has brought her handiwork to London and has set up an exhibition in Baker Street. 'Madame Tussaud's,' it is called." Irene smiled savagely. "You and I must visit it some day, when we return."

"How grotesque! I am amazed that another address on Baker Street could attract your notice, Irene, you are so taken with No. 221 B. But this girl's story is macabre, and quite sad. However violently she met death, she must not have feared the afterlife."

"How much better," Irene said, "had she not feared *earthly* life so much that she welcomed death with such visible joy. This lovely likeness is a monument to inhumanity, not to heaven, Nell. She has given up all hope. That is what much of so-called 'saintly resignation' amounts to and why I consider such virtues a sin."

I again studied the sculpture—no, the actual, dead face, preserved uncannily all these years. Those unpupiled eyes, that sad, slightly slack mouth. She could have been a seraph about to sing . . . or a ruined shop girl about to sink. Certainly she had been alive once; alive and obscure, not a curiosity for anyone to gawk upon.

I clasped my hands, suddenly aware that shadow chilled the dour old building, that stone and plaster and the endlessly lapping river water were cold comfort even to a corpse. The official crackled a stiff page of the ledger as his fingers tripped down another roll of the dead.

"Aha!" he announced. His finger stabbed a number with no name after it. A moment later he swung a huge hoop of keys from his belt and led us onward.

Now we went below to even colder climes. Shallow stairs coiled deeper and deeper into the building's dark belly, lit by oil-fed sconces that exhaled a thick smoke. Various chambers housed the dead in low-ceilinged, cellarlike rooms. We entered one and were ushered to a bier far less polished than Bram Stoker's dining table.

"How fortunate they have not yet removed the clothing," Irene said. I agreed with mute intensity. "What did you say, Godfrey, was our purported relationship to the corpse?"

"A former servant who had turned to the water trades."

"Ah." She nodded to the left hand that lay upon the rude wood. Its pallor emphasized the coarse black hairs clustered upon the first joints, the grime-caked fingernails, and especially the missing middle finger.

"An old wound," Godfrey said. "He might have been born so, save for the scars."

"And neatly done," Irene added, "as if by a cleaver, or a guillotine, hmm? No other finger has been nicked. There is a deliberate look to the injury, as on the man in Chelsea. Is that not so, Nell?"

"If you mean you expected raw tissue, I concede that there is a certain surgical neatness to the remaining joint. Wouldn't a physician have attended it afterwards?"

"Even a surgeon can't repair a ragged injury. I say this man *sacrificed* his finger, as did the drowning victim in Chelsea."

"Allowed it to be . . . taken?" Godfrey sounded dubious.

I also was skeptical. "But that was years ago, Irene. How can that be?"

"Perhaps both men lost their fingers at the same time, if not their lives." Irene smiled angelically at the attendant, a morose little man whose mustache ends drooped to his chest. "Mon-see-oor," she said in studied mispronunciation, "may we—that is—" Her dainty gloved fingers stuttered on a gesture that hovered on the brink of being French before she turned to Godfrey.

Godfrey intervened manfully with a string of French.

I stood absorbed in the exchange occurring before me. It was all writ plain on the attendant's sallow face: polite puzzlement, disbelief, a shocked glance to Irene and myself, stern resistance, uncertainty, reluctance, distaste. . . .

Through it all, Godfrey's French flowed like the Seine, placid and unceasing.

At last the attendant stepped to the corpse and began undoing the man's clothing with a last glance at us ladies. "*Anglais,*" he murmured in disgust.

I deeply resented *my* countrymen bearing the blame for Irene's brash American curiosity, but I was helpless to protest. And indeed, as the dead man's chest and shoulders were bared, I could not help feeling a pulse of anticipation: what if he, too, bore a strange ornamental tattoo? Would it mean only that both men—both drowning victims—had been sailors? Or that some other, less apparent, yet possibly sinister, link joined them in death, if not in life?

Irene sighed unhappily. I leaned past her shoulder to view the pitiful corpse. On a chest upon which black hairs coiled there lay another dark scrolling: the letter "S" in sinuous detail, at least three inches high.

Irene sighed again.

"Are you not pleased by this ghoulish discovery, Irene?" I drew out my notebook so that she could record the mark. I wished my diaries complete to the last detail, no matter how odious, since they had proven valuable before now. "Not only a tattoo, but another letter of the alphabet . . . and in the same rather rococo style. Proof that ties this poor creature to the man we saw on Bram Stoker's dining-room table so long ago, though what that can mean, I can hardly conceive . . . Irene?"

Irene herself rapidly sketched the mark, which Godfrey and I immediately compared to the original. The depiction was perfect.

She had ceased regarding the tattoo at all, a rather ungrateful reaction after all that Godfrey and I had undergone in order that she should see it. No, her gaze clung instead to the dead man's face, an unremarkable, full-featured expanse the color of overbleached table linen.

"What is it?" Godfrey leaned forward intently. The attendant rolled his eyes and muttered "*Anglais*" again.

"I have seen more than I expected," Irene said at last, straightening from her inspection and handing me the note pad. "The features are not French, but Celtic, as I expected. But I did not anticipate the bruises upon the throat. If only we had examined the Chelsea corpse more thoroughly! This man was throttled first and drowned as an afterthought. Perhaps the man in Chelsea was marked by attempted strangulation as well."

"Perhaps his rescuers caught him by the neck," Godfrey said. "Surely a more logical explanation."

"Forcefully enough to leave marks?" Irene sounded dubious. She noticed the attendant, plucked a lacy handkerchief from her reticule and dabbed her eyes, shaking her head.

"No, no . . . no! It is not poor Antoine after all." Her eyes, miraculously and suddenly red, turned on me. "Is that not true, Philippa? Not whom we seek at all. Thank you, Monsieur."

Godfrey translated this false speech to the attendant, but Irene's acting spoke more strongly than words: the fellow was already ushering us out.

I managed to trail the trio—I am always being overlooked; it must be due to my inbred Shropshire reticence—and had only moments in which to jot my last impressions into the note pad before the others reached the archway and I was compelled to join them.

We left en masse, as we had come, leaving the dead to their meditations. I could not resist a parting glance at the unearthly dead girl's face pinned like an albino butterfly to her dank stone wall.

Chapter Six

A SORDID SUMMONS

❧

''An Irish-linen handkerchief soaked in ammonia!"
Irene announced, producing this repellent item and waving
it. "An old melodrama trick."

"That explains how you can induce teary, crimson eyes on
cue, if not how you are to rid yourself of them," said I. "What
accounts for these two similar and serpentine initials?"

We three had gathered around the parlor table after dinner
to consider the sketches of these curious tattoos by lamplight.
Even Casanova had pressed against his cage bars, scrawny
head craned over the table and neck feathers ruffled.

"These letters are elaborate enough to decorate a medieval
manuscript," Godfrey complained, frowning handsomely.

"If only we had been able to record the tattoos with a
camera!" Irene said. "My eye or hand may have missed some
telling detail in the translation from skin to sketch pad.
Perhaps the resemblance to letters is meant to mislead us."

"You suggest that the meaning lies in the embellishment,
not in the central figure?" Godfrey liked the notion. "That
would be fiendishly clever."

"What of a mirror?" I inquired.

"Mirror?" they chimed in unison like a pair of well-timed
clocks.

"Perhaps the designs make more sense backwards."

Irene and Godfrey rushed to the pier glass in the hall, each clutching a sketch. A moment's study showed that the reflected images made no more sense than before.

"Why do you expect these letters to bear more than face value?" I queried. "Could they not simply be initials for 'Oliver' and 'Sidney,' or some such?"

"Why not 'Olivier' and 'St. Denys,' their French counterparts?" Godfrey asked. "Why need both be English?"

"Then why not 'Ophelia' and 'Serafina'?" I suggested.

"Excellent point, Nell!" Godfrey explored this new line of speculation by staring fixedly at the ceiling. "Men who acquire tattoos often choose to honor a lady of their acquaintance."

Our quickly widening circle of speculations annoyed Irene. "We must begin somewhere," she said, pressing the sketches against the glass and manipulating them like pieces of a jigsaw puzzle. "Initials seem logical. In any case, this is the only incident that shows any promise of developing into a curiosity at all." A long pause, and then she snatched the papers away. "Oh, I am so *bored* with France!"

With that she dropped the sketches and stormed into the music room, leaving Godfrey and myself to regard each other in the mottled old mirror. An excessively ferocious burst of Wagner soon thundered from the piano's elderly strings.

While I picked up the literal pieces, Godfrey retreated to the dining-room sideboard, where he poured a glass of sherry. Together we tiptoed to the music room, ignoring Casanova's raucous rendition of "The Pilgrim's Chorus."

Lucifer stood blinking on the rustic carpet, shaking his complacent black head. Obviously, he had been summarily evicted from slumber on the tufted-velvet piano bench. There Irene sat while she pounded out octave chords.

Godfrey diplomatically deposited the sherry glass atop the piano case, then brought a lit candelabra from the mantel to illuminate the music on the stand, a melodious and apparently irrelevant Schumann suite. Tonight Irene played from memory and emotion.

Godfrey arranged himself at the instrument's inward curve and assumed a stance of rapt attention. I settled upon an ottoman. Godfrey would have to deal with Irene's fit of pique, but I was far too curious about how he would manage it to withdraw discreetly, as I ought to have.

During my long association with Irene, I had occasionally been treated to the excesses of her artistic temperament; Godfrey was perhaps only beginning to comprehend that where brilliance and art blaze bright, there also flare impatience and frustration.

Irene's playing smoothed so gradually that I could not say when the moderation had begun. Perhaps a modicum of Godfrey's courtroom calm had reached her. The keys tinkled with the good-natured Schumann piece; then even that music faded as she paused to sip the sherry.

"It is true," Godfrey said in the sudden silence, "that we are strangers in a strange land, and further true that we are saddled with our own ghosts. But we are healthy, wealthy and wise, and we do have some resources at our disposal. You, my darling Irene, have your music and your mystery still; how many Paris ladies can arrange to be present at a sordid activity such as the removal of a corpse from the Seine? You, my dear Penelope—" Godfrey quite startled me by directing his thoughts my way; I preferred my "mouse-in-the-corner" view of things.

"You, my dear Penelope," he repeated, "are sustained by your habit of recording the world around you and observing life through others.

"Even I have found some slight place here, through my legal work. One never knows what will turn up. Only this week I found myself making a London referral on the testy matter of a French will that bridges the two nations. I realized, with some chagrin, that I could recommend no finer English inquiry agent to Monsieur Le Villard than Mr. Sherlock Holmes of Baker Street—"

Irene stood so abruptly that she nudged the piano. The keyboard cover clapped shut. "Godfrey, you didn't! You actually referred someone to Sherlock Holmes?"

"Not a mere 'someone,' my dear girl; François Le Villard is a prominent member of the French detective service. I felt that he would benefit from observing Mr. Holmes's methods. And now that *you* no longer operate in London, you would hardly begrudge a fellow sleuth the custom."

"Oh, Godfrey, you are incorrigible, outrageous! Why did you not tell me?"

The storm had evaporated. Irene was laughing as she sank again onto the piano bench. This engendered an injured cry and a frantic leap from Lucifer; the sly creature had taken instant advantage of her temporary desertion of the seat.

"It's a trifling matter, Irene," Godfrey went on. "Besides, I am interested to see what Holmes can do, and I am in no position myself to investigate the London arena. So, you see, life goes on despite upheaval, even despite outrageous good fortune. I am willing to wager my share of the Zone of Diamonds that you will decipher these troubling tattoos and the odd deaths of their bearers."

"But I am twice removed, Godfrey! As you and Nell so forcefully reminded me only minutes ago, I am on foreign ground, where even initials may speak a different language. London was an alien venue at first, but at least the tongue remained the same, if dialects did take strange twists. But here . . . here I am liable to assume more than I should."

"The tattoos seem a rather sordid matter," I ventured to say. "Perhaps a new puzzle, one involving a more highly elevated element of society, will present itself soon."

"Trips to the Petite Trianon instead of La Morgue, eh, Penelope?" Irene smiled fondly as she raised the keyboard cover and turned her gaze back to her husband. "You are right, Godfrey, as you were when I returned from Bohemia; I despair too soon. One might think I was a heroine of grand opera."

She struck a resounding chord that drove Lucifer from the room and ended our investigations for the evening.

My pathetic suggestion to Irene that evening soon proved so prophetic that I briefly considered obtaining a crystal ball and a skull-shaped lamp, the better to set up shop on the Rue Toucan.

The very next day a note from Godfrey arrived soon after lunch. "He has never felt it necessary to communicate so urgently before," Irene noted with a demi-smile.

I averted my eyes while she read, assuming that these billets-doux between spouses contain such excesses of affection that the reader might blush and the observer wish herself in Outer Mongolia.

"Well!" The hand with the message lowered to the table. Irene's cheeks were aglow with nothing so delicate as a blush; it was a glow more like a recurrence of the investigative fever I had seen before. "Listen to this! Ah, I will omit the, er, salutation." Here she did lower her lashes demurely. "At any rate, Godfrey is exceedingly short with the main import of his message. He requires our presence—"

"Our?"

"At an address in Paris I have never heard of."

"Then it cannot be respectable!" I wailed.

"Yes, you must be right." Irene grinned. "And that explains the rest of it, or at least part of it."

"The rest?"

"Yes. We are to bring a change of clothing for Godfrey— and for myself."

"A sudden journey? Oh, Irene, do you suppose—?"

"And my little revolver." Irene fairly scintillated with

satisfaction. "I see that Godfrey now repays my terse note commanding you to Bohemia so many months ago. No more explanation than I gave. Why?"

"He sent the message with the coachman. Why could he not have come himself?"

"Apparently it is more amusing to bewilder us, or else some situation compels him to remain in Paris. We shall go, of course. Immediately. What clothing do you suppose would suit a gentleman and lady about to . . . flee the country? Apply for work?"

"Something neat and restrained, Irene, is suitable for all occasions."

"What a pity. I have nothing that fits that description. I shall have to investigate your wardrobe, then." Thus it was that my gray plaid skirt and yellow shirtwaist joined Godfrey's change of clothing in my old, worn carpetbag.

André, our stoic coachman, rolled his eyes when Irene instructed him to take us to Godfrey, but he said nothing. It was now late afternoon. Waves of linnets lapped at the sunset-tinged clouds as the day's redolent breath grew chill with the onset of twilight.

"We shall never make Paris in daylight," I said.

"No," Irene agreed. She had been abstracted for most of our journey, not even noting when our horses' hooves rang on cobblestones instead of hard-packed country earth. She smiled suddenly. "But I do not think you would care to be observed arriving at this particular address."

"You said you did not know the address!"

"That is why I know it is not respectable, as you so swiftly discerned. And this . . ."—Irene lifted the revolver from her handbag—"this, too, is not a sanguine sign. Godfrey would not request my revolver unless he needed it—or believed that we might."

"I am amazed that you have not donned your 'walking clothes'," I answered.

"I had thought of it, Nell. But Godfrey told me to bring a change of clothing for myself; obviously, he expects me to be conventionally attired, as I do not have an entire wardrobe of men's clothing to choose from."

Our carriage wheel hit a loose paving stone and we lurched as the compartment bucked on its springs.

"We must be near our destination," Irene said, drawing aside the window covering to peer into the dusky streets.

I was reminded of our first hansom cab ride together when we had a murderer—the late Jefferson Hope—for a driver. It was down just such rough and twilight streets that our initial encounter had propelled us.

"I must admit, Irene," I said, "that I had begun to fear I had no use in your new situation, and no excuse to spend my days in idleness in a foreign land—" A jolt disconnected my thoughts for a moment.

"I suppose that amusement is not sufficient excuse?" Irene inquired calmly when the springs subsided.

"Certainly not! But I see now that it is fortunate that I am near at hand. Apparently Godfrey has a bent equal to your own for untoward events; at least I am here to see that you do not hurtle"—here the carriage swayed around a corner, hurling Irene and me like dice across the tufted leather upholstery—"into more difficulty than we . . . you . . . can manage."

"Folly does require an escort." Irene regained her spot in the seat opposite, pinning her hat in place.

"Why does André harry the horses so?!" I burst out.

Irene had been peeping through the shades again. "I believe he does not care for the ambiance of the vicinity."

"It is a slum?"

"It is worse than a slum; it is an extension of Montmartre—a place that attracts those in search of idle amusements. I think we turn toward the river."

"Why do you say that—? Oh." I, too, had inhaled the faint rank odor of cool, dark water.

Another jolt surprised us by being the last. We waited until André opened the walkway-side door. "Madame wishes me to wait?" he asked in his husky French.

Irene nodded and took his gnarled hand as she stepped out of the conveyance. I followed.

We stood on a narrow street, dark save for some lighted bistro windows at the corner, from whence wafted the scent of onion soup and the sound of drunken sea chanties.

André pulled his coat collar up around his neck and nodded to a flight of steps. *"Ici, Madame."*

"Et . . . Monsieur?" Irene asked. Only I could see that her handbag was slightly open so the revolver should be at the ready.

"Ici, Madame," André repeated with a nod toward the unsavory structure before us.

Even Irene paused before entering this unknown destination. A group of men who had been lurching down the street brushed by us on a wave of sour wine and garlic.

Many *"Excusez-mois"* and *"Mademoiselles"* were bandied from drunkard to drunkard. I felt a hand firmly clasp my forearm. Then Irene was propelling me up the dark stairs, through a peeling painted door and into a close, dim hall.

Here the odors were more confusing but no less unpleasant. A woman with a face like a dyspeptic bulldog sat behind a half-door.

"Oui?" she croaked.

"Monsieur Norton," Irene said.

What was left of the woman's eyebrows—a long, scant hair or two—lifted. She eyed us up and down, then mumbled something about the poor maligned *Anglais* again. A seamed palm extended for money.

Irene parted with a few sous.

The woman shrugged unhappily and nodded to a set of stairs even steeper and danker than those by which we had entered the establishment. "Upstairs," she said in French slow enough for me to follow. "Third room on the right."

The hag produced a cheap copper candleholder, a dirty plinth of wax impaled in its socket. The palm appeared again. For a sou, she pushed the light across the sill at us. For another, she offered a crude lucifer, which Irene struck on the wooden ledge, causing the woman's eyebrow hairs to waggle in surprise. Irene lit the candle, then drew a cigarette from her handbag and lit it, too, before the flame flickered out.

Now the shrewish concierge was truly piqued. Irene shook out the lucifer and thrust it into a wilted bouquet sitting on the sill.

I must confess that it was good to smell the sulfur of an expired lucifer and the tang of a cigarette instead of the leftover scents stewing in that close entryway.

We climbed the stairs, our shadows flung behind us. Irene went first, smoke haloing her bonnet like a veil as she puffed on the cigarette. I held the candle so that she might wield her cigarette and keep her other hand ready with the revolver.

On the first floor, light shone from under a dozen doors, lurid yellow light set into lengths like tallow. We climbed another set of stairs, each riser creaking abominably. I heard a groan behind me and stopped.

"Someone is being attacked—or attacks us!"

"I think not. We must go on."

"But I should—"

A woman's cry came, low and pained.

"Irene, we *must* intervene!"

I turned, but an iron grip stayed my candle-bearing arm.

"Our intervention would not be appreciated, Nell."

"Still, duty—"

"No one is being harmed," Irene said impatiently. "This is a house of assignation."

"A house of assignation? What, pray, is a house . . . of assignation? Oh, you mean—?"

"Yes, I do. The French call it a *hôtel particulier.*"

"Then that odious woman below must have taken us for—"

"Assuredly she did."

"But Godfrey is here!"

"Evidently."

"But why? How? What are we to do?"

"Go to the third door on the right on the next floor and find out."

"How humiliating! That woman thinks—"

"Who cares what she thinks?"

"No one! Except . . . she sneered at us."

Irene laughed. "I venture that she sneers at everybody; she has nothing better to do. But we do. Now, upward and onward! Only to the valiant come answers to unthinkable questions."

Chapter Seven

DEMOISELLE IN DISTRESS

No other woman could have encountered what we found in that room with the equanimity that Irene managed.

A shivering Godfrey opened the door to us. My candle, lifted to illuminate the scene, revealed tattered wallpaper, one feeble paraffin lamp on a table, and a brass bed so mounded with a dingy feather comforter that it seemed a storm cloud had fallen from the gray Parisian skies.

No fire warmed the grimy hearth. Godfrey was wrapped, Indian style, in a disreputable blanket he had found God knows where. His hair lay damp around his face, which was scored with deep scratches in rows as regular as those from a frenzied cat. Besides the door by which we entered, the room contained but one other, and it was braced shut with a tilted chair. Its doorknob shook as if ague-stricken, while enraged cries in French issued from beyond it. The voice was young and female.

"Either you have encountered an abusive variety of ghost," Irene remarked, removing her gloves and placing the revolver on the table, "or you have taken a prisoner. In either case, you shall certainly perish of influenza before you can tell the tale if we do not warm this room."

Irene went to the decrepit washstand, lifted the porcelain bowl and thoughtfully swirled the murky water around. In a moment she had moved the bowl to the table and had lifted the stand to smash it against the side of the fireplace.

The rickety wood splintered obligingly. Next, Irene drew a handful of wadded newspapers from where they had been jammed along the sole window and held it to her lit cigarette until the old paper caught fire. She deposited it gently on the remains of the washstand; in moments a fire was flickering in the mean, blackened, brick mouth of the chimney.

"So inventive, these Americans," Godfrey murmured, drawing a three-legged stool to the blaze.

I stood stupefied. Irene finished her cigarette and tossed it into the snapping flames. "Another chamber?" She nodded to the still-quivering door.

Godfrey looked abashed. "A closet. It was all I could find."

Irene noticed the screen askew in a corner. "Then you shall have to change clothing behind there, once you have dried off. I suppose she is as wet as you?"

"Yes."

"And not nearly so manageable?"

"No." He sighed.

"In heaven's name, Godfrey, why could you not have thought to light a fire? You shall catch your death! And she as well."

"At least *she* will be satisfied at last," he grumbled. "I was thinking only of the next steps, Irene; my present discomfort seemed little enough."

Irene sighed in her turn, and I edged nearer to the fire. It is uncanny how chill a room becomes at night, even in August, without a fire. If Irene was correct and this decrepit place was an illicit rendezvous, I could not imagine how the guilty parties could stand to commit even something as exhilarating as mortal sin in such icy surroundings.

"Nell is worried," Godfrey said to Irene.

She turned as if remembering me, then smiled. "Ah, yes. Keep a good grip upon that candle. We need all the light and warmth we can muster this night. If you are wondering, Godfrey has taken a bath in the Seine."

"Is that the . . . ah, the—" I came to a halt.

"*L'Essence de Seine* that you smell," Godfrey agreed, running a hand through his hair to dry it. "You find me in the fabled position of Bram Stoker: I have attempted to rescue a most uncooperative drowning victim."

The closet door swelled with blows as a torrent of fervid French issued from behind it.

Godfrey said, "I have listened to that for three hours, yet I dare not release her; she would rush immediately for the riverbank again. She has the strength of a madwoman and is quite unreasoning."

"Hence the scratches," Irene told me. "Poor Godfrey; we must wait until we get home to treat your face."

Godfrey winced as her fingers stroked the edge of his jaw. "I suppose I look a bloody mess. Madame DeFarge at the door certainly required a great many sous to make room for me, but I had to get the girl off the streets."

"I suppose she expects to make men pay extra for protesting girls," Irene said. "You look drier now, and the screen awaits."

Godfrey glumly rose, took the carpetbag and went behind the screen. It might have been embarrassing to hear the sounds of his attiring, but the hoarse protests of the rescued girl obscured them.

Irene looked down into the waning fire, then lifted her skirt and daintily kicked the stool into the embers. I stared at her. She shrugged.

"Godfrey does not need it now, and we shall soon be free of this place, though we will have our hands full with her. Between us, Godfrey and I have paid the woman at the door enough to incinerate the entire establishment."

"But, Irene, whatever the reason, to hold this woman against her will is tantamount to kidnapping!"

"That is why Godfrey sent for us. Perhaps we can instill some reason into her disordered brain."

"Us?"

"As soon as Godfrey is ready, we shall have to attend to her. She is no less subject to chill than he."

I turned toward the closet door, which still vibrated with curses and blows. Early in my governess days I had known a hysterical ten-year-old who held his breath until his face turned as scarlet as the Red Sea and his parents acquiesced to his every demand.

Irene squinted at the crude wooden chair Godfrey had braced under the doorknob. "Besides, we shall soon need that chair for the fire."

Godfrey emerged from behind the screen, looking more his usual self, save for the lurid scratches.

Irene pocketed the revolver, then nodded to the closet. Godfrey pulled away the chair. The door exploded open as a wet, disheveled creature shot into the room, then halted to blink at each of us in turn.

The sopping and tangled hair, the wild eyes, the raging energy so uncontained—I had seen them before. A tantrum carried to such extremes becomes dangerous.

Without thinking, I stepped forward to confront this overwrought, overgrown child, my French crudely accented perhaps, but every syllable imbued with a language I spoke much more fluently: discipline.

I heard my own commanding tones snap out like a ringmaster's whip; I spoke as a parent, as a governess.

"You will take charge of yourself," I ordered. "You will attend to the disorder in your dress, and then we will address the disorder in your thoughts. Enough of this screaming and kicking. You are not a child. You will behave as an adult. Now, to the fire, for soon you will be shaking with chills. I am Miss Huxleigh. Mrs. Norton and I will see to you. We mean you no harm, which is more than you can say for yourself.

What is your name, child? Speak up, we heard you well enough moments ago."

She muttered, "Louise."

"Ah, Louise, a most suitable name. Come then, there is not a moment to be wasted, child. You must be very tired."

Irene was waiting to drape Godfrey's cast-off blanket over the girl's shoulders, which began to heave with cold and the icy backwash of excessive emotion. She began sobbing and wailing, rather than kicking and flailing. Irene and I eyed each other over her bent head and nodded our mutual relief.

Irene spoke then, her French as fluid as the Seine, her tone musically coaxing, all solicitude and sympathy where I had been all iron and starch.

Godfrey observed us with almost comical amazement before drawing me aside. "The girl was absolutely incorrigible with me. When I insisted that she calm down, she called me a brute. When I soothed her, she accused me of being a seducer. Yet you and Irene play the same old tunes in quick succession and she gentles like a lamb."

"It is a matter of delicate timing and decisiveness, Godfrey," I said with some satisfaction as Irene crooned a French lullaby of little nothings in the girl's ear.

Once certified as reasonably dry, Godfrey was sent below to wait with the coachman. Irene and I remained above to extract the distraught girl from her wet clothes.

Irene repeatedly asked for her family's name.

"*Non, non!*" the waif wailed, shaking her damp hair until rattails whipped at our hovering faces.

Even when we had lured her to the privacy of the screen, she balked at removing her clothing. "*Ruinée,*" she moaned over and over. "*Je suis ruinée!*"

I am ruined. Even a sheltered spinster such as myself well knew what that meant. Obviously, a gently bred girl lay beneath the raw despair and hysteria. Some unprincipled man had lured her into a compromising situation. I thought of the angelic plaster face we had seen at the morgue. That poor girl's story had been sealed by death. No wonder the one before us had fought Godfrey so savagely for saving her life.

Irene unclasped the cameo pinned to the girl's soggy collar and handed it to me with a significant glance. Even I, with my dull appreciation of fine jewels, recognized an exquisite carving that surely dated to the last century.

A gold bracelet of good quality circled her right wrist; she fought briefly as I unclasped it. On her left hand, a gash across one knuckle mirrored the scratches Godfrey had suffered.

Once we began to undo her clothing, she began to struggle again. In vain did Irene urge my freshly laundered skirt and shirtwaist upon her. Louise's agonized charcoal-hued eyes darkened further and she shook her head, her arms crossed protectively over her chest.

"Child, you cannot go out into the night in these wet things," Irene said.

Her appeals succeeded by degrees; we managed to obtain Louise's wet petticoats and skirt in exchange for those we had brought. When it came to removing her basque, the girl began twisting and fighting, spinning into herself like a dervish.

"*Basta!*" Irene cried, exasperated into spitting out the Italian word for "enough," much used in opera librettos.

Irene's voice had once held opera audiences spellbound and had caused a callous king to weep. Now it sufficed to arrest the rising hysteria of one young French girl.

"You must remove your wet basque," Irene insisted, plucking at the clinging sleeve.

"I cannot," the girl sobbed, still girding herself with her arms. "I am ruined. Oh, the shame! And it is not my fault—"

"It generally is not indeed," Irene muttered in English before returning to her persuasive French. "My poor dear, we will not hurt you. I am an actress who has heard much both off and on the stage. Nothing is more shameful than a society, a people, who use shame as a weapon. Please, we are here to help you. Nothing can shock us. We are women of the world."

Here I could barely hold my tongue.

More tears squeezed through Louise's spiked eyelashes and down her pale cheeks to her collar. She regarded Irene with dawning awe. "An actress, really, Madame? Like the Divine Bernhardt?"

Irene smiled tolerantly. "Once upon a time. Now I am a respectable married woman—yes! You see how the past can be overcome."

The girl nodded and allowed us to begin unlatching the myriad hooks down her back. "But *my* stain will not wash away," she said on a rising note, "not even with time."

"All things fade with time," Irene hushed her.

"Not this!" Louise blazed with sudden fury, like a fire fed fresh fuel. She tore the bodice from her left shoulder, the hooks parting with a metallic wrench.

From concealment came revelation.

Irene and I stared transfixed at the tattoo glistening just above Louise's cameo-pale breast. It was a vivid, fresh representation of the letter "E."

Chapter Eight

A TROUBLE OF TATTOOS

''**It is** barbaric!" Godfrey paced our front parlor. "And she still refuses to return to her home?"

"She will not even say where she resides." Irene idly slid the third sketched initial across the polished tabletop.

"Awraaaac, barbaric!" the parrot seconded with its ready grasp of key new words.

Irene looked up to regard Casanova's one visible unblinking eye for a long moment. He spit "Cut the cackle" from the side of his beak and edged down his wooden perch.

"I believe that she is calm enough to tell you the tale now," Irene told Godfrey.

His pacing stopped. "I don't want to hear it." His hands lifted as if to repel an onslaught of candor. "The entire incident fairly makes my blood boil. This young woman is obviously from good family. If she were my sister—!"

Irene was unstirred. "You shall have to quell your imagined fraternal indignation and hear the facts, Godfrey. Louise owes her rescuer an explanation for her resistance, not to mention an apology for having disfigured his face for a fortnight. And you may discern some clue to the affair in her account."

Godfrey, newly attired and looking fresh in every respect, including the rawness of his wounds, grimaced in the direction of the mirror. I shared Irene's disturbance at seeing his not uncomely face so marked for having undertaken a singularly humanitarian act.

"I am not certain that I am as solicitous of the girl's welfare as I once was." Godfrey patted his cheek tenderly.

"Then what of my welfare?" Irene asked softly. His inquiring look brought plainer words. "I confess that the violence done this young woman draws me even more deeply into the puzzle of these tattooed dead men. I elicited but the bare bones of her story; you are a master of the courtroom query and may string the factual skeleton into some recognizable shape. Besides, Mademoiselle Louise must learn that not all men will misuse her. She could do no better than to begin that lesson with you."

"Thank you, Irene." Godfrey's jaw tightened; then he turned to me. "But I shall be lost without my faithful amanuensis. Nell, will you be so good as to take notes? We may as well treat this as a formal inquiry. If her family is as highly placed as I believe, the police may eventually figure in it."

"It may come to even more formality than a police inquiry," Irene said grimly. "Behind the disparate pieces of this puzzle there lurks a vastly complex scheme that has shadowed many lives and threatens to cripple others before it is ended." She went upstairs to fetch the unfortunate girl.

"Doesn't it strike you, Godfrey," said I in her absence, "that Irene weaves conspiracy on a very broad loom? The likelihood of your happening to rescue a suicidal girl whose distress is related to a pair of tattooed sailors drowned in two great rivers many years apart—"

"—is not the mad coincidence you hope, Nell." He smiled, then winced as the expression stretched his scratches. "I was strolling by the Seine, puzzling over the tattoos, and was very near the spot where you and Irene saw the dead man drawn from the water. It was then that I noticed Louise thrashing about in the river."

"But that low, dead sailor could have had nothing to do with a genteel girl such as Louise!"

Godfrey shrugged. "Irene is right. The sinews that bind together any sequence of events seldom resemble one another. Clues are no more than connective tissue, vital for their function, not for their substance."

Footfalls in the passage announced the girl's approach under Irene's gentle shepherding.

Louise entered, and we both stared. Dried, brushed and soothed by an actress's expert hands, she cut quite a different figure in our cozy, lamplit parlor, with its English chintz, rush-seated chairs and gathered draperies, than the one she had presented in the house of ill repute.

Louise was a more weighty young woman than she had appeared at first; no wonder Godfrey had been hard put to rescue her. The lamplight revealed large, expressive, almost black eyes and shining, nutmeg-colored hair, a piquant but decidedly stubborn profile, and hands that seemed far too dainty to have inflicted the scratches that even now seared Godfrey's cheeks.

Eyes cast down, she settled into the chair Irene indicated and crossed her ankles. I noticed that Irene's generosity had extended to the loan of my best black-kid house slippers and hoped that Louise's equally generous feet would not stretch them.

Godfrey and I knew, of course, that Irene already had plied our guest with soft, glancing queries; it was time for a concerted interrogation.

"You are feeling better?" Godfrey began courteously.

"I am dry, Monsieur, and warm. Yet I feel no better."

Even, white teeth pressed a pale lower lip. "Madame Norton has told you of the . . . attack?"

"You must not blame yourself. It was through no fault of yours. Perhaps you would care to share the circumstances with us." Louise remained silent. "As a barrister, I may find some way of discovering and punishing the culprits."

"What is there to discover?" the girl cried suddenly. "Except to know that these men are, were, mad!" The outburst propelled Louise forward, her white-knuckled hands clutching the arms of the chair.

She sank back, exhausted and troubled, looking twice her likely age. "Oh, Monsieur Norton, your wife has assured me that you are a wise and sympathetic man, that your own sister was the victim of a similar senseless attack—"

Here Godfrey and I looked to Irene, who shrugged as if to say: well, you gave me the notion, Godfrey. . . .

"I understand your interest," Louise went on, "and I truly apologize for resisting your noble efforts to save me. I was quite mad in my own way by then, having awakened in a strange place in an even stranger condition. It was unclear in my mind what had happened; I assumed the worst upon finding my basque disarranged. Then I felt a dull ache and discovered the . . . disfigurement. Not only had the villains abducted me, but they had marked me forever with their cruelty and my shame!"

"Barbaric," Godfrey murmured in a low, angry voice, so sincerely that Louise looked directly at him for the first time. She was barely twenty, I estimated, and certainly not immune to so dashing a champion as Godfrey.

"My dear young woman," he said, sensing his advantage, "you must tell me the exact circumstances if I am to help. Who were 'these villains'? When and where did they abduct you?"

Louise forced her hands to her lap, where they folded and remained as still as if cast in plaster.

"First, Monsieur, you must understand my position. I am of good family"—smug looks were exchanged at this confirmation of previous speculation—"though of impoverished circumstances. My mother died in childbirth and my father, distraught, began to lead the careless, dissolute existence that was to end his days prematurely.

"I became the care of my Aunt Honoria, no relative save by marriage, but devoted to me and very kind. Her husband became my guardian. Uncle Edouard was Father's older brother; to him had gone all the family's lands and assets.

"As I grew older, I learned of my father's weaknesses, particularly for games of chance. I also learned that my uncle might provide me with some small dowry should I prove myself a steady, well-behaved person prone to none of my father's follies.

"I cannot complain of my childhood, though Uncle Edouard was remote and stern, as if expecting me to follow in my father's footsteps. Aunt Honoria was my salvation, particularly when my father died in so shocking a manner."

Louise paused. We kept silent, each wondering how to broach the indelicate subject.

Casanova's voice floated from the other room: "What? What?" he croaked.

"What manner, you ask?" Poor Louise was so distracted that she had not noticed the nonhuman nature of her interlocutor. "By the rope. Oh, not by legal decree, but by his own hand. In Monte Carlo. The casino, you see. He had lost everything, the little that remained. I was only five. From that moment on, Uncle Edouard began to watch me as if I, too, would succumb at any instant to gambling fever, or to scandal, or to some misstep.

"It was only long after my father's death, which was highly publicized of course, that letters began coming to Uncle from Central America, London, the south of France, even from Africa. They began three years ago and upset him enormously. After one was received, he would glare at me as if I were a criminal. The entire household came to dread the appearance of one of these ominous missives upon the silver salver in the front hall. All of our breaths hushed, mistress and maid alike, until Uncle came home at six o'clock and read the post. The letters were sealed with a clot of marbled black-and-crimson wax impressed with some strange device. The sealing wax smelled of sandalwood."

"The wax was foreign, then?" Godfrey inquired.

"So it struck me."

"But the letters came from many nations," Irene put in.

"From a number of correspondents, then," Godfrey said.

"Or a single one who traveled widely," she amended.

"When did your father die?" Godfrey asked Louise.

"Fifteen years ago. It was a horrid scandal. That is why I must . . . erase myself somehow. I cannot face Uncle's disappointment and rage. Once I reached a certain age, he had his man accompany me upon the most innocent of errands, as if he suspected me of wrongdoing. Now that I am quite literally marked, I am worth no dowry. No man will wed me. I am as utterly ruined as if I had in truth followed in my father's profligate footsteps!"

Louise broke into soft sobs.

"Nonsense, my girl." I was surprised to hear myself speak. "You must not despair. I myself was orphaned before I was twenty, and my father, although a righteous country parson, had not a relative to whom to commend me, nor a pence in his pocket—save what he had collected from the parish poor box. You must convince your aunt and uncle of your innocence; if they spurn you, you can find work. Independence does wonders for a woman."

Louise gazed at me in horror through a shining glaze of tears. "Employment?"

I was about to sing the praises of self-support when Irene

interrupted. "Miss Huxleigh is certainly right; you must convince your guardians of your innocence."

"But how?" the silly child wailed.

Godfrey was ready with a concrete suggestion. "Continue your narrative. Who were these men who abducted you? How many? Where did the kidnapping occur? How was your uncle's man eluded?"

"Pierre? True, Pierre did not intervene." Louise frowned, then rubbed her temples. "My head aches so. I remember little from the time I was walking in the Bois de Boulogne until I awakened in that horrible room, discovered my injury, and staggered to the street to find the river awaiting me. It shone like a broad gold-and-silver braid in the late-afternoon sunlight. I—I could not live in this condition. I ran into the water. Its cold numbed me, like the sheets of a December bed. I was sinking into icy, sweet oblivion when Monsieur Norton appeared beside me and kept tugging me back to shore, back to shame, kept pulling me away from the cool, silent river!"

Irene rose and perched on the arm of Louise's chair, pressing a hand on the girl's quaking shoulders. "Shhh, my dear." She eyed us, saying softly, "I questioned her delicately while I arranged her toilette. I am convinced that the tattoo was the extent of the men's mischief, and further that they used chloroform to drug her, then dragged her into a waiting carriage."

"What of this Pierre?" Godfrey wondered.

"Duped. Or . . ."

"An accomplice," I breathed.

"It grows late, little one," Irene whispered into the girl's ear. "You must compose yourself and return home."

"Home? Never!"

"Soon," Irene insisted, "else our excuses for your unheralded absence will not ring true. We will say that you took ill

upon the street. My husband and I drove you away in our
carriage—for did we not do just that this very evening?—to
our quite respectable residence in Neuilly, where you did not
recover until now, when we promptly brought you home. The
maid has dried and freshened your clothing. You can return
home as if nothing has happened."

"But, but—" As more than one had done before her,
Louise fell speechless in the face of Irene's relentless will. "I
am utterly altered, Madame!"

"Tut, tut!" Irene brushed a tendril from her charge's cheek.
"I have a marvelous tinted cream that will obscure your . . .
um, interesting adornment. Some women willingly submit to
the tattoo artist's needle, did you know that? Perhaps not very
respectable women, but some who are quite famous."

"You, Madame?"

Irene's forefinger closed Louise's gaping mouth. "Not . . .
as yet."

"Irene!" I managed to choke out.

"But I have heard—" At this, Irene leaned close to
Louise's ear and whispered something. The girl's eyes grew as
round as her mouth had been.

"You are certain, Madame? She?"

"Indeed. So there may come a day when you will flaunt
your most interesting souvenir of an adventure. But for now,
you can easily hide it from even your maid, if you take care."

"Why should I perform such a charade when a letter may
come any day to my uncle announcing my alteration?"

"Why? Because we are going to get to the bottom of this
puzzle. Ah, that is an English turn of phrase, don't look so
bewildered; we are going to—"

"Find the villains," Godfrey said acerbically, with the look
of a Sidney Carton who has just seen his guillotine looming.

Irene adapted his phraseology without hesitation. "Find
the villains and—"

"—decipher the arcane meaning of the tattoo," I put in.

"Yes, of course, as Miss Huxleigh says. We must find out *why* a proper young Frenchwoman was seized from the Bois de Boulogne and forcibly tattooed. And then we will—" Irene paused, out of inspiration, as were we.

"Cut the cackle," a low voice suggested from the front parlor.

"And now we must cease talking and act!" Irene took the cue and stood. "Sophie will attend you." She nodded to the maid hovering in the passage. Our lost lamb moved to the doorway like a sleepwalker ordered to do so by the sandman himself, so persuasive were Irene's voice and manner when she cared to make them so.

"One last thing," Irene instructed the girl. "You must tell us your uncle's family name, else we cannot take you home."

Louise paused, cobalt shadows etched beneath those dark, doelike eyes. "Montpensier, Madame." Then she turned at Sophie's curtsy and followed the maid upstairs.

Godfrey stretched his legs as if uncramping them from a long and uncomfortable journey. "Montpensier. Good God, Irene! Montpensier was one of Napoleon's marshals of France. The uncle must be a grandson."

"Excellent." Irene collapsed into the vacated armchair, fatigued but aglow with satisfaction. "A first family of France. This puzzle is beginning to intrigue me."

Chapter Nine

THE FRENCH
CONNECTIONS

❦

Casanova, released from his cage for a few moments of freedom, gnawed the purple grape clutched in one leprous foot.

(Although I am no longer of the opinion that piano "legs" require sheathing from the view of the innocent, I am utterly convinced that all parrots should wear spats. My motivation is not the public morality, but aesthetics.)

The large bird was perched, like Mr. Poe's raven, upon a bust—one of Madame de Maintenon, the royal governess who became a royal mistress and then a queen, two commendable occupations out of three—atop the bookshelves. From his aerie he observed that plaster lady's imposing bosom, while far below, Irene perused "many a quaint and curious volume of forgotten lore," most of them obtained on expensive expeditions to Left Bank bookstalls.

Irene pored through books of ancient lettering forms, volumes on the arts of cipher and code, guides to the mysteries of Rosicrucians and Masons, compendiums of ancient maps and fabulous lost treasures, of arcane oriental tattooing practices, of sailors and the sea, and—I don't doubt—of cabbages and kings.

Irene sneezed. The parrot immediately produced a respectable imitation of the sound. Dust swirled in the lamplight, motes lifting like desert dervishes at each turn of a heavy parchment page. "Goodness!" she said. "I had no idea that 'toade spittal' was such a frequent ingredient of love potions. No wonder these elixirs work only in grand opera!"

I looked up from the eighteenth-century bible I studied. I held that the odd, tattooed letters were taken from an illuminated religious manuscript and when identified, should point to a particular passage that, if it did not solve the mystery, would at least enlighten us spiritually.

"What manner of book are you reading?" I asked Irene.

"A magician's *grimoire*—oh, the French have a way with a word: grim-wahr!" she enunciated breathily. "Think what dread formulas may lurk within."

" 'Gibberish'," I said. "That is the literal translation of the word *'grimoire'.* " Of course I pronounced it "grim-oh-are" despite my best efforts. "You will not decipher these tattoos in a book of magic."

"Nor you in a holy book," Godfrey added as he strolled in, his forefinger in a volume as thick as mine. "I remain convinced that the letters are taken from the motto on a coat of arms."

"O, S, E," Irene mused. "You think each letter begins a word in some Latin phrase. 'Omni Summa'—whatever. But it is impossible!" She banged her book shut and looked more closely at Godfrey's reference. "Coats of arms thrive in every country."

Godfrey turned his volume to reveal its title: *European Coats-of-Arms, Their Origin, Evolution and Significance, with Illustrations of All Major Family Modifications.*

"Oh!" Irene moaned, burying her face in her hands.

At that moment Sophie entered, curtsied and announced a visitor.

"At eight in the evening?" Godfrey asked.

Sophie, prepared for this objection, produced a visiting

card that caused Godfrey's eyebrows to leap for his hairline when he read it. He told Sophie to admit the caller.

"Well." He thumped his book atop an unsteady pile of volumes. "This should prove interesting. My dear Le Villard." He stepped to the threshold to greet a dapper man of olive complexion.

Monsieur Le Villard's palms brushed the sides of his pomaded hair—so black and shiny it resembled patent leather—before he bowed to Irene and myself in turn.

"You have found us mired in our homely evening pursuits, Monsieur," Irene said demurely. "Perhaps we could remove to the front parlor and send for refreshments."

"No, no!" The man began to pace, then realized that he was not in his own domain. He leaned forward to inspect Godfrey's face. "But, my friend, you have taken an injury!"

Godfrey laughed deprecatingly. "An encounter with a . . . rose bush while I was looking for the, ah, cat."

At that moment a raven-black shadow lofted down from an upper bookshelf: the elusive Lucifer seeking quieter sleeping quarters. We all jumped as if startled by a jack-in-the-box, then laughed in shared embarrassment.

"Yes," the Frenchman said, "even a cat may look at a queen, but more frequently it will lead its owner astray. May I recommend keeping a bird instead? Wonderful pets! Fascinating."

We paused. What was the best method of pointing out Casanova's eminent presence to a detective who had failed to notice it? Monsieur Le Villard was blind to our quandary as well. He took an elegant step, then whirled to confront us. One small hand made a fist that smacked the palm of his other hand. The French words rolled off his tongue so briskly that I had to listen closely to catch all he said.

"I have come, Monsieur, Madame—?"

"Mademoiselle." Irene nodded toward me.

Monsieur Le Villard stroked the thin strands of his jet-black mustache much like a cat grooming its whiskers after a bowl of cream. His next bow was profound. "Mademoiselle."

I was not impressed. He hastened on: "I have come—" he repeated, then lifted a graceful hand. "But I am being impolite. I have not thanked you, Monsieur Norton, for your aid in the matter of the will."

"You have made progress!" Irene divined. "Please draw up a chair, Monsieur, and share our table at least, if you will not eat or drink."

"Progress, yes!" He beamed at each of us in turn after he sat down. "The English consulting detective is what we Parisians call a man of many parts, a genius with an eye to the minutiae, a precision that would well endow a mathematician. I am translating his dissertations on various subjects so that the French detective service may once again come to the forefront of international crime-solving; our reputation has sagged a bit since the days of Vidoq. For this opportunity alone, I am most grateful, Monsieur Norton."

Another bow, this made while in a seated position. I was growing quite dizzy from so much bobbing and scraping.

"However"—one more furtive brush at the lip adornments, which rivaled a mandarin's for length—"I call not merely to express my gratitude. I fear—how can I say it but with brutal plainness? The matter that brings me to you at this inconvenient hour is the Montpensier tragedy."

We each sat upright as if inflicted by an outbreak of starch. Had Louise defied all sense of self-preservation and revealed the forced imposition of a tattoo upon her person?

"Montpensier?" Godfrey repeated dully.

"Tragedy?" Irene echoed.

Casanova and I exercised enough restraint to remain silent.

"Most tragic." Le Villard answered Irene's query first, perhaps deferring to the woman, which Frenchmen have made into a national pastime; perhaps merely addressing the issue that most concerned him. "The young lady, I fear, is gone."

"Louise? Vanished?" Irene looked indignant.

Godfrey sank back into his chair, his voice flat as if he were not surprised. "Dead, then?"

Monsieur Le Villard nodded soberly.

"Well, which is it?" I could not refrain from asking testily. Three such long faces at least owed me some clarity.

"Mademoiselle?"

I fixed the French detective with my governess's most gimlet eye. "Is the young lady dead, or merely vanished?"

"Both, I fear."

"How can that be?"

"An apt question, Mademoiselle—?"

"Huxleigh," I snapped, relieved to use a good English word that made no bones about its pronunciation—to me, at least, although some Americans insist on pronouncing it "Hux-lay" instead of "Hux-lee."

Monsieur Le Villard straightened at my intonation, adding paltry centimeters to his height. "Mademoiselle Montpensier is both dead . . . and gone. You will understand when you hear my account. You must pardon me, I cannot reveal many details. It is a shocking case, a girl so young and so pretty."

"But what has happened, for God's sake?" Godfrey demanded.

Irene stretched a hand to his over a pile of books. Godfrey was obviously shocked at hearing that the girl he had rescued but two days earlier was now truly lost. Irene's gesture, however, signified more than comfort; it called for caution. I saw that at once, if Godfrey was too overcome to notice.

Our position was delicate, to say the least. Louise's aunt and uncle, like the French police, knew nothing of the recent attack upon her or of her suicide attempt. Mentioning these sad facts now was not only futile, but possibly dangerous. We three could be held responsible for withholding the information, for not notifying her relations. Monsieur Le Villard's "tragedy" might indeed become one for all of us. I saw regret suffuse Irene's face as well as Godfrey's, and felt its sour bile in my own throat.

"How . . . did she die?" Godfrey asked.

The detective shook his gleaming head. "By water."

Godfrey nodded heavily. "That is why you recovered no corpse."

"Indeed." Le Villard bit his lip, which set his mustaches to quivering. "A sad scandal for an old and reputable family. I had the dreary duty of questioning the aunt—"

"Questioning the aunt?" Irene had risen and was leaning over the detective as if *she* interrogated him. "Honoria Montpensier is suspect? Of what?"

"Why, of murder, Madame. I am not insignificant in the Paris detective service. I do not attend mere accidental drownings."

"It was not an accident?" Godfrey's look of relief would have confused even the most optimistic bearer of bad news.

"No, my dear sir. I tell you, the circumstances are such—were cleverly arranged as such—that they might be taken as accidental, but there is the aunt's presence, of which the woman will not speak, and her utter silence to all questions. Most suspicious. Grief, of course, has driven the uncle to a terrible state; he is barely coherent. I tell you, the family is ruined!"

"But the *reason*, Monsieur," Irene said. "What is the aunt's reason for murdering her niece?"

Le Villard shrugged, a fatal gesture, for Irene could tolerate indifference no more than she could swallow stupidity. "I will find the reason, and when I do, it will be revealed as tawdry and feeble, as all such motives are."

"In the meantime," Irene said a trifle icily, "I hope you have no objection to our visiting the family and offering condolences. We have only just met, yet we feel—"

"Of course. And I also must ask you and your husband about your chance encounter with the young Louise only days ago. Did she strike you as fearing for her life?"

Considering the circumstances, we three remained blankly silent.

"No," Irene finally answered. "Nothing she did or said even vaguely suggested . . . foul play."

"No doubt it is some kind of domestic cancer that eats at the inner soul of a family," Le Villard diagnosed. "Such maladies seldom manifest themselves outwardly. So you have no information that might aid in the course of my investigation?"

"Nothing that would aid your murder investigation, no, Monsieur," Irene answered for all of us, rising as a queen does when an audience is over.

The French detective was admirably suggestible. He stood promptly to take her hand and kiss it lingeringly. Le Villard had not noticed that Irene's denial addressed only the assumption on which his investigation was based. No one could shred the truth finer than Irene and still avoid an outright lie. Such occasions always promised swift action on her part, and I found myself anticipating what it would be.

Once the maid had shown out the detective, Irene began to pace the chamber. "Such blind arrogance! He obviously considered our interrogation a mere formality. Monsieur Le Villard may be translating the works of Sherlock Holmes, but he has learned nothing of deduction, or of human nature. Madame Montpensier no more did away with young Louise than I did!"

"You met the woman only once, and briefly, Irene. How can you be so certain?" Godfrey had leaned his elbow on a pile of books, looking as worn as a student who has stayed up too late.

"You heard Louise herself say that her aunt was the only influence that made life in her uncle's house bearable. Oh, what an error has been made!"

"You refer to our decision to return Louise to her home as if nothing had happened?" I queried.

"I refer to *my* decision in returning Louise to her home at all! It was obvious. The poor child was so convinced that her ordeal would make her an outcast to her relatives that she attempted to drown herself. Even an idiot detective like Le Villard might have deduced a troubling severity in family life from that. But, no, I must concoct a method of hiding the girl's supposed fault, when the real flaw lay in the family situation. And into that situation I sent Louise, armed only with a jar of vanishing cream! Godfrey, we must visit the Montpensier residence at once. I will not rest until I discover what has happened to Louise, and by whose hands."

Chapter Ten

AUTUMN OF THE HOUSE OF MONTPENSIER

The House of Montpensier resembled the House of Usher in Mr. Poe's gloomy story. It was a gray, gaunt, raddled edifice. Stains veined the ancient mansard roof that drooped its hooded eyelids over the melancholy gabled windows.

Although travelers wax rapturous over the narrow residences of Paris, with their rows of tall French windows, I find such architecture pinched and consumptive-looking. And although fog and smoke seldom clog the parks of Paris as they smother the London byways, the same sooty tracks of crowded urban life that veil London streak Parisian landmarks.

So, in the chill rain through which we viewed it on that gray, early autumn afternoon, the house of Montpensier struck me as like some haughty French dowager whose face paint was melting.

Godfrey upheld a black umbrella broad enough to shield myself and Irene on either side. We each wore unadorned black, as suited visitors to a house of mourning.

Before we had left Neuilly, I had objected to my presence on the expedition, but Irene had overridden my protestations. "Of course you shall come, Nell! After all, you remember Louise, too. Besides, this is a most delicate mission. I will need all the aid I can get."

"How should it not be delicate?" I wondered aloud. "You have no connection whatsoever to the bereaved family. I am amazed that you would intrude at such a time."

"I must. How else can I make amends?"

Irene's expression of concern in no way resembled one of her habitual exaggerations for effect. I, too, sorrowfully recalled the soft brown rabbit who had been Louise Montpensier, alive in our Neuilly residence but days before.

"It is settled!" Irene declared, rejoicing in the face of my silence. I know of no one else who can always find such cause for optimism in mere hesitancy.

Godfrey took me aside moments later. "My dear Nell, I know it offends your sense of propriety to accompany Irene on her investigations"—I sniffed at the notion of ennobling this questionable outing with such a word—"but I also am most anxious to clear up matters. You, being less intimately involved in the tragedy, can offer a perspective unclouded by—"

"Guilt?" I suggested.

Godfrey nodded. "As a clergyman's daughter, you know better than most that such an emotion can poison . . . or purge."

"I see. I suppose that if you put my presence in the light of a spiritual advisor—"

"Exactly! You are so sensitive. You may perceive the true mind of the aunt, whom Irene believes to be falsely accused. You may detect—"

"The true guilt," I supplied.

"Indeed. We rely upon you."

"In that case, I shall object no more."

"Wonderful!" Godfrey clapped me on the shoulder as if I had volunteered for foreign service. I began to see myself as a shuttlecock tossed in the opposing pull of two highly persuasive threads of vastly different hue but of similar resilience.

Actually, I believe that the necessity of converting me to

their viewpoints provided both of my friends with a challenge they required on a daily basis, as athletes require exercise. I admit to taking a certain satisfaction in providing them with an opponent of some mettle.

Our living arrangement might strike some as bizarre, but in truth it suited each of our natures, as well as befitting social practice. It is not uncommon, of course, for inconvenient persons such as myself—that is to say, spinsters—to affix themselves to relations on some tenuous excuse and become family fixtures.

Indeed, the occupation of governess is predicated upon just such a system, save that there is no blood relation and the children's inevitable maturation forces a governess to change family circles from time to time.

Since I had no known relations, I was doomed to a solitary existence unless I sought a lodgings partner, as I had found in Irene. I felt quite capable of leading a solitary life; at times, in fact, I felt that I should insist upon it. But it was far more agreeable to reside with Irene, as before, and Godfrey, as now—the one my dear and longtime friend, the other my respected erstwhile employer and advocate.

Any fears of inadvertently interfering in their marital life soon had proven themselves moot. Godfrey and Irene were, for all their charm and bravado, obsessively private persons. I seldom glimpsed the more intimate side of their lives, or if I did, perhaps I was too inexperienced to mark its symptoms.

So we three lived as congenial members of one household, at times prone to differences or fits of pique, but always respecting one another and relishing the interplay that challenged our individual assumptions.

For myself, I enjoyed the role of ever-reliable brake to their imperious progress against the grain of propriety and convention. For their part, it cheered them enormously, I believe, to have so near at hand a person upon whom to exercise their considerable force of personality and persuasive abilities.

Nowadays Irene had no "audience" save me to manipulate, and Godfrey no "jury" but myself to argue before.

So we had forged a natural chain of three links that occasionally pulled one against the other, paradoxically reinforcing the strength of the connection rather than weakening it.

That is why we stood together in the twilight rain before the Montpensier manse. It is also why Irene and Godfrey solicited my opinion. They had seen the residence before; mine was the fresh eye.

"A forbidding place," I said.

"Of course, it is raining," Irene said doubtfully. "The house struck me simply as imposing on the evening that Godfrey and I returned little Louise to it."

Since her death, Louise had acquired the adjective "little," a sign that Irene's strong sense of injustice had been stirred to action.

"What were your impressions of the Montpensier couple?" I inquired in my role of uncompromised observer.

Irene and Godfrey consulted each other silently past the crepe veiling of my bonnet. I had never been so aware that they exceeded me in height until we huddled under the same umbrella.

"Strained," Irene pronounced.

"Suspicious," Godfrey said.

"Imagine how much more so they will be now that Louise is not merely overdue, but dead." It cheered me immensely to inject the proper sobriety into our expedition. "Shall we enter?"

The tall manservant who admitted us was as beefy as a pugilist, with a tuppence-size crimson mark on his left temple.

"Monsieur and Madame Norton, and Mademoiselle Hux-leigh, come to convey our sympathies to Monsieur and Madame Montpensier," Godfrey said.

"I will say you are here," the man promised after accepting our outer garments. He lumbered off in squeaking shoes.

"There is no fire in the grate," Irene whispered with a shiver. "And that servant seemed far too surly for a butler."

I, too, was struck by the icy, deathly still atmosphere. The hall's stone tiles darkened under our conjoined dripping until the floor resembled the carpet upon which Bram Stoker's unfortunate corpse had rained years before.

At length the dour manservant returned to lead us to a parlor. There we found the establishment's master, the uncle of Louise's narrative himself, standing staring down into the pallid flames of a dying fire.

I received an impression of hulking, tapestry-upholstered furniture, gilded legs and arms gleaming in the fitful firelight. So dark were the shadows that a circle of huge hounds with golden collars and halters might have been crouching silently around us. Certainly my imagination cast bogeymen into the corners of this gloomy chamber. The man occupying it did nothing to disperse them.

"Monsieur Montpensier." Irene glided to the fireside in a rustle of black taffeta. "Allow us to express our most sincere condolences on the loss of Louise. Monsieur Le Villard has told us the sad facts."

The man whirled to face her, revealing a scornful aristocratic aspect. He would have been distinguished in appearance had life not softened his character. World-weary features sagged over their bony underpinnings like melted wax. "What did the so-called detective tell you?" he demanded.

Godfrey stepped forward at the uncle's harsh tone. "He spoke of your niece's apparent death, Monsieur, of the difficulty it has caused your household."

"Difficulty! Hah." The man glanced to the servant, who still slouched on the threshold like a negligent guard. "You hear that, Pierre? The girl has been naught but a difficulty. This last is . . . only this last."

So this was Pierre, the uncle's personal servant who had dogged Louise's final footsteps. He was indeed a sinister figure. Yet he played butler in this awful house.

"How did she die? Where, when?" Irene was asking with true concern.

The uncle turned his back on us, fanned his hands over the fire, then gestured beyond the brocade-draped windows. "Behind the house lies an ancient mere. Animals are always falling into it. Louise was seen visiting it frequently by dark, or so the servants"—he glanced at Pierre—"reported even before her sudden 'illness' in the city. Two nights ago—a scant day after you returned her—Louise was observed leaving the house. Two cloaked figures met near the mere. When the house was alerted, I found only my wife there, and a silk scarf that Louise used to wear against the evening chill."

"Then there is no certainty—"

The man turned to stare at Godfrey, his once-handsome face as adamant as if carved in salt. "There is certainty," he said with satisfaction. "The gendarmes dredged the area. They raised a sunken tree limb; on it was snagged the bracelet Louise has worn since a girl. Her father had given it to her."

"May I see it?" Irene stepped forward, a graceful hand outstretched. Most men would have put something in it without thinking, for this was a woman who had received jewels from the King of Bohemia, as well as from the king of aristocratic commerce, Charles Lewis Tiffany.

"See it, Madame?" Monsieur Montpensier looked as if he would spit. "What is to see but a tawdry bauble my worthless brother bestowed long ago on his wife, and later on his daughter? They are all dead now, the end of an enervated line."

"Still, I would like to see it."

He looked away. "Honoria has hidden it. That is another quarrel the police have with her. She was always sentimental. The bracelet was, like my brother Claude, worth virtually nothing. The police may want its return as evidence if there is a trial." He seemed unconcerned that his wife would likely be in the dock should such an event transpire.

"Where is your wife?"

He nodded upward with a sharp, contemptuous motion. "The detectives questioned her, though she had no answers. Honoria is too milk-hearted to have drowned Louise. The girl's stubborn nature accounts for her death. Of late she grew absentminded and even more unreliable. Some frivolous errand or another was always drawing her to the heart of Paris."

"Which is why you assigned the dependable Pierre to escort her," Irene said with a smile.

"Someone had to watch the chit! You yourselves saw the trouble she had caused herself and others—evading Pierre, then falling faint among strangers. Oh, I suppose I am sorry for her passing, but she brought it upon herself, as her father did his fate, and I cannot excuse that."

"May we see your wife?" Irene asked. "I am sure the loss, coupled with these accusations, must threaten to unseat her reason."

"Reason! That's it. I ask you, what reason would my wife have to kill my niece? So I demanded of the detective, Le Villard. My niece was penniless as well as senseless. No one had anything to gain from her death, certainly not I or Honoria; that is why the idiotic detectives have had to cease questioning my wife. As for Honoria, she is mad herself. See her if you wish, and good luck to you!"

I was glad to retreat to the chamber doors after this dialogue. Pierre still stood guard there, his birthmark gleaming at us like a bloody coin in the fire-flash. Irene murmured thanks to the ungrateful uncle and we rustled out in our black garb to the forbidding hall.

Pierre fetched a candelabra; by its wavering light we were led up a long, dusty spiral of stairs. Near the top, gilt valances glittered above the windows. I almost expected to find the noxious Casanova perched upon one, ready to call down a greeting. "Nevermore," perhaps?

When Pierre knocked at a door in the upper hall, I was not prepared for the harsh, thick voice that answered. "Yes?" it croaked resentfully.

"Pierre," the servant said.

"Away, you ghoul!" a woman shouted, unaware of our presence.

Pierre shrugged with sour French indifference and turned to depart.

"Wait." Irene knocked gently on the chamber door. "Madame Montpensier, it is the American woman and the Englishman who found Louise several days ago. We would speak with you."

"No!"

"Madame, please, I beg you. We wish to offer our sympathies. We were quite taken with Louise—"

"Go away, can't you? I've had enough talk, enough questions!"

"Madame—"

Godfrey intercepted Irene's gloved hand before it could knock again and shook his head.

I shook mine as well. These two, master and mistress of courtroom and stage, had no notion of how to approach a sulking individual, especially one considered a likely murderess. Such a person must be firmly led. I neared the door and mustered my best French.

"Madame. It is possible that you yourself have slain your niece, in which case I can understand why you would not wish to see anyone. It is also possible that Louise's death was a terrible accident, in which case you would wish to know how kindly she spoke of you, only days past."

A long silence.

Then a lock turned, a hinge groaned, and the massive

wooden door swung inward. Shrinking behind it was a tiny woman with burnt-orange hair and a face the color of fresh snow. Pierre's candelabra blazed into eyes as dull as blueberries, sunk into maroon circles of skin. I had seen women painted in such lurid colors on posters around Paris, although Madame Montpensier's hues were the shades of deep distress, not of fevered gaiety.

Irene swept through the opening. Godfrey's prompt hand on my elbow urged me forward. I saw him bow sardonic thanks to Pierre before he firmly shut the chamber door upon us all and pointedly slammed the latch home.

This room was vast and chilly also, save for the fire in the grate. I heard a scratching sound and looked down to see a fat little spaniel waddling over to sniff our boots.

"It is—was—Louise's." Madame Montpensier bent to lift the creature.

No one in his right mind could question the ravages of emotion that had turned her face—undoubtedly once beautiful—into a gargoyle of grief. I looked at Godfrey and Irene. They, too, seemed thunderstruck by the woman's appearance.

"Hush, Chou-chou," Madame Montpensier chided the whimpering dog. "He knows something is amiss. But why have you come? How have you heard . . . what have you heard? That I—?"

"Please." Godfrey took the wriggling dog in one arm and guided Madame Montpensier to the high-backed chair that faced the fire. "Sit down. Perhaps you can enlighten us on how this terrible thing has happened to Louise. And to yourself."

She glanced up sharply. Godfrey Norton "leading" a witness, that is, posing questions that demand answers, was a phenomenon that even a statue would have had difficulty in resisting. I had seen him robed and bewigged in the Royal Courts of Justice on Fleet Street, his barrister's face assuming

an innocent concern, a profound understanding, that surpassed all suspicion. At such times, even a murderess might
forget herself and confess all.

Madame Montpensier drew herself up as if recognizing this
quality. She looked at Irene and then at me, wonderingly. "It
is kind of you to take an interest in our affairs."

"It is nothing of the sort," Irene said quickly. "We, after
all, feel responsible for having returned Louise to a situation
that has led to her apparent loss of life. And it is indeed our
business, in a way. We are"—she glanced roguishly at
Godfrey and myself—"experienced inquiry agents into matters criminal and, occasionally, merely puzzling. We wish to
see justice done."

The poor woman eyed me uncertainly.

Irene continued. "Miss, ah, Mademoiselle Huxleigh is our
valued friend and assistant. There is obviously more to this
matter than even the Paris police suspect, Madame. I think
you can tell us something more of it than you have hitherto
revealed."

The woman shrank into the chair while we gathered
around, our backs to the fire and basking in the fact. Godfrey
gently deposited the small spaniel in her lap. She absently
stroked the creature's silky ears while she spoke.

"I wonder that you discern so much of the situation from
such slight acquaintance with it—and us."

"Obviously," Irene put in, "Louise was kept under strict
supervision by her uncle. Few Paris demoiselles require the
unattractive likes of Pierre to shepherd them through the city.
One would think your husband feared kidnapping by pirates.
But we are not prescient, merely observant. Louise told us of
the mysterious letters that came to your husband. And of
another matter that we are sworn to keep secret—"

"You know even of *that?*" Madame Montpensier had
leaned forward in something like horror; now she drew back
in dismay. "You have told my husband?"

"Nothing. He did not seem interested. Besides, he is a suspect. Unlike the Paris police, we do not find it wise to settle too soon upon a candidate for suspicion."

"He is suspected of what?" I asked, shocked.

Irene's answers came readily. "Of ill will, at the most; indifference to his family, at the least. Am I not right, Madame Montpensier, in saying that this was a house of distress; that your husband ruled home and hearth with an iron poker; that he became even more vile-tempered after the letters began arriving three years ago?"

"True, Edouard was always high-tempered. It is understandable; he was the eldest of a family that was falling into ruin. He objected fiercely to his younger brother's marriage to a milliner, although Marianne was kind and pretty. I fear that the contempt of his brother drove Claude to seek his fortune at the tables of Monte Carlo. Of course, Claude found only further ruin there."

"And death," Irene said. "He took his own life."

Madame Montpensier did not deny it. "Marianne had died in childbirth; the infant had succumbed also. Louise was only five. I was surprised when Edouard took the child, but by then it was obvious that I myself could have none." A smile smoothed her haggard features as she rested her chin on the dog's blond head. "I welcomed Louise's presence. She was never any trouble, nothing but a joy. That is why it worried me when Edouard grew jealous of her movements as she grew older. A young girl should not be penned into an empty old house, dogged everywhere by a crude servant!"

"How old was Louise?"

"Just twenty when she . . . twenty last April."

"So when she matured, your husband's attitude toward her changed."

"He had been indifferent; then he became angry, suspicious, stifling. He became like a melodrama father, afraid that someone would steal away his daughter, save that Edouard

had never regarded Louise as anything but an encumbrance
. . . and a distraction for me, like Chou-chou."

"His manner changed exactly three years ago, when the
letters began coming?"

Madame Montpensier blinked, then considered the question. "Why, yes, about then."

"I must see one of those letters!"

Godfrey, who had been observing Irene's interrogation
with an expression of amused admiration, lifted his eyebrows
at that point. I was more blunt; I rolled my eyes.

"That is impossible, Madame Norton!" For the first time,
the woman showed spirit, even if in a cowardly cause. "My
husband has responded with nothing but unimaginable ire to
the appearance of the letters. They vanish immediately. No
one in the household would dare refer to them."

"You are his wife. You must know where he keeps them."

"No. I have glimpsed them only as they arrived; that is
enough for me to know that the entire household will suffer
for it for many days. That is all."

"Think!" Irene knelt beside the woman's chair. With the
veils of her mourning bonnet spilling around her pale face like
a black rose's wilting petals, her russet hair and entreating
expression, she reminded me of Mary, Queen of Scots,
pleading for her life with Queen Elizabeth. "Did he burn
them? Surely no woman—wife or servant—could resist
checking the grates the day after such a dire missive arrived.
That much must have been determined."

Madame Montpensier blinked again, as if just awakening.
She sat up straighter and lifted the dog absently—to my arms.
Of course I could do nothing but take it, heavy squirming
creature that it was. A pink tongue took liberties with my
bonnet strings while I tried to follow the scene unfolding
before me.

"No," Louise's aunt said, realization dawning in the
troubled skies of her lovely dark-blue eyes. "No! Not burned.

The distinctive heliotrope-and-sable-colored wax, the size of . . . of one of Chou-chou's paw prints, would have melted on the grate." She shuddered. "Wax like a clot of black blood. There was no peace in the house for a fortnight after such a missive's arrival. And the scent of it, heavy and foreign. No, Edouard could not have burned the letters. The fact would have been apparent to anyone in the house."

"Could he have buried them, or thrown them in the mere? It is convenient for necessary disappearances."

"Irene!" I hissed, appalled by her insensitive reference to Louise's last resting place.

"Don't worry, Nell. Louise Montpensier is no more in the mere than she is in Fleet Street . . . although she could more likely be there than in the mere, because she is not dead."

Madame Montpensier's face whitened. Godfrey made some sudden movement behind me. I inadvertently squeezed poor Chou-chou until he squealed like a little pig.

"My God, Madame Norton! You are—"

"No fool, thank you, Madame," Irene said modestly. "You see, your husband was quite right. Nobody had anything to gain from Louise's disappearance . . . except Louise. You yourself admitted that this house was a hell for her. I can imagine how the torment intensified when she was returned by strangers after having eluded Pierre and undergoing an unexplained absence of hours."

"But the bracelet dredged from the mere—" Godfrey began.

"A deliberate trail to a wrong conclusion. That is why Madame Montpensier has hidden it. I noticed it myself on Louise's wrist. If it were merely a foreign bangle—ivory or coral pieces strung upon elastic cords, for instance—it might conceivably catch upon a sunken tree limb and slip from a drowning victim's wrist. But this bracelet closed with a strong metal clasp, and gold would not break. Did it break, Madame?"

The woman shook her head.

"A mistake. You and Louise should have broken it first."

"She was too fond of it to harm it," the woman murmured.

"But—" I bent to deposit the leaden little dog on the stone floor "—if Louise is *not* dead and has left of her own will, why do you keep silent before the police, Madame?"

"She protects Louise's absence, is that not right, Madame Montpensier?" Godfrey put in. "She believes that it is better for herself to be accused of murder than it would be to keep Louise in this house a moment longer."

I could not accept this melodramatic answer. "Why cannot everyone know that Louise has left? Why must anyone suffer? The uncle is indifferent to Louise's well-being; the aunt is protective and willing to give up her niece. I do not understand."

"Because," said Irene, "the uncle may be indifferent to Louise's well-being, but he is not indifferent to the letters, and they involve Louise, intimately. I doubt that she has any idea of why, but she knows she is safer free, her whereabouts unknown by her uncle. It is better for him to think her dead than for him to know her alive."

At this point Madame Montpensier blinked several times. "But, Madame, you said you *knew*. I assumed—"

"Of course. I knew about the tattoo. We all did." Irene smiled pleasantly.

"But, Madame—Monsieur—Mademoiselle!" Louise's long-tried aunt was growing indignant. "I know nothing of any tattoo, and the letters, while mysterious, likely have nothing to do with Louise. She had to appear dead only in order to elope with her intended fiancé, a young American journalist. Edouard would have forbidden the match. Louise's only use to him was to marry well and bolster the Montpensier coffers. Why else did he marry me, although my dowry was far from splendid? You said you *knew!*"

Irene sat back on her heels, sinking into her dark garb like a funeral barge into its black silken sails from which all wind has fled. "An elopement. Well, no, I did not suspect that. Louise had said nothing. But then, I am not a romantic at heart."

Godfrey was laughing by the mantel, trying to bury his mirth in his mustache and a fan of fingers. I had never seen him behave in such an ungentlemanly fashion before. I was most amused.

"An elopement," Irene repeated. "How . . . unexpected. For Monsieur Montpensier, as well, if he knew."

"He must not!" Madame Montpensier looked terrified. "You must investigate this matter no further. If you were to alert Edouard to Louise's disobedience, I could not answer for it! Through all those years past, he was infuriated by his brother's profligacy; he even seemed to begrudge Claude his suicide, as if by it Claude had escaped Edouard's murderous rage. Now, with Louise—"

"We will remain as silent as the grave upon the matter, Madame," I promised. Someone had to take a responsible stance in this muddle. "I am most sorry for my friends' misconceptions and regret that their meddling has caused you worry. I can testify that they are reliable in most instances and will see to it that no news of this development reaches the ears of either your husband or Monsieur Le Villard." I turned to my companions. "Really, your curiosity has led us to seriously overstep the bounds of good sense."

Irene was biting her lips, whether from mortification or from laughter I could not tell, although it was the former if she had any shame in her.

Godfrey bent to assist Irene up from the floor, while Chou-chou took advantage of the rearrangement to claim Madame Montpensier's lap again.

"Thank you, Nell," Irene said with a sharp glance at me, "for your stirring apology on my behalf. I am convinced, however, that it is utterly unnecessary. Save for the addition of an American swain, I believe the situation sits much as it did before: Monsieur Montpensier is a dangerous individual with some secret interest in Louise that does her no good; Madame Montpensier is a courageous woman to shield her niece at the cost of her own reputation, but her silence may hurt Louise more than her speech would; the letters signify in some key manner, as do the tattoos, both old and new—no matter how lurid you personally may find these elements, my dear Nell.

"However, you are right that the facts must be held privately among us four," Irene continued. "You must trust us, Madame, to protect your niece and to unravel this mare's nest. Otherwise, I cannot be responsible."

In the course of a single speech, Irene had turned our heads around. I was possessed of a nearly irresistible urge to apologize for apologizing on Irene's behalf. Madame Montpensier leaned over the idiotically grinning Chou-chou, her hand to her heart, and herself apologizing.

"I tried to dissuade Louise from rash action, yet I could hardly advise her to remain in this house. She was so distraught after you returned her."

"If Louise did not tell me of her romantic involvement," Irene said gently, "she did not tell *you* of how she really fell into our hands. Godfrey rescued her from the Seine. She had cast herself into the water after having been unaccountably kidnapped from the Bois de Boulogne, rendered unconscious and tattooed upon the breast."

"My God, my God," the woman whispered, clasping Chou-chou in horror. "I had no notion. A suicide, like her father? Is Edouard right?" She seemed liable to throttle the dog accidentally in her emotion.

(I should note that the poor woman's profanity, which I reproduce, is understandable given the situation's gravity. For some obscure reason, the Lord's name seems less taken in vain when uttered in French, and the words *"Mon Dieu, mon*

Dieu" ring more graciously than their English translation— although, of course, the regrettable intent is precisely the same. Such are the mysteries of language.)

"Now I understand Louise's suicidal despair," Irene said, walking to and fro as if to put logic through its paces. "She undoubtedly often met the young American in the Bois de Boulogne." Irene smiled meaningfully at Godfrey. "Parks are famed as scenes of romantic rendezvous; I think of London's Regent Park in particular. But despite poor little Louise's fears that her suitor would reject her after such an *outré* episode, evidently he was more understanding than she thought. His must have been the second cloaked figure seen by the mere, the one taken to be Madame Montpensier when she was found alone on the sedge, with Louise gone. Now, Madame, I must have his name and the destination toward which the young lovers have fled."

I pitied the woman. Her face plainly showed the strain of having resisted all questions, domestic and official, for several days. Now she was being asked to put her faith in a stranger, and a foreigner at that.

Madame Montpensier shrugged ever so slightly. "Why else would strangers like yourselves desire to help Louise other than for the reasons you give, Madame Norton? The matter of the tattoo is troubling, especially the fact that Louise concealed it from me. I helped her to disrobe when she arrived home; how could I have missed seeing it?"

Irene's lifted hand spread thumb and forefinger. "A small jar of almost-magical cream, Madame. I gave it to Louise so that she could conceal the mark."

"You have more than magical creams up your sleeve, Madame Norton!" The woman's fleeting amusement showed her relief at passing her burden to another.

"I will perform one last magician's trick, Madame Montpensier, before I leave," Irene said. "But first, three answers for me—three wisps of information that I may weave into a solution: what is the name of Louise's fiancé; where did they go; and where would your husband keep the letters?"

The woman straightened, took a deep breath, and told us. "Caleb Winter of Boston; I believe they spoke of the Blue Coast; and the old library below holds many secrets. If the letters are anywhere, they are there. No one enters but Edouard. As a child, Louise liked to curl up there on gray days with a book, but Edouard was so angry to have his chamber disturbed that she learned to find books and reading facilities elsewhere."

Irene nodded at each morsel of information. Caleb Winter's name produced a moue of amusement, as if it reminded her of the inimitable character of her native land.

Mention of the fabled Blue Coast of France, overlooking the Mediterranean, elicited a pleased smile, as if this location figured in her speculations already.

And the existence of the sacrosanct study, from which even young girls were banned, positively inflamed her golden-brown eyes with the fever of pending challenge.

But first there was the promised magic trick.

Irene leaned against the mantel and glanced at Godfrey. In some ways, she looked as fatigued as she had when we returned to England after a sleepless five-day flight from the King of Bohemia's henchman. I would never forget her in the coach from Victoria Station, producing a cigarette from her man's suit coat. Smoke threaded through the carriage as Godfrey joined in that filthy ritual that yet manages to cloak one's memories in a hazy blue miasma, as fog blunts the sharp edges of London. We may cough at and revile them both, but fog and smoke are, alas, ineluctably romantic.

Now Godfrey produced a cigarette case and offered it to Irene before making his own selection. He lit their cigarettes with the remains of a long match from the fireplace. Irene tipped her head back, gazing dreamily through a mist of smoke as though consulting a crystal ball.

"Now I will tell you the location of Louise's bracelet."

Madame Montpensier gasped and clutched the dog upon her lap closer even as Irene leaned forward to pat the spaniel's shining head. Then her fingers burrowed into the thick blond fur at the dog's neck, and wrenched a bit of bright metal into the light.

"How did you know?" Madame Montpensier's morning-glory eyes shone in a face as guileless as a child's. "You are truly a miracle worker. Louise will be safe. I believe it now!"

"This room offers a thousand hiding places," Irene said, smiling, "but none so close to Louise as that dog, and none so likely to be ignored by your husband. That is the sad predictability of this house, that those in it will be ignored, as Louise was, until she became innocently involved in something too . . . exciting . . . to be ignored. That 'something' is what we will discover, Madame."

Irene cast the last of her cigarette into the logs. "Until then, Chou-chou may keep his collar, and you may rest easier. Louise is so far safe with her American suitor. At least we know now that there is indeed a mystery to solve."

Chapter Eleven

BURGLARS BY THE BOOK

❧

The following night no rain fell, but a full moon rode the darkness like a pearl set into an onyx mourning ring.

"Bah, humbug!" Irene drew back a chintz curtain and frowned at the moonlight bathing our front garden. "I loathe full moons."

She was clad again in utter black, on this occasion a well-cut gentleman's suit. Her dark hair's red-gold luster was snuffed by a black beret. Godfrey, also black-garbed from toe to collar, joined her at the window.

"You are no true romantic, Irene." He peered up at the moon's smug, waxen face. "Be grateful for its presence. We shall at least be in no danger of falling into the mere."

"Yes, but we are more likely to be taken for what we are—housebreakers!"

This was my signal for a small lecture. "The two of you look like Lucifer after a dip in the carp pond—black and sleek and too furtive for words."

The animal itself lay at my feet, toying kittenishly with a ball of cotton thread I was crocheting into a household object of use and beauty.

"We must see these fabled letters." Irene hefted a small black leather bag much like a physician's. It rattled as if concealing the family silver, although I suppose that what clattered was an array of housebreaking tools.

"We shall not even *take* the letters," Godfrey said.

"Of course not," I retorted. "That would give away your crime."

"We shall not need to take them," Irene said. "We have paper and pens—and lucifers, Godfrey?" she added in alarm.

He patted a bulging side pocket whose contents I did not care to speculate upon, although I had not recently seen Irene's ferocious little revolver. It, too, was black, in keeping with the mournful tone of the evening.

"Lucifers!" he announced.

"Surely you do not intend to *smoke* whilst flaunting the laws of France, not to mention those of hospitality?" I inquired.

"We must light our own interior moon, Nell." Irene lofted a shuttered lantern from the bag. It alone accounted for half of the clamor. My wince caused her to return it more softly. "We must be utterly quiet, Godfrey."

"We shall certainly endeavor to be so." He lifted a boot whose sole had been smeared with coal tar to smother his footfalls.

"I hope you do not leave a trail, as Lucifer does when he has been in the coal cellar," I said, crocheting so briskly that the animal under discussion began bobbing about in an attempt to pinion my ball of thread.

"No need to wait up, Nell," Irene advised, donning black gloves.

"I do not intend to." I rose and retreated to the parlor, where Casanova held forth from his cage.

I did not often have an evening to myself. I intended to make full use of it by plying the parrot with my French and studying the creature's pronunciation. This was an activity I did not care to pursue in public. So it was that I did not see them out, these charming housebreakers, although I peeped through the window with the lamp low. I saw the moon burnish their black shoulders to silver as they melted into the carriage that Godfrey would drive to the gloomy Montpensier residence.

When I turned back to the room, my insides were as knotted as my thread. Lucifer crouched by the bird cage, his fat tail twitching with unlawful appetite. "No, wicked cat! *Avaunt!* Leave my French tutor alone."

I offered Casanova a grape from the dining-room sideboard. The sly old reprobate sidled to the bars and cocked his head, presenting me with a suspicious eye as round and bright as a billiard ball.

"Pretty bird," I said stiffly, *"pairlay-vhoo franzay?"*

The ruffled neck darted forward. A flaking yellowed beak seized my bribe and would have snatched my fingertips had I not quickly pulled back. Casanova edged down the perch, which, despite daily attention from Sophie, still flaunted memoirs of chronic dropsy, so to speak. The bird transferred the grape from one talon to another, then eyed me, its head twisted at a conniving angle, looking like Long John Silver mentally measuring the captain of Stevenson's *Hispaniola* for a coffin.

"No, you foul bird," I admonished. "No escape. I've given you treasure, and you shall speak French. Now, *pairlay!"*

Thereafter Casanova trilled his French phrases, much to the irritation of Lucifer. I noted down phonetically the saucy but accurate pronunciations.

I did retire early, if only to demonstrate my absolute unconcern, but I did not sleep. The clock had struck two before I heard the sound of hooves in the lane; it struck three before my industrious criminal friends had installed the horses in the stable and crept into the house like the footpads they were.

"Well?" I met them on the stairs in my combing gown with lamp held high, feeling like an unlikely (not to mention anachronistic) offspring of Marley's ghost and Lady Macbeth. "I hope your entry to the Montpensier home was more discreet than this. You woke me from a sound sleep."

(A tiny untruth in the service of instilling guilt is permissible—even necessary—when dealing with wayward children and erring adults, as I had long since learned.)

"A pity." Godfrey grinned knowingly up at me. "Then I suppose you are too drowsy to hear our tale."

I sighed. "I doubt I shall sleep again, between your lumbering about the premises and that vicious bird gargling its gutturals all night."

Irene shook her hair loose from the beret. "We were in desperate need of your skills tonight, Nell. While you lay dreaming, I struggled to copy the penmanship of a drunken sailor."

"Then you found the mysterious letters!" I clattered downstairs to follow the miscreants into the parlor.

Godfrey was unshuttering the lantern to reveal the ragged pile of papers that Irene strewed over the shawl-covered table. I eagerly picked up one; because of my former profession of typist, paperwork has become my greatest weakness.

"Why, this is virtually illegible, Irene."

"You should have seen the original if you seek illegibility," she replied rather sharply. "I am not accustomed to writing by the light of a shuddering lantern while bent over a bookcase with my ears perked for a footfall at any moment."

"And this . . . what is this mess?" I demanded, staring at a veritable melee of crisscrossed lines.

"That is a sketch of the seal."

"Lucifer might have done better with his claws."

"Lucifer might have done better at the entire expedition," Godfrey said. "The window catches were so old they were rusted shut. The formidable Pierre makes the rounds of the house every forty-five minutes—and the library has high shelves reached only by a movable ladder so possessed of creaks that it mimics a pump handle."

"How dreadful." I sat down at the table, pulled out the pince-nez I happened to have ready in my gown pocket and propped it on the bridge of my nose. "Perhaps I can decipher this scrawl, Irene, in daylight. With time. But the seal is an impossible jumble."

"Exactly what I thought," she said, "until I realized that the blurred appearance was intentional because it *is* a jumble, a jigsaw puzzle. The wax was not imprinted with one massive seal, but overprinted with several. And I think—oh, where are the previous sketches?"

Godfrey fetched them from the desk where she had left them rolled into pigeonholes.

"Where were the missives found?" I asked Godfrey, watching Irene's hands shuffle pages around on the tabletop as if consulting an ouija board.

"On the top shelf of the farthest bookcase," he said. "A false back hid them. We had to remove two shelves with all of their books. Quietly. Within minutes."

"Oh, dear. How did you ever know to look behind that particular bookcase?"

"I did not. Irene did." He nodded at her tumbled auburn curls, all we could see of her face as she pored over the copies. "You must ask her to explain the logic; I cannot. It has something to do with a Provençal cookbook being on the top shelf."

"Well, of course!" said I. "Who would put a cookbook on a *top* shelf? Only someone who expected that shelf never to be disturbed. No woman worth her house sense would do it, but a man would, if he wanted to conceal a hiding place with books and wasn't particular of the volumes he selected."

"I see," said Godfrey, sounding unconvinced. Male logic often trips over such small but telling details.

Irene suddenly lifted a sketch to the lantern light, then another and another. Her face was rapt with dawning excitement.

"Yes! If I turn this one . . . so . . . and this that way, and do this with the third—Yes! Now, where is the sketch of the seal?"

Godfrey fetched it. She held it so close to the unshuttered lantern that I feared it might catch fire.

"Yes! The seal blends all three letters we have seen tattooed on three vastly dissimilar people."

"How extraordinary," I admitted.

"And not the half of it. Look! There is yet another letter impressed into the seal. I believe—I am convinced!—that it is an 'N'."

"What does it all mean?" Godfrey asked, as a barrister will.

Irene sat back with a great sigh. "I don't know. Certainly these two dead men and a young French girl are connected in a matter that involves at least one other person, perhaps several."

"What did the letters say?" I asked quite sensibly.

"Oh. A lot." Irene seemed too distracted by her puzzle pieces to go further, so Godfrey continued.

"I read them over Irene's shoulder as she took notes. They were decidedly odd, even ominous. The earliest-dated ones referred to the 'lamentable and curious' death of Claude Montpensier and told Edouard of a matter in which Claude's nearest relative, Louise, would figure. The letters said that although Louise was not of legal age, it made no difference, that the uncle should arrange for her to be contacted by the writer, in secret."

Irene nodded as I stared in confusion. She said, "Now the uncle's actions become understandable. The proposal to meet with an undefended young girl without her guardian's knowledge of the specifics is most bizarre."

"At this point, cruel Uncle Edouard sounds a hero," said I.

Godfrey shrugged. "Later letters grew more urgent, saying that it would be to Louise's 'advantage' to respond to the request, that many people were involved in the matter, which was highly secret, and that the uncle's demands for information were inappropriate, since he was merely a conduit and not the nearest relation of the dead man and thus not entitled to know more."

"And all of these letters were written in French?"

"Grammatical French for some, others not," Irene said. "Most were written in *different* hands and posted from various points on the globe. Some took months to arrive. The tone increases in urgency; the last letter came but a month before Louise was kidnapped and tattooed."

"It seems some vast old plot, like *Treasure Island!*"

"Exactly, Nell." Godfrey lit a cigarette and leaned against the window. "This is a sinister affair, I think, involving a number of desperate men. Louise's uncle has violated some long-standing agreement by keeping his niece from these men. I doubt they mean to harm her."

"But the assault! The tattoo!" I burst out.

"These are likely men of a seafaring nature, Nell, remember," Irene said, "considering the far-flung correspondence. They are not apt to weigh the effect of a forced tattoo upon a well-bred young woman. In fact, they seem to have been striving to meet some obligation owed her father. With Louise presumed dead, I wonder what they will do."

"Perhaps," Godfrey said, "they will do what a solicitor would do in the case of a deceased heir. They will approach the next nearest relation."

"Uncle Edouard!" Irene abruptly straightened. "Yes, he has not underestimated the import of the letters, else why hide them? And he has kept Louise from them. Perhaps he wished to force the writers' frankness; perhaps he too saw some gain in it . . . for himself."

"And now that he thinks the poor girl dead—" I put in.

"He may deal with this . . . company . . . himself! To his own profit!" Irene's glance sought our concurrence. "He may force himself upon them."

"What is this scheme?" I wondered aloud. "And why would tattoos be the method of its initiation?"

Irene swept the papers into a pile and rose to lift a candle. "Excellent questions to sleep upon. I shall be most interested to hear your suppositions in the morning, Nell. In the meantime, Godfrey and I shall consult the sandman."

I picked up my lamp and followed her to the stair.

"For myself," she continued, "I see but one sensible course. I must visit Sarah Bernhardt first thing tomorrow . . . or rather, tomorrow afternoon, as she never rises before noon."

I glanced with amazement and dismay at Godfrey. He knew what I thought of that hussy, Divine Voice or not.

"And you must accompany me, Nell." Irene's voice floated down from the dark at the top landing, her lone candle winking like a bright star. "Sarah has been most eager to meet you."

Godfrey was just swift enough to take the lamp from my nerveless fingers before I dropped it to the floor.

Chapter Twelve

RAPT IN BABYLON

M a d a m e   S a r a h reclined upon a divan that was draped with oriental cloths.

Madam Irene lounged upon a pile of cushions.

Miss Huxleigh sat upright upon a chair.

A diaphanous scarf draped the Thin One's no doubt scrawny neck, but her famous strawberry-blond mane spilled around her pallid face like a fiery fountain. Irene's hair had been styled for the occasion in a similar free-flowing mode: she looked very French and more than somewhat wicked. I was sure that Godfrey would not approve but that Edward Burne-Jones would want to paint her. Then I reconsidered my conclusion about Godfrey.

I wore a gray-felt bonnet with a few pheasant feathers.

A cat that made Lucifer look saintly prowled among the heaped pillows, its sharp withers knifing the smoky air, its spotted amber hide shifting with each muscular step. I have never favored leopards as domestic pets.

Plant leaves as extravagantly broad as the ostrich-feather fan our hostess waved tickled the ceiling. Green tendrils snaked over the furnishings. An arrangement of peacock feathers brushed my nose if I did not sit absolutely still.

Somewhere in that crowded salon, I was given to understand, a serpent lurked. Certainly Adam and Eve had already long left this garden of excess, and Lilith herself was my hostess for tea.

Little in the ornate façade of the actress's modern house on the Boulevard Péreire had prepared me for this ungoverned interior. Perhaps the "S.B." carved above the door should have alerted me that I was entering a temple of vanity.

Irene and I were shown into the main salon, whose crimson-damask walls reminded me of Mr. Poe's Chamber of the Red Death. These bloody walls bristled with antlers, exotic masks, and weapons of sinuous oriental design. I nearly tripped on the massive open jaws of a brown bear when I entered. Many such still-carnivorous skins littered the carpets, as did pots of scent-heavy tropical blooms profuse enough to induce a swoon.

No wonder the Divine Sarah reclined upon her divan in the semi-stuporous pose she had made famous.

"So this is the admirable Nell you mention, Irene," said the only animal exhibit in the chamber capable of speaking. The Divine Sarah coiled forward to peer at me.

I remained tongue-tied. My French certainly would not survive exposure to a wicked woman who declaimed in that language as if divinely inspired.

"I have had many lovers," the actress went on to Irene, "but seldom a devoted woman friend. Now this Miss Uxleigh"—(That is how she pronounced my surname; I was delighted that even the Divine Sarah could be flummoxed by foreign words.)—"is indeed a rarity of world stature."

"*Merci,*" I murmured modestly. Perhaps she was not so very wicked as I had thought.

"A jewel beyond price," Irene said airily. "Have you visited the cafés of late?"

"Ah, our amusing masquerade. We were quite dashing, were we not? I really think you ought to have fought that duel, dear Irene. My son, Maurice, has fought duels twice in my honor since he has turned sixteen. Swords are so dramatic . . . and so harmless these days. I wonder how they ever won wars with them."

"They didn't." Irene twisted in her pillows to pluck an apple from a basket. I gasped to see a fat, serpentine form slithering away as her hand reached out. "They used ships, cannon and cavalry, then guns. Swords were always mainly ornamental. Men can be so vain."

"Almost as vain as women," Sarah agreed with a laugh. "I imagine that Miss Uxleigh is not vain."

"Oh, no. She is most refreshing, and almost always honest."

"Almost always!" I squeaked.

"What an *original* pronunciation," the actress said enthusiastically. I cringed in irritation as she spoke on. "A pity that I can master no English. I believe I would have as charming an accent in that language as Miss Uxleigh has in mine. There is no single advantage a woman of truly enduring fascination can possess that is so splendid as speaking with a foreign accent, whatever her origin."

"Really?" I said in English, sitting more upright.

The actress's painted red lips parted over white teeth that struck me as rather too large and pointed. *"Vraiment,"* she said to me simply, with a smile. Truly . . . really.

Then she turned to Irene. "I do so long to speak Monsieur Shakespeare as written, but to attempt to do so would draw attention to me rather than to the part. Please speak a bit for me, my dear. It is such a pleasure to hear Shakespeare in his own words."

Irene complied by rising nearly as sinuously as I had seen our hostess do and launching into Katharina's curtain speech from *The Taming of the Shrew.*

Sarah Bernhardt listened almost visibly, a palm pressed to one temple, her spread fingers as white as an ivory comb against her flowing hair, her eyes closed and her pale profile tilted to the ceiling. The actress's every pose seemed designed for a photograph or a portrait. Even as I recognized the art—and artifice—behind the façade, I felt mute admiration for such adept self-presentation.

Despite the magnetism Bernhardt exerted even when frozen into a complicated pose, Irene managed to divert my attention. She gave a quietly ironic reading of the famous "advice to wives" speech that pretends to submission but in truth urges subtle rebellion. I had seen Irene act before, of course, usually in musical surroundings—in Gilbert and Sullivan, for example, or before the intervention of an aria. This informal performance moved me more, perhaps because there was only Irene to create the illusion. Her character's sly sincerity shone through the bizarre environment.

"*Brava, brava!*" Sarah cried at the end, clapping her hands over her head and lowering her small, feral face so that the wild waves of blondish hair made a frizzled mane behind her. "I could never play the shrew: there is no murder or suicide in the plot."

Irene sat down again, searching for her half-finished apple.

"Utterly gone, my dear. Eaten. Panache tidies up so diligently. He is an anaconda. So much more useful than the boa constrictor that ate my sofa cushions. I had to shoot Otto."

"S-shoot him?" I said faintly.

The Divine Sarah leveled her ostrich fan at an ottoman of particularly mottled design. "Otto. I did not even have to change his name."

I need not report every odd detail of that bizarre meeting, or, perhaps I should say, every bizarre detail of that odd meeting. In the salon of Sarah Bernhardt, eccentricity came and went an honored guest.

What was most bizarre was that the great actress—and I

could see that S.B. indeed would be formidable upon the stage—welcomed me, the soul of convention, as an intriguing new eccentricity in her chaotic domestic mise-en-scene. Perhaps excess always ultimately admires its opposite.

Yet I sensed that Irene's visit to Sarah Bernhardt was another sudden, inexplicable turn of my friend's own particular genius. Even as I kept alert for encroaching snakes or vines, I knew to my bones that Irene had a serious reason for consulting her acquaintance.

Someone, or something, tapped my shoulder. I turned to find a blue-and-yellow parrot perched upon my best woolserge basque with the rather smart new epaulets. The bird's loathsome scaly feet curled around the extravagant satin braid of my left epaulet as if it were a luxurious perch.

"Away!" I ordered in my best imitation-Casanova grumble. The bird jumped to a pillow embroidered with La Bernhardt's ever-present personal motto, *Quand même*, "in spite of everything," upon which it deposited a final exclamation point. Even the odious Casanova would not have so presumed.

But amidst so much clutter, what was one parrot dropping?

"Ah," the actress was intoning, "I have played Shakespeare only once. Ophelia in *Hamlet*, here in Paris, but the run was brief and costly. I was forced to tour South America to rebuild my gold reserves. I took one hundred curtain calls in Rio, and the millionaires of Buenos Aires made a carpet of their pocket handkerchiefs for me to walk on from my carriage to the stage door—so gallant, these Hispanics. And in Peru, the Indians gave me a necklace made of human eyes. I wear it now—"

She lifted a strand from among the strings of beads swagging her breast, but I hastily averted my . . . ah, eyes.

"That was the tour on which I lost both my poor maid and my wonderful impresario, the Terrible Mr. Jarrett—a pet name, you understand. I also fell and injured my knee while trying to avoid a pot of heather on shipboard coming home. Such vile luck, heather. Never let it come near you, my dears."

"Fear not," Irene said, getting a word in at last. "I have had quite an aversion to herbs since I was in Bohemia." She cast me a sidelong glance and an ironic smile that were quite lost on Madame Sarah.

"At least I was able to net a delicious Andean wildcat from the tour . . . and Otto, of course, and two hundred fifty thousand francs in profit, which made possible this new house and my first production of Shakespeare."

"You would make a splendid Ophelia," Irene said politely.

Madame Sarah's smile shrank into a pout. "I did, but the audience booed my darling Phillipe as Hamlet. I was forced to close the play quickly."

"Well, then," said Irene briskly, "if your audiences did not like your Hamlet, why not replace him?"

"I could not! Phillipe is . . . quite close to me."

"Sentiment cannot overcome profits. Obviously, your production featured the wrong Hamlet. You must do the play again with a more correct casting."

Bernhardt writhed upright in her robes and upon her divan, as slowly as a queen cobra lifting to fan its hood and sway seductively before its entranced victim. She assumed the aspect of an angry empress considering the beheading of her immediate family. She was Theodora, her greatest role. I wondered that Irene should be so bold as to contradict this fiery Parisian wildcat.

"Whom would you suggest for the title role, Madame?" the Divine One demanded imperiously.

"Why yourself, naturally."

"Myself?!"

"Indeed. Hamlet is perhaps the greatest role in the English language; why should you not make it the greatest role in the French?"

"But . . . my beauty—"

Was more applied than inborn.

"My . . . fabled femininity—"

Was more stage-managed than inherent.

"My . . . youth—"

Madame Sarah was well past forty.

"True . . ." Irene consented sadly. "It would be a violent casting against type. But Hamlet is the pinnacle of leading roles. Remember, my friend, our expedition in gentlemen's dress to the cafés? How you deceived them all! Why should you play the mere supporting role of Ophelia, no matter how appealingly she goes mad, with her dress disordered and her hair wild? It is a role originally essayed by some shallow Elizabethan young *man*, when you—you, the toast of the modern world—could take the plum part for yourself and amaze all with your forceful art that overcomes even so great a barrier as sex, hmm?"

Irene took a grape from the fruit basket and offered it to the parrot.

Madame Sarah sank back into her rich cloths like a snake coiling into its cast-off skin. Her piquant face had assumed a thoughtful expression that had not a particle of pose in it.

"Play Hamlet? I suppose I could. I've played a youthful trouser role or two, but Hamlet himself? 'To be or not to be, that is the question'."

"To be or not to be Hamlet. Exactly." Irene peeled a grape. "I merely mention the idea, of course. Women in opera often play trouser roles. I myself, because of my deeper soprano, have done a few. It is seldom tried of late in the theater; perhaps the concept is too bold for these cautious days. It would be too great a gamble. Better that one go to Monte Carlo and have some fun with one's money, no?" Irene smiled conspiratorially.

My ears perked up when the words "Monte Carlo" fell from Irene's lips. At last! The nub of the matter. I needed to extract my note pad discreetly and transcribe any clues that might fall from those painted red lips. I sought a spot upon which to deposit the teacup and saucer I had clutched before my bosom like a shield since our arrival. The maid who brought it had never returned, and there was no flat surface in sight that could be considered a "table".

While I was thus fruitlessly engaged, the conversation bounded on.

"Ah, you like to ride the wheel of fortune, too?" Madame Sarah asked Irene.

"In a modest sense."

"My dears, there is nothing modest about Monte Carlo. Everything is on the grand scale there, like an opera, or like one of my plays. You have been, of course?"

"No, I have not. To tell the truth, I'm afraid that Miss Huxleigh has dissuaded me from going. She is most adamant that gambling is not only wickedly wasteful, but that it leads to other sensual indulgences, including drink, drugs and, alas, such losses that suicide may seem the only solution."

"Lies!" Sarah shouted before I could say the exact same thing.

Although Irene had properly conveyed my opinions on the pastimes of the rich and idle, I had never sought to stop her from going to Monte Carlo, simply because she had never before expressed a wish to go. Besides, how was I to interfere in the movements of a married woman? It was her husband's business to dissuade her, and I was sure that Godfrey would indeed quash any such frivolous scheme, much as he had tried to dissuade me two years ago from foolishly going to Bohemia on the mere say-so of Irene's cablegram.

"Libel," Bernhardt continued, drowning out my feeble protests.

I at last set the cup on a low stool upholstered in a jungle print and surreptitiously withdrew my note pad so as to record Irene's calumnious use of my opinions and my character.

"Monte Carlo," declaimed the actress, "is a divine oasis of warm winds, fanning palms and sparkling waters, much like my beloved Rio. You must go! And take Godfrey. Take even this most amusing Miss Uxleigh. Perhaps she will prove lucky; the most unlikely people often do in Monte. The wheel of fortune has strange favorites."

"And stranger ways of repaying former favorites," I finally put in. "Many losing players commit suicide. How can such a hellish place be a paradise?"

"That is the work of these hostile cartoonists. See how they have pilloried me in the press, and I am nothing like their scandalous rail-thin depictions, no?"

I was not so sure, but I held my tongue.

"If we are to go to Monte—" Irene began.

I braced myself at that "we."

"—how would we make ourselves known there?" she continued.

Madame Sarah took Irene's meaning instantly. "You will have an introduction from myself to the queen of Monte Carlo herself. Well, princess, not queen, and her position is quite unofficial—as yet. Dear Prince Charles rules Monaco so operatically, although he is allergic to flowers—can you imagine?—and thus cannot spend much time there. You must stay at the Hotel de Paris and eat at the Grand, where Cesar Ritz reigns over the menu."

Irene interrupted to nod at me. "You are recording that, Nell?"

"Religiously," I gritted through my teeth in English.

Madame Sarah went on. "You must, Irene, lure that handsome Godfrey of yours into long, open carriage rides along the coast, but bring a sunshade for privacy, my dear; men go quite mad in the subtropical climate. You must be sure to acquire some—" Madame Sarah eyed me "—some attractive clothing for this English wren and find her a rich husband. And you must go first to my dear Alice Blue-gown. She is

American, yes! And, like myself, has blonde hair and blue eyes."

Madame Sarah batted the lampblacked lashes shading those expressive blue-green orbs. "In fact, my dear Irene—" here she forsook her languor long enough to edge confidentially close to my friend "—Alice may have some small awkwardness intruding into her future that you may be able to settle. I hear that you have a way with small awkwardnesses. She would be most grateful, and Monte Carlo would be your plum . . . as Hamlet may yet be mine, no?"

"Alice—?"

"Alice Heine of New Orleans, courtesy of the family Heine of Hamburg. Banking interests. The poet, Heinrich, is an ancestor. Now Alice is the young and widowed Duchesse de Richelieu. Her father is my trusted financial advisor, and sometimes a very fierce lecturer, let me say! Despite my ardent attentions to the gaming tables, my dear 'golden pig' has a bank big enough to make such things as this house possible."

"Then the duchess is prominent in Monte Carlo social circles?" Irene asked eagerly, beaming at me as the opportunity to introduce the true purpose of our visit fell into her lap. "I am most anxious to pursue a rather urgent inquiry there. Could she help me, do you think?"

"Of course. Alice is rich, and pretty. She may soon become the first American princess of Monaco, if poor Prince Albert can outlive his father, Prince Charles. Albert is divorced, a long story and like all long stories, unsuitable for telling. Alice will adore you and your Godfrey and Miss Uxleigh. She has a great love for the opera and art . . . and for my acting, of course. She will make a splendid princess. I have decided! You must go to Monte and stage-manage this situation, my dear Irene. You will put a crown upon an American head, and—a pity you are otherwise engaged; it's so bourgeois to be married—you may even snare a princeling. Oh, but Miss

Uxleigh is unmarried, no? Ah, we must work upon Miss Uxleigh. . . ."

Here those piercing blue eyes turned rapaciously in my direction. At that exact moment, I heard a crash of china. We all looked down to see the "footstool" at my ankles undulating over the carpeting through the remains of my shattered tea things. I had never been so grateful for such an odious distraction in my life.

Chapter Thirteen

ENTER THE DETECTIVE

❧

''**A sorry** business, Watson.''

My friend Sherlock Holmes looked up. A sheaf of foreign notepaper dangled from his thin fingers as he lounged in the velvet armchair as carelessly as only Holmes could.

I smiled at the legs thrust straight out, the long arms cast over the chair's sides; even at rest, Holmes's figure possessed a tense, geometric energy that implied imminent action.

"One of your European cases, no doubt." I nodded to the limp papers. "It must be complicated."

"To the contrary, Watson." Holmes sighed. "A supremely simple matter. It is the police who make it complicated. Still, it requires looking into. I am no Mycroft, who can fabricate webs from a cosy corner at the Foreign Office or at the Diogenes Club. I must examine the scene of the crime, and the domestic scenery against which it took place. Legwork, Watson, this will require legwork! Le Villard is puzzled, a sign that there may be one or two interesting threads woven into the patchwork of tawdry passions and familial greed usually present in such a case."

"A murder, then?"

"Le Villard is not so sure. It seems that an English barrister living in Paris has convinced him that the primary suspect may be innocent. And there is no body."

"What will you examine, then?"

Holmes gave that short, sharp laugh so like the bark of a hunt dog about to begin the chase. "You are a physician, Watson, and rely upon physical evidence. I find the *absence* of a body far greater evidence of crime than its presence. The deed, however, may not be what it appears . . . or is meant to appear to be."

"I suppose this resembles your curious 'incident of the dog in the nighttime' not barking—more remarkable for what has not happened than what has."

"You suppose, Watson! Let us call the matter closed, then: Watson supposes and Holmes disposes. I don't know why I bother to open my correspondence or answer my door when whatever case may come to me is supposed to be 'like' a previous one. Crime can be cut from patterns, then. It becomes merely a question of imposing the particular outline upon a new set of facts?"

"You know quite well that's not what I meant to say, Holmes. I merely wondered how you would proceed without a body to study."

"I will study the bodies available to me, notably the person of the suspected murderess, Madame Montpensier—a heretofore respectable woman who is aunt by marriage to the vanished girl.

"A woman is thought to have murdered her own niece?"

"Crime grows apace in France." Holmes rubbed his hands together. "I confess that a foreign environment may prove stimulating. Also, I'd like to see how Le Villard's translation of my monographs gets on. Yes, time for a sea voyage, even if only a humble channel crossing. A pity you are wrapped up in your practice at the moment."

"My banker does not consider it so," I said dryly. "But as a doctor confined to physical evidence, I must admit that I rejoice to see you in high spirits again, Holmes. If I may make so bold, I could think of no better prescription for you, were you my patient, than a short sojourn abroad."

"So Watson not only supposes, but approves! With that benediction, I will embark tomorrow. I don't want to flatten your hopes, but I doubt I shall retrieve a story suitable for your burgeoning literary efforts. These foreign crimes are all too often cramped, tangled matters in which pride plays too great a role. More the stuff of opera than your brand of breathless journalism."

"Breathless! I hardly would describe my reports as breathless."

"Hmm. But it takes a certain melodrama to find a way into print these days, to judge by the newspapers. Just look at how they go on about the Whitechapel business. Compared to that, the Montpensier disappearance should merit no more than a footnote even in your records of my exploits."

"This opinion is based, I suppose, on deduction."

"Heavens, no, Watson! It is based, like most opinions, on no reasonable basis whatsoever. For that very reason, I must go to France; although that sounds a contradiction truly worth investigating. Hand me the schedule for Waterloo Station, Watson; just as a child must crawl before he can walk, so even the world's greatest consulting detective must go by rail before he can set sail . . . or rather, get up a head of steam."

Chapter Fourteen

SNAKES IN THE GRASSE

❦

"**I am** so glad that we are leaving Paris!" Irene commented fiercely as our train rolled out of the gloomy terminal yard toward the sunny south of France.

"Why?" I asked.

Godfrey answered for her. "It's best to withdraw from the Montpensier investigation before Le Villard realizes that we know more about the matter than he does and that we have concealed facts in the case. The police in any country become abominably testy about such things."

"And we must not forget Louise," Irene added. "I doubt she is in immediate danger in the company of her fiancé, but that may change. She has been abducted and brutalized once already. Until we know why . . ." Irene settled uneasily against the burgundy velveteen seat.

I did not see how Louise's presence in Monte Carlo, an obvious attempt to learn more of her father's death, would clarify any of the matters before us, but I was glad enough to be leaving Paris myself. It was entirely too French for my tastes.

Our iron steed for this mission was a charger in the Ouest line; the train would speed southward through the soft, fertile lands cupped between the long arm of the Loire and the trailing fingers of the Seine—and later the Rhone—rivers. We would traverse some four hundred miles, roughly the length of Irene's and my escape route from Bohemia eighteen months before.

I settled against the seat's upholstered back, assured of viewing only tranquil countryside. Even the towns through which we would pass were sleepy in the extreme, bland yet fabled communities that the French interior hoards like fallen apples—Dijon, Lyon, Avignon, Arles. Then, at last, we would reach the bustling Mediterranean seaport of Marseilles.

I felt a nervous flutter about entering this unsavory city. I also harbored misgivings at leaving Casanova and Lucifer in the care of Sophie. Our maidservant was reliable but no match, I feared, for those devious creatures, each the arch-demon of its species. Not that I would miss the beasts' bedeviling company, of course, but I do take my responsibilities seriously. And among them was Irene Norton, *née* Adler.

Irene remained pensive, watching the confluence of tracks near the station dwindle to a single set of rails alongside our own and then vanish utterly. No doubt she was troubled by leaving Madame Montpensier to face false accusations alone. Godfrey also seemed distracted, his pale gray eyes as dull as steel. His forefinger lifted absently to smooth his mustache, something I had never previously seen him do.

I wondered if events deeper than I suspected unsettled my friends. Both were too unlike themselves to note the other's abstraction. That is the advantage of being a third party; I alone could offer the objective viewpoint.

For now my objectivity submerged itself in the small excitement of traveling through foreign countryside. In fact, I secretly hoped that Monte Carlo would prove so removed from such lurid phenomena as tattooed girls, drowned sailors and mysterious capital letters that it would forever cure Irene of interfering in matters more fit for the police, with whom she imagined herself to be engaged in some game of wits. Not that Fate had ever much respected my hopes.

We left Paris in the morning. The train's lavatory facilities were primitive, so Irene and I gratefully availed ourselves of the accommodation at the simple country restaurant when we lunched in Lyon, halfway to our goal. The journey from there to Avignon was horrific, including a long stretch when we hurtled ahead at more than thirty miles an hour, over rough tracks through bleak terrain. But Avignon was very near Marseilles; the Mediterranean coast lay but an hour or two away over gentler landscape.

While Irene puzzled over sketches of tattoos and Godfrey read a volume on French estate law, I watched the cows and the countryside roll by until the monotony and the railway car's rocking rhythm lulled me to sleep.

I awoke to civilization, or the imitation of it, a steep, thronging town raked down like an amphitheater to the stage of a vast blue rippling sea and bracketed by fierce-looking fortresses. Masts made a barbed forest in the harbor, against a cobalt sky already paling before the final bloodbath of sunset. For our arrival, Marseilles pelted our compartment windows with bouquets of strong sea smell, while waves of white gulls fluttered against the sunset-drenched sky like streamers of white ribbon.

Marseilles' wet cobblestone streets sparkled with fish scales as bright as cut steel. The men's faces had a robust, sun-charred cast; I saw more than one parrot perched on a seaman's jerseyed shoulder.

We found rooms at a hotel overlooking the Vieux-Port, since a train to Monte Carlo would not depart until the next morning. I remained there that evening, while Godfrey and Irene ventured into the raucous city streets to dine, they claimed, on *bouillabaisse*, oysters and champagne. My stomach was too uneasy after the rough trip and the commotions of Marseilles. I supped on the French bread and cheese Godfrey had found at a local market, which were quite tasty, save that the cheese had a musty flavor and the bread crust was prone to crumble. So much for the fabled French cooking!

Still, by morning I was my cheery, uncomplaining self again and ready to resume our impetuous progress. I even welcomed the sight of our steel steed gleaming deep green in the sunlight as its pistons kicked up clods of steam and a docile herd of railway cars panted in line at the Gare Saint Charles. Ahead of us lay the spectacular mountainous sea-coast to Cannes, with the perfume-bearing hills of Grasse, the great French scent district, beyond it, and then on to Monte Carlo.

"Oh, but wait!" Irene cried as we prepared to board. Even the attendant stowing our luggage on the inside rack paused at her clarion call. "I saw some wonderfully amusing postcards in the station last night. I must buy some."

I stared at her openmouthed. "You are presumed dead, Irene; you cannot send postcards. And to whom?"

She shrugged gaily. "At least I can keep them as memen-tos. I saw a most macabre one of a suicide victim hanging outside the casino in Monte Carlo."

Now I understood. I made the sound with which the parsonage housekeeper in Shropshire used to call the chick-ens. Novelists represent it as "tsk-tsk," which hardly does justice to its implications and effect.

"Ah, postcards of Monte Carlo," said I. "No doubt that is how Mr. Sherlock Holmes begins to investigate a new region. Who knows what hidden depths may be concealed within a simple postcard?"

"Exactly!" Irene ignored my sarcasm, an oversight I found most unsatisfying. "Godfrey will see you aboard, Nell."

"Don't miss the train!" I elevated my voice to an unladylike level, to no avail; Irene had turned and moved swiftly against the current of the boarding crowd.

Godfrey took my elbow reassuringly. "Rest easy, Nell; Irene is not so careless as to miss this train, though the last train we missed—the St. Gothard-line excursion over the Alps—spared us a fiery death in thin air."

"No one could claim that the air of Marseilles is the least bit thin," I retorted. "It's as thick and steamy with corruption and clatter as *bouillabaisse,* perhaps even more populated by strange, whiskered denizens of the deep. It is my sincere hope that this chug-chug across France will lead to nothing but twiddling our thumbs."

At that moment a rough fellow in a striped jersey jostled past, ramming me into the side of the compartment.

"Be careful, man!" Godfrey exclaimed in French.

The uncouth creature turned and grinned, revealing a checkerboard of yellowed and blackened teeth. "So sorry, Your Highness," the man said with a sneer, "but a first-class ticket makes this my compartment as well as yours."

"Bridle your tongue before a lady!" Godfrey advised.

"Why don't we discuss the state of my tongue inside this compartment, Your Grace? And the lady, too. Step in, now."

Godfrey was about to do nothing of the sort; then his face tightened. I turned to see that the lout blocking our way had caused a queue to form behind us . . . if one shriveled Indian man may be considered the start of a queue. I was struck by the notion that our fellow first-class passengers looked as if they had been lifted directly from the deck of a river scow.

Before I could communicate this interesting observation to Godfrey, he gripped my arm and impelled me into the empty compartment, where our baggage already lay in the overhead racks. The rude man pushed me into a seat near the center.

Of a sudden I understood the reason for Godfrey's compliance. As the Indian followed him inside, I saw the thick, curved knife blade the ruffian pressed into Godfrey's side.

"Godfrey!" I half rose, but the man in the jersey pushed me back down.

"Stay put, Madame," he said, "and close your mouth. Your husband and I have a matter to settle. If you happen to be present, it is your misfortune."

Godfrey and I stared at each other in confusion. He glanced to the window, then quickly away. Beyond his shoulder I glimpsed the flow of people on the platform outside. Among them I spied Irene emerging from the station building, her eyes lowered as she examined the tiny fan of postcards in her hand.

Jerseyman jerked his head at his swarthy accomplice, then at the window. The Indian oozed over in a thrice and began drawing the curtains on their brass rods. (Only the French would be frivolous enough to install velvet curtains in a railway car!)

Irene glanced up from her purchase to look for us, seeking the compartment window framing our waiting faces. Alas, we were not there. Puzzlement—as well as a new alertness—crossed her face.

Then that familiar face was shuttered from our view as the Indian pulled the fabric shut. It was like watching opera curtains close on Irene at the end of an act: first the relentless advance of heavy cloth narrowing her figure to a mere sliver, then nothing.

Godfrey's face showed relief just as the curtains closed, plunging the compartment into a rather ominous dusk. Although I applauded his manly intent to spare his wife danger, I was not sure I was pleased to be taken for that wife in such a situation.

The Indian slipped to the door to perform the same service with the drapes there. I noticed only then that he was barefooted—and black-footed, so grimy were his toes!

"The gaslight?" Godfrey suggested quickly, before the last daylight had been banished.

Jerseyman nodded permission. Godfrey scratched a lucifer on his boot bottom and reached up to light the gasolier that depended from the ceiling. In the artificial light, the compartment's brass trimmings—ceiling scrolls, baggage racks and curtain rods—glittered as if for an audience. The burgundy velvet upholstery and curtains radiated a deep, gemlike sheen.

Given our unseemly companions, the civilized scene was ludicrous. The mingled odors of sulfur and gaslights reminded me of an opera box during a performance of "Faust."

"Might I smoke?" Godfrey still held his burning lucifer.

"I always grant a man a last wish," Jerseyman said. I realized that his French bore a cockney twist. "And give me one, Guv." Godfrey complied. "I've had naught but bottom ends for the past few weeks." Jerseyman lit up, then blew out a putrid stream of smoke.

With the curtains drawn, Godfrey and I were gestured toward the window seats. Jerseyman barred the door, sitting at Godfrey's side. My seat partner was the silent Indian, who promptly lifted his filthy feet to the velvet cushion and crossed his ankles, knees akimbo. He set between us a woven basket of a peculiarly flat shape. I appreciated any barrier, however homely, that would separate myself and my strange captor.

For we were prisoners, that was clear. The Indian rested the dreadful knife across his draped thigh; he wore no trousers, only some foreign cloth, similar to a dresser scarf, wrapped around his nether regions.

Jerseyman flaunted his own knife, less exotic but equally visible. And very dirty fingernails.

The scene reminded me of the occasion when the King of Bohemia's henchman had trapped me in a train compartment during the escape from Prague, save that this time no Irene with cane in hand and pistol in pocket would come to rescue me.

There was Godfrey, of course, but his use in a crisis of this type was unproven. Smoking serenely now as if we four made a congenial party of fellow travelers, he eyed Jerseyman with a lively interest.

"I presume you have a reason for your most curious form of introduction," Godfrey said.

The Jerseyman's evil grin was his answer, along with a deep inhalation upon the cigarette Godfrey had given him. I recalled demons who were said to breathe fire.

Around us, the compartment throbbed with the train's prelude to departure. Godfrey and I eyed each other, imagining Irene hunting us and failing.

"Your reason, man!" Godfrey demanded more urgently.

Jerseyman, almost genteel now that his lungs were sufficiently smoke-clogged, smiled and spoke in English. "Your friend on the platform will just have to do without your company."

"F-friend?" I inquired.

The miserable oaf regarded me with cocked head, as the vile Casanova was wont to do at his most uncooperative. His eye whites were as unappetizingly yellowed as his teeth. "Your friend, too, Missus, I suppose. She's better out of it," he said gruffly. " 'The beauty,' the concierge in the hotel here called her, and right the old harridan was. 'The beauty' will have to get on alone now."

I swallowed at the finality of that declaration even as the train gave a preliminary jolt. Would Irene decide not to board when she couldn't find us? "What do you hold against us?" I demanded. "What can the likes of you possibly hold against us?"

"Even the likes of me has friends, Missus . . . or business acquaintances." As he leaned forward to pierce me with a look, a strange rustle came from beside me. The abominable basket was shaking with some interior disruption!

"Oh!" I shrank against the window frame. "I don't doubt

that you have friends . . . such as this fine Indian gentleman."

He laughed until his eyes ran and his nose turned a decidedly unattractive cherry-red. "Singh's a gentleman and I'm a lemming! And you two have much to answer for, or you're a tragic railway accident. The track follows the coast from here to Toulon. An open window, a wee push . . . it's a long bounce down the seaside cliffs to the water, milady."

"Look here!" Godfrey leaned forward, perhaps to distract the man. He was rewarded with a knife point in the chest. "If you've some quarrel with me, out with it. Let me answer, and leave the lady unharmed. I've done nothing to earn any man's emnity."

"Then it's a dull life you've lived!" Jerseyman wheezed with bitter laughter. "I've done naught but earn enemies, some undeserved, some not. It's sweet to see a fellow speak up for his wife, but it's a woman I too would avenge, a girl really."

"Girl?!" I echoed, judging our captor to be well past sixty.

"A girl of good family. You done her in." He turned on Godfrey with casual threat, jerking the knife tip to his throat.

I gasped in comprehension. "Louise! You must refer to Louise Montpensier!"

"At least the lady admits it. Likely you had little to do with it, Missus, though you may have aided his villainy."

"Godfrey villainous?" I couldn't help sounding incredulous.

"You're his wife; you have to defend him."

"I beg your pardon, I'm not—"

Godfrey's glower would have frozen the medusa to silence. It sufficed to persuade me to change my tune. "I'm . . . not obliged to support my, er, husband if he commits a wrong."

This statement adhered to my philosophy; furthermore, it did not actually claim Godfrey for my husband. The idea was ludicrous to me, as I'm sure it was to Godfrey. Evidently

Jerseyman had presumed the English people in the party to be man and wife and the American the odd woman out.

The train's initial exertions soon turned to the bump, hiss and clatter of actual speed. I felt truly frightened.

Jerseyman waved his blade in my direction. "If you're not bound to help out your husband here, then why did you and your lady friend come running to the L'Oiseau Blanc in Paris? Didn't you guess what kind of place it was? A *hôtel particular*, as they call it?"

"No! Not until I arrived there."

Jerseyman prodded Godfrey's collar with his knife point. Luckily, it was well starched—the collar, not the knife point.

"What kind of worm, Guv, would drag his own wife and another apparently respectable lady to such a place, as well as a young girl?"

Godfrey had no opportunity to answer, for besides resenting the "apparently respectable," I was struck by an insight I could not help expressing. "Then you, sir, consider yourself a *friend* to Louise Montpensier!"

This gave the man pause. "I can't say I ever met the young lady face-to-face."

"Then why avenge her upon those who did her no harm?" Godfrey inquired with a barrister's reasonableness.

"No harm!" The knife sawed the air near Godfrey's Adam's apple, which appeared about to become apple cobbler between the ruffian's threats and the train's abominable shaking. "First you force her into a low, vile place like that—I should know, I've slept under such roofs before—and you have the gall to call your own wife and another lady there. Then you take her away in a carriage. Within days, Mademoiselle Montpensier is gone, vanished! We put a lot of time into that girl; we don't like losing her."

"*You* don't like losing her?" Godfrey's voice clapped with the thunder of righteous indignation, at which he excelled in court. It was a pity our questioners did not wear white

horsehair wigs and abide by the English system of jurispru-
dence. "How do you think *we* feel? I pulled that child from
the cold, wet grasp of death itself that afternoon. Of course I
brought her to the nearest shelter! She was soaked, chilled
and distraught, yet to involve the police would be to brand
her as an attempted suicide. Naturally, I asked my . . . er,
wife and her friend to help with Louise. For this you threaten
me?"

"You didn't bring her to that place to misuse her?"

"Of course not!" Godfrey's eyes narrowed to steel-bright
slits as he saw our captor dueling with doubt. He pressed his
advantage: "And how do *you* know of that incident? Did you
see Louise jump into the Seine? Were you following her?
Why? Do you know why she was determined to destroy
herself?"

"To get away from you, I'd think." Jerseyman had decided
to rely upon first impressions. "Young girl like that, her uncle
so careful that he had a man assigned to follow her. We've all
been careful of her. Then you take her to that place and the
next thing we know, she's gone, sunk like a stone, and not
even in a proper body of water. We got an investment in that
girl an' if it's gone for good, I guess I'll satisfy meself by takin'
it out of your hide—"

"Sir!" said I.

Jerseyman and Godfrey stared at me as if I'd gone mad. In
the ensuing silence, I heard a new rustling from the basket,
which shook as if with an ague. The Indian was smiling, an
expression that emphasized a shallow, sinuous scar meandering from one bottom eyelid to his chin like a single
tear track—an elongated "S," as in the tattoo! Were the
scar bas-relief rather than engraved, it would have resembled . . . a snake.

"Sir," I repeated, thinking to distract Jerseyman from
threatening Godfrey further, "am I to understand that you
consider yourself a . . . a Dutch uncle?"

"The Dutch have nothing to do with it, lady! That's one breed we haven't got in our company, the Dutch."

I cast frantically about for a more felicitous expression and, God forgive me, found it. "Is it possible, sir, that you and your"—the basket beside me was heaving closer—"companion are secret friends to dear Louise? Guardian angels, so to speak?"

It was sheer blasphemy to attach such an elevated designation—and a Romanish one at that—to the debased examples of humanity before me, but I am told that the Deity welcomes the lost sheep. Perhaps He may extend mercy even to a heathen Indian holding captive something decidedly unlamblike in a basket.

"Guardian angels?" The man laughed and nodded. "So you might say. We look after her interests, Singh and I. Have for years."

"How . . . nice." The Jerseyman was so intrigued by my question that he had lowered the knife an inch or two from Godfrey's throat. "I assure you that we meant her no harm, did her no harm, mean her no harm."

"Mean?" Jerseyman pounced on the present tense.

I was speechless in the face of my misstep.

"Louise is alive, we believe," Godfrey said quietly, "though the Paris police think her dead." He waited until the knife was withdrawn fully before speaking again. "I see the story now. You and your henchman here drugged and tattooed Louise. You left her to awaken alone and discover her fiendish alteration. Why was it not you who pulled her from the river into which she cast herself after your infamy? Why was it left to me?"

"Lost her for a bit," the Jerseyman said sourly. "So she dove in herself? I didn't know what to think. When next we spied her, she was wet and with you. Then you forced her into that low place. After that, the two gentleladies arrived in a fine carriage—and when next I look in at the Montpensier house, the police are coming and going and the neighbors say that Louise drowned in the mere. I figured she'd killed herself, like her dad, over what you'd done to her."

"Good God, man, it was *you* and that foul tattoo that forced her to the river! *I* saved her from drowning!"

"Uh." The Jerseyman's grunt echoed my traditional interjection with quite different effect. His seamed, sly face grew sheepish, although I doubt that even the Deity would have found it pleasant. "We made sure the girl was fast asleep for the needle. She couldn't have felt a thing. Singh has a touch of velvet; he did me when I was cold sober. Why would Louise do herself in over a little tattoo? Pretty, too. Singh does a first-rate job. He's a bloody artist, and he's got all these foreign curlicues to his work. 'Course, her dad was a despondent sort. Had to have been to kill himself, don't you think? Especially with—"

"My dear sir!" I imbued those undeservedly polite words with scorn and disbelief. "Have you no idea of how an abduction would horrify a young girl of tender upbringing? Of how she would feel to awaken in a strange, vile place, her clothing disarranged? To have no memory of events, nothing but a foul, disfiguring tattoo inked across her hitherto unblemished flesh? Had you considered how she would explain such a thing to the aunt who loved her? To the maid who assisted her in dressing? To her stern uncle and guardian? To her future husband? Sir, you are an uncivil and ignorant creature, as benighted as this poor heathen sitting on his heels here."

Jerseyman blinked at my tirade. "It had to be done, Missus, for the girl's own good. If Louise was to keep a finger on the compass, so to speak, in her father's stead, it had to be done. What other way was there? The uncle wouldn't deal, and would Louise heed the likes of us if we sashayed up to her on the street and proposed she let us ink a little picture on her skin?"

"I take it," Godfrey said, "that you are responsible for the servant Pierre's dereliction of duty on that fateful day."

"You may take it and put bows upon it, sir! We managed to delay the brute long enough that he lost sight of Louise. It's a wonderful thing, is it not, what care her uncle takes of her? He was fiercer than a Tibetan terrier to get past, but by him we did get. Singh draws with pins and needles and I tell him what to do. Singh an' me might be all that's left of our Quarter." Jerseyman frowned. "But you don't know anything 'bout that and never will."

The Indian beside me had followed the conversation thus far with scant understanding but with quick intelligence. I noticed that the knife had vanished from his knee, a sign that our captors were no longer determined to blame Louise's ruin upon us. Still, the oddly animated basket continued its creep toward my skirt folds. Godfrey had been so intent upon convincing the Jerseyman that he failed to notice this anomaly, although I was conscious of every quiver within the woven reeds.

Jerseyman himself was disarmed now, the knife tucked into some hidden place upon his disreputable person, a servile grin upon his face. "I can see that Singh and me has jumped to conclusions about you two. And if you claim Louise is still about and kicking, so much the better. We'll be takin' our leave now, but you two must sit still and keep mum—"

"Wait. Did you and your friend here follow me in Paris?" Godfrey asked.

"Follow you, yes. We took you for the villain of the piece."

"Godfrey!" I couldn't keep from interrupting. "You were followed about in Paris?"

"Yes, after Louise's presumed death. It was one reason I wished to get Ire—er, to remove *you* and our mutual friend from the city to calmer surroundings, my dear."

"Most thoughtful," said I, "though you could have warned

her—I mean, of course, myself. You are entirely too protective of female sensibilities, Godfrey."

"Perhaps." He turned again to Jerseyman. "Paris must have been a hard berth for seasoned tars like yourselves. Was it you who sent the letters to Monsieur Montpensier?"

Jerseyman turned his head as if to spit. "Hard as two-sou nails, that uncle. His brother was likable enough, considering his family pretensions, but I couldn't get nowhere with the elder brother and I dared not tell him of my mission. Nor will I tell you, sir, no matter how smoothly you wiggle around to it. Consider yourself lucky to be out of this business. Take your lady wife and her friend for a nice jaunt along the Riviera and forget Louise Montpensier and us two."

As the fellow rose, our compartment door burst open. Godfrey leaped up to confine Jerseyman, while the Indian screamed shrilly and hurtled like a monkey to Godfrey's back. No knife blades flashed in the gaslight; it had happened too fast for anyone to produce one.

A capped silhouette stood in the passage against the background of blinding daylight that poured through the hall windows; that was all.

"Tickets," this intruder called loudly in French into the shadowed chaos within.

At that moment the awful basket rolled from seat to floor, its latch springing open as it struck the boards. A round of dirty greenish rope spilled out. I bent to seize it with some notion of binding our attackers when the rope began lifting of its own accord, rising up . . . up . . . up. Tiny eyes shone like jet beads in the darkness.

I screamed and jumped up onto the seat.

Just above me, the gasolier swung like a censor, emitting an incense of pungent fumes. The Indian, alerted to the escape of his captive, gave up on Godfrey and began patting the seat cushions in the gloom, plaintively mewling for his pet.

Into this tangle came the ticket-collector, not pausing to aid Godfrey in containing the Jerseyman or to assist myself in eluding the detestable snake, or even to help the Indian, now crawling upon the floor pleading for his missing property's return.

No. Instead, he stepped smartly through the cramped scene to the window, where he jerked the curtains open.

Daylight fell upon our befuddled party. Placid countryside clicked past our window in a rapid series of stereopticon images. Godfrey had pinioned Jerseyman to the seat corner opposite with one knee and both hands. Crawling about on the floorboards, his basket open and empty, the Indian looked even smaller from my elevated height.

I saw that the ticket-collector by the window, for all his official cap—and there is no nation like the French for officious uniforms on the most insignificant persons—had somehow fused his lower limbs and resembled a chessman with a pedestal base.

Nowhere did I see the snake.

Nothing meant anything to me so long as the horrid serpent was loose in the compartment.

The ticket-collector pointed to me like a figure from a Christmas pantomime. I did not see myself as the main character in the confusion, despite my elevated position and the almost insuperable difficulty of maintaining it in a moving train. I certainly would not forsake it. To have the vile snake so much as slither over my foot . . . oh! it would be an act too hideous to contemplate.

The ticket-collector was still pointing, as if struck dumb. Slowly Jerseyman, Godfrey, and the Indian gave up their separate struggles to gaze up at me. I stared down into faces frozen in horror, then realized that they were looking not at me, but at the gasolier swaying rather hypnotically just beyond my face.

Despite the absence of my trusty pince-nez, I too regarded

it—a tangle of tarnished brass, with the usual array of arms and lamps—and noted a dull, coiling design about the central pole that was quite serpentine in shape, shade and movement. Movement! I shrieked, appalled to see the elusive serpent writhe upon its perch, dangle horribly like a living pendant, and then vanish.

Yet no one in the compartment looked down. Their upturned faces grew even more horror-struck, if possible. I still quivered from the snake's odious proximity. Nothing on heaven or earth could have persuaded me to leave my lofty pedestal or to touch a boot toe to that infested floor, not even the Angel Gabriel and the trumps of Last Judgment.

The ticket-collector spoke, jabbing his finger idiotically at me. "Nell! Your bonnet! Your bonnet!"

Caught within the net of a nightmare, I found elements mixing madly. The French ticket-collector spoke with Irene's voice and wanted my bonnet?

Godfrey abruptly released the Jerseyman. Before I could open my mouth to protest his carelessness, he had bounded onto the seat beside me, torn the bonnet from my head—and I always pin my bonnets quite firmly in case of an unpredictable wind—and cast it to the floor.

I shrieked again, this time in pain. "Are you all mad? Look, he's getting away! Godfrey, how could you? My best bonnet, the only purchase I deigned to make in Paris!"

He ignored me, leaping down to stamp upon my pitiful bit of festooned straw as if demented, while the Indian crawled about the compartment wailing disconsolately.

Fate and the train picked this moment to enter a tunnel.

The swaying gaslight was a beacon of sanity in that disordered cell out of Wonderland. Our train lurched around a curve and unbalanced me. I caught the gasolier as I fell; my fingers recoiled from the notion of touching anything associated with the snake, but my presence of mind overruled my distaste.

I swung for a dreadful moment while the fixture groaned its disapproval of myself as a pendant. Then the train burst from the tunnel, and illumination again flooded our compartment. My fingers slipped, but Irene and Godfrey reached up to cushion my fall. We tumbled together to the seat, dazed by the light.

I sat up immediately, lifting my feet from the floor. The compartment was deserted, save for ourselves.

We looked around. My bonnet, sadly crushed, lay upon the floorboards. Of the basket, the snake, the lithe Indian and the menacing Jerseyman there was no trace. And of the ticket-collector there remained only a fallen cap.

"Well." Irene sat up and brushed locks of loose hair from her face.

"How have you managed to mimic me in losing your bonnet?" I asked.

She pointed mutely to the floor and the ticket-collector's cap.

"You were . . . he?"

She began undoing her jacket's gleaming brass buttons; I hadn't noticed her attire until now. Underneath was her charcoal-gray traveling gown. No wonder the ticket-collector had looked as if he sat upon a pedestal—he had been Irene in skirts!

She laughed as I stared at her transformation. "I only had time to bribe the ticket-collector for his cap and jacket. My object was to startle the miscreants, but I underestimated your ability, Nell, to single-handedly distract them with gymnastic exhibitions." She turned swiftly. "Godfrey, my dear, are you quite all right?"

"Quite," he replied, laughing, his collar sadly askew. "A queer pair of villains, almost out of Gilbert and Sullivan's light operas, far adrift from their normal environment. Though they did keep their sea legs better on this rolling train than we."

"Legs," I said bitterly. "If you must be so indelicate as to mention 'legs,' Godfrey, what of the one *without* legs? Where is . . . it?"

"I believe that Singh entrapped it in the basket during the confusion; certainly he would not have left without it."

"I do devoutly hope so. But *what* was it?"

Godfrey struggled to reinstate his collar without benefit of mirror. "Difficult to tell. It was somewhat smaller than a cobra—"

I gasped.

"—and too mildly colored for a water snake."

I moaned.

"I might suspect a *fer-de-lance*—"

"A *French* snake?" I demanded.

"Only the name. Indian by origin. Its bite is—"

"Yes?"

Godfrey paused, obviously determined to spare me.

"Deadly," Irene intoned, pushing Godfrey's hands from his throat, where they had seemed more likely to strangle him than straighten his collar. "Now, your collar is tidy and I am in proper guise again. And, Nell, here is your bonnet."

"Leave it!" I shuddered.

"Paris millinery?" She tsk-tsked and bent to retrieve the cap, its braid winking in the conjoined brightness of daylight and the swaying gasolier. "I must return this to our generous —and generously paid—ticket-collector."

"How did you find us?" Godfrey stood and stretched his whole height to dim the gaslight.

"A process of elimination. I spent the better part of half an hour jostling from car to car. How fortunate that these new European trains offer interconnected carriages, rather than isolated cars that may be entered only one by one from the outside. Progress has its benefits."

"What of our assailants?" I asked. "Surely we are not going to simply let them escape?"

Godfrey bent to the window to peer at the rapidly passing countryside. "I fear we are. They could jump off safely at any point along here—we are slowing for our entry to Cannes—although Singh's pet may escape again and lose itself in the long grasses of Grasse rather than among your bonnet plumes, Nell."

"I do hope so! That is the proper place for a snake . . . in the grass. How did you explain your bizarre request for his uniform to the ticket-collector, Irene?"

"I told him that I had an eccentric friend at whose expense I wished to have some merriment."

"You implied that *I* was eccentric? How could you say such falsehoods about me, even in the service of our rescue?"

"My dear," said Irene, smoothing my untidy hair with nanny-like amusement as she propelled me into the passage, "when he sees your present state, he shall be completely convinced."

Chapter Fifteen

STRANGERS IN PARADISE

❧

After Marseilles and the sordid struggle in the railway compartment, I was thoroughly convinced that France had nothing to offer but hubris and a few slightly superior varieties of mushroom.

So when our train wound around the low cliffs overlooking the Mediterranean and a vista shimmered in the hazy blue distance that resembled the Heavenly Gates—all white and gleaming—it was some consolation to reflect that Monaco was a principality in its own right and thus not part of France.

"How glorious!" Irene cried.

She and Godfrey had crowded to the compartment window like eager children, his trousered knees and her skirt folds pressing the tufted-velvet upholstery of the lower carriage walls.

I studied our nearing destination. Monaco and Monte Carlo lived up to their lofty implications; a promontory ringed with sheer cliff faces commanded a view of the shimmering cobalt water lapping at its rocky roots. Like a mountain, its summit was snowcapped. Strong sunlight danced off cupolas and towers of white marble, its brilliance making my eyes water.

"It resembles a wedding cake," Irene observed, "a great, frosted wedding cake."

As we neared, we saw ragged green palm fans brushing the white buildings, indicating a soft, warm breeze at play.

"Surely nothing too unpleasant could occur in such a place," I ventured.

"On the contrary," Godfrey put in sharply. "Claude Montpensier hung himself in view of these balmy palms and that glittering sea."

"Yes, we forget why we came." Irene leaned back to extract a slim selection of postcards from her reticule. She thrust one at me.

It showed a baroque building rising from a manicured landscape. In the upper right-hand corner, a top-hatted gentleman with a flower in his lapel hung by the neck. At the lower left, a breeches-clad lackey came bearing a giant scissors with which to cut down the unfortunate suicide.

"How grotesque, Irene! And callous toward the loser's fate."

"Realistic, perhaps, Nell. And so are the casinos, and the governors of these fair gambling centers. Guns are not allowed in Monte Carlo, nor poisons, although these strictures do not stop suicides—or prevent those lethal means from entering the principality. It is said that during the seventies, one suicide victim a day was found . . . and quickly spirited away. Still, it does not stop pleasure-seekers from coming."

Godfrey eyed the fanned postcards, then drew one as if an ace from a deck of cards. "And here on this one we are pictured en route to this paradise of sun, sea and temperate weather. Irene and I are the handsome foreground couple, but I believe that if the lady mounting the carriage steps would turn, she'd wear Nell's features."

I viewed the scene askance. The postcard showed a "Train des Moutons" bound for Monaco; its "passengers," about to board, were well-hatted sheep dressed in the latest fashions.

"We are not here to be shorn," Irene said with spirit. "We

are wolves, not sheep. We hunt a vanished girl and the source
of the mysterious tattoos. And perhaps a missing snake. Poor
Mr. Singh was so patient. I wonder what a 'Quarter' is. While
I waited my opportunity to enter the compartment, I heard
Nell's 'Jerseyman' mention that word."

"Three months," I answered promptly.

"Not to those two sailors who accosted us on the train."

"Sailors?"

Godfrey nodded. "Seamen of the old-tar school. They are
not here only to follow us, flattering as that assumption may
be. This is their home ground, this great inland sea of the
Mediterranean."

Irene smiled. "That is why the letters to Louise's uncle
came from so many corners of the world—all of them
seaports, you noticed."

"No, Irene, I did not. I am not interested in seaports . . .
or sailors." I directed my second remark to Godfrey, who
shook his head in mock sorrow.

"Perhaps you are interested in American princesses-to-be,"
Irene suggested.

"Hardly. I was not even impressed by an American
queen-to-be in Bohemia," I responded tartly.

"You will have little to occupy you in Monte Carlo, I fear,"
Irene said, "for our business involves princesses, old tars and,
I suspect, sealing wax, if not cabbages and kings."

"I had enough of kings in Bohemia."

"Indeed." Irene eyed Godfrey, who was busy checking his
pocket watch. "I have had my fill of that species also. But the
real aristocracy of Monte Carlo is not old King Charles the
Third, who is blind, or Lady Luck, who is even blinder. It
is not even Prince Albert, who will soon inherit this mecca
on the Mediterranean. No, Monaco's reigning monarch
is the gambler, who nightly risks thousands of francs,
dollars, pounds and marks in the temple of gaming called
a casino."

"It is a Whited Sepulchre," said I, pinning the bonnet Irene had lent me firmly to my hair.

Within hours we were ensconced in airy adjoining suites at the Hotel de Paris. Long French windows opened onto the sea view from every room, although one could hardly spy the blue sparkle of the water through the tumbling vines of exotic flowers that spilled from the balcony tubs and down the landscape toward the lapping waves.

In my own chamber, I inhaled a melange of strange scents along with a lungful of warm, salt-seasoned air. How delicious to be free of Casanova's continual croakings! Really, one cannot comprehend how it dampens all emotion to be saddled with the constant company of a chronic intoner of gloom and doom. Outside my window, vivid scarlet and cerise blossoms nodded their fragrant agreement.

I admitted to myself a small thrill of conversion to the Riviera, beginning with the open carriage Godfrey had engaged at the train station. We had ridden in nodding, smiling splendor up the cramped, winding, cobblestoned streets of the Condamine, the portion that occupies the low ground between the city of Monte Carlo itself and the Rock of Monaco, the principality's sparkling summit. Flower-draped villas clung to precipices between, as they had along the railroad line into Monte Carlo. The scene seemed painted in a slapdash hand of blue and white, enhanced with flashes of green foliage and crimson blooms.

"Smell the scents on the air! This suggests the American South, though I have never seen it," Irene said. Her eager features turned every which way as if to devour each exotic detail. "I adore it, Godfrey! We must honeymoon here every year."

He laughed and tipped his hat to a passing party in an open equipage who, in turn, greeted us out of sheer exuberance for the climate rather than for acquaintanceship.

"This," said I, "is how I imagined Paris to be. Bright, warm and gay."

"Certainly it is not London," Irene said. She frowned through the spidery latticework of her veil. "This is such a happy spot that it must be doubly dire to face ruin here."

Godfrey's schoolboy grin vanished. "We are here on grim business, it is true. I shall look into the suicide of Claude Montpensier as soon as I can make the rounds of the local legal and journalistic offices next week."

"Ah, excellent!" Irene melted into the cushioned carriage seat with catlike luxury. "Legal and journalistic sources are so divinely dull! You attend to unearthing the tedious facts, dearest Godfrey, at which you so excel. Nell and I shall concentrate on such frivolities as finding the unfortunate Louise and meeting the Duchesse de Richelieu, my American cousin, so to speak."

He laughed at this high-handed division of labor even as I sputtered my objections to climbing the social ladder in yet another unknown city.

"First we will have a day or two to enjoy the sea air," Godfrey said. "I recommend it; in fact, I prescribe it. Meetings and maneuvering can wait!"

I did so admire Godfrey when he managed to deter Irene's unfortunate curiosity into all that was obscure, salacious and none of our affair. A pity his masterfulness didn't last.

The weekend was spent in driving, dining and walking. I made certain that my two friends had sufficient time to themselves by pleading correspondence or my diary and remaining in the hotel.

"To Hellespont with your everlasting diaries!" Irene said once, drawing on cerise kid gloves. "It is yet another glorious day."

"You do not complain of my diaries when they produce needed notations for your purposes," I answered mildly. "I cannot be precise if I do not cultivate and weed them daily."

"What have you to write of here, save sunshine and flowers and Monsieur Escoffier's crepes at the Grand Hotel?"

"For one thing, the bearded gentleman who has been following us."

"Following us? When?" Irene was indignant.

"Bearded? Like a sailor? Where?" Godfrey cross-examined me.

How satisfying to note their mutual amazement; I did not often surprise either one. Now I was happy to answer their questions in sequence.

"Since we arrived at the hotel this morning. Bearded—more like a gentleman. Everywhere."

"Why did you say nothing?" Godfrey demanded.

"I assumed that you both noticed his presence and forebore mentioning the fact to spare me worry. He was no Pinkerton, to be sure, and they are most obvious, as Irene herself has bewailed on many an occasion."

Irene was laughing by now, torn between admiring the protective glint in Godfrey's eyes and snuffing the smugness in mine. Despite my retiring intentions, she swept me along for a stroll along the promenade skirting the sea. "Nell, you sly boots! Describe your anonymous admirer."

"He most certainly is not!"

"You are a lone third to our pair. Why shouldn't you attract the attention of an unattached gentleman?"

"In Monte Carlo? Irene, please! The very parlor palms conceal beautiful American heiresses and Continental adventuresses. Why should some gentleman waste his time observing me?"

"Perhaps," Godfrey said gallantly, "he has discernment. But describe him to us."

"He is of middle years, though not old; well groomed save for the beard—not that it is not well groomed, but you know that I much prefer a clean-shaven man. A mustache, of course, is acceptable."

"Thank you," Godfrey put in, twitching his. "I know your standards are rigorous."

"And purely my own. As I say, he is not evil-looking, but quite respectable. Dark hair and eyes. Curiously neat hands . . . or rather, curiously precise hands, like an accountant's. He looks, in fact, quite utterly harmless. No doubt I slander the man by even mentioning him. I wouldn't want to cause an innocent stranger undeserved difficulties!"

The longer I spoke, the more convinced I became that I was hanging a lamb for a sheep. Oh, the responsibility of presuming to read the actions of one's fellow men! Truly, I was usurping the prerogatives of godhead.

"No doubt you are quite right and he is harmless," Godfrey agreed.

"Still," Irene suggested silkily, "point the fellow out when you see him. Merely to satisfy our curiosity, of course."

"You would not . . . confront him?"

"Confront him? Certainly not." Irene sounded rather wounded. "My methods are never confrontational. You should know that, my dear Nell."

Irene spoke only the truth, but it was no consolation. On our last walk along the promenade, no palm top could scrub the soapy clouds and clean blue sky above us without my examining its trunk for glimpses of a lurking homburg, a manicured dark beard or a worn but well-polished shoe.

I carried a green silk parasol Irene had insisted I buy at one of the principality's expensive milliners. She strolled on Godfrey's other side, her parasol handle dashingly cocked over her shoulder, her arm through his, lounging along as if a Monégasque born.

The sun and shade jousted for possession of her lovely features. I welcomed our southern adventure merely for the mute rapport that sparkled between man and wife, as if he were the great, glittering blue sea and she the sharp, dancing sunlight that glinted from its surface.

I was, in fact, composing a most lyrical diary entry on the subject of conjugal affection—an emotion I was no doubt never to experience personally, for my callow entoilment with the poor parson, Jasper Higgenbottom, last heard of laboring in some mission's foreign field, had evaporated. Now that I had known so fine a gentleman as Godfrey, I doubted that the mere mortal men common to my station in life would satisfy me. I was, as I report, waxing quite poetic and resigned when Irene spun to face Godfrey and myself, making us into a tight, conspiratorial triumvirate.

"There! Is that he, Nell? Our shadow? Our gentlemanly accountant? Don't turn! Glance coquettishly under your parasol flounce . . . well, glance *slowly* at least, as if you were admiring a flower. Is that he?"

I glanced, whether as subtly as prescribed, I cannot say. "Yes," I whispered, whirling back to them. "Is he watching us?"

"He is now," Irene said drily. "I must teach you the art of the indirect look as soon as we return to the hotel."

Godfrey presented his arms to us and turned smartly on the walk. By this simple strategem, we were all facing back toward the object of our interest and could amble in his direction.

"I told you he was respectable," I hissed as we neared the man in question. "He wears a hat and carries a cane."

"So did Doctor Jekyll," Irene reminded me. "What do you think, Godfrey?"

"That Nell is astute. A professional man, though not rich—look at those shoes—but certainly more than an accountant, I think. His gaze does not falter."

Mine faltered, dramatically, as we neared the place where he stood. What if Irene should suddenly greet him, naming me as the one who had drawn their attention to him?

"Never fear, Nell," she murmured in my ear. "I won't disgrace you."

As we passed him, I breathed again. Before us lay the rococo Hotel de Paris, set in a bezel of pots of red geraniums. Irene presented Godfrey and myself with her cheek for farewell kisses.

"Now, my darlings, you must continue your walk, as I have a frightful headache. It must be this strong Mediterranean sun. I will return to the suite."

"I will go with—"

"No, Nell, you must walk to and fro with Godfrey until you determine if the bearded gentleman is watching you—or if he was watching me, which has been known to happen—or if he is observing cockatoos in the palm trees. I shall be fine. Really, I insist."

She was gone, leaving Godfrey and me to meekly follow orders. We strolled up and down the promenade so many times that the bearded gentleman finally deposited himself upon a bench. I began to wish for such a mercy.

Godfrey remained calm, discussing the history of the casino, inquiring into my Shropshire girlhood, and even treading dangerously near the subject of my sentimental attachments. This effectively distracted me from all but the mild weather, the endless pacing and the unfading presence of the bearded man.

At last Godfrey turned us back toward the hotel. The sun was blushing in readiness for its evening ablution in the sea. My parasol's carved handle had impressed a heathen dragon shape into my palm. Even the promenade had grown deserted, and I could detect the pale glow of gaslights from the casino next to the hotel.

A solitary stroller, a young man with copious facial hair and wearing a pale holiday suit, went by with a tip of his slouch-brimmed hat. Godfrey nodded in passing and steered me for the hotel, which although pretentious, offered innumerable opportunities for *sitting down*.

At the door I could not resist turning. Under the cover of my now-unnecessary sunshade I glanced back at the bench the bearded man had occupied for the past forty-five minutes. It was empty.

"Godfrey—!"

He drew my gloved hand gently through his arm and led me in. "It's quite all right, Nell. Irene is following him."

Chapter Sixteen

INTERVIEW WITH A
DUCHESS

❧

I did not see Irene again until breakfast on Monday.

She and Godfrey had settled at a table upon the hotel terrace, the picture of the serene married couple. He was dressed for the day and peering at the fine print of the newspaper's legal notices, and Irene, wearing a lace-cascading cashmere breakfast jacket, was feeding small songbirds a croissant flake by flake.

"My dear Penelope!" Godfrey rose to greet me. "You look pale and drawn. Are you ill?"

"Not at all, but I did have difficulty sleeping. I kept imagining Irene being waylaid by a bearded man and thrown to the bottom of the cliffs."

She looked up, surprised, from her dainty little friends. Each bird would have made one bite for the absent Lucifer.

"My dear Nell, surely you were not worried! I would have bid you good night, but the hour was so late that it was early when I returned. I feared waking you."

"Needlessly, it seems," I said, accepting the hot tea the waiter had brought. "Then you successfully followed the bearded man, else you wouldn't have stayed out so long."

"Indeed." She raised an eyebrow. "He went first to the palace, where he waited incognito for some time. Finally, at one in the morning, a heavily veiled lady emerged. He escorted her to a nondescript house not far from there. He stayed for an hour, then returned to his residence, a small hotel near the base of the city. I was home by three o'clock."

I turned to her unruffled spouse. "And you, Godfrey, will no doubt tell me that you were not worried."

"Of course I was worried, but what good did it do me? Irene returned safely and berated me for remaining awake."

"At least *you* knew of her return."

"At least *you* escaped her lecture," he returned with a twinkling eye. "It was fierce."

Suspicious still, I turned again to Irene. "And you mean to say that you were in no danger last night, that the bearded man never suspected your presence?"

"Never," she answered. "I assure you that I was safer on the streets of Monaco than I would have been here in the hotel, where a jewel thief might have entered and rapped me on the head."

"There were no untoward incidents?" I pressed.

"None." Irene produced a strange smile. "Except for a gentleman who made a rather shocking proposal in passing."

"You see!" I waited until both Godfrey and Irene gave me their full attention. "Someone *did* see through your male disguise! A woman is not safe alone at night, or at any other time, in any guise."

"He did *not* see through my disguise, dear Nell. Indeed, he would have been most disappointed if he had," Irene said. Her odd half smile was both amused and indulgent, I fear at my expense.

"I'm afraid I don't understand, Irene. And you needn't hide behind the newspaper, Godfrey; I can tell you're laughing. At any rate, I still hold that these solo expeditions are likely to catch up with you one day, Irene, and then there will be a terrible scandal."

"I forever seem to flirt with one scandal or another," she answered lightly. "But that is the advantage in being dead to the world. Who can harm me now?"

"You are still mortal," I warned.

"My dear Nell," Godfrey said, "our cautions fall on deaf ears. Irene has been doing as she will since long before I—or even you—met her."

"Yes. And given her predilections now, one must wonder what she was about before we knew her."

I detected a hint of confusion on my friend's features and was about to pounce upon the issue of her past while she was still feeling guilty about her lone midnight lark. But a waiter swooped between us like a crow, presenting a silver salver to Irene.

"A message, Madame Norton. The bearer said it was urgent."

Irene lifted the thick parchment envelope from the tray, all other topics forgotten. I should not forget, of course, but would obtain no answer now to any of my questions. With an unknown item before her, Irene was like Lucifer about to pounce upon a dust mote: feral concentration embodied.

She drew a hat pin from the tangle of lace and silk flowers dressing her hair and, with its six-inch steel barb, slit the envelope as neatly as a surgeon might. Before she withdrew the contents, she pricked the thick puddle of scarlet sealing wax upon the flap with her miniature rapier.

"The paper alone costs a pound a sheaf. The sealing wax is crimson . . . and scented," she declared after lifting it to her nose.

"Not—?" I began.

"Not sandalwood-scented, no. And the insignia is so ornate that it is unreadable."

"Then it must be French," said I.

"Are you going to analyze the envelope, or open it?" Godfrey asked.

Irene smiled at our eager curiosity. Her fingertip traced the impetuous scrawl across the envelope's face. "A woman, I think, in a hurry now, but quick to act even when there is no reason to. The loops are smudged, she was writing so speedily. The handwriting itself is conventional, save that the letters are cramped and angular. She will appear to obey the letter of the law, this woman, but her heart will always flout convention."

"Another actress!" I complained. "Say it is not true that Sarah Bernhardt is visiting Monaco."

"Not Sarah." Irene drew out a piece of ivory parchment folded once in half. "There is not enough scent upon it."

Godfrey had risen to lean over Irene's chair as she read the letter. Her eyebrows raised, then she reread it.

"Interesting," Godfrey commented.

"Very," said she, sitting back to read it yet again.

"Well?" I demanded.

Irene passed the letter across the table to me. "It is from Alice, Duchess of Richelieu, *née* Alice Heine of New Orleans. Sarah's friend."

"I should have known!" I pulled the pince-nez from my reticule to begin translating the ungoverned handwriting. The French was perfect but the writing outraced the meaning; letters were dropped, and even the occasional word, so that I found it hard going.

"She wishes to see you!" I said at last.

"Naturally. It was only a matter of time."

"And Godfrey also."

"Possibly because he is a barrister as well as my husband."

"And your . . . your *sister!*"

Irene beamed at my incredulity. "Alice, Duchess of Richelieu, is a discerning woman. Her Paris salon in the Faubourg-St.-Honore attracts the leading wits, politicians, writers and artists of Paris, although she somehow overlooked inviting myself; living incognito can be an inconvenience."

"What does the woman have to do with *me*, pray? Would she invite your entire family if she knew any more of them than Godfrey and I do?"

"I merely point out that Her Grace is not unintelligent and that she has included you in the invitation; apparently she recognizes you as a key member of our . . . association."

"But this is not a social invitation!" I said, exasperated.

Irene smiled with extreme self-satisfaction. "No, is it not. It is a business invitation. My first . . . case . . . as Madame Irene Norton. And I owe it all to Sarah Bernhardt."

"The world owes much that is unfortunate to Sarah Bernhardt," said I darkly, "including the notion that women may go about doing as they wish with no consequences."

"Oh, there are consequences," Godfrey said, draining the last of his coffee with a thoughtful expression. The imbibing of that disgusting brew was a habit he had acquired from Irene. "And it is consequences that cause crime, which in turn provokes more consequences. I had best begin inquiring after poor Montpensier; I must return by three for this command appearance before the duchess. Perhaps I shall know more of the suicide of Louise's father's then."

"That would be nice." Irene smiled as if Godfrey were promising her some tasty bon-bon, her hand pausing on his.

"Someone must tell this woman that I am not your sister," I said when he had left. "First I am taken for Godfrey's wife, and now for your sister, which is equally ludicrous."

"Godfrey's wife? But, Nell, who would—? Not the ruffians on the train! Poor darling, you seem to be forever miscast by both the highest and the lowest elements of society. Being my sister is not so awful a role, is it?"

"I would that I were; I could probably sing on key and I might even be pretty."

"You're pretty as you are; you simply don't dress for it."

"Oh, Irene, you always think clothes make the woman."

A wicked gleam enhanced her already bright eyes. "Let me

prove it. I will attire you this afternoon as my mythical sister. We will see what the duchess thinks of you then."

"I am more concerned with what I think of the duchess."

"You are always thinking of others, and never of yourself, Nell. We will take one small step toward correcting that today. You will see; you will not know yourself. Besides, it will divert my mind from the excitement of my appointment with the duchess, will it not? And you do wish to be useful, don't you?"

I was, as always with Irene, trapped by my own credo.

We walked to the duchess's home that afternoon. Irene said she knew the way. In Monte Carlo, walking was not a sign of poverty but, rather, a display of ease and idleness and the means to afford it. Here it was called "taking the air," or "strolling," never a "necessity."

Yet walking any distance from the public promenades was hazardous, for the streets were steep and winding. Godfrey offered each of us an arm, delighted, he claimed, to squire two such beauties about the town.

Irene had indulged in two happy hours devoted to my reconstruction, trilling snippets of arias as she snipped off frills of my hair. She became so enraptured by her vocalizing that she waved the hot curling iron as if it were a conductor's baton. Such play, she said, reminded her of her performing days.

If at any point I objected to a particularly frivolous placement of a curl, or to such enhancements as rouge delivered on a rabbit's foot or soot pooled around my eyes, I was instructed not to be silly; she was using only the lightest of subterfuges.

I was curious to see how she would transform me into her "sister." I had not forgotten the aged housekeeper she had created on my features before she and Godfrey fled

England, the King of Bohemia and Mr. Sherlock Holmes in London.

"A pity you would not permit the henna rinse," Irene said as her fingers poked my frizzled locks into a final semblance of disorder. "Your hair is unremittingly brown otherwise. Now the bonnet."

She lowered a beribboned concoction atop my plain brown head. A pale-blue ostrich plume trembled above the felt bonnet in time with the matching flutter of the curls fringing my face.

The gown was of brown grosgrain silk, with broad, blue satin skirt reveres and sleeves on which a brown cut-velvet pattern provided rich shadings. Pleated blue canton crepe circled my neck and cascaded down my bodice, emphasized here and there with blue satin bows.

Irene led me to the pier glass and while I confronted myself, gave me one last examination.

"Well?"

I studied myself, who indeed did not resemble myself, and next I studied Irene. Then I laughed.

"You do not like it? Nell, you ingrate!"

"I do not look like your sister—I look like you! And you look like a laundry girl! Irene, the price of making me into a silk purse has transformed you into a . . . I do not wish to be explicit."

"I know the adage, Nell."

Irene frowned at herself in the looking glass. Her long labors over my coiffure had caused her own hair to fall from grace. Her face was pale, her brows knitted, her expression distracted.

"We have less than half an hour before we must meet Godfrey in the lobby," I reminded her gently. I stepped to the room's center and turned slowly. "Of course, I am ready."

"And I will be in a moment," she said, seating herself at

the dressing table. In mere minutes she had worked the same transformation upon herself that it had taken her two hours to achieve with me.

Irene spurned personal maids; her long experience with theatrical paint and hairdressing made her more skilled at her own toilette than any servant would be. And indeed, she moved with a magician's swift surety, her fingers darting to the precise powder puff or rouge pot she required. Her hair bowed to the admonishment of a boar-bristle brush and was quickly piled and gleaming auburn again, without benefit of henna. She soon rose to doff her combing gown. I helped her don a handsome visiting costume of pink lace and corded satin.

We shortly stood before the mirror again. Now there was nothing laughable about her appearance, save that mine suffered by comparison.

"You look divine," Irene said, bracing me. "How unfortunate that your nature takes so little delight in feminine frivolities."

"It's a pity that feminine frivolities take so much time! Your beauty is inborn, Irene. That's why you can enhance it in a moment. Mine must be erected brick by brick from a dull foundation."

"Nonsense. It is a matter of motivation. We must find you a charming gentleman to dazzle."

"You were beautiful before you met Godfrey."

"And you have your own virtues, both inner and outer, Nell. Neither need be skimped upon."

Irene thrust toward me a blue silk parasol decorated with an exceedingly silly array of bows. I backed away. "Not another parasol, I beg you!"

"A parasol will not kill you, and it is ever so elegant in Monte. We must not let the sun darken our porcelain complexions."

"And how could it, with all this powder we have pressed upon them?"

But Irene would not be denied. I took the idiotic thing. Thus we rustled downstairs to greet Godfrey, whose surprised attention and complimentary opinion greatly embarrassed me and brought many unwanted glances to our party and myself.

Now I was bemoaning my fragile apparel as my thin-soled kidskin slippers skidded on the rough cobblestones and the soft, constant sea zephyrs blew curls and furbelows into my eyes.

"The very house, as I thought!" Irene said, stopping before a villa that crouched in the shadow of the palace. The wind had tousled the curls around her face into a rich russet furl; on her, disarray seemed neither an impediment nor a detraction.

"This is where the bearded man escorted the woman from the palace?" Godfrey sounded doubtful.

"Exactly. I stood there—" Irene pointed to a narrow side alley "—and smoked a cigarette while waiting for him to come out."

We were expected—and urgently—for a houseman opened the duchess's door before Godfrey could ring. He bowed us down a short hall to a side parlor.

Although the house's pale stucco exterior was in need of paint and some of the shutters had broken struts, within all was elegant in that French manner that makes wicker stools and flowers in pitchers seem the careless height of fashion. Oscar Wilde would have adored it . . . and probably did.

Sunny yellow silk covered the parlor walls; gray velvet pussy willows studded bare stalks arching from vases set around the chamber. Bowls of blue Japanese porcelain bloomed against this temperate background like Holland tulips.

The duchess rustled in unannounced, clad in a striped house gown of hyacinth and mint-green taffeta bearing multitudes of heliotrope ribbons.

My long association with Irene had given me an opportunity to meet the day's most acclaimed beauties: in London, Lillie Langtry and Florence Wilde; in Paris, Sarah Bernhardt. I was always struck upon first meeting them by how their reputations had not only preceded them, but exceeded them.

It is perhaps testimony to my partiality, or to the cruel obscurity in which the most deserving almost always languish, that none of them could hold so much as a beeswax taper to Irene's incandescent loveliness.

Alice, Duchess of Richelieu, was another disappointment, although some would find her enormous blue eyes piquant. Certainly her blond hair was striking, but her nose and chin were excessively long and would coarsen with age. Now, of course, like Irene, Alice Heine was but thirty. Unlike Irene, she was already a mother—of a boy, Marie Odeon, and a girl, Odile—and a widow for longer than she had been wed.

Such facts had Godfrey produced from his inquiries with those who record us all for posterity: journalists and lawyers.

"My dear Mr. and Mrs. Norton," the duchess said in English. "And Miss—?" Bright blue eyes as unblinking as buttons were fixed upon me.

"Miss Penelope Huxleigh," Irene said quickly.

"Then you are English by ancestry, if not by birth," the youthful duchess said quickly, still taking me for Irene's sister and thus assuming that Huxleigh had been Irene's maiden name.

Apparently it suited Irene to have her think so. "Not—quite," said she.

"But you were born in America. Sarah says so."

"The North." Irene said no more.

"I lived in the South, the penultimate south of New Orleans. If you have seen it, you understand why I love the French, and love particularly Monte Carlo. Perhaps you know New Orleans?"

"No. My travels have been predominantly abroad."

"You must have been young when you left the States. I detect no accent."

"As a singer, I am at home in many languages."

"I see." Again the lively blue eyes pecked at Godfrey and myself, darting from buttonholes to gloves to faces to empty chairs about the chamber. "You must be seated and we will have tea. Are you enjoying Monte Carlo? Mr. Norton? Miss Huxleigh?"

"Splendidly," Godfrey said, "although I am now engaged in poring over obscure documents rather than strolling in the sunshine."

"Indeed, I have heard that your grasp of both English and French law has been useful to many in Paris. It is becoming a fluid world, is it not? We are all mixes of this and of that and live in this land and that."

A maid appeared among us and began quietly laying out a tea fit for an emperor.

"Certainly, Your Grace," Irene said, "but our roots remain. I detect a New Orleans glide upon your vowels in both English and French."

Alice smiled so sunnily that I revised my opinion of her beauty. "I am an utter melange, it is true: half French, half Jewish and of the Catholic faith!" She laughed at her self-contradictions. "I am a young woman still, but a mother and a widow. I am wealthy, yet unable to buy my heart's desire. I am a friend to starving writers and artists, yet would be a princess. Can you help me, Mrs. Norton? Sarah said you are a mistress of the awkward situation."

Irene sipped the exotically colored tea in a Sevres porcelain cup. "How awkward?"

"Very," replied the duchess. "I am, you see, an impetuous woman."

I stared, recalling that Irene had discerned that very characteristic in her handwriting.

The duchess went on as one accustomed to talking and

being heeded, not from vanity but from the effervescent force of her personality.

"I wed just two weeks past my seventeenth birthday and bore my first child within the year."

"That is indeed impetuous," Irene murmured into her teacup.

"Armand died in Athens scarcely more than four years after our marriage. In the meanwhile, my father had left New Orleans to join his family's banking firm in Paris, Heine Freres, second only to the Rothschilds in prominence. Father would say the Rothschilds are second."

Irene nodded sagely. "Sarah Bernhardt credits your father for the fact that any of her wealth accrues at all, given her spending habits."

"Sarah is an artist. She holds nothing back, especially money. When she comes to Monte, my father bombards me with letters pleading that I keep her from the gaming tables."

"Do you?" Godfrey asked.

She regarded him for a long moment, during which she both measured his attractions and read his imperviousness. "No, Mr. Norton. Only one thing would distract Sarah from gaming, and then not for long enough. Besides, my father asks the wrong persuader. He has had scant luck at dissuading me from my, ah, intense interests."

"How intense?" Irene asked softly.

Alice sighed, folded her hands in her lap, then tilted her head to eye us each in turn. The maid had long since departed. In the silence, a cheerful trill came from a cage of canaries almost lost from view against the yellow silk-covered walls.

"Sarah knows, of course, the entire story. Did she tell you?"

"No," Irene said. "Sarah is discreet about her friends."

Alice smiled. "A pity she cannot be discreet about herself.

Neither can I. You are an odd triumvirate to whom to entrust my deepest secrets. I feel that by rights, Mrs. Norton, we should be rivals; and that we, Mr. Norton, should be romantic intriguers; and that we, Miss Huxleigh—" she leaned forward to fix me with a long stare "—should be sisters. Yet there is something steady and reassuring about you all. I sense perhaps that you also have seen more of the world than most."

I did not know whether to resent more being taken yet again for a harmless sister or the assumption that I was hardened to the world's uglier side.

"Certainly we *see* more than most," Irene said. "Your Grace—"

"No, no! Alice. Simple Alice from New Orleans—though my title enraptures my father to the buttons on his spats. That's what has always worried him, you see, that after the coup of capturing Armand, Duc de Richelieu, one of the oldest, most esteemed titles in *tout France,* I should waste myself on someone unworthy."

Irene contemplated the chirping canaries. "Would 'some-one unworthy' have precise hands and wear a beard?"

Alice drew back, surprised into silence for once. She regarded her entwined fingers and spoke on. "I was but twenty-two when Armand died. I did not show the proper spirit of wishing to vanish utterly from the sight of the world. My father exported me to the isle of Madeira, off the coast of Africa. There I was to bask in the sunshine, stroll lost in melancholy along the beach and in general wither for a decent period of time.

"Instead, I met Emile. He was a doctor and Jewish. Neither characteristic pleased my father. He descended on the capital city of Funchal like a well-dressed torrent, humiliating Emile and whisking me away to Biarritz to 'recuperate' in peace."

Alice shrugged. "Biarritz also had doctors. I met Jacob,

also Jewish, also a physician and also poor, relatively speaking. This time I was not to be swayed by my father's wrath. My money was my own, as was my will."

Irene frowned. "Where does His Highness, Prince Albert, come into this?"

Alice dimpled, clearly delighting in recounting her shocking story. "I had met him briefly in Funchal. He was leading an expedition to conduct deep-sea diving experiments near Madeira. He was titled and rich, all that Father would want for me, but of course Father must rush me from Madiera to separate me from Emile."

"Was the prince not also married?" Godfrey asked coolly. When she stared at him, he smiled. "Such facts are always recorded in cramped handwriting in dusty offices. I have spent my morning in such unpleasant places."

"Albert's wife left him years ago, while still carrying his son. The marriage had been arranged, and she was Scotch," Alice added disdainfully, as if the last fact certainly explained all previous ones.

"But you have jumped to the conclusion of my tale," she continued. "Albert was also a neighbor of mine in Paris. Our brief meeting in Funchal was not our last. His first marriage had been annulled in the church and dissolved by the divorce courts. We were free to marry, save that his father, Prince Charles, forbid it. He found me flighty. So it sits, with Albert and myself living our lives in Paris and Monte Carlo, waiting for . . . the inevitable, when we will do the inevitable, and marry as we wish."

"What is your difficulty?" Irene inquired. "You are willing to wait, and worldly enough—both of you, from what I hear of the prince's younger days—to make the wait pleasant."

"The problem is Emile," Alice said.

"The bearded man," Irene prompted.

Alice appeared dazed. "You know him?"

"I have seen him, which is enough. You set him to follow us."

"I wished to know more about those to whom I would confide such delicate matters. Then, too, Emile himself was suspicious. He thought you might even be the source of our problem."

"Which is—?" Godfrey put in.

"Blackmail," Irene answered promptly for the duchess. "Someone wishes to acquaint Prince Edward with your indiscretions. Though the prince himself had a scandalous youth—"

"He is a shy man who hides behind the worldly façade expected of princes. Has not the same phenomenon dogged your own Prince of Wales, Mr. Norton and Miss Huxleigh?"

I finally got a word in edgewise. "I am no apologist for the excesses of *England's* Prince Edward," I said smartly. "You must justify Monaco's prince without my support."

Alice took in my stiff denial, then said, "So it stands, with Edward and myself peacefully waiting to formalize our love. Now some . . . unknown person . . . has determined to stir up the scandal of my earlier liaisons. I am not the mistress of my heart. Indeed, I am not certain I would not have been better off living an obscure life with my dear and glorious physician."

"Physicians," I corrected.

We regarded each other, the confident blond duchess and myself. I anticipated being asked to leave. Then she laughed.

"You are so very British, Miss Huxleigh, as bracing as a sirocco from the shores of Africa. I would keep you as a court critic if I could, a voice of rectitude to toll the minutes of my sins like some relentless clock upon a church tower. I cannot tell you how wearisome it is to have everyone agree with me."

"Not everyone," said a voice from the doorway.

The bearded man entered.

"Emile!" The duchess began to stand, but he moved quickly to lay a dissuading hand upon her shoulder. "Dr. Emile Hoffman," she introduced him. He all too obviously knew who we were. "Emile doubts the wisdom of sharing our delicate situation with strangers."

"Better than sharing it with friends," Irene put in crisply. "Why is he involved, pray? You said that your liaison was long over."

The doctor flushed, as if less inured than the duchess and Irene to such frank realities. "It was I who was contacted by these wretches. The first letter threatened to damage Alice's reputation with the prince, and with the public."

"My reputation, *cherie*," she said with a smile, "is partly why I am so well regarded."

"So said Marie Antoinette once," the doctor returned. He eyed us all in turn, then sat down on a tapestry-upholstered chair.

Unlike most men taking the Riviera air, he wore dark, sober clothing. Even his vest was of charcoal-striped sateen. Perhaps professional dignity was why he chose to wear a beard. He was much better-looking than first glimpse promised, with dark, curly hair and a set of keen, twinkling eyes that gave him the look of an amiable schoolboy rather than a dignified medical man. Yet even while uneasy, he radiated an energetic charm that would explain the duchess's attachment.

Godfrey had been studying the pair himself, for quite different reasons. His mild gray eyes sharpened as he leaned forward to address them.

"These are very serious blackmailers, I suspect. They approached the doctor first to impress the duchess with how much they know and to amplify your mutual fears. I assume, Doctor, that it would not harm your practice if all—"

"I am now in Nice."

"—if all Nice knew of your former relationship with the duchess?"

Dr. Hoffman's smile was rueful. "Indeed, it might enhance it."

"Then she alone is the target," Godfrey declared. "Although using you as intermediary has the interesting effect of renewing your association and further compromising her."

The duchess sighed. "Yes. It is most unfortunate. Albert's and my wedding has not only been forbidden by Prince Charles, but by the Bishop of Monaco as well. We will marry when Charles dies, but a scandal before then will not convince the bishop or the people to accept me as Princess of Monaco. I am already hampered by being an American and half Jewish."

"You believe that the prince will stand by you?" Irene asked. "Once his father dies, he may decide he must serve the line and marry into the aristocracy."

Alice's bright blue eyes clouded, then cleared. "I *am* the aristocracy, Irene. The aristocracy of New World money. American heiresses are becoming quite the fashion for European noble houses to marry."

Irene answered drily "Kings and princes can be fickle."

I knew she recalled her disastrous encounter with the current King of Bohemia, who had pursued her as a prince but was ready to disavow her when he inherited the throne.

"Anyone can be fickle, my dear Irene."

"Unfortunately, not blackmailers," Godfrey said. "We know what they propose to reveal. What do they want?"

The duchess and the doctor exchanged a quick, uneasy glance.

"That's just it," she said at last. "They won't say. Or rather, they say they will tell us when the time comes. You see why it is so distressing."

"When the time comes?" Irene was suddenly alert. "What time? For what?"

"Alas . . ." The doctor spread his hands with a medical man's precision. "We are told only to wait and see."

"How do they convey this extraordinary instruction?"

"By letter," the doctor answered.

"May I see it?" Irene's gloved hand was extended.

Dr. Hoffman reached into his breast pocket and withdrew a sadly wrinkled document. Irene scanned it quickly.

"In French, but execrable French. Cheap paper, and filthy. This is not the handiwork of a society blackmailer."

"Perhaps some servant thinks to grow wealthy on forbidden knowledge," Godfrey speculated.

Irene shook her head. "This is an ignorant, crude attempt, but not pointless. Or without guile." She eyed the doctor. "How did it come?"

"By post."

"You have the envelope?"

"I . . . not here." He seemed confused. "I left it, ah . . . in Alice's sitting room."

"May I see it?"

"Of course." He rose, bobbed the women a bow and darted off.

The four of us carefully avoided regarding one another. Obviously, Dr. Hoffman still enjoyed a certain familiarity with the duchess.

Hurrying footsteps announced the physician's return. He brought the envelope directly to Irene, who snatched it eagerly. She ignored the address on the front and turned it over.

"As I thought!" she announced, her eyes shining as if she had just received an ovation at La Scala in Milan.

We stared, uncomprehending.

"The sealing wax! The scent of sandalwood. The senders of the mysterious letters to Louise Montpensier's uncle!"

"Of course," I murmured dully.

"By Jove—" Godfrey began.

But Alice, Duchess of Richelieu, had the last and most shocking words.

"Louise Montpensier? Little Louise? You know her, too?"

Chapter Seventeen

AULD ACQUAINTANCE NOT FORGOT

❦

Prince Albert of Monaco, the Duchess of Richelieu on his stiffly cocked arm, was circling the ballroom to my side, and there was nothing I could do to prevent it.

There was no mistaking his direction, nor his identity. Two diamond stars of office blazed from the dark cloth of his navy-wool dress uniform. Gold braid entwined upon his collar and cuffs, while genuine gold glinted from the hilt of the ceremonial sword at his side. A ribbon of rank slashed from his right epaulet to his left hip.

I felt that I played some third-rate opera company Cinderella, delivered to the ball and then abandoned, like an inconvenient pumpkin, to the oncoming prince. Irene sang for the guests, at the behest of the duchess, in a more intimate salon, while Godfrey circulated in search of news and clues. I was left to join the dowagers lining the walls, under orders to "learn what I could" of everyone, but especially of Louise. Her safety and the solution of the puzzles involving her were the underlying reasons for this social expedition.

Onward came the quasi-royal couple. Her Grace's Worth gown of billowing cerise taffeta added sparkle to the prince's intimidating appearance. With his stoutness, heavy-lidded eyes, straight nose and closely trimmed beard, he looked bored and overstuffed, as the Prince of Wales often did. It was hard to imagine this man marrying the vivacious woman beside him—although it was true that the stolid Prince of Wales had wed the beautiful and formidable Princess Alexandra.

"Mademoiselle Huxleigh, how charming you look!" The duchess addressed me in French. "Prince Albert so enjoyed hearing Irene sing. I had no idea that we had a diva of such skill among us. A pity the prince's social duties drew us away beforetimes. I adore the opera! One day soon, Monaco shall have a splendid opera house worthy of Irene and other artists."

Despite the threat of blackmail, the duchess seemed undeterred from her ambitions of a princess-to-be. "Albert," she went on, "Mademoiselle Huxleigh is English."

A flicker of interest stirred in the prince's wan brown eyes. "Ah, English. So many Americans flock to Monte Carlo now that I fear we have lost many of our English friends. American women dazzle but are unpredictable. They ride astride and are forever appearing in the newspapers. I believe that a woman should appear in the press at only three times: at birth, at her marriage, and at her death."

"I quite agree, Your Highness."

"Excellent! Discretion in a woman is as honesty in a man, a cardinal virtue."

With that, the prince moved on, the duchess pausing long enough to whisper to me, "You must ignore Albert's mothballed ideas; his father is an ogre of convention. The important news is that Louise and her American are here tonight. Irene was particularly happy to know that. Louise's American is, of course, one of those detestable journalists who put women in the newspapers! Let us hope that Irene's investigations will ensure the prince's peace of mind by keeping my past affairs from the public print."

She swept away, a gaily colored marzipan figure of cerise flounces, golden hair and blue eyes. I felt some sympathy for her. If a good fairy had given Alice Heine wealth, beauty and title, a less friendly benefactor had taken from her also: first a young husband, then two men who had clearly attracted her. Now her past threatened her present: a prince and a principality.

Women milled around me, their skirts draped and swagged like the rococo ballroom itself. Brilliant facets of gemstones and crystal exploded everywhere, sending forth fireworks of diamond, ruby and sapphire. Gilded pillars and polished mahogany and carved plasterwork mounted to high ceilings from which hung ornate, glittering chandeliers.

"There you are."

Godfrey, dashing in formal dress, had brought me a cup of iced punch, a boon in the crowd-warmed room.

"We are here tonight on the duchess's whim—and Irene with scant notice for her Riviera debut. Even so, her singing is staggering the audience," he noted with forgivable pride. "No one had the slightest inkling that the unknown 'Madame Norton' could even hum so much as 'Frere Jacques.' "

"It may be satisfying, but is it safe for Irene to sing?"

"Far safer than some of her other pursuits." He glanced to a crown of glowing crystal above us. "Safer than snakes and swinging from lighting fixtures on moving trains, I should think."

"It was not my idea to travel south, nor to stir up sailors and aristocrats."

"Odd, isn't it, how highborn and lowborn persons mingle in these two vastly separate puzzles." Godfrey stared into the distance. "Now their threads entangle again! For there stands Louise Montpensier, looking far happier than when we last saw her. "Thank God she is all right!"

"We must detain her, Godfrey, before she vanishes in this mob and Irene accuses us of incompetence!"

"Indeed."

Together we wove through the room until we reached the missing girl. I would not have recognized her. The sallow, dispirited young woman was now animated and attractive. Perhaps the young gentleman beside her had accomplished this change. I liked him immediately. There was honesty in his sun-darkened face and eager, open eyes; some would find him naive. I persisted in finding him refreshing.

Louise paled as she recognized Godfrey. He bowed over her hand. "Mademoiselle Montpensier. And Mister Caleb Winter of Boston, is it not?"

"Look here," the young American said immediately, "if you're an agent of Louise's uncle, you'll have a fight if you try to force her back to Paris."

"My dear sir, I'm nothing of the sort."

Louise tugged at her champion's woolen sleeve. "This gentleman rescued me from . . . from those who tattooed me," she confided. "Please do not harm him."

Godfrey smiled at her. "Your fiancé is the second party to take my service to you in the wrong way. You have more defenders than you know, Mademoiselle. It is a pity that you are dead."

"Dead?" The color faded from her face. "You know all, then?"

"We could visit the terrace for some fresh air," Godfrey proposed.

I slipped to Louise's side. In a few chaotic days, the poor girl had gone from despair to elation, and now to shock.

"Mademoiselle Huxleigh!" She gave me a look of even deeper shock. "You have altered."

"I am dressed for a soiree, that is all. Come, we will sit outside, where we may talk in private."

The night was cool, but the heat of the ballroom had been so overpowering that we welcomed the change. A far-flung chandelier of stars glittered against the night's india-ink skies.

Floral scents drifted from the surrounding bushes. While couples strolled in the gardens, none came close enough to intrude upon our party.

Louise and I sat down upon a bench, our skirts puffing like sails and making it impossible for the gentlemen to sit also. That did not matter: Louise's young gentleman took up a protective post behind her. Godfrey paced.

"We are pleased to see you alive, Mademoiselle," Godfrey said at last. "But to the Paris police, your uncle and his neighbors, you are dead, drowned in the mere behind your home."

Louise twisted her gloved hands. "I had to flee. When I found that Caleb would not abandon me after my misfortune, I was overjoyed. He convinced me that we must run away and be married, and that his acquaintance, the Duchess of Richelieu, would help us. And my uncle—"

"We have seen your uncle," I said. "Therefore we understand why you might flee. Didn't you guess that your so-called death would be blamed upon your aunt?"

"My aunt? No! Is she—?"

"There is no proof," Godfrey said gently, "so she is safe for the present. But you must return and tell the police the truth."

"Yes, yes. But first Caleb and I must find the truth of my father's death here in Monte Carlo. I . . . I no longer believe him a suicide, a coward who lost all he had and so threw away his life. I no longer believe my uncle's story of his death."

"Louise has had a raw deal, Mr. Norton," the young American said in his colorful manner. "I can't figure it out." She swears there's no money in the family anymore. That don't matter a fig to me, but maybe someone has an eye on the inheritance he thinks she has. Anyway, Louise has a right to know about her father, and I'm going to find out the facts. I'm a correspondent for *The Boston Clarion*. I know how to dig up the truth."

"Truth is not a buried bone," said a voice behind us. "It takes more than a good nose to find it."

We turned to find Irene watching our conference with some amusement. Louise had never seen her in full plumage and the young American had never seen her at all, so they stared with mouths agape. She wore an evening gown of changeable violet silk, with iridescent black coq feathers bristling from the shoulders and hem. The effect was, as the French would say, *"formidable!"* Caught between the moonlight and the soft blur of the ballroom's candlelight, Irene seemed a figure conjured from a Byronic ode, beautiful and slightly sinister.

She greeted Louise with a reprimand. "It was most foolish of you to run away." She turned to the journalist with another. "And even more foolish of you to abet her. You have brought her to the very heart of danger."

"I'm not afraid of danger," he replied.

"Then you are certainly too young to face it." Irene eyed Louise again. "How did you come to meet the duchess?"

"Caleb did," Louise said. "The duchess is very fond of Americans. He proposed to interview her for his newspaper. We thought she would know those in Monte Carlo who would remember my father's death. She was most sympathetic."

Irene's impatient gesture with a black-velvet-gloved hand made an amethyst and zircon bangle dispense cold fire. "Sympathy is as misleading as truth. What have you learned of your father?"

The two exchanged a glance. "Why, nothing yet, Madame," Louise said politely. "It is too soon, and his death was long ago and hushed up."

Irene turned to Godfrey, who was lounging against a stone balustrade with the air of a playgoer during an intermission. "What have *you* learned so far, Godfrey?"

"That Claude Montpensier had the honor of being among

the first fatalities of the casino in eighteen seventy-three, when we were, all of us, mere children. Much that we see surrounding the casino today was not yet constructed, but ill luck was firmly installed, as it always is in gaming palaces. Suicide was the hidden scandal behind Monte Carlo's dazzling wheel of fortune. The facts in such cases—and the bodies as well—were often suppressed.

"From what little I have learned, Claude Montpensier was found at one o'clock in the morning dangling from the chandelier in an unused parlor at his hotel. His pockets were empty, hence the supposition that gaming losses caused his suicide."

"That's all?" Irene sounded indignant. "Empty pockets and they assume a suicide?"

"There was the rope."

She bridled like an offended peacock. "Rope. Anyone can commit murder by providing rope and a dead man. No one saw him losing money in the casino? No one knows for sure that he died by his own hand?"

"Irene, no one took responsibility for victims of the wheel of fortune in those days; no one had foreseen the likelihood of suicide becoming as much a part of Monte Carlo as the palm trees and the sea. I have the name of a doctor who *may* have attended the body at that time, but he himself may also be dead."

She turned to the young reporter. "Godfrey is a mere barrister, yet he has ferreted out more facts than a fearless correspondent, and in less time. As for truth, who is to determine it after so many years have passed?"

"We will come with you to see this doctor," the young man, unabashed, told Godfrey.

Irene mutely but eloquently beseeched the heavens for deliverance, but there was none. Our party had acquired a pair of babes in the woods.

We agreed to meet upon the morrow and seek out the

elderly physician. Irene, Godfrey and I departed through the ballroom, our progress halted frequently as admirers offered congratulations on Irene's singing. We finally stood, cloaked, on the palace steps, awaiting our equipage.

"A most unsatisfactory evening," I mentioned.

Irene smiled. "Really? I thought it went rather well. Especially the Schubert."

"I meant our investigation, not your singing."

"'Our' investigation did discover Louise and her fiancé."

"And now we are burdened with them!"

"Better than letting them blunder about on their own and run into danger," Godfrey said, nodding toward the drive as our carriage clattered to a stop.

"But is it wise—?" I began.

Godfrey assisted us both into the conveyance. "It may not be wise, but it is necessary," he said softly. "One fact only did I keep from Louise and her swain. The official records of her father's death mention the presence of a tattoo."

Chapter Eighteen

A DETECTIVE IN TRANSIT

❧

Poor old Watson! Here I sit usurping one of his rare privileges, that of recording my investigative adventures for "posterity."

Posterity, I fear, will little mark nor long remember the current case, a straightforward matter of a young woman's apparent murder. As far as Watson knows, I went to Paris as a courtesy to my colleague in its Prefecture of Police, Monsieur Le Villard. This promising detective communicated his distress and eagerness for myself to come and take a look in person.

In fact, I was also eager to preview his translations of my monographs into French, my works' debut in foreign print. It is perhaps my authorship of various monographs that allows me to tolerate my friend Watson's literary ambitions and related vanities.

Watson would take offense at the notion of my jotting down the facts of my own efforts, but his thus-far-unpublished accounts of my cases convince me of the value of recording events as they occur. Of course, my memoirs are far more likely to see print than Watson's sensationalized versions, but there is no sense in pointing out the obvious to the oblivious. And he means well, as always.

Watson seldom inquires into my jaunts abroad, recognizing that they often involve heads of state, some of them crowned, and require strict secrecy. The current journey will draw me into such deep waters, though I dare not even hint at these delicate matters other than to say that they involve hemophilia, the succession of an important European duchy and a certain deadly species of camellia.

"My dear Holmes!" M. Le Villard greeted me from the threshold of my hotel parlor on the evening of my arrival. "How kind of you to come so far to assist in this troubling problem of mine."

"And how thoughtful of you to have brought the typeset pages of my monographs," said I.

The French detective lifted the parcel wrapped in brown paper that had been tucked under his arm. "But how—?"

"You would not be bringing me a sheaf of musical scores, my dear fellow. Although I play the violin, you could hardly know that, and besides, my repertoire is written on the staffs of my memory, not on paper. May I see them?"

"But of course! You did not say that you knew French."

"Oh, I speak it enough to make myself understood, but not well enough to translate my own writings."

I unveiled the printers' galleys, not failing to notice that they had accompanied my French friend to lunch, where he had enjoyed a filet of sole somewhat overweighted with garlic and had partaken of a rather inferior sauterne in the company of a one-armed bistro-keeper.

Of the man himself, neat as a monkey and as genial as a poodle, the particulars were as unexceptional as his lunch. He had served in the French Army until requiring retirement for an injured back; he had been born left-handed, but early and diligent correction had changed him to right-handed in all respects save tying his shoes, an exception of mild interest; he was married and had three children, one of whom was deaf. And he was a fair translator, to judge by a glance at the galleys.

"I am grateful, Monsieur Le Villard, for your interest in translating my monographs. They will no doubt prove most instructive to the French detective force."

"My pleasure, Monsieur Holmes. I admit to marveling evermore at your range of esoteric knowledge as I labored over the translation. Unfortunately, pure genius is not to be translated."

"You underestimate me. I am a man of science and system rather than one prone to bursts of inspiration. That is always translatable."

"That is what is so admirable, my dear Holmes!—the consistency with which you approach a variety of problems, and with which you obtain results. Yet it cannot all be method; there must be some passion in it."

How like the French to find passion even in science. "My friend Watson would argue with you. He accuses me of a stunning lack of curiosity about my fellow humans' deepest emotions. He would call my methods bloodless, however successful."

"If your methods are successful, then bloodshed may be avoided in many cases; that is a bloodlessness to be desired. And I hope that shall be true of my current case as well."

"What is the problem?"

Le Villard shrugged, taking the seat I indicated. "I am puzzled not so much by the facts of the case as by my own unease regarding it. The enforcement of the law is my passion, hence my enthusiasm for your monographs. I have watched men whom my work has convicted meet Madame Guillotine and have felt no regret. But in this case, I find myself harboring the doubts that afflict the timid. Perhaps I am wrong in accusing the murderess."

"A woman who murders always impales men's consciences upon the double barbs of law and chivalry."

"Madame Montpensier is not a strikingly sympathetic figure in any obvious sense. She is not young and beautiful, although the victim was. She is a suspect primarily because she was last seen with her niece in a clandestine meeting alongside a mere behind the house. A misty, dank, forsaken spot, Monsieur Holmes! From its marshy waters was later recovered the missing girl's bracelet."

"But no body?"

"No."

"And you believe—?"

"I believe that Madame Montpensier is the most likely suspect, a position she reinforces by refusing to talk to the police. We are not ogres."

"Assuredly not," I reassured him before lighting my pipe. In physical appearance, Le Villard was a small, neat man with peculiarly barbered whiskers and a scent of Macassar oil about his person. By no stretch of the imagination—which Watson insists that I do not possess—was he reminiscent of an ogre.

"If the woman in question will not submit to an interview with you," I said, "will she see myself?"

He shrugged again. "She is a woman. She may be intrigued by the famous English detective's interest."

I laughed, what Watson no doubt would have described as "a cynical bark of mirth."

"My dear Le Villard, no murderer is sufficiently intrigued by even the Queen of Spain to wish to unburden himself, or herself, to a pursuer."

"She has insisted privately that the girl is not dead."

"She has, has she? What are the facts?"

"Louise Montpensier is an orphan of decent family. For most of her life she has resided with her father's elder brother, Edouard, and his wife."

"Then the aunt is unrelated by blood."

"That is true, and another reason she is a suspect."

"How comforting to know that if Watson, say, were to be found throttled, I would be the likeliest suspect because we are unrelated. I propose to you, Le Villard, that relationship is always a more plausible motive for murder than not. She is wealthy, this Louise Montpensier?"

"No. Nor is her uncle."

"And the aunt?"

"She brought some wealth to her husband. The Montpensier family had money once, but the fortune dissipated. The suicide of the girl's father, Claude, in Monte Carlo, did not help the family finances. But that was years ago."

"Since you have asked it, my friend—and have brought me this excellent reading material—I will attempt to see Madame Montpensier, but not in my own guise."

"Yes, I have heard that the art of concealment is another you have mastered."

"All arts are subservient to science for the detective. You must let me go about this in my own way. Merely give me the address. I will report when my explorations are done."

"But I wished to observe your methods."

"A good detective moves mysteriously, Le Villard, like a planet in transit across the heavens. The effects, rather than the process, are all that should be seen. I will inform you when I know more."

Chapter Nineteen

THE ROSE TATTOO

❦

''**A tattoo,** sir, indeed the most bizarre tattoo I have ever seen. I remember it well. To find a tattoo upon a gentleman is most unusual. And then the manner of death. . . .''

Dr. Jarnac straightened slowly over a Marechal Niel rose. Our party stood surrounded by rosebushes in full bloom and of dizzying scent. The white stones of Monte Carlo sparkled on the horizon like a low cloud bank. Below us, the sea snapped at a strand of sand and rock. We were high on a headland, in the garden behind a simple cottage.

But such a garden! Its small environs illustrated why the Beaulieu coast was called La Petite Afrique. Alongside magnificent roses grew miniaturized examples of the tropical vegetation that only this small, sun-seared slice of Western Europe would nurture: gum and calabash trees, banana trees and date palms, mangoes, prickly pears and Indian figs. Dr. Jarnac had pointed out each to us. Godfrey's eyes had narrowed as he surveyed this lush property, estimating what such a desirable location would bring on the current market.

"This tattoo?" Irene had drawn her sketch of Louise's defacement from her handbag. The wind whipped at us; she had to use both hands to hold the paper up to the doctor's faded brown eyes.

"Like it, Madame. Like it. I cannot say. It was many years

ago." He bent to sniff a full-blown beauty too ripe to pick. "The senses dull with time, but even age cannot blunt the perfume of these lovelies."

"The dead man was my father," Louise said suddenly. "We must know the circumstances."

The doctor straightened to regard her with as much tender concern as he did his roses. "Who can know the exact circumstances but God, Mademoiselle? I have lived long enough to know *that*."

He was a small man, and shrunken, so he seemed a strangely elderly child among us. Yet we hung on his words, even Irene, who often disdained to take words at face value. This frail man had arrived upon the scene shortly after Claude Montpensier had died.

Dr. Jarnac offered Louise the Marechal Niel he had plucked. "Have faith, my child." He turned to a ravishing scarlet variety. Use-rusted shears snapped through a tough stem. Irene graciously accepted the vivid flower he extended. "And hope, Madame."

He faced the roses again. I heard the snip of the scissors. When he turned to me, a yellow rose shone buttercup-bright in his palsied hand. "And you, Mademoiselle, charity."

The physician's courtliness instilled an odd virtue in all of us: patience. We smiled at each other and watched him dodder to a stone bench overlooking the sea.

He laid his shears and straw hat beside him, sighed, then began his story. "I was already old when I attended the body of Claude Montpensier. It was in the early seventies, I think—"

"Seventy-three."

The old man nodded at Godfrey's prompting. "Dates blur, but certain particulars remain vivid. Emotions never fade, and I was distressed to see such a fine young man dead by his own hand. I am glad I retired soon after; many more have chosen to embrace the rope after the dice disappoint them."

"What of the tattoo?" Irene asked.

"It was here, over the heart. An odd placement."

"Fresh?" Godfrey inquired.

The doctor tilted his snowy head. Freckles lay scattered like sand beneath his thinning locks and flecked his hands and face. "I doubt it. That is what was surprising, beyond the issue of his station in life. A new tattoo has a sheen; this one had dulled to become one with the skin."

"And the marks of death?"

Dr. Jarnac glanced at Irene's intent face. "That is why I gave you the ruddy rose, Madame; you are implacable in the face of opposition, even death. Yes, he bore all of the marks of his suicide. The rope welt around his throat, the broken voice box, the bruises upon his calves and shins where his feet flailed."

Louise made a sharp sound and buried her face in her hands.

"Were there any other signs about the body?"

"Other, Madame? Only a bruise at the base of the skull, where the knot had pressed during and after death. Some abrasions at the wrists. Perhaps the poor devil had lifted his hands at the last to fight the rope and his starched cuffs had grazed his skin."

Irene inhaled deeply of the crimson rose, as if to perfume her thoughts. "Wrists. I was afraid of that. Perhaps, Doctor, his wrists were *bound* and later released."

"Bound? But why? How could he—?"

"How could he indeed? And there was nothing on his person? No coins, no cards, no personal effects?"

"Not even tobacco flakes in his pockets, Madame."

"Then how did you determine his identity?" I demanded.

The doctor smiled sadly. "It was a difficulty. His death was reported in the papers, of course, and his description. No one stepped forward. He was about to be buried in a pauper's grave when a lascar from one of the ships in the harbor visited my office with a torn clipping of the death report and a note identifying the man as Claude Montpensier of Paris. The police there located his brother."

"And he still had a pauper's funeral," Louise said thickly. "Uncle would not hear of him being brought back to Paris for burial, or of us coming to Monaco to attend his interment."

"There was not time, child." Dr. Jarnac stood. "This balmy air does not permit long delay for the dead."

"Do you know where he lies?" the American asked.

The old man shook his head. "No. It was out of my hands. All I have to offer are my memories."

"And they are excellent, Doctor." Irene advanced to take his hand. "I suppose that there was no signature on the note revealing his identity."

"None."

"And the lascar?"

"Gone. Surly, filthy sort of fellow. Looked as if he hardly understood English."

We walked through the gardens and around the simple stone cottage to the front, where our open carriage waited to take us down the winding corniche road to Monte Carlo. Even the sun of a Côte d'Azur day could not banish the chill of early, wrongful death that touched each of us.

We settled in the carriage, looking, I'm sure, like a party of revelers. Louise tucked her rose at her waist, I fastened mine to a lapel, and Irene thrust hers into her hair at her bonnet rim, a gesture of dash and melodrama that suited her perfectly.

I remember the drive back, with the sun beating down on our hatted heads, the sea's endless sapphire sparkling on our right and the rough foothills of the coast hunched at our left.

"Someone cared for him," Irene said abruptly, turning from gazing at the sea. She smiled at Louise. "Enough to alert

the authorities to his identity. It was good-hearted, but a
mistake. Their first mistake. It has not been their last."

"Who," I asked Irene when we had returned to the Hotel
de Paris and were sitting in the Nortons' suite parlor, "who are
'they'?"

"I don't know. Do you?"

"Of course I don't. I don't even know that a 'they' exists.
Nor do you."

"They move in exceeding mysterious ways, it is true, dear
Nell. But so does God, and you believe in His existence."

"I will not be diverted into theological culs-de-sac. If you
do indeed know something about these puzzling events, be so
kind as to share your knowledge. Louise's happiness may rest
upon it."

"My opinions are still forming." Irene lay on the chaise
longue, onto which she had thrown herself after donning
combing gown and house slippers. She was never one to sit
about in corsets and full dress if she could escape such
confinement. She drew a brown Egyptian cigarette from the
small table at her side, inserted it into a mother-of-pearl
holder she had bought in Paris and lit it with a lucifer, letting
the smoke lift like a thin blue veil past her face before she
spoke again.

" 'They' are vague in number. Certainly the men who
tattooed Louise, then accosted you and Godfrey on the train,
are two of them. So was the lascar beneath Dr. Jarnac's notice
fifteen years ago. And Claude Montpensier was one of them."

"Claude Montpensier? Irene, you go too far."

"Not far enough." Godfrey entered the room in a smoking
jacket of handsome emerald brocade.

"You approve of this wild surmising, Godfrey?"

"I approve of almost anything Irene does, wild or tame."

"Almost?" she objected. The glitter in her amber-velvet
eyes promised even wilder surmising to come. "Not only are

Claude Montpensier's death and the two seamen who accosted his daughter linked, but so is the tattooed sailor we found dead in London years ago, as well as the one we saw more recently in Paris."

"To join these persons and events, the connection would have to extend back fifteen years!"

"More, Nell," Godfrey corrected me. "Perhaps twenty."

"Twenty," Irene agreed. "Moreover, all these people were, I suspect, involved in the same scheme, and were on the same side in that scheme. One thing that strikes me is that their numbers are decreasing with time."

"Save," Godfrey reminded her, "for the addition of Louise Montpensier—if the tattoos are the password in this strange conspiracy."

"Louise takes her father's place," she mused.

"Why wait so long?" he countered.

"Because, my almost-always-perceptive husband, affairs reach a head now. Perhaps Louise's two ugly fairy godfathers hoped to protect her by waiting until the last possible moment to brand her with the mark of the conspiracy.

" 'Mark of the conspiracy'? Comes to 'a head'?"

They ignored me.

"And the uncle?" Godfrey's head tilted close to Irene's.

She let her head loll back and slitted her eyes in thought— or in an attempt to keep the cigarette smoke out of them. I had never seen her more resemble Lucifer at his feline laziest. "An unexpected problem. He was to have been a conduit to Louise, who would take her father's place, but then . . . well, you have seen him. He would not take second place in anything, and this is clearly a joint venture."

"What 'venture'?"

"Then, too," she said, "somehow the blackmail of the duchess is connected."

"The duchess as well? Irene, this is too much," I expostulated.

"Really," Godfrey said, "even I must balk at including the duchess. You go too far at last."

"And the prince," she intoned dreamily. "His role is key, if somewhat foggy. I must know more about his courtship of the American-born duchess."

Godfrey leaned forward to remove the cigarette holder from her languid fingers. The last sinuous strands of smoke floated past their faces. He regarded her with an expression I could not interpret.

"I really think, my dear Irene, that you must put surmising aside for a while. It cannot be good for your constitution," he admonished, a smile tugging at his lips.

Her eyes suddenly widened. "I am tired," she said. Her glance found me. "And obviously too lost in my speculations to answer your astute questions, Nell."

"Of course," said I, rising. "Too much sun and too much smoke will addle the brain. I plan to rest before dinner and suggest that you both do so also."

"An excellent idea," Godfrey said in a voice like French silk.

"I will certainly take your advice under consideration," Irene said.

I thought her answer most evasive but said nothing. I saw them as I left the room, Godfrey's face close to Irene's. They watched me leave with a curious intensity, like matched leopards too lazy to bound after an innocent passing gazelle.

While I did not comprehend the odd change in their moods, I stole quietly away to a most refreshing nap.

By day, the casino in Monte Carlo had the atmosphere of a church or a theater when no service or performance is scheduled. Visitors still milled about in the high-ceilinged grandeur, yet the building's very vastness and rich ornamentation made the enterprise seem strangely deserted.

The casino was no church, but rather a Temple of Gaming.

(I was still speechless from regarding the most recent decorative addition—the new ceiling fresco of the bar, which
boasted an excessive number of nude ladies puffing on cigars
and cigarettes, each one taking modest pains to keep her *feet*
concealed!) The various rooms, known by the French as
salles, bristled with high oriel windows and half-shell niches,
with pillars, Palladian casements, massive paintings of a
secular—even a pagan—nature, and huge gaming tables
covered with green baize.

Irene and I eyed the empty bustle within the main *salle*, the
Duchess of Richelieu at our side.

"I hate it!" our noble guide said passionately, upon
observing the lethargic gamblers still slumped at the tables,
driven to wager until their heads should nod onto a pillow of
green baize. "But I am told that on this rock—the two
million gold francs the casino has brought to the Grimaldi
treasury—lies the security of the entire principality and its
citizens."

Irene strolled among the tables, watching the fall of dice,
the collapse of losing hands of cards, the fateful spins of the
red-and-black wheel of fortune.

I followed her through this bizarre foreign temple, where
money changed hands in the form of colored chips and no
discernible reason governed the process but luck. The duchess seemed amused by our awe of the great perpetual-motion
gambling machine, the eternal inner clockworks of the icy
white-marble exterior that baked in the Mediterranean sun.

We paused at a roulette table, the duchess remaining
slightly behind us that we might better view the action.

"Sarah is an inveterate gambler," she noted, sighing. "She
spends her money as liberally as she has spent herself on the
stage and lives far beyond her means. Still, she comes here to
risk even more capital. Eager as I am to see her, I hate to see
her ride this fickle wheel of fortune. But then . . . she is
Sarah. She will do as she wishes."

"The theatrical life," Irene said with a nostalgic smile, "often encourages excess off the stage. So much emotion is spent in make-believe that real life can seem tame by contrast. I imagine that Sarah winning and losing at the wheel is as artful a performance as any she has given on the boards."

"Oh, yes. Losing is always a tragedy." The duchess dropped her eyes. "Sometimes it is even a real tragedy. As with Louise's father's death. You know that Eleanora Duse never gambles anymore? Do you know why?"

I shook my head, awed that our guide knew Duse, the Italian mistress of heartfelt emotion.

"It happened at this very table." The duchess swept a hand past the oblivious seated souls. "A desperate young woman—a child, really—lost and lost again. Losers are common; few are noticed in the mob. Duse noticed, however, being ever alert to the human drama. The girl's face grew more ashen, her eyes sank into banked fires. A final loss, and she reached into her reticule and dragged out a colored vial. She threw her head back and drank. In moments she collapsed, dead of some poison. Duse's death scenes have been even more wrenching since but she has never gambled here—or anywhere else—again."

"But why did the poor girl destroy herself?" I asked, shocked. "Who was she? Why would one so young be so set on gambling?"

"Duse survives, and the story, but not the origin of its true, tragic heroine. She was likely some well-brought-up young woman introduced to the pleasures of wagering by a worldly man. Losing more than she should have, she caught the gambling fever and wagered more than she had, until she could not face her losses. Obviously, she had counted on one favorable turn of the wheel to redeem all. When it didn't— Who knows where she came from, or where her body lies? She is a lesson for the history books, at least, because she was young and presumably beautiful and her death was such a waste. And because Duse witnessed it and was touched."

"*Les inconnues de la roulette,*" Irene murmured.

"Your pardon?" said the duchess.

"I was only thinking, Your Grace," Irene said, "that there are many forms of self-destruction for tender and willful young women. Some are prettier than others."

We had passed through the *salles privées*. The chatter of roulette balls, dice and gamblers' tongues muted to a patter like distant rain as the duchess led us into a richly appointed office.

"Call me Alice," she entreated Irene again. "I like hearing an American pronunciation. It is my father who is so enamored of titles." She smiled at me. "And I long to address you as 'Penelope', Miss Huxleigh. I have never known a Penelope. I will feel like a character in one of dear Oscar's plays when I can call you Penelope. It is almost as perfect a name as Gwendolyn."

"If Your Grace is certain that it would be proper."

"Proper! You are the soul of propriety, Penelope. At the hint of your slightest disapproval, improper persons the world over must blanch in concert. Call me Alice, please. I am rich and titled, but not well endowed with friends. I trusted you both from the first, and your admirable husband, Irene. I envy you him, your extraordinary ordinary man, despite my noble marriage. In truth, the aristocracy can be such a bore. Do sit down."

We sat on the indicated glossy-black horsehair sofa. A tea service of Georgian silver stood at shining attention on a table before us. Alice sat opposite us on a charming little Louis XV chair and poured the tea.

Irene smiled indulgently at our titled hostess. "For all your impatience with nobility and ceremony and your distaste for gambling, Alice, you may well become the reigning princess of this artificial little hothouse world."

"My dear Irene, I would have done so long since had Prince Charles, blind in more ways than one, not managed to hang on to life for so long."

Alice's blue eyes twinkled like the seas surrounding this fevered, rockbound principality. "The elder prince believes that his son's sober nature requires a less lively wife." She laughed, obviously enjoying our girlish chat. "Yet Albert is a melange of opposites, like myself. He had a wicked reputation with the ladies after his divorce—yes, my dear Penelope, he did! On the other hand, he is shy with women and quite ready to settle down. As for my own youthful enthusiasms—"

"Dr. Tweedledum and Dr. Tweedledee," Irene put in laconically.

Alice roared with decidedly un-duchess-like laughter. "You have Sarah's delicious sense of satire, Irene. That is why I liked you at the outset. My indiscretions are in the past. I plan to be as proper a princess as our dear Penelope would make, had she any inclination toward royalty."

"I? Dear me, no."

"Save for the blackmailer," Irene pointed out.

Alice sipped her tea. "Hmm. Indeed. But you and your cohorts will dispatch him shortly, I'm sure. At any rate, except for such vexing obstacles as a stern father and an unknown blackmailer, Albert and I have no other barrier to our happiness."

"The prince is interested in forms of sea life?" Irene inquired mildly, a sure sign that she considered the answer significant.

"Oceanography, it's called, my dear. He is quite a pioneer, though you would not know it to look at him. After he resigned his youthful commission in the French Navy, Albert studied under Professor Milne-Edwards. He most admires the work of a one-time American naval officer, Maury, on the mysteries of winds and currents. To Albert, nothing is so fascinating as that which breathes saltwater. He pursues

submarine zoology and chemical oceanography as madly as
most men would pursue mistresses. On one of his expeditions,
he managed to collect specimens as deep as nine thousand
feet. Perhaps they are mermaids! All this involves deep-sea
diving apparatus and such, as from a story by Jules Verne. You
may have noticed the abundance of seawater that surrounds
the principality," she added drily.

"But this second physician—"

Alice dimpled at the memory, then glanced at me. "Let us
be frank. I am, to an extent, a commodity on the international marriage market. Like many Americans, my father wants
me to obtain a title in exchange for bringing my new blood
and money into a European nobility exhausted of both. I have
followed my heart—Armand was madly in love with me, and
so is the prince, as were my darling doctors—but I am also
aware that I am well suited for the life that an aristocratic
marriage entails.

"Yet, I am human. I was widowed and lonely, and these
were brilliant men interested in my welfare, and most
charming, both of them. Perhaps it is the poetic nature in me
from my grand-uncle, Heinrich Heine. To the world, I am the
'beautiful blond American' who would be princess. To myself,
I am much more complicated."

"We see that, Alice," Irene said, speaking for herself.
"And we see that marriage to a prince entails compromises
perhaps not always foreseen. I am delighted to hear that yours
has such a strong interest in the science of the ocean. Has it
always been so?"

"Since his youth."

Irene nodded with extreme satisfaction. I looked at her
suspiciously. She said, "It is obvious that you admire men of a
scientific bent."

Alice dimpled again. "I can also admire a man of a
nonscientific disposition, such as a barrister, Irene. No doubt
you, too, could have married a prince, with your beauty and

talent, but there are rich compensations to be found with the uncommon common man."

Irene remained strangely silent, sitting like the Mona Lisa, a faint, half smile upon her lips. Only I knew how close to the tender truth Alice had trod. Indeed, Irene had all of the qualifications for a royal life, save she had not had the money to persuade one of royal lineage to accept her lack of royal blood.

"We all make the choices most suitable for ourselves," Irene said blandly. She turned to me. "Since I am already spoken for, perhaps Alice can exercise her matchmaking talents to find someone suitable for you, Nell."

"No!" I nearly spilled my tea into the saucer.

"You do not wish to marry?" Alice asked, curious.

"I have no objection to the state." I colored faintly to recall my girlish attachment to the young curate, Jasper Higgenbottom, and an inexplicable faintness in the presence of One Other Gentleman clearly beyond my reach. "I will have to do for myself in this regard, however."

"I'm sure you will do excellently, my dear," Alice assured me. "All my friends find you utterly delightful."

"Oscar," Irene put in impishly, "was most taken with our Nell in London, before his marriage."

"Oscar was always being taken with some woman in those days—Lillie Langtry, for one. Now he seems to have overcome the habit quite dramatically," Alice said.

I was glad to hear of our old acquaintance's reformation. It struck me that there was always hope. If Oscar Wilde could change his womanizing ways, perhaps someday I could find a suitable spouse.

Drifting into a rosy study, I considered what kind of man would constitute a suitable spouse for myself now. Certainly not the rawboned Jasper. No, I was a more worldly woman these days. Thanks to Irene, I had seen much more of life than a Shropshire parsonage would have ever allowed. I could drink tea with a woman who admitted to liaisons with two men to whom she had never been married, and I winced only mildly. The road to hell is paved with such subtle progress.

"That will be our next project, Miss Huxleigh's acquisition of a new surname, once we have disposed of this trifling matter of the blackmail," Alice declared.

Irene stood. "An excellent idea. I shall suggest it to Godfrey immediately. But blackmail is never trifling. I must learn what progress he has made in his inquiries."

"I'm delighted you could join me for tea. I must remain behind to speak to the manager, Monsieur Blanc. He frets that my distaste for gambling will influence the prince to disown his legacy, so I must reassure the old dear that I, too, am fond of gold louies. But I wanted you to see the casino, it is so splendid architecturally. I only wish that I could convert some of the tragedy it has caused into a source of innocent happiness and pleasure."

"I am certain that you will think of something." Irene's eyes narrowed as if she already had. "Thank you for your unusual hospitality, Alice—a ladies' tea in a gambling casino. I will let you know the moment our investigation bears fruit."

Irene and I paused by the door. The beautiful blond duchess stood like an all-too-breakable Dresden figurine amid the heavy red velvet and burnished-mahogany splendor of the office. I recalled how vulnerable Irene had been in Prague at the hands of the prince's hostile family and felt a twinge of pity for our hostess, despite the irregularities in her life.

"I will await news eagerly," Alice said. "I have heard that the renowned English consulting detective, Sherlock Holmes, is visiting Monte. Perhaps you can collaborate."

Irene's face washed white, then rosy. "Sherlock Holmes? In Monte Carlo?"

Alice shrugged. "So I am told. Another of these uncommon common men, no doubt."

We bowed and left, threading our way through the various *salles*. Irene expertly avoided the occasional dazed gambler who veered into our path and finally led us into the brilliant daylight. I stood blinking after the dark interior of the casino, hearing gulls shrieking in the distance.

"An uncommon coincidence, Nell," Irene murmured finally, "if true. Sherlock Holmes in Monte Carlo. It is ludicrous! But not a coincidence. *Why is he here?*"

Her fiery and demanding gaze pinned me to my silence. Answering impossible questions was Irene's province, and she was clearly feeling out of her depth.

"Sherlock Holmes?" Godfrey looked as disturbed as Irene when he heard. "Again? That man has a gift for meddling in your affairs."

"Or vice versa," Irene said softly. "And just when I was beginning to make progress."

"We cannot be certain that he is here for any reason involving our inquiry," I pointed out.

They regarded me with something very like the pity one extends to the feeble-brained. I ignored their reaction, distressed to see my friends so concerned.

"I'm going to put cornflower oil on my eyelids and lie down and think," Irene said, rustling off to her bedchamber without a backward glance to me or Godfrey.

I eyed him in some trepidation. "What can the man do, after all?" I demanded. "He can only go 'round and ask questions as we have done. He may be here on business having nothing to do with our matters. He may simply like to gamble—well, it's possible. You have no evidence to the contrary. Why is his presence so problematical?"

Godfrey came near and leaned his hands on the arms of my chair so that his face was close to mine. I was fond of that face and it was not unpleasant, but the proximity allowed me to see the worry shrouding the familiar features.

"Because, dear Nell, Sherlock Holmes is a premier problem-solver and travels nowhere without a first-class problem to solve. Because Monaco is small, and visitors, like ourselves, are easily noticed. Because we are juggling a host of problems, with no solution yet in sight. Because, worst of all, Irene and I are supposed to be dead—and are not. He could recognize us and report that fact. And, most important, because Irene has always been intrigued by the blasted fellow and I'm a bit jealous."

I swallowed and was silent. I could not fault Godfrey's logic.

Chapter Twenty

ACCOSTED EN SUITE

Irene and Godfrey did not come down for breakfast the following morning. I occupied myself by taking an unescorted stroll along the promenade. At least I was safe from discovery, as Mr. Sherlock Holmes had last seen me in the guise of Irene's elderly housekeeper in the St. John's Wood villa in London.

I did not take a parasol. The morning was fine, with wild parakeets bursting like rainbows from the trees and bushes. Their flagrant colors—bright green and blue—made me momentarily homesick for Casanova's feathered coat of many colors, although his raucous comments were not missed.

An elderly woman in half-mourning, whom I'd noticed before on my strolls, was feeding the gulls and pigeons. I paused to discourse with her on the attractions and depredations of birds and their suitability to a wild state. She was most interested to learn of Casanova's offensive habits and language, and sympathized heartily on my trials with the creature.

I did not return to the hotel until almost noon, pleased with having entertained myself and with my delicacy in recognizing my friends' need for sober withdrawal at news that Mr. Sherlock Holmes lurked in the neighborhood.

Their third-floor rooms were still quiet. When I knocked,

the door edged open slightly. French maids are famous for disrespecting closed doors, either by blithely opening them or by leaving them unlatched for the next innocent party to blunder through.

I entered to find the parlor deserted and stood perplexed. Had Irene and Godfrey gone out for an early luncheon? Or had they risen at all?

A burrowing sound issued from the bedchamber, a hasty rummaging rustle that reminded me of an animal or a child getting into mischief. I approached the door, which was also ajar, my footfalls muffled by the heavy Turkey carpet.

I heard a sharp intake of breath, a moment's silence, and then again the fevered rustling. At that moment I appreciated the figure of speech about being on the threshold of a decision. Should I enter, and risk an embarrassing intrusion? Should I retreat, perhaps permitting a sneak thief to steal at his leisure? Should I remain as I was, poised like a statue on the threshold?

A renewed burrowing noise decided me. I swung the door wider and stepped through. The bedchamber was shrouded in that lazy, secret semi-darkness that exists only when one knows that bright sunlight is pressing against the closed curtains.

The bed had not been made and, much as I disapproved of this state, I was relieved to see that it stood unoccupied as well as disheveled. Unfortunately, the room itself was not unoccupied. I stared at the swarthy man who, half bent over an open bureau drawer, stared back at me.

"You trespass, sir!"

He gazed at me uncomprehendingly, frozen in a posture I can only describe as being "caught in the act." As a governess, I had often apprehended children so. My recourse then had been stern reprimand. I saw no reason not to apply the back of my tongue to this intruder while I hastily contemplated how to make my escape.

"You are in the wrong room, sir." I edged toward the open door.

"Not likely," said he in rough-spoken French, stepping toward me.

Even in the dim light I could see matted black hair escaping a filthy wool cap and the crooked line of a scar along his equally crooked nose. An aroma of the sea—or rather, of fish—assaulted my nostrils and mixed uneasily with the perfume of Irene's favorite Parma violets.

In backing away, I caught my heel in the rug. I fell against the door, which in turn fell shut, immuring me in the darkness with the thief.

He was on me in a thrice, his fingers loosely circling my wrist, his face bowed to snarl into mine. "I'll thank you to keep quiet."

"Oh, I will be quiet," I whispered with some irritation. "But I must know what you are about on the premises."

"Lifting a watch," the fellow said with a grin, elevating Godfrey's pocket timepiece by its long golden chain. The man's breath reeked of onions, and I averted my face.

"Aren't we nice? You'll not say anything to anyone about me?"

I shook my head vigorously while shrinking against the door to avoid any contact with this disreputable person's clothing. At first I might have suspected Irene in disguise, but there was no way that her magical touch with theatrical paint could extend her height by several inches or enlarge her hands. This man had the aspect of a powerful street bully.

"Promise?" A yellowed eye rolled in that shadowed, brutal, unshaven face with its white-streaked mustache.

"On my honor. But please go! You don't want to be caught by my friends, do you?"

"Caught? A slim chance that anyone catches Black Otto at his work," he cackled. "A good thing that the room is dark and you haven't had a good look at my face, or—"

He released my wrist as if he found me as unappetizing as I did him, and slouched to the window.

A billow of French brocade puffed toward him. Then the drapery was snatched back, revealing a figure limned against the violent daylight.

"Irene!" I shrieked in warning and, I admit, relief, for I had grown to expect her mastery of any situation.

The thief never hesitated. As Irene moved into the room, he entwined her in a grotesque mazurka against the bright windows, lifting her as if she weighed no more than a fashion doll and swinging her around. I shrieked as Irene whirled in the man's grasp, her feet flying above the floor.

Another screamed with me: Irene. "No!" she shouted. "No, you idiot, put me down!"

"Never, Madame!" he boldly shouted back. "I am an unrepentant ruffian who will never free you for as long as I live."

Such a threat was too much for me. I seized a parasol leaning by the door and fell upon Irene's captor, raining blows of split bamboo and ruffled silk upon his shoulders and head.

The uproar, if anything, increased. Irene called "No, no, no!" The man cried "Stop!" and I—admonishing him to be "Away!"—continued my assault.

Somehow, in the melee we three became tangled with the draperies. An awful crack resounded, followed by a deluge of brocade and dust. I found myself foundering in the fallen fabric, coughing. Near me, Irene was gasping, "Stop, I beg you!" And laughing.

So was the thief. Laughing. And coughing.

In the blazing light of the denuded French windows, Irene surfaced from the billowing brocade with tears furrowing her cheeks and her face convulsed with merriment.

The blackguard in our midst was neatly swaddled by the curtains, but when I raised the broken handle of Irene's parasol for a final blow, she stopped me. She did not stop laughing, however.

"I fail to see what amuses you, Irene. We have captured a desperate villain rifling your rooms!"

"My parasol!" She pointed. "Poor thing!"

I felt it unbecoming of her to display toward an inanimate object the concern she ought to have felt for me.

Irene, immune to my feelings, was burrowing in the hummocks of fabric, pushing them aside to reveal our catch. The same swarthy, sly, unappealing face I had glimpsed in the shadows emerged into broad daylight, along with a grin as wide as a window.

"Nell," Irene said, proceeding to brush matted hair from the brute's grimy forehead, "you have given Godfrey quite a fright."

"Godfrey!?" The man's evil grin only widened. Despite the use of lampblack on a pair of teeth, I saw that indeed some semblance of himself lurked under the surface. I was tempted to employ the parasol once more to eliminate a grin obviously at my expense.

"I surrender," Godfrey offered meekly in his normal tone. "Had I known what a tigress you were with a sunshade, I would have revealed myself sooner."

I levered myself upright with the shattered parasol, refusing all aid with the conviction that only the indignant can muster.

"Really! You are a pair of schoolchildren, two of a sort. Scamps of the first water." I slapped dust off my hands and sneezed, ardently. "What has this charade accomplished, save that the draperies have had a good dusting?"

"At least," said Irene, rising, "we know that Godfrey's disguise was sufficient to deceive a friend."

"You take liberties with that description of our relationship after this incident," I said sternly. "What is the point of making Godfrey resemble a pirate?"

He stood in turn, gingerly, having borne the brunt of the curtain rod. "So I can go to the harbor and investigate among the sailors, and also elude Sherlock Holmes," he said as if by rote. Obviously, the guise was Irene's idea.

"That ensemble would not gull an albatross. And we do not even know that Mr. Holmes has the slightest interest in our activities. The rumor of his presence may be just that. And why do you want to make inquiries in the harbor?"

Godfrey jerked his head in Irene's direction. "*She* says it is necessary."

"Irene says much is necessary when it is merely intriguing to her."

"Well." Ignoring our revenge upon her, Irene began dusting off Godfrey's worn pea jacket. "I must say Godfrey makes a dashing old tar. Appearances before the bar are superb preparation for thespian endeavors. I'm satisfied he can prowl the waterfront bistros tonight with a rolling gait and a squint and be perfectly safe among the rough sort to be found there. And my survey of the balcony shows Black Otto can come and go discreetly. At least—" Irene eyed me rebukingly "—*I* am not attempting to assume this role myself."

"Thank God." I turned to survey the damage. "Will the hotel be able to reinstate these curtains by nightfall?"

"That matters little," Irene answered irrepressibly. "Godfrey will be out 'til all hours of the morning with his fellow old salts. We shall not need the privacy of curtains until tomorrow."

"A most unfortunate accident with the parasol," Irene told the hotel manager that afternoon. "It snapped as I was walking by. I caught hold of the curtain to keep from falling, and you see the rest."

The manager, a slight man in a morning coat, blinked primly behind his spectacles. It was difficult to imagine the delicate hand that Irene waved so airily bringing down the massive curtain rod and yards of brocade. As Delilah, she was believable; as Samson, not.

He shrugged, his position requiring not belief, but discretion. "Madame is correct. The curtains cannot be replaced until tomorrow. I will move you and your husband."

"Oh, no, Monsieur. We will stay here."

"Without draperies?"

"For one night, why not?"

The pomaded head so like a sleek black seal's shook dolefully. Soulful seal's eyes grew resigned, and he agreed. Visitors to Monte Carlo were known to indulge in high jinks of a volatile nature. It was not a hotel manager's place to question his guests.

When he had gone, Irene breathed a sigh of relief. "Godfrey will be coming back early in the morning to these very French windows. I do not want him returning to an empty suite, or finding a zealous hotel employee tidying up."

I went to the windows and pushed one open. A mock balcony rose waist-high. "Irene, our room is on the third story."

"Godfrey cannot enter the Hotel de Paris at an ungodly hour in his sailor guise; he would never be admitted. He will have to climb."

"But four floors! And the ground floor alone must be twenty feet high."

"That is why men wear trousers: so they can climb when necessary. I have already surveyed the route. He will manage it; more, he will consider it an adventure."

"And where will *we* be while Godfrey is slinking through the seamy bistros in the harbor?"

"We will have a picnic in the parlor."

"A picnic in the parlor?"

"Don't echo me; you sound like Casanova. It will be like old times in Saffron Hill. A loaf of French bread, a jug of country Burgundy, and thou."

She took my elbow to steer me into the parlor, where indeed a large wicker basket ordered from the hotel kitchen waited upon the Aubusson rug. Irene lifted the lid with the prideful expression of a stage magician revealing a lady, or a tiger, within.

"How can we consume such a great quantity of food?" I studied the array of breads, meats, mustards, fruits, cheeses and the mentioned bottle of wine—two bottles, in fact.

"We will have a long evening waiting for Godfrey," Irene explained simply. "And he will be hungry when he returns, as we will be ravenous for news of his expedition."

Chapter Twenty-one

LADIES LUNCH, MEN CAROUSE

⚜

"**What is** this?" I asked Irene sometime after midnight.

"What is what?"

"This brown mess in a tin."

"A famous French delicacy."

"Then it must consist of something disgusting; I have learned that much about French cuisine."

"Pass it to me, then. Paté de foie gras is too precious to waste on the stomachs of the idiotic English, whose cuisine features disgusting things like pig-brain puddings, and is boring to boot."

The hour was too late and the level in the first wine bottle too low for me to argue. Irene and I reclined against the tapestry bergères, the remnants of our feast spread on a gros-point ottoman. Our feet were slippered and our hair lay loose over our shoulders. I had returned to my suite to don a combing gown before joining Irene for our informal indoor picnic. Her lavender satin robe billowed around her like a frothy wave.

I felt a schoolgirl again and suspected that we both looked it. We had not enjoyed so casual yet pleasant an evening for years, not since we had shared quarters in London before Irene's opera career drew her to the Continent and her unfortunate adventures there. Certainly we had not had an opportunity for such a satisfying conference since her marriage to Godfrey. What Godfrey would think of us when he returned, I could not guess.

The Meissen clock on the mantel tinged once for the half hour. Irene lay her head against the gilt chair arm and stared dreamily into a half-full goblet of Burgundy.

"One could write a monograph on the national characteristics of clock chimes. English clocks are no-nonsense and spout grand basso booms, like Big Ben—dong, dong, dong. French clocks are coquettes, their tones light, amusing, almost teasing. Ting. There. And ting again."

"What of German clocks?"

"Oh, they are strict, like the English clocks, but they break a simple 'dong' into smithereens. Clicks and nudges, preparatory *rurrrring* gears. Much marching of the hands into position and then, harumph—bang bang bang."

"What of Swiss cuckoo clocks?"

"The same, only gone quite mad."

"And Italian clocks?"

She closed her eyes. "Sonorous. Dignified. Long, sustained notes. Mellifluous." She practically sang the last word and I laughed, for her description of each country's clockworks had summarized the national character. The stage of any land had lost a premiere performer with Irene in retirement. The notion saddened me, or perhaps it was the uncustomary wine.

"What of American clocks?" I asked.

She considered. "I have not heard one in a decade. All business, bustle, and as bright as new brass. Full of self-important alarm and as ready to broadcast danger as to intone such mundane practicalities as the time. Fire! Flood! Foreigners! Indians!"

"Indians? Really? In New Jersey?"

She laughed. "Yes, but not since the French and Indian

wars. Only cigar-store Indians nowadays, Nell, not the genuine untamed variety. Oh, sometimes I wish I had gone West instead of East."

"There are no opera houses in the American West."

"Not so! Culture is creeping its way out West. European performers are in demand, even on the frontier."

"You are not a European performer," I pointed out.

"No, I am not even a performer at all anymore."

"You will always be a performer, as I will always be a parson's daughter."

"You think so?" Irene smeared a clot of the vile brown stuff on a cracker and crunched, oblivious to the crumbs that studded her dressing gown.

"Your life is a performance."

"One could say that of anyone. We each are handed our prime roles at birth. Penelope Huxleigh: Parson's Daughter, modest and conventional, with few expectations but many surprises waiting."

This nettled me, although I could not say why. Perhaps because it was true. "What of Godfrey?"

"Godfrey Norton: Wronged Woman's Son, hardworking and honorable, law-abiding, conventional and extraordinary."

"And yourself, Irene?"

Her eyes shone with mischief and more, a kind of melancholy. "Irene Adler: Itinerant Adventuress, actress and stage manager of other lives, independent and unconventional."

"You define Godfrey and myself by our parents, yet you stand alone. What of your antecedents? Have they had no influence?"

"I do stand alone," she said firmly. "I am my own creation and no one's creature, as the King of Bohemia discovered to his discomfiture, if not to his sorrow."

"Oh, he was sorry, Irene. If you had seen him at the last, when he and Mr. Holmes and Dr. Watson came to St. John's

Wood to find you gone. He cast himself about like a bewildered, lost and angry child. I do not think he had ever before failed to have anything he truly wanted."

"You did not tell me that Willie was so humbled!"

"You did not ask me," I said drily. "You had ears only for what Mr. Holmes said and did."

She was silent for a moment. "And if I had not been gone, Nell? What would the repentant Willie have done? He would have gloated at recovering my one poor weapon against his royal force; he would have relished my besting. He might even have repeated his dishonorable offer, as a sop to a desperate and broken woman. If I had lost, rather than won, His Highness would have dispensed a fatal generosity, the kind such men always offer when they wish to kill a woman with kindness. Or for it."

I had never heard Irene speak with such fire before, the anger in her voice barely bridled.

"What mercy would Mr. Holmes have offered?"

"Respect, at least, even in victory. And I think he is sufficiently self-assured to offer it in defeat, which is remarkable in a modern man."

"Surely men are not such a sorry lot!"

"They have not been reared to be anything better, at least toward women. The long-cherished notion of 'chivalry' disguises an arrogant disregard of a woman's deepest concerns. We women are much to blame, for asking no more of them."

"For all your disdain of the Lords of Creation, you are a married woman, and I am not."

Irene smiled. "Isn't it amazing? What did Alice call Godfrey—an extraordinary ordinary man? She meant, I think, that he has no noble blood but great nobility of character. That's true also of Sherlock Holmes, I suspect. Willie, king or not, is a pauper in the aristocracy of mind and soul. He shall never win any man or woman's esteem, only their fear or obedience."

"Why did you describe Godfrey as conventional, then, a moment ago?"

"Because he is, bless him. You have no idea of the persuasions it took to transform him into Black Otto and send him forth to spy. Deception is anathema to his character, as it is to yours, for different reasons. You have ingested the churchly tenets of truth-telling no matter what. He saw hypocrisy crucify his mother upon a cross of social disapproval. He is a crusader, our Godfrey; he wishes to make what is wrong right. He may even be heroic for having such an aim. And that makes him supremely conventional."

"Do you not wish to right wrongs? Else why rush to the aid of Louise Montpensier and her aunt?"

Irene sat back like a demure schoolgirl. "I wish only to amuse myself, to occupy my idle hours, to stretch my slack brain. To have fun."

I rose to my knees in outrage at her self-deprecation and was surprised to find the room spinning a bit.

"Irene, you will never convince me that only selfish motivations rule your actions. I know your game! Your role is to torment the conventional, to prick bubbles and shatter complacency. You impel us—Godfrey, myself—beyond the bounds forced upon us. You are freer than we; I don't know if you were born that way, or became it, or if it's just that American brashness you hear in the clock chimes. But *you* are an alarum, and you peal us both out of our sleepy beds, blinking our eyes at the world and the danger hidden all around us, danger that we would never see without your caroling."

I expected an amused dismissal. I expected Irene's habitual sleight of speech to glide over my sudden passion and slide into other topics. Instead, she regarded me soberly—which was quite remarkable, considering that she had consumed the preponderance of the wine.

"Am I right, though," she asked, "to counter society's assumption of common sense and tradition? Is it wise to encourage Godfrey to don a false face, to send him amongst lascars, thugs and tarry old salts? You are correct, Nell; danger *does* lurk beyond the safe social strictures of ordinary life. Real, physical danger. I have brought you to its brink on occasion, and now, Godfrey." She glanced at the open door to the bedchamber. "If he should not return through that window, if he—"

"He will! Godfrey is most capable of handling difficult situations, even those you create for him. I am surprised. I thought you quite unconscionable when lashing one of us to outré endeavors."

She shrugged. "Some responsibilities I take seriously."

I smiled cautiously. "Irene, we have never spoken of your past. I have grown not to mind, only—"

"It is good that you do not mind, for I am not minded to discuss it."

"—I question the present. Why did you, with all your scoffing at convention, with your almost frantic disdain for its impediments, why on earth did you marry Godfrey?"

"Perhaps you have noticed, Nell. He is a most prepossessing and persuasive man," she said.

"Certainly I have noticed," I snapped. "He is handsome and clever and kind. You are deliriously lucky to have him. Perhaps my spinsterhood makes me thick about such things—"

"Perhaps?" One eyebrow raised.

"It is true that my experience of the intercourse between a man and a woman is somewhat limited—"

"Somewhat?"

"Oh, do stop mimicking me like Casanova! I know that I am lamentably naive on such matters. But why, with so little

regard for convention on your part, did you marry Godfrey?
Why do you not do as your friend Sarah Bernhardt does, as
the Duchesse de Richelieu and her prince do?"

Irene tucked her knees up and rested her chin upon them.
"I never thought that I would hear you urging so improper a
course as taking a lover."

"I do *not* urge it! I merely question why you resisted it,
when your philosophy does not object."

"You mention Sarah and Alice's irregular romantic lives.
Both of them are independent women, by temperament and
by virtue of economic freedom. Both set the course of their
romances. Alice even ventured to love far beneath her
station, not once, but twice. Yet she remains prisoner of her
sex. Her millions are inherited from father and husband. The
husband may be dead and unable to say anything about her
behavior, but the father is ever ready to rush into his grown
daughter's life and govern her actions."

"She is too dutiful," I concluded slowly, amazed at myself.
"Had she been truly unconventional, she'd have never given
up the doctor . . . er, doctors."

"Yes. Above all, the Great God Hypocrisy rules her life.
Despite her family roots, her own father objects to her
association with a Jew, and enforces it. Alice is free only by
appearances. Sarah is free to her soul, yet pays for it. As much
as men applaud and pursue her—and often achieve her for a
moment—they resent her, for she does not docilely meet
their ideals of womanhood. She is cruelly caricatured by the
cartoonists, who depict her as a garden rake. Why do you
think she wears her signature scarves about her neck? To
disguise its thinness. Why affect such flowing robes? Again, to
hide the fact that she does not fit the model of female
voluptuousness currently in vogue. She is an urchin at heart,
Sarah, and ever at war with her world even when she rules it."

"So their freedom is an illusion."

"Yet they have more than Lillie Langtry, who has truly

surrendered to the man's game and is little more than what the French so aptly call La Grande Horizontale, a woman who rises in the world via a reclining position. She moves from man to man, title to title, millionaire to millionaire. One day she will be old and no longer negotiable, like paper money that has passed through too many hands."

I shuddered. "Still, you have not said why you married Godfrey."

"He wished me to do so."

"Irene! You never do anything merely because someone wishes it."

"And he is one of those 'uncommon common men' Alice so envies me."

"You never did anything merely to make others envy you."

"And there are his personal attractions."

"The King of Bohemia had as many personal attractions, in his way, and you did not marry him."

"Ah, Penelope, but I would have. Once. When I was young."

"You would not now?"

"Never!"

"Then . . . Godfrey?"

Irene swept her hands wide. "You are a merciless inquisitor, Nell; I shall have to set you on a suspect. Who can interpret the human heart? He is peculiarly suited to my odd brand of honor. Godfrey grew up counter to his beast of a father. When his mother could stand no more of her husband and dared to take her three sons and support them by her novel-writing, Godfrey saw her shunned by the same society that had tolerated her husband's abuse. Then he watched that that society's regulatory system, the courts and the law, support his father's claim to all money that his wife had earned, even while living apart from him.

"Marriage does not protect a woman, as is commonly put forth; it confines her. Caroline Norton found that out, and so did her son. So perhaps Godfrey is the *only* man I would dare marry, that I would ever care to marry, the one man who will not make a prison of his love."

"Love. You finally mention that."

"Love is not to be discussed as casually as the weather, unless it is only casual love. I will say this: that while in the relationships between men and women there is much stuff of comedy and tragedy, there can be found in the marital bed an intimacy that mingles the best of the human and the divine."

Her words brought me far over a threshold I had merely meant to peep past. I don't know if I colored, but I could not keep myself from asking one last thing.

"Irene, I've never inquired about your past experience of . . . men. You seem to grasp this mystery by some . . . some mysterious process."

"It is not a mystery, Nell. It is merely kept so to most women, for their own 'protection'."

"Well, do you think, possibly, that I, I might someday—"

She regarded me with tilted head and a frank expression. "I cannot say, Nell. You have been reared to be a perfect ass on the subject, you know."

"I'm not as indifferent as I might seem. In fact, before my father died and I was cast adrift on the world far from Shropshire, I had conceived an . . . affection for a curate in the neighborhood. Jasper Higgenbottom. He was, of course, unaware of my interest—"

"Of course."

"—and I naturally was unwilling and unable to make plain my regard—"

"Not naturally, but go on."

"—and I frankly have virtually forgotten him, for a wider experience of the world has shown me that he was narrow in more senses than his features—"

"Brava, Nell."

"—and later, when I was governess for a family, I did

experience a fleeting . . . discomfiture with my charges' young uncle, who, of course, was far above my station, and I may have been imagining that he even paused to notice me in any sense whatsoever. Still, naturally—"

"Yes, Nell? Naturally and of course. The point?"

"Do you think it possible that I could overcome my extreme ignorance of the sex and . . . make friends with one? A man, I mean."

"Aren't you friends with Godfrey?"

"Of course, but he's different."

"Why?"

"He's . . . yours."

"But you met him before I did. You worked as a typist for him. You had every opportunity to snap him up."

"But I didn't! Godfrey is—was—above my station." I thought for a moment. As embarrassing as this conversation had been, some glimmer of enlightenment was sizzling through my brain. "But you say all talk of station is non-sense."

"Is and should be. Still, it rules most of England."

"I suppose I need not regard myself as beneath anybody. Any man, even."

"No, Nell, you need not regard yourself as beneath any man, unless . . . ah, but I am getting too risqué for a parson's daughter." Irene suddenly seized my elbows, nearly causing me to spill the last bit of wine in my glass. "You have had a wonderful insight tonight. You have seen in a glance what is wrong with the world and put it into one simple phrase, one motto, one undeniable truth and inalienable right: you need not regard yourself as beneath any man! There, go forth now, my child, and act upon it. Then who may say what you will do, and with whom, and when?"

"Really, Irene? You think that there's hope, that I shall not have always to pine after the uninteresting Jasper? Really and truly?"

A noise from the next chamber ended my moment of dazzling lucidity regarding my purpose in life.

"Godfrey!" Irene whispered, hastily rising. The expression of mingled relief, joy and anticipation on her face told me more than had all of the words we'd exchanged.

I, too, felt eager to ascertain his safety, and even more eager to learn about his outing. We rushed into the adjoining room to find one French window banging open. Godfrey was climbing over the stone balustrade outside it.

"Godfrey!" Irene pulled him into the room, and then through the door into the parlor. "How did it go?"

"Excellently, if you consider breaking a wine bottle over the head of an Algerian navigator and fleeing a mob of Monégasque police through the streets of the Condamine worthwhile."

"Poor dear. Have some paté de foie gras. Some crackers. Breaking a wine bottle? How wasteful." She poured him a full measure of Burgundy, which he downed like milk. He also gulped the disgusting crackers without complaint.

The lamplight revealed smudges of dirt upon his threadbare sailor's jersey. Irene brushed at the revolting hair matted to his ear.

"Your sailor's sunburn, applied by myself, has faded at the edges. Lucky that you visited dark bistros, not the open docks in daylight."

"Lucky that I had the dark of night to shadow my retreat."

"But you were accepted as what you appeared to be?"

"All too well," Godfrey complained. "They are a brawl-minded lot in the bistros. When I inquired after our quarry, I got more questions than answers."

"But—?" Irene seemed certain that more words would follow.

"But. The two tars who accosted Nell and myself in the train are indeed known, and have been seen in town. 'Gravesend Gerry and his Heathen,' they are called. Many strange sailors sail into port these days, and so does one whom we know as no sailor whatsoever."

"Who?" Irene demanded.

"Who, indeed, should I find in the old salts' lair, asking questions like myself, but Louise's wretched uncle? He didn't recognize me."

"Louise's uncle," I repeated. "He must have hounded the child to Monte Carlo."

Godfrey shook his disreputable head. "It wasn't Louise he was asking after. He was hunting the same quarry we sought—one seaman, Gerald by name. He didn't get far, though, since he had no description, unlike me."

"How lucky—" Irene stared into the distance as she mulled Godfrey's tale "—that Gerry and the Heathen decided to accost you on the train. Otherwise, we'd be as lost as the uncle."

"Aren't we anyway?" I asked.

"No, we are not. I begin to see a common thread to this affair. Godfrey! You must go tomorrow to the registry of ships. And we must recruit Mr. Winter as a researcher as well; we have no time to waste!"

"In what guise do I go?" he asked sardonically.

"Why, as yourself," she replied. "Your handsome, brave, clever and kind self, of course." He looked a bit taken aback at this surfeit of praise, but Irene galloped on. "I have it on impeccable authority that you are all these things. Surely even a registrar of ships will succumb to such virtue and tell you all we wish to know. If not, I myself will have to persuade him."

Of the next few days' activities I was mercifully kept ignorant. Irene recruited me as a sort of governess again, for into my hands was given the shepherding of Louise. Now that her formidable uncle had been seen about the harbor, she must be kept out of sight.

With her customary appropriation of all decisions, Irene ordered Louise and myself to holiday at one of the picturesque villages halfway up the mountainside. So much for "three heads are better than one." How she decided to trust us two to ourselves, I cannot say, but Louise's young man was required in Monaco, so it was a sisterly jaunt we made to the simple village of Eze.

Louise brought a sketch pad, and I my diaries. We spent placid days sitting atop the bluffs, gazing on the Mediterranean's frowzy surface, munching picnic lunches of sausage and cheese. It was, if I may say so, quite a bohemian existence, and the most pleasurable part of my sojourn in France.

Louise, I found, despite her impetuous flight with the young American, a most delightful and docile girl. She felt keenly her aunt's predicament and asked me many questions of that lady's state of health and mind.

"She is a woman determined to endure," I said at last. "May the Lord have mercy on your uncle."

"Is he a bad man, do you think? I have never liked him, but he *is* my uncle." A wisp of wind blew a hat ribbon over her shoulder like a strand of cherry-colored hair.

It was quite pleasant to be consulted so earnestly. Certainly there was little of that when Irene was about. "It is difficult to say. He is a hard man, I would judge, in his disowning of your father."

"Perhaps he is in the neighborhood because he feels it his duty to find me."

I found myself smiling the smile Irene offered me on occasion. "It is good to think as well as one can of one's uncle. But it is more likely that his motives serve himself, not duty."

She bent her head to her sketch pad for some moments. "Mademoiselle Huxleigh—"

"Nell, please."

"Nell. I have been very happy here. I do not like Paris, I have discovered."

"My sentiments exactly."

"Really? Then when Caleb and I marry, it would not be so dreadful if I went to the United States with him? Aunt would—"

"Aunt would understand. But first we must settle your uncle's role in this affair. We cannot abandon your aunt with your death still hanging over her head, or in danger of your uncle's anger."

"What exactly is 'this affair'?"

"We are not certain, which is why it is an 'affair.' Perhaps it is an assassination attempt—"

"No!"

"—or some scheme to defraud you of money due you."

"I am an heiress? I can do as I please?"

"You most certainly cannot. Not even the duchess can do as she pleases, and she is an heiress to make all others pale."

"She has been very good to Caleb and myself, as have you and Madame and Monsieur Norton." Louise suddenly giggled. "Oh, it is not funny, for I felt most terribly desperate that day, but poor Monsieur Norton. I fear I was most ungrateful to him for saving me from the Seine."

"Godfrey has a gift for surviving ingrates."

Louise drew herself up. "If I am an heiress, I will give him a reward for saving my life."

"That is most responsible of you," I said with a smile.

"There is no danger to what they are doing, do you think?"

"A little perhaps, but your American seems braced for it. And I can assure you that Irene thrives upon it, and Godfrey survives it quite adequately."

"And you, Nell?"

"I abhor it. Danger is unpredictable. It tends to make a fool of one." I envisioned myself swinging from the snake-draped gasolier in the railway carriage. "It is unnecessary to a well-regulated life."

"This is more fun than danger," Louise said with a sudden dimpling smile. What an adorable child she was, after all. She handed me her sketch pad. "What do you think?"

I studied a pencil portrait of myself. "It's quite good, but I don't think my nose is so long."

"I had to change it to make the pince-nez fit. Spectacles are dreadfully difficult to draw."

"So I see. As are collar pins, apparently."

"Do you think they will tell us when we get back?"

"Tell us what?"

"Tell us everything that they did, they saw, they learned. It is exciting to think of so many people acting on my behalf."

"No, Louise. They will tell us only what pleases them. That is why they have sent us here to the country. But we shall have our revenge."

"How so?" she asked with twenty-year-old innocence.

I smiled conspiratorially. "We shall enjoy ourselves."

Chapter Twenty-two

A BIT OF BLACKMAIL

My bucolic idyll ended when Caleb Winter arrived at our rustic pension that night to assume the duty of safeguarding Louise. The search at the registry of ships was not done; apparently my clerical prowess was called for, or so I was told.

I reluctantly took Caleb's hired coach back down the precipitous corniche road to the Hotel de Paris, leaving the lovebirds to share the attractions of the mountainside unchaperoned, and arriving so late that I merely greeted Irene and Godfrey in their rooms before retiring to my own chambers.

We three breakfasted early the next morning. I was eager to catch up on Irene and Godfrey's investigations and looked forward to attacking the musty documents at the registry of ships. There is something about old papers that I find irresistible. Imagine my disappointment when I learned I was not to see that fountainhead of official foolscap after all: a summons to the duchess's villa came during breakfast, in the person of a harried Dr. Hoffman.

"It is urgent, Madame!" the personable physician told Irene, refusing the seat she urged upon him. His lively eyes paused on Godfrey and myself. "Monsieur. Mademoiselle."

So polite, these French; they must observe the social amenities even while bearing dire news.

"What has happened?" Godfrey wanted to know.

Dr. Hoffman's worried eyes belied his shrug. "I must let the duchess tell you the particulars. But the blackmailer has made clear the price of his silence."

"And?" Irene asked.

The doctor's well-kept hands slapped his sides helplessly. "It is a most extraordinary—nigh impossible—demand. And Alice—" he glanced as if overconscious of my presence "—the duchess is frantic with worry."

"We will come at once," Irene promised. "Only wait in the hotel foyer until we have dressed."

He nodded and bowed politely to me on his way out.

"I was minded to pursue the past today," Irene murmured, "but it seems that the present has reared its ugly head."

And so we ventured forth to witness the next act in the melodrama of the duchess's life. When we arrived, we were shown directly to the sunny parlor. She herself had moved beyond puzzlement and indignation to numb bewilderment. She handed Irene a letter.

"This came—?" Irene was already reading the missive as she spoke.

"Sometime in the night."

"How?"

"Slipped under my bedchamber door."

Irene's eyes lifted from the paper. "You were alone?"

"Yes, but—"

"But the blackmailer wishes you to see how close at hand he may be. What does he refer to, 'the royal expedition'?"

Alice sighed and sat down, thereby permitting the rest of us to sink to whatever seat was near. "Albert is always poking around underwater—or, rather, mounting expeditions to do so. He had planned next to visit Corsica."

"This communication instructs you to see that he goes to Crete."

"How can I? Oceanography is Albert's pastime, as balls and good works are mine. If I were to venture my opinion, if I were to *insist* in this matter, Albert would . . . well, he is not about to heed a woman in such an area as science. I cannot even think of a plausible reason to give him."

"Oh, there are always reasons," Irene said absently, "plausible or not. You can blame your charming feminine whimsy and declare an immediate need for a sea voyage. Corsica is too close, you require a greater change of atmosphere. You are becoming quite mad with the predictable social rounds, the delay in your nuptials, et cetera, et cetera. I believe you know the speech if you would but put your mind to it."

"Albert is stubborn about some things," she said.

"So are you," Irene answered with a smile. "No, I do not think the difficulty is in persuading Albert, by hook or by crook, to go where he is wanted. The problem is *why* should he? Why should *we* let this anonymous correspondent force us in his direction?"

"The revelation of my past," said Alice bitterly.

"What Irene means," Godfrey put in, "is that this letter proves that the blackmail is a side issue, a means rather than an end. It comes from one who has no personal wish to destroy your happiness, but one who only wants to use you to move the prince to a particular point at a particular time. Why? What will the blackmailer gain by Prince Albert's arrival on Crete?"

"Or removal from here?" the doctor put in suddenly.

Irene smiled at him. "Splendidly put, Doctor. Is our oceangoing prince a mere pawn on the board, or the point of the game?"

"It is not a game!" the duchess burst out. "It is my future."

"The blackmailer cares naught for your future," Irene said, "only for the whereabouts of the prince. That is what you should consider."

In the silence, I found myself speaking. "Do you imply, Irene, that the prince could be a target?"

Alice paled as Irene answered, "We have such a thorny knot of disparate odds and ends in hand that not one skein seems to join another; all are loose ends. Something more deeply sinister than anything we have guessed may underly these puzzling events."

"Speak more frankly," the doctor urged, drawing his chair closer.

Irene frowned. "Consider your position, Alice. You are the pivotal figure in a political dispute. Although the prince would wed you in a minute, the true civil power in this principality, his father, Prince Charles, forbids it, as does the religious authority that governs Monaco, the bishop. Despite this, you persist in an unlawful relationship. I see opportunities here for many plots—the death of the elderly prince, of the bishop, of yourself, of Prince Albert."

"That is ridiculous! This is civilized Europe. I am a well-known and wealthy woman, with a title that commands great weight in France. We will merely wait until Prince Charles dies—he is not well. No one would gain by assassinating any figure in such a tiny principality as Monaco."

"It is a principality, Alice; it is European, not American, as I was reminded regarding another kingdom and another prince." Irene paused to direct a tight smile at me. "You are a woman following her heart, not her head. The elixir of love makes you feel superior to all obstacles. You forget that you are at the center of a perplexing political dispute and that even tiny principalities may play politics on the grand scale . . . for keeps."

"Then you think," asked the doctor, frowning, "that Alice is in personal danger?"

"Not necessarily." Irene laughed at her own apparent inconsistency. "I think that she should keep in mind that she may be. What most concerns me is, why Crete?"

"That's simple," I burst out. "Because it is not Corsica!"

Alice and the doctor gazed at me with exquisite politeness,

as if they thought me mad but were far too well-bred to show it.

Irene clapped her hands. "Excellent, Nell! 'Because it is not Corsica' indeed. But what is Corsica?"

"An . . . island," Alice answered.

"As is Crete. That must mean something. Has the prince shown any desire to explore Crete?"

"Not that I know of."

"Then we must manufacture a reason." Irene turned inquiringly to Godfrey, who nodded.

"I will add a visit to the local archaeologist to my agenda, along with the registry of ships." he said. "Is the prince intrigued by past seafaring feats, or is he purely interested in the possibilities afforded by modern methods?"

Alice shook her head. Her face and hair today seemed the same pallid wheat color, a sign to me of blond women's insipid appeal. Such women fade into old age without a fight.

"I confess that I have paid scant attention to Albert's oceanographic exploits, although he plans to christen a ship after me. When his father dies, of course," she added with irony.

"No matter," said Godfrey kindly. "I will discover the best approach." He turned to Irene. "I trust that if further investigation of a seafaring nature is required, I can go as a yachtsman rather than as a deckhand."

The doctor and the duchess stared at this—to them—non sequitur.

Irene smiled. "We shall see," she said, "what the times require."

Chapter Twenty-three

OF SHIPS AND SEALING WAX

Louise and Caleb returned, on being summoned that afternoon, to discover Irene, myself, and the disreputable sailor, Black Otto, plying our separate oars at fever pitch. We made an unlikely quintet around the table in Irene and Godfrey's parlor suite as we reported our individual triumphs of the day.

"Louise's uncle," said Godfrey, "has taken a room in the same hotel that Dr. Hoffman occupies and shows no suspicion of Louise's presence here, or even of her survival. He lounges about the bistros interrogating sailors, save for an afternoon spent at the registry of ships in the unwitting company of Black Otto. He searches, but has small knowledge of what it is he seeks. As long as Louise can restrain herself from patronizing the bistros, she is safe from discovery."

"She will be even more secure," Irene put in, "after I accomplish some alterations upon her appearance—in the name of beautification, of course. You will not have to be banished to the country again, my dear."

Louise and I exchanged a look. Banishment did not properly describe our delightful sojourn in the hills, although our busy-bee friends would never understand.

"What success have you had in locating the British sailor and his Indian companion?" Irene asked Godfrey.

He scratched his crooked nose, augmented with sticking plaster, and smiled a crooked Black Otto smile. "I hope to see friend Gerry at Le Cochon Qui Fumar this very night."

"I am tempted to join you at The Smoking Pig," Irene said with genuine regret. "However, my singing debut at the casino ball has garnered an invitation to perform privately for the prince's closest friends."

"I trust one of them is not Sherlock Holmes," I put in.

Irene's magnificent topaz eyes narrowed. "Of the elusive Mr. Holmes no trace has been heard or seen. Perhaps the rumor of his presence is just that. I shall have to take my chances. He is not expecting to see me, surely, and that is already to my advantage. Besides, Mr. Holmes has no reason to begrudge me life and limb, even if he *has* heard of my supposed death in the train wreck. No, the least of our problems is Mr. Sherlock Holmes."

Privately, I disagreed. If Irene had stumbled onto a plot that webbed all of Monte Carlo, a detective of Mr. Holmes's reputation could hardly fail to discern it as well. However, Irene had little opportunity to perform; I was not about to discourage one of the few harmless pursuits in which she indulged.

"Godfrey," Irene said with a mock shiver, "you have played Black Otto for too long. You sound quite bloodthirsty. Perhaps Mr. Winter should accompany you to The Smoking Pig tonight. Separately, of course."

"Capital!" exclaimed the American. "I can't speak this French lingo to save my Aunt Agatha, but I'm keen to see one of these local waterfront saloons. And if it looks like Mr. Norton needs a helping hand, why, fists speak any language, ma'am."

"I shall," Irene said, "sing my high C's serenely, with you on watchdog duty, Mr. Winter."

"And I and Louise?" I inquired.

"Will join me at the palace. We separate this evening: ladies to culture in the salon, gentleman to manlier entertainments in the saloon."

"This puzzle again sorts itself by extremes," said Godfrey, placing the briarwood pipe that Black Otto affected between his rot-festooned teeth. "High and low, prince and sailor boy, clues hot and cold."

At this moment there came a knock on the parlor door. We kept silent as Irene rose to answer it. She returned slowly, a box and a missive in hand.

"From Alice. A posy for tonight's concert, and an envelope."

As Irene opened the box, Louise gasped at the sight of the "posy"—a florid entwining of orchids, roses and gold lace— and then took charge of its container. Irene put the corsage on the table and opened the missive, pulling a folded sheet of thick pink paper from the envelope.

"Ah, an invitation to tonight's recital, on the palace stationery. Alice wished me to have a memento; how deliciously thoughtful. 'His Royal Highness, Prince Albert Grimaldi of Monaco, requests the pleasure of your attendance for the Monte Carlo debut of Madame—'Madame' does sound so professional!—'Madame Irene Norton, mezzo-soprano, singing selections from the Schumann Leider.' If I must be pseudonymous, in a fashion," Irene said, "at least I perform for a rarefied circle."

She shuffled the invitation into its blank envelope and cast it facedown on the table.

"Now I must rest for this evening," she said, picking up the corsage and moving toward the bedchamber, already rapt in envisioning the night's presentation. "The rehearsal with the pianist this morning was most arduous. I am no longer used to the rigors of performance—"

"Irene!" She was nearly out of the room. "Irene!"

She turned back to me with an incurious air.

"The invitation!" I stared at the tabletop as if I saw before me, incredibly, poor Singh's escaped reptile.

The rest were equally tardy to observe the great anomaly in our midst. It lay before our very eyes, and we all had overlooked it.

"Irene, are you not fond of a certain story of Mr. Poe's, about a purloined letter? One that was sought in every conceivable hiding place?"

"Except in plain sight, among the other letters upon a desk. It illustrates that the most obvious clue is often the most vital. What is your point, Penelope?"

"There. That is my point." And I rather impolitely pointed.

Eyes all around the table focused on the abandoned invitation, then narrowed in sudden comprehension, for there it lay like one of Dr. Jarnac's overblown blood-red roses: an untidy blot of crimson sealing wax, the Grimaldi coat of arms pressed into its smooth, hard surface.

The palace wax was black and crimson, wafting the faint odor of sandalwood.

The Duchess of Richelieu, aglow with diamonds, came swooping through the door on the heels of her light rap, into the chamber assigned to Irene as a dressing room. Louise and I, attending our diva friend, had little to do but watch admiringly as she completed her toilette.

Irene wore sapphire-blue velvet and the Marie Antoinette solitaire at her throat. The ornate corsage was cradled on the swell of her décolletage. Even orchids could not outbloom her beauty. Urns of additional floral tribute filled the chamber.

Alice bent to brush cheeks with Irene, then fell back in admiration of Louise and myself, both of us transformed by Irene—Louise because she required disguising, I because I was near at hand.

"A pity all of you do not sing. We could introduce you as the Three Graces," Alice said.

"Not after I had performed," I put in.

"Nor I!" Louise seconded me. "I sing like a frog."

"Certainly you would decorate an angelic chorus, my dears, even if you never opened your mouths," Alice said. She was never one to be deflected easily from a notion.

"So kind of you," Irene said, thrusting a delicate pink orchid into her hair, "to send the invitation. I have fallen in love with—of all things—the sealing wax. Such scent, so rich a color! I must have some."

"Oh, dear." Alice's high spirits sank. "I am glad that you like it, but you can't have it. It is simply not to be had by anyone. It is the royal house's custom sealing wax, used since before the French Revolution. The formula is secret."

"No wonder it is so exquisite," Irene said admiringly. "Monaco is truly a fairy-tale princedom, with even the magical proscriptions—the rose that can never be plucked, the threshold that must never be crossed—"

"It may ruffle our egalitarian American sensibilities, Irene, but Europeans are wedded to their hereditary privileges. I'd give you buckets of the stuff, really I would, darling, but Albert would be dreadfully piqued. The wax appears only on palace or personal royal correspondence."

"You are right. In America, the commercial instinct would ferret out the formula and produce it in quantity for Mrs. Grundy to apply to her bridge-party invitations. It must be manufactured within the principality, then?"

"I believe so," Alice said vaguely. "Despite its critics, Monaco produces more than the money spent by pleasure-seekers. Oh, Irene, how I wish you and Godfrey—and Nell, of course—would take a summer villa here! With Sarah a frequent visitor, we could establish a circle of culture that would easily counter Monaco's reputation for all that is fast, fashionable and frivolous. When I marry Albert at last, I would love to install an opera house, but I do not know where upon this tiny rock to find room for one."

Irene's eyes had taken fire from the duchess's ambitions. "Why not within the casino? Convert a grand *salle* to the purpose, or use the theater. Everyone will know where the opera house is, at least."

"The casino? Art installed within a temple of Champagne and Chance?"

"Is not Art the greatest creation of Chance? And vice versa? And Chance merely another form of Opportunity?"

Alice laughed until her remarkable blue eyes were lost in pleats of wrinkles. "Like Sarah, you let nothing stop you. I cannot even decide whether or not to change the course of Albert's explorations—quite literally—for no reason, save that it is forced upon me."

"You must." Irene had grown still. "And you must also discover more about the Grimaldi sealing wax—its history, manufacture and who might have access to it."

"Sealing wax, Irene? You are serious? I tremble to ask what Godfrey is up to this evening."

"He is dealing with ships," Irene answered with impish promptitude, "while I dispense with sealing wax. Nell may have cabbages, and I will leave kings to you and Sarah."

"Thank you very much," said I, "for assigning me a common vegetable."

"At least it is not rutabaga." Louise wrinkled her upturned nose.

A knock indicated that the concert was imminent. Louise and I rose to wish Irene luck, although her performing skills were far too formidable to require such haphazard assistance. We followed Alice to a splendid chamber, where a gilded grand piano crouched like a Chinese lion bristling with a curling mane of ormolu. Under the high, painted ceiling was assembled a gay and glittering crowd.

"I am so looking forward to hearing Madame Norton sing," Louise confided.

"So," said I, sitting down, "am I."

It was only when the final applause was fading that my mind drifted to the very different songs that Caleb Winter and Godfrey must be hearing in the smoky waterfront bistros.

Lost in my speculations, I remained seated long after the audience had dispersed. When I shook myself out of my brown study and visited the refreshment table, I found myself utterly redundant. All introductions had been made, all compliments tendered, and all the evening's clusterings begun.

I drifted by groups speaking rapid French, then surrendered and searched for Louise and Irene. Louise was easy to locate, even with her hair shining under a new halo of henna and her eyelashes blackened with burnt cork. She was a shy moon in Alice's scintillating social orbit, which circled always around the prince's dignified figure.

"Where is Irene?" I hissed as I joined Louise.

Surprised, she inventoried the room. "How odd. I last saw her accepting the ardent admiration of a distinguished-looking gentleman. Perhaps in the dressing room?"

I doubted it, but made my way there. The room was empty except for our cloaks and the suffocating scent of roses. Disturbed, I rustled discreetly down halls and peered through open doors. Grand, empty rooms stretched in every direction. I should need a footman to guide me through them.

Yet servants were nowhere to be seen, not even to direct me back to the recital chamber, now hopelessly distant. What if I blundered into some private area of the palace? My cheeks felt feverish. I moved down an uncarpeted hall, my footfalls echoing against the double line of mirrors that reflected my confusion.

A steady murmur reached my ears, and I rushed toward it.

Beyond another pair of gilded double doors I found another empty receiving room, and beyond that, another echoing hall accoutered with paintings, mirrors and chandeliers.

The voices still lured like sirens of the Rhine from far away. I fluttered after them, and finally found the sound's source in a pillar-bracketed niche, wherein rested a massive portrait of the naked Venus dismounting from her clamshell, which was pulled by an odd hybird of dolphin and horse.

"Irene!"

She turned with a start. "Nell, you have found us."

Irene was seldom one to state the obvious. I stood blinking, wishing I had worn my pince-nez so that I could put the indiscreet painting quite effectively out of focus, for I can see either far or near, but never both at once.

"Nell, this is Viscount D'Enrique, a cousin of the prince. Miss Huxleigh, a dear friend."

"A step-cousin of the prince," this gentleman corrected, bowing deeply.

The viscount was as sleek and animated as the prince was stolid and wooden. Save for the heavy-lidded dark eyes and the beard, they had little in common, and the viscount's piercing yet veiled regard instilled in me a deep distrust.

"Viscount D'Enrique was showing me the palace art collection," Irene said.

He lifted her hand for a prolonged kiss upon the wrist. "Madame Norton is the most fabled artwork of all."

"She is an artist, and thus works very hard and must be off early to bed," said I tartly, then turned to Irene and added, "Louise is also weary, as am I."

"The night is but a playful kitten," the viscount remonstrated, his dark, hidden eyes speaking dark, hidden things. "It will soon stretch its long, black back and become a cat—a panther on the prowl, with the moon for its plaything. Surely you do not propose to take Madame Norton away from me."

"That is exactly what I suggest. She has obligations."

"No." Again his eyes clung to Irene. "No, the world is obligated to her. She owes nothing to anyone but the pleasure of her company."

Irene was strangely silent, strangely complacent, in the face of this fulsome flattery. Could her recent obscurity have instilled an appetite for recognition that outweighed her ordinary good sense? If so, I must protect her from herself.

"Please, Irene, I have the headache, and Louise is most worried about her fiancé, who may be out late tonight and in who knows what difficulty," I said pointedly. "We must return to the hotel."

"The hotel—?" the odious viscount prompted.

"—de Paris," Irene answerèd without a qualm.

"Where your husband awaits," said I. "Poor Godfrey." I turned to the viscount. "As a barrister, he has much taxing work in Monaco, else he would have attended the recital. Godfrey never leaves Irene's side if he can help it."

"Apparently none of her friends do either." His suave comment carried a sting in its tail. "I quite appreciate the sentiment. Adieu then, until—"

"Good night," said I, sharply, taking Irene's arm and leading her down the hall. I was still utterly lost but determined to manage a confident retreat, if such a thing is possible.

At the long hall's end, Irene paused, then turned to the right. "This way, Nell."

We went through a room, then right again, then left, down a hall, left, right . . . I can no longer recall the sequence of directions. In short order we had returned to the dressing room, where Louise was waiting with our cloaks.

"Whyever did you waste so much time with that odious man?" I admonished Irene.

She regarded me with amusement. "He is not odious at all, but a gentleman of the old school and cousin to the prince."

"Step-cousin," I corrected her, as he had corrected me not long before. "There must be a reason."

Irene smiled dreamily, reminding me of the empty-headed serenity I had observed in Lillie Langtry as she acknowledged the excessive admiration of her circle of gentlemen. I had never expected Irene to tolerate, much less welcome, such superficial tribute. Perhaps Godfrey was spending too much time in the bistros as Black Otto. I would find some subtle way to warn him that he should keep closer to home. So I resolved as we three made our way back to the hotel by foot.

Alas, I failed to mention to Godfrey the odious attentions of the Viscount D'Enrique, with dire results. This confession, however, is an addendum to my diaries, made from hindsight.

I forgot the viscount for excellent reason: our return to the hotel found a fellow plotter already there, with such shocking news that unseemly palace incidents and the apparently minor issue of the royal sealing wax simply melted away for the moment.

Chapter Twenty-four

DEAD SAILORS THREE

❧

"**Dead?**" **Irene** repeated on the threshold. Her jet-spangled net evening scarf drifted around her face like cloud shadows around a highwayman's moon. "And Godfrey?"

"Gone," Mr. Caleb Winter muttered, his usually frank eyes cast down.

He, too, had donned seaman's garb for the expedition. Such rough clothing suited his blunt American features, a melange of many offshoots of the Anglo-Saxon race. Now, however, his face was ghastly and drawn. His hair dripped mist, or worse, and his pea coat reeked of wet wool and an odd piscine perfume.

"Caleb," Louise cried, going to him despite his redolent state.

His raised hand stopped her. "No, Louise. No time to waste on me. All I can tell you, Mrs. Norton, is that we found the Indian fellow, Singh, all right, but when we followed him out of The Smoking Pig, we lost him—until Mr. Norton tripped over a mess of wet rags by the strand, only to discover that it was what was left of this Singh."

"Dead? How?"

Caleb Winter indulged a racking cough before speaking. "Too dark to tell, especially by the sole light of a damp lucifer.

Mr. Norton lit many lucifers to permit me to record this—"
He pulled a wrinkled paper from inside his pea coat. "I'm a bit
of a sketch artist; have to be in my line. He insisted I copy this
down. And when some drunkards wheeled past singing
'Farewell to Liverpool,' Mr. Norton was up in a flash to join
'em and steer 'em away from me and my morbid work. That's
what I got, that little drawing there, and it's not the fair piece
of work I'd do with decent light and any time on my hands."

Another cough overtook him. Irene brought the fragile
scrap to the table, where she smoothed it out under the glare
of a paraffin lamp.

"Another tattoo! And a new design," she breathed. "That
much I can tell at a glance. But what of Godfrey?"

"Off with the sailors. He went willingly, that's all I can say.
I finished my sketch moments later and returned, expecting to
find him arrived here before me."

"How long ago was that, Mr. Winter?"

"Half an hour. When I heard the door, I thought for sure it
was he."

"Not by the door. Black Otto enters by the bedchamber
window." Even as Irene spoke, she hastened to the aperture
in question. She returned instantly, shaking her head.
"Nothing yet. Nell, some brandy from the sideboard for Mr.
Winter. I shall be back in a thrice." She slipped quickly into
the bedchamber.

I was annoyed that my dislike of spirits had caused me to
overlook Mr. Winter's medicinal need for the bracing warmth
of brandy. He tossed the liquid down through chattering
teeth.

"Did you . . . encounter some body of water?" I asked.

"No, Miss Huxleigh, but when the day's sun-warmed water
meets the night chill, a fog rises from the waves and weaves
through every byway, especially by the water. A seaport's an
eerie place, no doubt, threaded through with rogues, foreign
folk and wanderers. There's small elbow room for pistols in

those narrow streets, but a knife comes in handy. I wager that's what did in Singh."

Louise and I stood rapt at his evocation of the waterfront. When Caleb Winter waxed descriptive, one realized why he followed the newsman's trade. The brandy had stopped his ague, but suddenly his eyes fixed behind us, as if he'd seen a ghost. I wheeled around.

A silhouette in dark trousers and a pea coat hovered in the bedroom doorway.

"Mr. Norton!" A pulse of relief throbbed in the American's voice.

"No, *Mrs.* Norton," said I, sorry to disappoint him.

Irene briskly strode in, the full lamplight revealing her male-clad figure's delicacy as compared to Godfrey's more substantial presence.

"Ready, Mr. Winter? You must show me where you last saw Godfrey."

He rose, letting the blanket Louise had draped over his shoulders slide to the floor. "You'd pass for a lad in the shadows, but I won't be responsible for what transpires if a sailor laddie spots a woman in that getup."

"I don't expect you to be responsible, Mr. Winter." Irene produced the smuggled revolver from a side pocket, expertly checking its readiness. "Simply show me where Godfrey left you. I will proceed from there."

"But that's where that poor devil Singh lies dead!"

"All the better. I'd prefer to see the body where it fell. And I must examine the tattoo for myself as well. Shall we go?"

He was speechless, a rare condition in an American, I have observed.

"I will go also," I burst out before they could take a step.

"In a watered-silk gown, Nell?"

"I will change clothes."

"Mr. Winter is right; women are not welcome in that quarter."

"I will dress as you do."

That halted Irene. "An interesting offer, but there is no time to implement it. We must be off immediately. Mr. Winter, are you composed enough to climb down the trellis below the bedroom balcony?"

"I have not had that much brandy."

"I meant the depredations of the evening." Irene smiled and led him into the bedchamber.

I followed, Louise trailing me as speechlessly as her American suitor.

"Irene! What if Godfrey returns and you are gone?" I asked as she leaned over the balcony to verify a clear coast below.

"Then he will wait until we return also."

"What if he insists on going after you two?"

She swung a leg over the stone balustrade as casually as a man swings astride a horse. "Then we shall chase each other all night until dawn comes, and we cannot fail to find one another."

Her cap-covered head slipped below the railing. I rushed to the window, seeing only her gloved hands clutching the bottom of the balustrade. "What if Godfrey does *not* return?" I demanded in a hoarse whisper.

"Then we shall not, until we have him," came the diminishing answer. Mr. Winter catapulted over the railing as soon as Irene had vanished. I heard much agitation among the flowering vines below, and then silence.

"Oh, Nell," Louise whispered at my back, "are they all mad? I should kill myself if my muddled affairs were to cause Caleb's death! Or Mr. Norton's death, or Mrs. Norton's, of course."

"Nonsense," said I, turning. They also serve who only stand and wait upon the weaker among us. "You have tried that once for less reason, and it did not go well. Now sit down and have some brandy, and do not bestir your mind or your body until they have all returned safe and sound."

Louise knew my uncompromising tone by now and went meekly to an armchair. She accepted the glass of brandy I brought and sipped it as if it were milk, but then these French introduce their children to wine at a shockingly early age.

"It is so awful to wait, Nell," said she. "What will you do?"

I sat at the table. "First, I will copy over this unsightly drawing onto a fresh sheet of paper. Your Mr. Winter shows a talented hand, but I fear he was forced to use his knee as a sketch pad."

"What . . . what is the tattoo like?" she asked tremulously.

"Come and see," said I, knowing that curiosity is the first sign of a reviving morale. She did so.

"It is a whole, brand-new letter that your fiancé has discovered. No wonder that Godfrey wished to ensure that he worked undisturbed. You see, under all these wriggling curlicues there lurks the noble 'N'."

"Oh," wailed Louise, sinking onto a chair beside me in tears.

"What is it now?"

" 'N', as in N-N-Norton."

" 'N' as in 'no, not likely.' They will be all right. They have always been all right. It is you and I who are in danger, my dear girl, in danger of being ninnies. I must enter this latest episode into my diary. Perhaps you could compare this new tattoo to the others I keep here, between the pages. Some people store pressed flowers within their diary pages, but, no, I must harbor tattoos. It is quite a topsy-turvy world, Louise, as you will discover when you have been in it longer. Now, we must try to make some sense of this new clue, so that we have something to show for our time when the others return."

Chapter Twenty-five

A CONSPIRACY OF CRETANS

❦

Within an hour, time proved me to be not only a model of sensible decorum, but a prophet, although we had failed utterly to make any sense of the "N."

A veritable sirocco in the greenery brought Louise and myself rushing to the bedchamber window. Up they came, scaling the trellis like long-lost monkeys: Irene first, then Mr. Winter and, at last, Godfrey!

Louise embraced me with a happy gratitude as pleasant as it was misplaced. I had done nothing to ensure the prodigals' return; I had only occupied her mind during their absence. To the young, that can seem miraculous.

Godfrey and Irene closeted themselves in the bedchamber to change clothes while we three waited impatiently in the parlor. Irene emerged first, wearing a voluminous violet taffeta wrapper. Shortly afterward came Godfrey in his emerald brocade smoking jacket. With Black Otto's features rinsed away at the washstand, he looked as if he had risen from a sound sleep instead of from a chill, roistering night on the wharves. He pronounced himself no worse for wear, save for too many toasts with cheap rum among his sailor friends.

"My first object was to lead them away from Singh's body, but then I couldn't get away. Convivial, custodial arms thrown around shoulders, toasts shouted to the wickedest captains of the seven seas and all that. I did learn where our Gerry lifts his tankard. We can seek him out tomorrow if our heads will stand it."

Caleb Winter groaned but took another tot of brandy anyway. Cold had painted his nose a cherry-red, or perhaps the brandy had. "I've never before seen a dead man; no, not in all my reporting years."

"You barely did," Irene reminded him. "The body was gone when we returned to the spot. Who's to say it will ever appear again?"

"Gone!" I felt an odd stab of loss, remembering the Indian's mute presence on that dreadful train ride. He had done me no harm, save by the cosseting of a sinuous pet. "Murdered then, for certain!"

"Another tattooed sailor sunk from sight," Godfrey intoned a trifle more morosely than he might have done without so much rum.

"Another sailor," Irene agreed, frowning as if she did not truly concur and could not say why.

"And another tattooed letter discovered," Louise said brightly, indicating the sketches, which she had arranged into a cross before her. "An Esse, Ay, Oh and an En."

Irene smiled, struck, as was I, by the extreme French accent with which Louise spoke the English she had learned from, and for, her American swain. "We had surmised the 'N' from the multi-lettered seal on your uncle's letter. Still, surmise is not as good as certainty!"

"E-N-O-S," Godfrey spelled aloud. "Enos? Something biblical?"

"E-O-N-S?" Mr. Winter suggested. "Or O-N-E-S? That might signify the conspirators." He smiled modestly. "I work with words, you know."

"N-O-S-E!" I blurted, an unconsidered inspiration that met blank stares all around.

Irene shook her head at each of us in turn. "You presume that the word, if these letters do indeed spell a word, is English. What does Louise make of them in French?"

The girl's eyes brightened at Irene's invitation. "I can only think of the French word *once*, which has three of these four letters and means 'ounce,' or—less commonly—a snow leopard."

"*Snow* leopard!" Caleb Winter clasped his fiancée's hands triumphantly. "That must be it, for the phonetic English spelling of snow could be S-N-O-E."

"Snow in Monte Carlo?" I queried.

"I can think of no other word," Louise said wearily. "There is no 'W' in French."

"There is no 'W' in French," Irene repeated pensively, her dark eyes glinting. She leaned over the sketched letters, moving them around and around in the crosslike configuration Louise had chosen: two above each other, two beside the central pair. Then she clapped her hands.

"Of course! So simple. I should have suspected on the train!"

We blinked in conjoined weariness and waited.

"What rail line took us all to Monte Carlo?" she demanded.

Godfrey had forgotten this minor detail, but I had the advantage in having jotted down such facts in my diary. My dear father considered the act of writing a great aid to memory.

"The Ouest line, Irene, although only the French would call a railway line 'West' when it travels south."

"West indeed! But there is no 'W' in French, so they spell it—?" She eyed Louise, her eyes sparkling with anticipation.

"O-U-E-S-T."

"Exactly. Ou-west. The English west. The other words begin the same initial even in French: *Nord, Sud, Est.*"

"North, South, East and West," Godfrey repeated.

"And what do modern sailors navigate by but . . . compass points? Capitalized, as these tattooed letters are. When I place them in the proper position—North above, South below, East to the right, and West (in this case, Ouwest) to the left—and move them over one another so the decorative scrolling intersects in just the correct way, it is likely that we will have a design, an arcane clue to this conspiracy."

We stared politely at the assembled compass rose, dubious, but hopeful of conversion.

"We must find a better way to overlay the sketches," Irene admitted. "Nell?"

"Tracing paper!" I suggested. "I employed it as a child when practicing my penmanship."

"Very well. Louise and Mr. Winter will procure some tracing paper tomorrow"—Irene glanced at the dawn-burnished windows—"later today, rather. Nell will copy the individual tattoos onto it, overlapping their forms. Godfrey—" Here Irene's face showed regret. "Godfrey will resurrect the unlovely Black Otto long enough to discover if news of the missing Singh spreads in the bistros. And I . . ." She sighed. "I will try to discover how Monaco Palace's private sealing wax came to be on letters mailed by unlettered sailors from ports whole continents distant."

Despite the sleepless night, weariness fled that morning as we went about our appointed tasks.

Luckily, Monaco attracts legions of would-be artists, and Louise and Mr. Winter soon returned with a thick pad of delicate tracing paper. I set to work. I was so taken with my task that I went over my pencil work with india ink, the better to slide one tracing over the other and still see through several layers.

Louise and her young man hung admiringly over my shoulder for most of the morning, slipping away only for luncheon. They returned with a tray for me and a pitcher of black coffee with cream. I found myself imbibing this rank liquid in hopes of keeping my eyelids from fluttering shut while I pursued my exacting work.

At last my task was done. We eagerly ushered the four pieces of tracing paper over each other. They made patterns as suggestive of hidden shapes as Chinese damask, but no telling configuration pointed to any purpose other than that of a compass rose.

"A jumble." Mr. Winter huffed unhappily as he collapsed on a chair.

Louise frowned, trying with the stubbornness of the born puzzle-solver to interlace the letters' scrollwork into a new configuration.

I shook my head. "Perhaps Irene will have some insight when she returns from the palace."

She did not do so until late afternoon. The young people had left long before that to return to their—separate, I am happy to say—hotels and recover from the arduous and wakeful night.

I attempted to nap in my bedchamber but found myself staring at the ceiling, an overblown expanse plastered with overweight cherubs. Nothing, not even a heavenly vista however ill-executed, could persuade me to close my eyes. I felt exceedingly nervous, forcing myself to remain supine, listening to the birds' aggravating chatter outside my window and waiting for our party to assemble again for another unpredictable night.

A light knock on my door roused me from a sort of waking stupor. I answered it to find Irene bonneted in rose faille, bowed with chiffon under the chin, and clad in a black-lace fichu from shoulder to peplum, through which her faille visiting gown in the shade known as Rose Du Barry peeped most charmingly. A pity her urgent manner did not match her amiable ensemble.

"A message from Godfrey awaited my return to the hotel,"

said she breathlessly. "We must meet him at a café near the bay."

"A café?"

"Quickly! Fetch your bonnet. I am fearfully late in returning from the palace. Godfrey's message has been waiting for more than an hour."

I pinned my bonnet on askew and tied its chin ribbons tightly. The wind would blow hard nearer the water. In minutes Irene and I were rushing down the steep streets to a destination known as Le Café de Mouettes. Monaco has now become renowned for its cafés, but then such places were barely respectable for women, although I was happy to see Irene going out, for once, as herself.

The day was very fine. Clouds scudded through the sea-blue sky as gracefully as the full-sailed yachts puffing about the harbor below. Monte Carlo was hardly the commercial seaport that Marseilles was. No, this blue bay at the base of great white cliffs of stone studded with stucco residences was a Croesus' port. Still, sailors were required to make all those pretty boats go; nearer the water, a whiff of the briny deep wafted among the cafés, bistros and fishmongers.

We found Godfrey in his Black Otto guise. How soon Irene had subverted him to her nefarious devices! He was sitting with the elusive Gerry, the villain I had christened Jerseyman, at a large, round table covered in a green-and-white checked cloth.

Jerseyman seemed shriveled and morose now. I marveled that he had ever had the power to terrify. He nodded meekly when we ladies sat down, his only courtesy. A tankard before him was filled with some murky liquid. We were too far from England for it to be ale.

"No sign?" Irene asked.

Godfrey shook his head.

"He's over the rail and into the arms of Mother Ocean,

ma'am," Jerseyman intoned. "Dragged out to sea and down the coast, feedin' the fishes, poor old Singh, that never ate a living thing in his life. Some heathen quirk of his kind, I guess."

"Who would kill him?" Irene asked.

Jerseyman shot her a glance but remained silent.

"One of his Quarter?" she persisted.

Jerseyman's face grew as jaundiced as his eye whites. He stiffened suspiciously. "*You* was on the train at the last! Likely overheard that. No, it weren't none of our Quarter. We're not ones to do in our own mates."

"How were the Quarters selected? By station? Chance? Choice?"

The man hoisted his tankard. A waiter approached our table, looking disapproving. No doubt the sight of the rough seafaring men in the company of gentlewomen was uncommon. Godfrey ordered Vichy water for Irene and myself. It soon arrived—in tankards!

"Lots," said the Jerseyman suddenly, after a deep swallow of his dark, unknown libation. "We drew lots. But most of our Quarter were the lowly and unlucky folk. Montpensier was the only gent, and he done himself in early."

"You and Singh were most thoughtful to inform the authorities of his identity, so he shouldn't die unknown."

"Singh didn't think of it," the man said sourly. "Them from his country don't look on the ceremonies of death the same as the white man. He was just a messenger. I figured they'd forget about it if someone like Singh, who didn't speak any Christian lingo, brought the message. Young Montpensier was a decent sort, never looked down on the rest o' us. As for the others, one or two stopped showin' up in port years ago. They weren't shipmates like me and Singh always were. Maybe the last of 'em'll blow in now."

"Your compass must have had a center," Irene speculated.

"Someone who kept track of all the Quarters through the years."

"Poor old Singh," the man said, ignoring her remark. "As solid a mate as a salt can have. We hacked round the Horn together, by God. Now some coward sticks him for a few sous he didn't even have. I always carry the coin. I was off talkin' to your man here," he added with a glance at me, "or I'd been there to give them that did in Singh the what-for."

He bent to lift a basket from the floor to the tabletop. I recognized it with a thrill of horror. "This'll be all old Singh had, this damned little green vine snake. Treated it like a child, you know. Petted it and called it names in that long-syllabled lingo of his and fed it warm milk in a saucer." He lifted the latch and peered in. "Don't know how long it's been since it had a bite—"

"Please!" I beseeched.

His bleary eye noted me. He shrugged and shut the basket again. "Harmless, it is, just like Singh. I always looked out for him. Lots of folk don't like to traffic with foreign ways, but Singh was no more harm than a fruit fly. Pity him going off like that so soon before—"

His eyes darted around, suddenly sharp. He drank from his tankard, the fingers of his left hand idly petting the serpent's basket. I gasped when I noticed that the man was missing the middle finger on that hand, a phenomenon I had been too distressed to observe while on the train.

"I don't think that Mr. Singh died randomly," Irene said. "I believe he was murdered for his portion of the Quarter, like the other two sailors."

"Other two? Which?" Jerseyman frowned with anxious suspicion.

Godfrey answered. "One was an old man found in the early eighties in London. Lean, but strong. Missing a middle finger on his left hand and tattooed with the letter 'O.' Despite a powerful effort to rescue him, he drowned himself in the Thames, as if the Hounds of Hell were after him."

"Grimes!" The sailor huddled into his jersey until they both seemed shrunken. "'Tis not true! 'Tis some game you're playin' with me. Grimes was lost overboard somewhere in the Adriatic."

Irene nodded grimly. "Lost overboard, all right, from the Thames passenger steamer *Twilight*. We saw him dead, I and my friend here." She nodded at me.

The man grasped the wicker basket as if clinging to a piece of flotsam and gazed at me. "Truly, Missus, truly? You said you'd not lie, even to defend your own husband."

"Godfrey's not . . . I'm not . . ." The misconception was too ingrained to deny it now. "No, I wouldn't lie. As my friend says, I saw the man—the awful absence of his finger, the presence of the tattoo, still wet from the river."

"How murdered?" he demanded.

Irene shook her head. "He acted as if he wanted to drown, an odd impulse for a seaman, don't you think? Perhaps his food or drink had been doctored with some potion that unseats reason. Perhaps he saw someone pursuing him whom he had no desire to confront."

"Grimes was old," the sailor said doubtfully.

"The man these two ladies saw recently pulled from the Seine was not," Godfrey added.

Jerseyman looked at him, waiting.

"Missing a middle finger and bearing a tattoo of the letter 'S'," Godfrey confirmed.

The man plunged his seamed face into his hands. "That's it, then. I'm the last of our Quarter. And Paddy must have been on the way here if he was as far inland as Paris. Recently, you say? By God—" the face that lifted to regard us had hardened until the eyes were as bright and as black as the snake's "—if there's foul doings afoot, I won't have it! Our Quarter's the one that's been cast to the four winds and the seven seas all these years, trustin' to the others to do right, trustin' to our betters," he said bitterly. "There's no common interest between common folk and highborn sorts, save for young Montpensier; he'd have played fair."

"Perhaps that is why he is dead," Irene said quietly. "His death may not have been a suicide, either. I think it unlikely, although assassination would be impossible to prove at this late date."

"By God! Then it's a miracle I sit here a living man, ma'am. But why Singh, poor devil? He never even had a proper share. I was going to hook him in on my part. He couldn't say so much as 'good day' in English or French or any other white man's lingo. He followed his ways and hurt no one. And if his goddesses sometimes had as many arms as an octopus, whose business was it but his? Who'd he hurt? Why Singh?"

The man's grief for his fellow sailor was as sincere as it was roughly expressed. I was minded to say something comforting along the lines of "generations of grass mown down," or "resting in the bosom of the Almighty," but I wasn't sure that the bosom of the late Mr. Singh's almighty was the sort one rested in.

"Perhaps," said Godfrey in a kindly way that warred with Black Otto's grim features, "you will tell us the entire tale."

Oddly enough, Jerseyman seemed to take some comfort in Godfrey's bearded, scarred face. He nodded solemnly. "I'll tell. I've wanted to spill it on a hundred nights in a thousand seaports, for it's a story to make Sinbad drool . . . and we seventeen forced to keep separate and silent about it so long. Now I'm the last o' my Quarter; likely I'll draw my lungs full of water or blood with no one to avenge me.

"I'll tell, by God, though we all lose by it. It's not worth the lives of my Quarter, nor so much as the soul that stirs Singh's little snake here. Strange, but the thinkin' of it, the waitin' and the dreamin'. . . the knowin' that Singh and me, someday, would come back here and pick it up like a plum out of a Christmas pudding—well, that was the taste of it, ladies. That was the sweet and the bitter part. It was the idea of the adventure rather than the rewards that made it worth the candle, worth the fingers all we sailors sacrificed so's we'd be recognized if we turned toes up some day, for our closest relation could claim the prize, if we had any relations who'd care to acknowledge us."

"That's why Louise was only tattooed," Irene said softly.

"I'm not about to nick the finger of a little lady like that! Not needed, anyways. We left the father out of it, too. 'Twas a sailors' pact. A tattoo is a wee tingle and sting and a bottle of brandy. Fingers, now that's a sweating man's chore. Oh, I drank right royal the night Grimes took mine. Held me hand out and he cut nice as you please between the fingers—no easy job. Nerve needed on both sides, yes indeed. Never missed it, though, and most folks never noticed it was gone."

"I confess that I did not, in the train."

The man smiled at me rather condescendingly, considering his position. "You was more concerned over this little rope of muscle and scales, Missus. Ah, I'll miss old Singh, and the odd part is, we never talked the same lingo. We just knew, I guess, what the other was about."

"I said before," Irene said, "there must be some central party to whom you all reported, who notified you when to assemble again."

"I heard you. And you're right. But it's a good tale and I'll tell it as I've always wanted to, with a full tankard before me and open eyes and ears all around and the sea within sight."

Godfrey took the hint and signaled the waiter for a fresh round of Vichy water and . . . whatever. Jerseyman hunched over his basket and his fresh tankard and looked to each of us in turn.

"It was a pleasure jaunt, for the passengers at least. For us sailors, it was pull and haul and trim and sweat. A pretty swell on the sea, this very one that blinks so blue and innocent just beyond the piers. Almost twenty years ago. Little Louise was newborn, and this small snake right here was likely thousands of generations from its getting.

"We lifted anchor out of Monte Carlo, bound for Crete. Oh, the ladies was twirling their parasols on deck, and we barefoot boys was playing monkeys in the rigging, and the captain was struttin' afore the fancy folk on deck. We tacked merrily down the boot of Italy and eastward to the Aegean for two days. The third dawned unlucky.

"A wind came up, fast as a clap of hands. Ahead of the sirocco season, but black and bitter for all that. Well, it was pipe-my-boys-jolly for some time, an' all the slackin' of sail and tackin' of ship didn't keep us from being hit amidships like that—boom! Knocked bloody over by a wave as high as Big Ben. Off it sped for the shore and we sat swamped and sinkin'. We swam for it, those as could. Those as couldn't, or those as couldn't find some flotsam to cling to—well, there was a lot of parasols afloat, and a wide-brimmed straw hat or two.

"We dragged ourselves ashore by ones and twos, those of us left. Singh came aground but thirty yards from meself. Montpensier was washing back and forth in the surf, so Singh and me pulled him out. At first we didn't know where we was, and it could have been the Greek isles, or Crete, for all we knew, the wind had blown us about that much. The skies was still scrubbed dirty gray and the sand kicked up like to rub your skin off your body.

"Lucky we was, though, Singh and me and the young Frenchman. Found a cave. Started a fire and settled in to rest up and dry off. By daylight we found the others bit by bit—some passengers, no women; none of the ladies lived. No captain, no first mate, a few sailors. We had to stick together until a ship would come by and pluck us off whatever we was on, and it didn't much matter, island or coastline, for it was deserted through and through, and little in the way of fresh water.

"But the rest joined us in the cave we three had hunkered in on the first night. Must have been almost twenty of 'em, and we never learned each other's names. It was while we was settlin' in the cave, pushing deep with our makeshift torches, for fire was easier to come by than water there, that we stumbled upon a shallow pool. Well, there was drinking on bellies and faces dipped in to the eyebrows—and brackish sour water it was, but still less salty than Mother Mediterranean.

"And we're down on our bellies swillin' the water, and the torches glimmerin' on the little ripples we make, when we see it shining gold like a city under the waves. Montpensier wades in—he'd been off his head since we found him—and he's knockin' his shins on some stones in the water. Big ones, like for a cathedral, rough and broken. Then the others are in there, too, pulling things from the water, things crusted like ancient crabs. Crowns, we find out. Golden crowns under a shell of rock and sand. Broken a bit, but real gold crowns. And neckpieces, pagan-like—heavy and thick. Things to eat and drink from, looking like strange rocks, all crusted and brown, but underneath it, the golden glint, you see!

"And finally Grimes and a Frenchy—I never caught his name—strip and go under, deep, holdin' their breath. They come up asking for rope. Rope! We stranded without knowin' where, with what flotsam we can burn and what foul water we can drink and what grass we can chew—and they want rope! But we find some washed up the next day, and they dive again and we all pull away in the shallows of the pool, and the torchlight catches it as up it comes up—big as a mastiff and covered in barnacles, but with the glint of gold shining. 'Twas a great golden man with the head of a horned beast—maybe Singh could tell you what it was—and we all gathered 'round and chipped at it with stones and watched the brittle barnacles fall off like a suit of armor. Oh, it was bright beneath. We never made much headway, I grant you, but we could see what we had. And there was more of it below, who knows how much?"

"Treasure!" I breathed. "Ancient treasure."

"Archaeological treasure," Irene said, caution in her voice. "Of course you couldn't admit to it; the whole world would want a piece of the discovery."

"As it turned out, couldn't indeed. The winds had never quit. We heard them howling outside the cave. Inside, the pool was boiling. Maybe the gods of the golden man were angry with our meddling. Maybe the sea still had a finger in it. Anyway, we were sleeping and dreaming of wealth, every man jack of us, lord and lowborn, and that night the water washed in, racked the rocks that had been our shelter, filled up the cave like to drown us right then.

"Most of us struggled out and lay quaking on the sand. And lucky we were, for behind us, the cave—it already was half-submerged—simply cracked and crumbled into the tide. All that stone and sand and gold washing out to sea. In the morning we found a few pieces, a broken bit of crown, a pot of glass. But the golden man-beast was gone.

"We sat right down and wrote an oath in the sand, each and every one of us, that we would tell no one, but would return and claim the treasure secretly when we could. The tattoos was my idea, Singh bein' handy and we havin' time to occupy until we was rescued. His oilskin pouch of inks and needles had never left his waist. It diverted the party, you see.

"One of the Frenchmen went up on a prominence and sketched the shoreline. Then we counted that there was seventeen still alive, so we divided into quarters, each oath-bound to keep track of one another. The others wouldn't admit Singh to our company, him being heathen, though I always figured, like I said, to share my portion with him. So poor Singh did the needlework; for all he wasn't worthy of a share, he was worth double most of the others. Each man of a Quarter bears on his breast one point of the compass and a fourth portion of the shoreline where the treasure lay.

"Later, when Montpensier died, I had Singh tattoo my portion on hisself. Singh and I could count for two now, I figured. Claude was always talking of his little daughter, so I swore to see that Louise got her share when the time came. Our pact allowed that if one of us died aforetimes."

"But *several* of you died aforetimes," Godfrey noted.

Jerseyman nodded and tightened his three-fingered grip on the tankard.

"How were you rescued?" I ventured in the silence.

"Greek freighter, full of olives, bound for Marseilles. Saw our signal fire a half a league off and scooped us all up like we was guppies in a pond."

"Someone," Irene repeated, as if barely heeding Jerseyman's exotic tale, "had to oversee the whole."

"The gennelman," Jerseyman admitted at last.

"What gentleman?"

"Don't know. That was the idea of the tattoos, wasn't it, that names didn't matter? Though two Quarters were sea folk like ourselves, eight of the survivors were passengers, gennelmen all. One undertook to direct this scheme."

"There must have been a way for you to communicate."

"Monte Carlo. This very café."

"For almost twenty years?" Godfrey sounded skeptical. "The café might have vanished."

"Didn't, though, did it?" Jerseyman looked smug despite his grief. "Maybe the gennelman saw to it. And there was the system."

"Ah." Irene looked intensely interested. "What was it?"

"We was to write here once yearly and to slap a special sealing wax on our letters as a sign that we were in a Quarter.

When the time was ripe for a go at the hoard, we'd get a letter
with the selfsame wax upon it, and head here. Then off we'd
all scamper to get our loot at last."

"How could you be sure that others in the league wouldn't
precede you to the treasure?" Godfrey wondered.

"Beg pardon, sir?"

"That they wouldn't beat you to it?"

The sailor shrugged. "Couldn't be sure, save that it'd take a
crew to raise that lot, and who'd keep themselves mum but
those that stood to gain by it? 'Course, there's nothing to say
that some villain couldn't cut the Quarters down so there'd be
less to share."

"And the special sealing wax, how did you come by it?"

Jerseyman regarded Irene with eyes nearly screwed shut.
"We all got a chunk of it as big as your fist—or my fist, ma'am.
Parceled out like gold at these very tables nigh twenty years
ago, and seals for each point of the French compass."

"Parceled out by the 'gennelman'?" Irene asked sardonically.

"Yes'm."

"Yet you used this scarce wax on your letters to Louise's
uncle—"

"To put an air of importance on the letters. An' it was
Quarter business, after all. Looked right royal on the envelopes, official-like, even if the insides was unlettered. Grimes,
rest him, could only print. We relied on Paddy for the
French—his mother was Calais born—though we gave him
an idea of what to say."

"Apparently your 'gennelman' gave you more than enough
sealing wax for side ventures. You have no recollection of
what he looked like?"

"Oh, I do, 'deed I do. Only that was twenty years ago and I
look nothin' like meself then. But he was a young fellow,
quiet and gennelmanly, of ordinary height, dark-brown hair,

eyes like muddy water, and wearing sideburns and mutton chops. But a man's facial adornments may change in twenty years."

"But not a tattoo."

"No'm. Not a tattoo."

Irene sighed. "Was he French?"

"French? Yes."

Godfrey leaned forward, looking particularly villainous in his Black Otto guise. "How many of your survivors were French?"

"Why, almost all, sir. Save for Singh, Paddy, meself and Grimes."

Irene sighed more deeply and sat back on her flimsy wooden chair.

Jerseyman shook his head. "Don't know what I'll do without Singh. Depended on that little blighter. Don't know what I'll do with the bloody serpent. Could turn it loose, I suppose."

My feet shifted nervously on the paving stones beneath the table.

"Or drown it," he said.

A silence prevailed, broken only by the reptilian rasp from within the basket of the creature under discussion.

"Sir," said I, astonished to find that I cared, "that seems poor repayment for the serpent's companionship to your late friend."

"If it were a bird, I could tolerate it," he said. "A nice fat parrot with glossy feathers—now there's a proper pet. And it might even say a word or two to you now and again."

"Feathers and scales are not much different," I pointed out, "and God found room for all creatures great and small, and even, I daresay, slimy."

"Oh, he's not slimy, Missus. Dry as a landsman's hand, him. Take a look; mayhap you'd keep him for a parlor pet."

"I?!" I glanced wildly from Irene to Godfrey, both of whom were sitting back with firmly noncommittal expressions. "Of course not; it's out of the question."

"He showed a bit of a preference for you on the train, now didn't he? Never known the little blighter to escape his basket like that before. He's just a wee slip of a thing—"

The man, popping the lid open, pushed the basket toward me. I smothered a scream and an impulse to flee. Through the partially raised lid and by the light of the oil lamp on our table, a small, flat head lifted. Two dark eyes, as polished as shoe buttons, stared at me. It struck me that there was an anxious cast to the low-browed head. So, I imagine, Gulliver must have felt in his cage among the giant Brobdingnagians. How nonsensical to imagine that the small serpent could understand that its very fate was under macabre discussion! But certainly it might miss its dead master on some primitive level.

"What on earth would it eat?" I wondered aloud.

"Much on earth," grinned Jerseyman, "but Singh gave it milk and some other delicacies."

"Godfrey? Irene?" I looked to my companions.

They were mute.

"I suppose, if you are bent on destroying it, I . . . we could take it back to the hotel and release it in the garden. You are sure it is harmless?"

"Safe as a shoelace," Jerseyman said with a grin. "Singh used to wrap it around his head like a turban."

"I have nothing that cozy in mind," I warned as the sailor latched the basket and pushed it further toward me.

"Well, Nell," Irene said, rising, "it appears that you have gotten more out of this evening than we. What will you call it?"

"Call it? Nothing. It is a snake." I glanced indignantly at Godfrey, grinning now behind his barbaric beard, and suffered an inspiration. The scandalous Sarah Bernhardt had already appropriated the name "Otto" for a serpent, or I should have named it after Godfrey's current incarnation. Instead, another candidate for namesake occurred to me. "Or, rather, I will call it Oscar, after our mutual acquaintance."

Chapter Twenty-six

A SNAKE AT LARGE

❧

We were not to return to the Hotel de Paris without incident.

Immediately outside Le Café de Mouettes, we encountered Louise's uncle. We froze at once, paralyzed by surprise, even as we saw that he was walking at a brisk clip with his head cast down. He'd careen into us did we not have the wit to move.

Irene and I began to scatter in unison, bumping into each other and managing to make an even tighter knot. In the melee, the snake's basket, which Godfrey had been kind enough to carry, swung like a pendulum, its lid flapping.

"Oscar!" I screeched in English, seeing a bright green ribbon flutter to the ground.

At that very moment, Monsieur Montpensier collided with me. The impact roused him from his reverie. He favored me with a most intimidating glower.

"My—" I sought the French word for snake and found none "—my cobra has gotten away," I muttered in my usual execrable French.

"*Pardon, Mademoiselle,*" he said in tones that asked no one's pardon, favoring Godfrey and Irene with a piercing stare.

Godfrey he dismissed as quickly as he had myself; Irene he

regarded burningly for a good half-minute. She broke the spell of his regard by loosing a flood of silly French, perfectly pronounced. *Her dear friend, Fifi, means to say, of course, that her adorable pet serpent has taken an unsanctioned walk. Or can serpents be said to "walk"? Certainly, it is such a little snake—no cobra at all—and quite charming. Monsieur is not to be afraid. If he would watch where he steps—*

Monsieur Montpensier did no such thing, stomping onward with, if anything, a harsher tread. We regarded his departure in silence. Then Irene crouched to inspect the walk.

"Is . . . it missing?" I asked hopefully.

"Here!" Godfrey announced, lifting a wriggling length of green from the shrubbery. He dropped it into the basket and closed the latch.

Irene had risen and was staring after our unsociable acquaintance. "A near thing. Thank goodness Godfrey was in disguise, and Nell has been altered by my cosmetic attentions. Myself he has not only seen, but spoken with. Odd that he did not recognize me. I think he is too full of himself and his plans to do so. Certainly the strategem of the snake was brilliantly done. Thank you, Godfrey. While Nell and I blundered into each other like headless chickens, you at least had the sense to loose a distraction."

I was incredulous. "You mean to say that you released Oscar deliberately?"

"Yes, my dear Nell, I did. Now tell me, are you angry because you were exposed to the unbridled presence of the serpent, or because your new pet might have been lost or injured?"

I studied their eyes; they were brimming with mischief. "You are growing as incorrigible as Irene, Godfrey. I had cherished hopes that you would provide a leveling influence for her."

"Oh, he is very leveling," Irene said impudently, taking

Black Otto's disreputable arm, thus causing strangers to eye our party. She merely laughed at their obvious disdain.

We returned to the hotel arm in arm, parting only on the promenade. Irene and I entered by the grand front lobby, while Godfrey skulked to the usual rear entrance.

We arrived at their parlor just after him. "A treat for Oscar," he said, emptying something from his pocket into the basket.

I forbore asking what it was; certainly I would have to consult a herpetologist quickly, although I understood that snakes do not dine daily. If the creature was in my charge, I could not let it starve, however disgusting its appetite.

"Well." Irene unpinned her rose-colored bonnet and lay it on the table next to our assembled sketches. "Crete, then. Jerseyman and his partners obviously washed ashore there, ironically making their destination in an unanticipated way. And the 'horned beast' can only be a representation of the Minotaur of classical legend and labyrinth. We shall require a detailed map of the Cretan coast, particularly the northern one. The compass rose we have assembled from the individual tattoos must provide some still-arcane clue to the exact location. Somehow we must make compass and map tell us the secret."

"I presume that when details are called for, you will turn to me?" Godfrey surmised.

"Indeed. And please dispense with Black Otto from now on. I find the blackened teeth wearing."

Godfrey produced one last revealing grin and vanished into the bedchamber.

Irene tapped the drawings. "We know what and we know how, Nell, but we still do not know who."

"Irene, you astound me. Certainly we know that resurrection of the lost treasure is the aim of the conspiracy, but how on earth are they to attempt it?"

"Not on earth at all, but by sea. The prince's forthcoming

oceanographic expedition. That is why the voyage must be diverted from Corsica, and why someone has resorted to blackmailing Alice to accomplish the diversion. Her royal lover's research has provided the means of redeeming this sunken booty. His expedition will unwittingly become a reclamation project."

"I see now why Alice is being blackmailed in this manner, but it's impossible!"

"How so?"

"This will be an official scientific expedition. No one could conceal the act of raising a bulky treasure from ancient times. Such a deception would be impossible under the eyes of the prince, the crew, the captain—"

"Difficult is not a synonym for 'impossible.' You forget, Nell, being forthright like the prince himself, that others are not so direct. But one man in the diving party could move the treasure to shallow water so that cohorts might collect it easily by dark of night. Even an outsider like myself could arrange for Black Otto to become a crew member—"

"Irene! You would not allow Godfrey to attempt something so dangerous as deep-sea diving? This begins to resemble an episode from Mr. Verne's *Twenty Thousand Leagues Beneath the Sea.* Have you no regard for Godfrey's safety?"

"None," the gentleman in question himself answered, coming from the other room while fastening his collar. He paused to let Irene supervise the artistic arrangement of his tie. "Irene, I refuse to be used as a piece of rather large bait off the coast of Crete, even in theory. You never asked, but I do not swim. Being expected to perform the unauthorized transport of unknown snakes is danger enough."

"You do not swim?" Irene beamed at Godfrey, as if elated at discovering a new facet to his personal accomplishments. "Then we must bathe on the beach as soon as this vexing matter is done with. I will teach you to dog paddle."

"A human being," I put in, "was not made to so much as duck paddle."

"On that I concur with Nell." Godfrey took my intervention as an opportunity to snatch up his hat. "I must be on the trail of a map of Crete. Please leave something of the puzzle unsolved for my return."

"I did not know that you swam," I told Irene when he had gone.

She smiled nostalgically. "I did not so much swim as to appear to. My dear Nell, I was once a mermaid."

"A mermaid?"

"Yes. For Merlin the Miraculous, a magician in Philadelphia. I wore a sea-green bathing costume that had a single lower extremity and I submerged myself in a large tank of water with my hair loose, blowing bubbles for exactly one hundred and eight seconds. That was how long it took for the Miraculous Merlin to replace me in the tank with a trained seal—or rather, for myself and the intelligent seal to accomplish the transference. The Miraculous Merlin actually had very little to do with the feat."

"You blew bubbles, underwater, for a hundred and eight seconds? Without breathing?"

"Of course. Singers have excellent lung capacity, you know."

A soft knock on the door interrupted this fascinating reminiscence that offered more than I had learned of Irene's past in the seven years of our association.

"Godfrey?" I wondered.

It was only the maid with a letter.

I heard the envelope flap tear free and glimpsed the heavy parchment in Irene's hand as she read; then came a sudden stiffening of her shoulders. I edged around her to view the missive, but she turned and went to the window.

"What is it, Irene?"

"Nothing of consequence, save the seal." She lifted the

envelope so I could see the fat blob of palace wax she had
broken to open it. She read the contents again, quickly, then
folded the message and replaced it in the envelope. "We must
see Alice. Let us hope she is in when we call."

"Now? But it is teatime."

"My dear Nell, the Americans and the French do not
take tea with such fervor as the British. We shall have to
risk it."

I naturally assumed that Alice's message contained some
new development and that I should shortly know every detail
of it. And I was all too correct.

"My dear Irene, you are positively prescient!"

So the duchess greeted us, rustling into her yellow morning
room in an ecru-lace tea gown that must have cost a thousand
francs. "Please sit down, Nell, Irene. I have been told the
date."

One would have thought from Alice's flushed cheeks and
excited manner that the prince had chosen a wedding day.

"How were you told?" Irene wanted to know, shaking her
head to refuse the tea Alice offered.

I accepted my cup with a genteel nod. Alice Heine might
have been born American and have married French, but she
knew how to select and serve a most satisfactory tea.

"By letter, of course," she said, delivering my cup gracefully. "With that same seal that fascinates you, the same
overpressed signet device. And the palace wax."

"I believe we know how that is come by," I put in.

Alice's blue eyes widened, if that was possible.

"Or how it was come by almost twenty years ago, in
quantity," Irene modified. "Would that have been possible?"

Alice nodded. "Like all accoutrements of royal houses, the
wax is a fusty old formula from forever ago. 'A fusty old
formula from forever ago' . . . that line would sing well in an
operetta. Irene, your suggestion for installing an opera hall

within the casino may well be possible. Then I will write an operetta to accompany my line and you shall sing it."

"First we must settle the present business," Irene rejoined. Enthusiasm ever tended to distract the duchess from present necessities; but then, there must be some reward in being a duchess. "So you would say that it is feasible for someone to have removed a sizable bit of sealing wax from the palace years ago?" Irene prompted.

"I presume so, were that someone familiar with palace routine. The wax is of secret manufacture, but it is hardly a state secret, though it was more significant during the French Revolution, when a forebear of Albert's was imprisoned and the principality was temporary swallowed by the squat Corsican. It was used for clandestine communications."

"Corsica." Irene considered. "Luckily, on a global scale, the prince's first destination is not far from Crete."

"No. Nor is the date far off by which I am to have Albert leave for Crete. The twenty-second of September."

"Not much time," Irene murmured.

"For what?" Alice asked.

"To . . . make arrangements. So the wax is at least a hundred years old. That is the charm of a principality, I imagine; traditions do not change."

"I wish that they would," Alice answered with feeling. "Then Albert and I could marry."

"Quite remarkable, the way the Grimaldi line extends back six centuries and has endured despite the frequent perambulations of national borders all around it. After my concert, Viscount D'Enrique explained the Grimaldi continuity and showed me several imposing paintings of princely ancestors."

Alice rolled her eyes. "Oh, he is most charming, that one, but more interested in arts other than painting, my dear Irene."

"So I gathered. His family, however, has been loyal to the prince for some time."

"Ages," Alice said with a very American groan. "That is the politics of this little principality. Such a lot of families with precedence. Victor—Viscount D'Enrique, that is— comes from a family of palace right-hand men; he has practically grown up with the prince. In fact—" Alice glanced cautiously in my direction "—when Albert was a royal carouser, Victor was his most constant companion. Albert, I am happy to say, has reformed completely. Victor, alas, is incorrigible."

Irene produced a polite, distracted smile. I could tell that her agile mind had fastened on some crumb of information that had fallen from the duchess's voluble lips and that she was busy milling it to the fineness of face powder. What it was, I could not imagine, but that is the constant state of the lesser intelligence.

At that moment the maid stepped in. "Dr. Hoffman, Your Grace."

The doctor bustled in with his usual efficient manner. Even on social occasions, the good physician regarded people with the sharp eye of a diagnostician with symptoms on his mind.

"Alice, you look ravishing but a bit overexcited. My dear Mrs. Norton—" he took Irene's hand warmly, then narrowed his dark eyes, studying her "—you have not been sleeping enough lately. Your beauty is not faded, but it is a bit . . . crinkled."

Irene laughed in great good temper. "You are quite right, Doctor, I have missed a bit of sleep recently." She turned to wink at me. Only Irene could accomplish that vulgar gesture with supreme style.

The doctor next bent his attention on my humble self. "But Miss Huxleigh has lost no beauty sleep; she practically blooms! The Blue Coast is salubrious for you, Miss Huxleigh; it has given you fine color."

Certainly I blushed as scarlet as a rose at his compliments, knowing my appearance to have been abetted by Irene's beauty potions.

"This appears to be a council of war," he jested, turning to survey the three of us. "Has anything happened?"

"Another letter has arrived," Alice admitted, "saying that I must have Albert and his ship on the north coast of Crete by the twenty-second of September."

"And what does the formidable Madame Norton think of this directive?"

Irene smiled again, that dreamy, removed smile that looks so innocent and is in fact so dangerous. "She thinks that Her Grace must follow the instructions precisely. My inquiry has hit heavy waters, Dr. Hoffman. I fear I can offer no advice but compliance."

"From you and your charming companion, a course of compliance is all that is to be desired," he said with a bow that had me blushing again.

"I think," Irene said as we left the house moments later, "that the good doctor is harboring an admiration for you, Nell."

"Impossible," I murmured. "The duchess is a famous beauty, and you are even more deserving of that sobriquet. I am a wren in the company of birds of paradise. Besides, it is your theatrical tricks with my appearance."

"Whatever," she said airily. "I am married and Alice is sworn to be. You, though, are a single woman."

"Irene! You cannot be serious! Dr. Hoffman is no doubt a dedicated man of medicine and most charming, but we will leave Monte Carlo and I will likely never see him again."

"Oh, I am sure we will return. Someone must teach Godfrey to dog paddle; we appear to have no time for it this trip."

"Irene!"

She stopped walking up the steep cobblestoned byway and

turned to confront me. "Odd, isn't it, that Alice persists in her attraction to men of science: first Dr. Hoffman on Madiera, then the doctor in Biarritz; now the prince, who is an oceanographer."

"She is at least consistent in her preferences." I was somewhat bewildered by the change of topic.

Irene's face grew extremely pleased, as if I had just uttered some perfect pearl of philosophy. "Yes, people do not change, do they, in their preferences?"

"Not usually," I said. "I, for one, shall never regard the odious Casanova with affection, nor could I ever have any strong attachment to a snake."

Irene laughed. "You are a rare and discerning woman, Nell. You have no idea of the number of women who become intimately attached . . . to a snake!"

And off she went ahead of me, striding up the hill, humming an aria I did not recognize. I could only conclude that Irene had learned something that day—some fact, some clue—that she, and only she, could put to the proper, or improper, use.

Chapter Twenty-seven

SEALED WITH WAX

❧

I miss the fogs of London.

Watson, I suspect, would be pleased to know that my
ventures abroad always bring home to me the rare affinity
between my own rather melancholy nature and that of my
nation's great capital city.

One cannot think properly under a blazing Mediterrean
sun, which is no doubt why pleasure-seekers flock to balmier
climates. Curses, I say, upon sunny seas and starry skies, upon
idle holiday mobs and fresh warm breezes as clean as a French
laundress's linen sheets.

Such relentlessly open and bright atmospheres are no
proper milieu for the spawning of intelligent crime. Oh, the
crimes of passion, certainly, can flourish here as floridly as do
the native blossoms, but they are lurid events that run
interminably in the papers and are as simple to solve as what
comes after A,B,C. Even Lestrade could do it.

No, such sojourns as my current visit to Monte Carlo
remind me forcibly of what delicious kinks, crooked as a black
cat's broken tail, crime can take on a lonely moor or in a
crowded back alley of Saffron Hill. Give me smoky, stygian
air, creeping damp, and a dank, rancid river fog running
through it all; nights on which both murderer's and victim's

breath leave a visible if ephemeral trail in the chill murk. Give me the devious schemes that arise when some four millions of people are crowded into a great spinning, creaking clockwork of a city.

Give me, in short, England, and let Le Villard and his ilk bask in this filthy sunshine.

At least I have had an opportunity to acquaint Le Villard with the full range of exact knowledge in which he is so lamentably lacking. Otherwise, I find him a quick study, with that Celtic intuition so useful to the policeman. As a translator, he is merely competent, but it is my hope that his work with my monographs will inspire him to emulate my methods, if he cannot equal my success. In truth, I am eager to have done with Monte Carlo and to proceed to the infinitely more important and intriguing affair that awaits me in a more northerly quarter of the globe.

However, I have committed to the Montpensier matter. The case took on some small interest when Edouard Montpensier disappeared from Paris with the circumstances of his niece's banishment still pending.

Madame Montpensier's distress, if possible, went up another note on the scale of hysteria.

"You are concealing something, Madame," I challenged the lady brusquely.

She wrung her hands and looked left, right and down, at last, to the useless yellow spaniel in her lap. Then it came out: the flight of her niece with a young American admirer, the odd intervention of an English couple named Norton, her husband's disappearance . . . despite the suspicious odor it lent him in the matter of his missing niece. And she told me of the letters that had arrived over the years, and of the English couple's interest in these same missives.

It was child's play to find the letters. My suspicions fastened, as had the Nortons' previously, on the house's large old library. Once there—Watson knows my methods and takes far more pleasure in detailing them than I—it was a simple matter to find the false shelf-back and the very documents behind them. The dust fields atop the books on that shelf had been recently disturbed by two sets of hands, one set remarkably dainty to be found at such a height.

Unlike the ubiquitous Nortons, I removed the papers. My examination produced several interesting facts as to the types of persons—yes, there was more than one—who had written them, from where they had been posted, et cetera. I need not go into detail here; Watson can ferret all that out should I decide to tell him anything about the affair, which depends on how secret it needs to be kept.

The papers were of no interest except for their variety of origin: a cheap oatmeal-pulp stock attainable only in Calais; a limp parchment with a meaningless watermark that is manufactured in Barcelona; and a flimsy, pale-blue notepaper of wretched texture that I have seen emanate only from the South American nation of Argentina. What intrigued me most was the sealing wax, a particularly creamy variety that blended the colors of black and crimson into a marbleized, swirling pattern. The quality of the wax far surpassed the quality of the envelopes, the paper, and the literary level within.

So sealing wax, rather than missing heiresses who stand to inherit no money, vanishing uncles and falsely murderous aunts, is the one sure strand in this tangle. A physical clue is always the most solid. I have traced the wax to a small stationer's establishment in the Condamine at Monte Carlo on the Côte d'Azur, and to that shop I will go tomorrow.

Chapter Twenty-eight

BARED WITH IMPUNITY

❦

Godfrey had returned from his errand with not one but four maps of the Cretan coastline, each drawn on heavy parchment and folded until the creases had obliterated some of the ink. The maps covered the parlor table like ungainly dressmaker's patterns. I was dismayed by the profusion of these large guides to the island's silhouette.

"So many fussy ins and outs per inch! I may as well attempt to decipher Battenberg lace," I said, firmly applying the pince-nez to the bridge of my nose.

An arm embraced my shoulders. "You will do it, Nell! You have an impeccable eye for detail."

Despite Irene's confidence, I surveyed the intimidating tablecloth of overlapping maps with little appetite. "And if no length of coastline matches the configuration of any of the tattooed letters' scrolls?"

"Then we shall have eliminated *that* idea and can concoct a new one," she said cheerfully. "You will have performed a most valuable service."

I groaned, a sound that escalated as I saw Godfrey peep into the snake's basket by the window. "Godfrey, are you feeding the creature something dreadful?"

He smiled as he latched the lid. "Something delectable, to snakes at any rate."

I could not rebuke him further, being grateful that he at least tended the creature's needs so that I should not have to. I began work immediately, and tedious it was. The thick pad of tracing paper that the young people purchased had struck me as wasteful when first I saw it. Now I was tearing through it, tracing intricacies of coastline, then reducing my traceries enough to compare them with the intertwined scrolls of the N, E, O and S.

Yet it captured me, the enormity of the task and the remote possibility that I could actually demonstrate some synchronicity between Crete's coastline and these fanciful scrolls of the late Singh's manufacture.

I declined to join Irene and Godfrey for dinner but supped on onion soup, roast beef, cheese and a vanilla pudding sent up on a tray. What had begun as the search for a needle in a haystack or a jig in a whirligig soon proved to be a matter of straining grains of sand through cheesecloth. Too many inlets mocked the curves of the scrollwork to make the one answer apparent.

My taskmasters returned in an expansive mood, perfumed with the dubious scents of post-prandial brandy and Turkish cigarettes.

"Nell! Still working?" Irene said. "You shall get the headache."

"I *have* the headache."

"Then you must rest," Godfrey prescribed, coming over to grasp the back of my chair.

"Only another minute! I must copy this last curlicue of coastline; this may be the very spot we seek . . . oh, but not quite. Perhaps one more tracing—"

The chair shook in a light, admonishing way. "My dear Nell, it is past midnight," Godfrey said. "We had no idea that you would work so long."

"Midnight!" I pushed the ebbing pince-nez back on my nose.

Then I frowned at my companions' flushed faces and

celebratory air. Godfrey, with his raven hair and pale-gray eyes, looked as devastating in the crisp black-and-white of men's evening dress as any man I had seen. Marie Antoinette's diamond flashed at Irene's throat, barely competing with the Worth evening gown of jade-green brocaded tulle that bared her shoulders and swirled around her figure in a sea foam of swags, draperies, and folds. The Tiffany pin that Godfrey had given her in Paris, of an intertwined musical note and a key, reposed on the tulle at the cleft of her bosom.

"You are up very late," I commented.

"So are you." Godfrey pulled back the chair with me on it, then firmly took my elbow. "You must give it a rest, Nell, and return to your rooms. The maps will be here tomorrow."

"Of course, but I am very near—"

"Wonderful!" Irene spoke with hearty insincerity, brushing my cheek with a good-night kiss. "We must see it all . . . in the morning."

In the passage, feeling quite like a bird flushed from its favorite cage, I paused to pat my skirt pocket for the key to my room. From behind the parlor door there issued the sound of soft laughter—not at my cartographic obsession, in fact having nothing to do with tattoos or maps. And then it abruptly stopped.

By morning my eyes were refreshed and I saw new possibilities in my tracings. Alas, Godfrey and Irene did not.

"These look like hieroglyphs." Godfrey squinted at several sheets, then set them down again.

"More like decorative braid," Irene agreed to disagree. "Perhaps I've set you on an impossible task," she told me with regret. For one whose talents were creatively expressive and came naturally, the notion of repetitive, boring work was appalling. Now the size of the assignment she had given me was weighing on Irene's ordinarily cast-iron conscience.

"Perhaps we—you—should drop the notion," she said. "Alice has invited us to the palace."

"What will Godfrey do?"

He smiled at my question. "What else would Godfrey do in a landscape of sun and sea and waving palm trees? I will seclude myself in the Office of Maritime Records and hunt for a shipwreck near Crete around eighteen sixty-eight."

"Irene never gives you any amusing assignments," I said.

"Not 'never'," he replied, giving her a glance I could not read. "And I prefer the Office of Maritime Records to the palace. It harbors some amazing old gents with even more amazing old stories." With that and the addition of his hat, he was off for the day upon as dry a mission as my own.

Irene left me to my tracery, retiring to her bedchamber and warning me that I must stop for lunch and then be ready to stroll to the palace for a most interesting demonstration. She had an odd look upon her face; it made me wonder if she was on the verge of a discovery that would render Godfrey's and my own work moot.

My hand was cramped and my neck stiff by the late forenoon. I was only too pleased to lay aside pencil and pen and refresh myself in my room. When I collected Irene, I learned the reason for her withdrawal all morning.

She stood before me a fashion plate, magnificent in a black silk gown brocaded with clusters of pink barley spikes. Pink ruffles ran up and down the skirt and bodice and festooned a black lace parasol. Neither the broad girdle of pink that encircled and emphasized her slender waist nor the black velvet bonnet with its explosion of pink bows at one ear did anything to detract from the utter, feminine splendor of her toilette.

"We . . . we are only going to see Alice?" I ascertained.

"I did not say we were going to see Alice—" Irene drew on pink kid gloves "—only that Alice had invited us to a demonstration at the palace. So we are expected, but I don't expect Alice to be there."

By now my blue-and-white striped skirt train was cascading alongside Irene's wake of pink ruffles down the grand marble stairway of the hotel, while every head in the place turned toward us—or rather, toward my companion. Irene rustled through the lobby, oblivious. The faint flush on her cheeks disturbed me. I had seen that glow before, and it was always the same: the bright, feverish expression of a huntress upon the track.

"Irene," said I. We had paused on the hotel terrace while she unfurled her extravagant parasol, dousing her flaming expression in filtered pink shade. "Why will you not tell me what you have in mind?"

"Because you possibly will betray my intentions."

"I would not! Indeed, I have rarely known them."

"Exactly why you would give them away if you did." She marched, not strolled, smartly down the promenade toward the palace.

I sighed, then clattered after her like a tardy child.

We were indeed expected at the palace. The liveried footman admitted us at once and led us toward the building's rear, and deep within it. I felt vaguely like a trespasser when he flourished open a set of double doors and bowed: "Madame. Mademoiselle."

The room beyond was vast but so overlit by gaslight that the same architectural details that were charming and whimsical above seemed glaringly gaudy below. Parlor palms thrived somehow in that bright dungeon, while standing coats of armor glittered like gunmetal specters along the walls. These walls were plainer than those above and on them hung strange artifacts: crossed rapiers and leather sacks, bizarre masks of metal mesh, clubs, shields and pistols.

"Madame Norton!" came a jubilant, welcoming voice. "You answer my note with your presence."

We turned to see a gentleman walking toward us. In that enormous, unfurnished chamber, our entering footfalls had sounded like repeated claps of doom. Yet this man's steps were soundless. He approached us as if treading water, his silent reflection driving deep into the polished marble floor.

I recognized the Viscount D'Enrique despite his bizarre dress: a striped jersey like a sailor's, baggy trousers of some cotton stuff, and—now I saw the reason for the stealthy soft-footedness—lace-up shoes as flimsy as spats, with no visible soles.

"I am delighted that you and Miss Huxleigh could come today." He nodded to me, then bowed over Irene's hand to kiss the shell-pink kid. "Alice said that you were intrigued by the pugilistic art."

"I am intrigued by any art, Viscount," she responded in tones as silken and dark as her gown, "when it is well done."

Our host was, of course, the same odious viscount who had steered Irene so far down the palace halls on the night of her concert. I liked him no better by day.

"Pugilistic?" I hissed nervously to Irene as he turned away. She shook her head imperceptibly and I subsided.

"Ladies, let me show you the ring," the viscount offered. "An impromptu space, but it serves."

His great, silent strides took him to a farther corner of the ballroom-sized space. Upon the floor a painted rectangle defaced the shining stone.

"But it is square," I noted in confusion.

Irene smiled. "The term is traditional, Nell, from the time when fisticuffs were street affairs, bound only by the ring of men surrounding the contestants."

"Fisticuffs?" I was horrified. "You call that an art form?"

"No, my dear," Irene said, "but when gentlemen do it and it is called 'pugilism,' it is considered an art form. Fisticuffs is mere survival."

The viscount's greasy smile grew slicker. "Madame is

obviously an aficionado of the sport, a rarity in a woman. But then she is a rare woman, is she not, Miss Huxleigh?"

"Rare, indeed," I choked out.

Irene lifted her furled parasol, which she had braced on the floor like a decorative cane, to point to the wall. "Those, I suppose, are the protective gloves."

"Those?" Was Irene blind as well as mad? I wondered, observing the fat leather bags she indicated.

"Indeed." The viscount, smiling still, looked her up and down as if she were a painting. "I have taken the liberty of asking an equerry to play the role of sparring partner so that you ladies may observe the science of an actual encounter in the ring."

I stared again at the *square* on the floor, but I held my tongue. Obviously, these were deep waters, and Irene had seen to it that I should have neither chart nor sextant. I looked up, startled to note the presence of another man in the room. He, too, had arrived soundlessly and was attired as eccentrically as the viscount.

The two men stepped to the wall to take down the clumsy bags, then plunged their hands into them, the viscount lacing the equerry's closed. He turned to Irene, expecting her to perform the same service for him. She went about it as surely as if she were lacing a corset, not some bizarre appliance for a cruel and even more bizarre sport.

Then the men faced each other. The viscount glanced to me. "Miss Huxleigh," he said in rebuke, looking at my feet.

I discovered that I was standing on the ridiculous line that indicated the square ring and stepped back, as Irene had. The men began bouncing on their toes and dancing in and out, swooping at each other with their swollen gloves.

Irene prowled the drawn perimeter like a visitor to a zoological garden inspecting a prime exhibit. I stood speechless, watching the viscount strike snake-fast at the equerry, whose head snapped away from the blow. The sound, like a muffled slap, disquieted me.

Many more such sounds ensued. The gleam in the viscount's eye showed a feral concentration; he took this "sport" very seriously indeed. The equerry was no match for him—how could he be, given the vast difference in their station?—and the viscount soon finished pummeling the man's resigned features and nodded brusquely to end the match.

He crossed to us like a lion proud of a kill, his face damp with effort, his jersey darkening in places from the same source.

"Well? Was it what you expected, Madame? Mademoiselle?"

"I expected nothing," I said pointedly, more to Irene than to the viscount.

She smiled and unlaced the hideous gloves. I performed the same chore for the poor equerry, who looked quite faint. Irene regarded the viscount's overheated state.

"It is warm work," he said, not in a properly apologetic tone, but in one of boast.

Irene merely smiled again and remained silent.

"You are disappointed, Madame?" he asked. "I could have knocked him down easily."

"No, no," she said at last. "I do not require knockdowns, and your skill was most impressive. I should certainly not wish to drive you to violence, Viscount. It's that I'm American by birth, and in the United States, pugilistic pursuits are not so . . . formal."

I had no idea of what she was talking about, but the viscount laughed like a man who has just been dealt a fine hand of cards.

"America! No doubt, Madame, you are used to bloody knuckles and bare chests."

Irene shrugged ever so slightly and smiled like Mona Lisa.

Despite her elegant pink-and-black gown, I was reminded of a cat who had just released its jaws from a mouse.

"It can be done that way here, Madame," the viscount said, his voice going low and husky, "but not in the palace. The prince would find it in poor taste. He has found much that he and I used to enjoy together in poor taste since he has become enamored of your American friend, the duchess. I hear now that she wishes to put an opera house in the casino! Opera houses are all very well, and you sing quite ably"— Irene bristled at the comment, I was glad to see—"but the casino! I see, however, that you are a woman of another stripe."

The conversation's undercurrent was horrendous. I felt like a swimmer sinking in a rank, dark tide of innuendo and intrigue. Of course I had not the slightest notion of Irene's purpose, but I wished myself gone. I wished Irene gone. I wished the Viscount D'Enrique gone also, but first I wished Godfrey to arrive and punch the man in his sneering, smiling face. It never occurred to me that I was asking rather more of my imaginary Godfrey than he might accomplish against so seasoned an opponent of the "ring."

Irene said nothing. In the silence, the viscount barked "Jacques!" at the departing equerry. The man froze like a fox at the first call to hounds. Beside me, Irene's kid gloves made fists for the merest moment.

With a particularly slimy smile, the viscount crossed his arms and grasped the hem of his striped jersey. "We will have another go at it. No one need know. Madame will be well satisfied." He made to pull the jersey up—up and off.

"No!" said I.

"You may wait outside," Irene said without looking toward me. Instead, she was staring at the viscount like a snake at a bird. I could hear my heart beating and the soft shuffle of the reluctant Jacques as he approached the "ring" again. I glimpsed a wedge of cheese-white flesh, a sprinkle of black hair, as the viscount's jersey peeled upward.

"Really, this is most improper and quite unnecessary," I stammered. Irene caught my arm in a tight, cautionary grip.

In that awkward, frozen instant, I heard a door open and hard-soled shoes cross the stones. The viscount dropped his jersey. Irene dropped my hand. The equerry's face lost its look of dread.

"There you are, D'Enrique," came the prince's bland voice. "I thought we'd have a go at some of the official correspondence, but here you are, dressed for boxing. A demonstration for the ladies, I see."

We all bowed.

"I will attend Your Highness within a quarter of an hour," the viscount promised formally.

The prince's smile and limpid wave of hand indicated that the two were on far easier terms than the viscount's public manner hinted.

"No hurry, my dear fellow. I've no wish to shorten the ladies' pleasure. I've quite a good gymnasium here; used it myself in my youth, but now leave that to D'Enrique. I do my exercising at the Ritz *table d'hôte.*" He laughed at his own jest and left us.

"Well, my dear ladies . . ." The viscount bowed. "Perhaps another day?"

"Indeed," Irene said, pivoting on the point of her parasol and rustling out beside me.

Our echoing steps prevented further conversation. My last glimpse of the wretched human punching bag, Jacques, was to see him vanish down a lower hall.

We left the palace in silence. I found the frank splash of the Monte Carlo sunshine a relief, like light that is cast upon some dank, damp place.

Irene inhaled deeply of the fragrant air and sighed. "So close."

"Close to public offense! That wretched viscount was about to remove his shirt."

"I had so hoped, Penelope." She sighed again.

"Irene! That is hardly the sort of answer I would expect of you."

"Surely you did not think I had any interest in viewing that pasty, puffy expanse? If he had more than helpless equerries to practice on, the viscount would spend his time in pugilistics staring at the ceiling."

"Then why did you go to observe him?"

"To observe him? I wished to see if he bore a tattoo."

"The viscount?"

"Not the equerry, surely!"

"Irene, you didn't tell me."

"I never dreamed that you would interfere."

"Even if you had truly had a legitimate aim, I would have been obliged to object. Really, there must be some other way to find out than by tricking a man into removing his shirt in the presence of ladies!"

"There is another way—" Irene's face had a speculative look "—and the advantage to it is that you would not be required to cooperate, since it would be a private ruse as opposed to a public one."

"What is that?"

"I could accede to the viscount's obvious intentions to seduce me and . . . be seduced long enough to learn what I need."

"Worse! Truly depraved! You would compromise yourself beyond redemption. You might not be able to escape him. There would be a terrible scandal. Godfrey would—"

"Yes," she agreed glumly, "Godfrey would. There are some severe drawbacks to marriage for the investigator." She glowered at me. "Also for the investigator who has well-intentioned friends. She schemes best who schemes alone.

Well. No harm done. I shall simply have to find another method of inspecting the viscount's chest."

"I can suggest one," I said grimly.

"What?" I had caught Irene off guard.

"Drown him," I proposed with some pleasure. "Then pretend to find the body. As we both have seen, a dead man may be bared with impunity and cause no scandal whatsoever."

"Murder before impropriety!" Irene unfurled her parasol along with her sunniest laughter. "It never fails to shock me—what a properly brought-up Englishwoman will condone to ensure her blessed propriety."

Chapter Twenty-nine

LADIES *EN GARDE*

❧

On the way back to the hotel, we stopped at the telegram office. Irene sent a message to Milan.

When I asked her to whom the telegram was directed, she tightened her lips and said, "Desperate questions require desperate measures. I have sent for aid."

"Outside aid? That is not like you, Irene."

"You would not let me ply my feminine wiles on the viscount; now wait and see to what lengths you have driven me."

"Surely the viscount cannot be that important!"

"If I am right, he is the key to the whole affair. It is vital to determine . . . what I was on the verge of determining this morning when you so prudishly interfered."

"And if the prince had found us with the viscount in a state of undress? I mean the viscount, of course."

"He would have tsked and wandered off. A great many more scandalous things than that occur in Monte Carlo every quarter hour."

Somehow Irene had twisted my upright position askew. I changed tactics. "Why are you so certain that the viscount is involved in your investigations? You seem to have picked him out of thin air."

"On the contrary, he picked me. I found that interesting and asked Alice about him. A dangerous man, she said, one who once had great influence over the prince, one who has lost it since she came into Albert's life. Did you not hear the prince himself this morning ask the viscount to assist with the royal correspondence? D'Enrique is, and has been for years, the prince's social secretary. Alice told me that, too, on the night of the concert. He has now, and would have had long ago, access to the palace sealing wax. In fact, only he could be sure that it was an item no one else could duplicate. I believe he is your Jerseyman's 'gennelman'."

"Would a man with such a title allow himself to be tattooed?"

"Why not? From the gossip I have heard of the prince's early life, he and his cronies indulged in all sorts of pranks. A tattoo is the sort of debauchery that might appeal to a man of D'Enrique's rank and reputation. And obviously he has no money, or he would not affix himself to a minor prince in a subsidiary role. He would live his own life."

"Then you admit that he is no suitable acquaintance for a lady!"

"I admit only that he is a perfectly suitable suspect in this Cretan conspiracy." She sighed vastly. "This morning I hoped to prove it in front of witnesses—but the equerry was too terrified to aid us, and you were too squeamish to permit the necessary steps."

"*Squeamish?* I do not think I am squeamish, Irene. Reserved, perhaps, but not squeamish."

She shook her head until her bonnet ribbons rustled. "It does not matter, Nell; I have resolved to take another course. This time I shall unveil the viscount publicly, so there will be no scandal of the sort you fear."

"How will you do this?"

Irene merely smiled cryptically and would say no more, not even about the mysterious telegram.

Naturally Godfrey was still gone when we returned to the hotel. The man was tireless in the pursuit of information— but I suppose that is an admirable characteristic in a barrister.

Irene picked up the latest communication bearing the palace seal. I realized only now that it must have been the invitation from that vile man to watch him hit an equerry.

"Unfortunately, to convince Alice that I was enough of a sportswoman to be interested in palace pugilism, I had to create one or two wrong impressions." Irene spoke as if mulling these thoughts, rather than addressing me, but my blood chilled.

"What wrong impressions have you given her?"

"That I—and you—are sports enthusiasts. She invited us for a bicycle tour of the city."

"On these narrow, steep streets? We could kill someone, or, worse, ourselves. Irene, no!"

"I replied that such exercise was a trifle vigorous for city mice like ourselves."

"Thank heavens."

"She then suggested a sail on a small yacht crewed only by two sailors. She found it most thrilling to be so close to the wind and the waves—"

"And the fish and the octopi."

"But I thought the expedition too time-consuming to arrange."

"I am relieved."

"So I consented to join her in a ladies' exercise class held in a ballroom of this very hotel. Most convenient."

"Irene! My most vigorous exertion is to change the water in Casanova's cage!"

"We will need to wear something simple. A tennis skirt and a loose blouse or jersey. No corsets, of course. And flat-soled shoes."

"Irene, I have no tennis skirt. I have no flat-soled shoes. As for a jersey, from what I have seen of that piece of apparel lately—or from *whom* I have seen wearing it, whether highborn or low—I am convinced that it is not a suitable garment for a lady."

She pouted with no real conviction, like an actress in a melodrama. "I, at least, can concoct something appropriate. But we must hurry, for we are expected at four."

"I am amazed that you require my presence, since you found it so hindersome earlier today."

"This is different, Nell; this is all ladies. You will see nothing to object to, I assure you."

I could not help feeling that she was underestimating me, but off she went to her bedchamber, leaving me to repair to my own and exchange my walking suit for a house gown.

When next I saw Irene, her attire was even more a disguise than were her men's "walking clothes," although it did nothing to conceal her femininity.

Her skirt was of cream-white flannelette with turquoise-blue wool peeping between the pleats. A striped turquoise-and-cream jersey clung to her uncorseted figure, looking most laissez-faire. The collar was loose, held half-open with a soft tie; all in all, a most nautical ensemble, an overtone of the common sailor in its every line. Her hair was drawn into a queue at the back of her neck, held in place by another soft tie.

"Where did you acquire those clothes?"

"Alice," she said, turning. "She wears them when yachting or for lawn tennis."

"*When* did you acquire these clothes?"

Irene laughed. "When you were conjoined with the maps upon the parlor table." She made my tedious map-making sound almost scandalous.

"To which I must return. Godfrey shall come back with the information you desire, yet we shall be no wiser as to where the sunken treasure lies than before."

"Come down at least and see that it is a harmless pursuit I indulge in this time. Then you can work unworried on the maps."

"Perhaps." But, too consumed with curiosity to resist, I went—garbed in my periwinkle-blue house gown, suitable for receiving visitors, if not for bounding about.

The ballroom reminded me of the palace gymnasium, save that the floor was a parquet of rich woods rather than an expanse of stone. Irene bounced on the balls of her feet as she tested the floor in her soft-soled shoes. "Excellent. Better for spring," said she.

"It is almost autumn now," said I. She gave me a cryptic and somewhat condescending smile.

Three other women were in attendance, each similarly attired. That did not relieve me. They lounged against the opposite wall; indeed, one of them had braced her right foot upon a small stool and placed her hand upon her hip, a most swashbuckling posture for a lady, if I may be allowed to make that observation. Another stood with a cane braced in front of her, a narrow, shining silver cane.

I saw more canes lying about and soon discerned their real form—rapiers, the needlelike swords used in fencing. The same wire-mesh masks I had seen at the palace gymnasium lay scattered hither and yon, looking like misplaced utensils from Torquemada's kitchen.

As I eyed this display, Alice entered the room, dressed as casually as Irene, a long scarlet sash looped around her waist and caught low at the back of her skirt in a knot. Her blond hair was in the same simple arrangement as Irene's.

"Wonderful!" she said. "We shall have new blood in the class—a figure of speech, my dear Nell. I was beginning to anticipate my usual partner's moves."

"I am here merely to observe," said I quickly.

"Of course," answered Alice, so unruffled that I resented it. Irene had gone to inspect the foils, flexing one's thin, lethal length. A woman tossed her a buckskin gauntlet, which she donned.

"Beatrice is our instructress," Alice said, nodding to the tall, rawboned woman, exactly the sort of female whom I imagined took pleasure in men's athletics. "Why don't you show her what level you're on? You'll have to be in very poor practice to be my partner."

Irene nodded, her face as blank as any fencing mask. Beatrice bent to pluck two of these ungainly items from the floor.

"We can dispense with those," Irene said with a slight smile. "We will hardly go at it that hard the first time."

Beatrice frowned. "I do not wish to be responsible—"

"Then I will be." Irene moved to the middle of the floor, hand on hip, foil raised but not engaged. She stood sideways to her sword arm and smiled down the long silver length as coolly as a seamstress might sight down a yardstick.

Alice joined me where I stood near the wall. "This should be interesting. Beatrice is quick and skilled, but Irene is as cold as coins. I did not even know she fenced."

"Neither did I!"

Alice gave me a startled look. "Perhaps . . . the masks? It would be a pity if Irene were to acquire a scar."

But it was too late. Beatrice was annoyed by Irene's calm air of command, I suspected as Irene intended her to be. She stood sideways to Irene—a taller, broader woman with a longer, more powerful arm; even I could see that. Irene was neither short nor long, but retained a dainty, catlike beauty that one never envisions winning by main force. For the first time, I worried.

Then the blades crossed. I studied the buttons blunting the tips. Suppose one should dislodge? Suppose . . . The sound of metal foils shearing off each other was like the slice of a giant pair of scissor blades.

The two danced back and forth, one lunging and the other

retreating. It did not look like hard work; in fact, there was a graceful dexterity to their motions that I found strangely feminine despite the weapons they wielded. Yet I saw upon Irene's face the look of utter concentration she wore when immersed in a mental effort that consumed her every fiber. It was play, this ladies' duel . . . deadly, serious play.

I cannot describe the sequence of moves, only that despite Irene's daintier aspect, the line of her arm and the foil seemed made of conjoined strands of steel cable. Larger, stronger Beatrice began to lunge awkwardly and to retreat more frequently. Her feet landed heavily, while Irene's soft soles still scarcely whispered over the wooden floor. Beatrice's forehead knotted and she bit her lower lip.

In one instant the foils sliced over and over each other in quick succession. Irene's weapon was suddenly bent, its point fixed to the jersey over Beatrice's heart. I feared it would break, had broken, but Irene stepped back and I felt as if a ballet dance had ended.

Beatrice's face had drowned in a red tide of anger. She whirled on Alice. "Why did you not tell us—me—that your friend was an expert fencer?"

"I did not know." Alice's eyes were as large and as round as marbles.

"And I am not," Irene said with a smile. "I merely playact it."

"You playact it well enough to need no lessons from me."

"We all need lessons. I was not sure I remembered enough to engage foils with a stranger."

Beatrice shrugged, defeated by Irene's verbal feints as much as by her physical ones.

"You are perfection!" Alice exclaimed, going over to Irene. "Where did you learn to fence so well?"

"Where I learned all things. On the stage. I have sung an opera or two—"

"In America," Alice said.

"There and about," Irene murmured vaguely. "My voice is suited to trouser roles, ergo I am expected to carry a sword. Most opera companies have a fencing master, and performers have idle hours, so I studied when I could, purely for my own gratification. But I feared I had forgotten it."

Alice glanced to Beatrice, who was busying herself among the equipment. "Obviously not. You certainly inspire us, Irene. That is just how I wish to look with a foil—lovely and lethal. And when you suggested fencing without the masks! I know the points are guarded, but still, an accident . . . this is only a sport, Irene."

"No, it is not, no more than the viscount's pugilism is a sport."

"You saw him then?"

"We did."

Alice glanced at me, surprised. "You both did? Do you find him as formidable an adversary as I do? We *are* adversaries, you know; we both seek to influence Albert."

"He is formidable as a bully is formidable. He is not skilled, merely ruthless. But that often serves as well."

Alice shivered prettily. "You have measured him as a man would, my dear Irene, as if you would be willing to meet him on his own terms."

"Of course," she said. "That is the only way to measure such a man. But you mistake me. I would never meet him on his own terms, only on mine, although I might be forced to meet him on his own ground."

"He worries me," Alice confessed. "If news of my early indiscretions reaches him, he will know how to use it against me."

"I would not worry about the Viscount D'Enrique," Irene advised her. "He will soon have more pressing affairs with which to deal than your long-dead romances."

Irene handed the foil to Alice, who accepted it awkwardly, and we left.

"What did that gain us?" I asked as we returned upstairs.

"Knowledge," Irene said. "You see how central the viscount is to the tendrils of this puzzle if he is indeed the 'gennelman'? He has it all at his fingertips: treasure and sealing wax; prince and the duchess's indiscretions. Perhaps Godfrey will have unearthed a likely wreck and a passenger list that names him."

"Perhaps. Irene, did you have to antagonize that woman? Couldn't you have let her feel more as if she could have won?"

She paused on the step above me and turned, her face stern. "I was not there to make her feel good, Nell; I was there to learn how well I can still fence. Had I not antagonized her, I could not be sure that she used her full skill and strength."

"Yes, but, Irene, to do so might inflame her to become vindictive, to try to hurt you."

"She did," Irene said with a tight smile. "Several times. You think I did well?"

"Incredibly. I never thought for a moment that you were not in complete control."

"That is why I won and she lost. But she is a feeble opponent. I will have to find better."

"Better? But why?"

"Winning is nothing unless the opponent is worthy."

Chapter Thirty

THE WICKED UNCLE

❦

"**Louise!**" **cried** her uncle. "You are alive!"

We sat thunderstruck on the terrace of the Hotel de Paris, our merry fivesome, staring at the ferociously erect figure of Edouard Montpensier.

Irene, as usual, was the first to recover. "As are you," she said. "Is this not a happy coincidence?"

Her remark drew Monsieur Montpensier's attention from the quivering Louise, who had grasped my hand beneath the table.

"And you, Madame—I recognize you at last! You are that American hussy who called upon me in Paris with false protestations of grief at Louise's demise. And this mild-faced person I have seen before . . . also under false circumstances," he added, staring at me.

Godfrey rose. "Your present state of mortality will suffer, Monsieur, if you continue to libel ladies in public in this fashion, especially since one of them is my wife."

"That's as may be, Englishman, but this chit is my niece. I should have expected to see her in this unwholesome climate, and in the company of some fortune hunter." He had at last honored Caleb Winter with his coruscating eye and tongue.

This American gentleman leaped to his feet. "By heaven,

sir, you won't take after my fiancée like that, even if you are kin, without us coming to blows about it here and now."

"It is so comforting," Irene commented in flawless French, "to view an uncle's sincere joy at the discovery of his niece's unsuspected well-being."

This mild remark slipped through Edouard Montpensier's guard like a rapier through butter. He belatedly removed his hat. "I am surprised to seé the girl alive," he said gruffly, "that is all. As for her 'fiancé,' this robust young man may have her if he will, but he can expect no dower."

"What of your fortune-hunter remark?" came Godfrey's lawyerly verbal pounce.

Edouard Montpensier shrugged with Gallic elegance. "An uncle's overprotective instincts, Monsieur . . . Norton."

"I think not," Irene said, thoughtfully stirring her coffee. "I believe that Louise stands to inherit a substantial amount from her father's Quarter. Oh, do sit down, Monsieur Montpensier. You look as if the sun has drained your strength."

He accepted the chair Godfrey appropriated from an adjoining empty table, bracing himself upon his gold-headed cane. His face was now the color of tracing paper, and almost as transparent.

"You know about the Quarter, Madame Norton?"

"Of course, but how do you?"

"I suspected something. The last letter requesting to contact my niece was posted from Monte Carlo. After her presumed death, I decided the matter merited a journey south to investigate. I assumed a nautical correspondent on the basis of the postings."

"Bravo," Irene said. "And I assume you now realize that much is at stake. But why did you find it necessary to kill the Indian?"

"The British sailor's pet? I did not!"

"Yet you know of the Quarter," Godfrey said.

Edouard looked from face to face around the table, as if importuning a jury. "I swear to you, I have killed no one! And you can see that Louise is safe enough. True, I have learned of these Quarters from the British sailor."

"How?"

"By the simple means of telling him of Louise's . . . drowning. He hinted at a cache of money of which part would come to Louise."

"And now to yourself, since Louise was presumed dead," Godfrey said. "That is why you were so surprised to see her alive, and why you called Mr. Winter a fortune hunter. Now *you* are disinherited."

Edouard Montpensier was silent, his gloved hands throttling the greyhound's head that topped his cane.

"We must ask ourselves," Irene said, "whether Louise is safe now that her uncle knows of both her part in the cache and her continued good health."

"I would not hurt her!" Montpensier's eyes fired with fresh surprise. "I am not about to lose money that is due my family, but I am no murderer."

None of us looked convinced.

"Uncle." Louise's voice fell strangely sweet into the unkind silence that gripped our table. "I would never allow the one who had reared me to be excluded from my good fortune."

His hands went limp on the cane's sleek gold head. "You would not, Louise? Even after—?"

"No, I would not. But the thing we seek is by no means guaranteed. It may be beyond everyone's reach."

Irene extracted a Turkish cigarette from her reticule and lit it daintily. "Go back to Paris, Monsieur," she urged, her words wreathed in a film of smoke. "You clutter up an already overpopulated landscape. Go back to Paris and clear your wife's name, tell her of Louise's safety. Comfort the poor woman, and hope for future fortune."

"I may have business—"

"It is likely that Mr. Sherlock Holmes is investigating Louise's disappearance at the request of the Paris detective force. He is in Monte Carlo. You have heard of Sherlock Holmes? He will not overlook your actions in this affair; he has no reason to be wary of Louise's feelings. Go back to Paris."

The gilded greyhound at the top of the cane received one last wrenching as Edouard Montpensier lifted his hat from his knee and stood. "Very well, Madame. I can see the field is too crowded for a mere uncle," he said bitterly. "Messieurs. Mademoiselles." Erect as a flagpole, he left the terrace.

Irene turned to Louise. "Really, generous child? You would admit your uncle to some share of your portion of the treasure?"

Louise smiled. "I said I would share with the one who had reared me. That was my Aunt Honoria. If Uncle wishes to partake in her good fortune, he shall have to earn her good will."

"A Solomon come to judgment!" Godfrey proclaimed. "Whether he goes or stays, your aunt will be well treated in any case."

I squeezed Louise's hand encouragingly as she withdrew it from beneath the table.

Irene frowned and extinguished her cigarette in the crystal dish provided. "No one can raise the treasure without the aid of the prince's expedition. We can only openly enlist His Highness's cooperation. The treasure will have to be shared with the government of Crete, with the prince, with the world of wonder seekers who uproot the past. There may be little left."

"Fine by me, Mrs. Norton," Caleb Winter said stoutly. "All I ask of Louise is her hand in marriage and that she be willing to accompany me home."

"To America? Really, Caleb?" Louise sounded delighted.

"It's where I earn my living, Louise. We make our own way in America."

"So I have seen," Godfrey put in under his breath, with an amused glance at Irene.

I spoke at last. "Do you think Louise's uncle will leave merely because you have asked him to do so, Irene?"

"He will leave because matters have been taken out of his hands," she replied. She turned to the young couple. "And it would be best if you followed his example. We shall have less to worry about, including Sherlock Holmes discovering that Louise is alive."

The pair exchanged a glance.

"I reckon you're right, Mrs. Norton," the young man said. "I've pushed my stay as it is. My editor isn't about to swallow a Paris assignment that becomes an extended jaunt to the Blue Coast. Besides, I'm eager to show Louise the other side of the Atlantic. We can always come back for a visit when things settle down."

"Excellent sense!" Irene said. "I recommend a speedy wedding—Alice will help, I'm sure—and immediate departure for Paris, then London, then to America by ship. I cannot wax too extreme in my recommendation of impetuous nuptials," she finished, a twinkle in her demure brown eyes.

As witness, I stood the next day beside Louise in Alice's buttercup-yellow parlor while a local priest performed the marriage ceremony in sonorous Latin. Luckily, Caleb Winter was of the Roman Catholic faith, so there was no barrier to the couple's swift coupling, as Monaco did not require civil ceremonies first.

Louise had chosen myself as her attendant over my protestations that Irene would better serve. Godfrey upheld the groom. I wore one of Irene's gauzy tea gowns, as did Louise. Hers was arranged in multiple shades of pink, and she bloomed like a brunette rose in a pastel garden. Mr. Winter bore a more serious demeanor than I had ever seen in the young, energetic American, and so it should be when a man pledges his life and future to a woman.

Having missed Irene and Godfrey's nuptials, I avenged myself by shedding copious tears at this ceremony. In fact, I had become exceedingly fond of Louise. I was not untouched to see her jet-black eyes glaze as we made our farewell embrace and promised to write each other faithfully. (A promise I kept to a greater degree than we had then imagined, since so much transpired after the new-wed pair left the Blue Coast.)

Alice served a dainty tea afterward. Then her coachman drove the handsome young couple to the railway station.

"Well," said Alice, her blue eyes misted, " 'all's well that ends well.' Forgive my repetitiveness, but I am much relieved to have Louise and her suitor safely married."

"And safe," Irene added, brushing tart crumbs from her rose, Nile-green and brown-striped changeable silk skirt.

"You think real danger remains?" Alice sounded doubtful. "I have persuaded Albert to sail to Crete at the time demanded. Surely that will satisfy the blackmailer. Since you know the object of the voyage, you and Godfrey can arrange to have the authorities intervene in time to end the conspiracy."

"I would rather it ended before the voyage begins, my dear Alice. We will all rest much easier."

"But how, Irene? You say that many loose ends remain."

"Then we must gather them all into one knot and start from there."

"How?" Alice repeated.

"I don't know," Irene replied, "but something will come to mind."

Chapter Thirty-one

A DIVINE VISITATION

❦

Finally allowed to return to my map tracings, I was startled that evening when the maid brought yet another missive, this one for myself.

"You were not in your chambers, Miss Uxleigh," she said in English, handing me the envelope with a curtsy. All of the maids at the Hotel de Paris were polite, efficient and pretty.

My envelope bore no sealing wax. Irene passed me a long, rather lethal hat pin and I slit the flap.

"It is from Dr. Hoffman! He wishes to call with news of interest to us. This was clearly meant for you." I handed the note to Irene.

"But it is addressed to you, dear Nell. Perhaps the good doctor wishes to ensure your presence."

"Surely not. He must misapprehend my importance in the affair."

"Surely not," Godfrey echoed me with a smile. He pointed to the innumerable pieces of tracing paper floating like flotsam on the map-laden table. "This is exacting work, Nell."

"Yes, Nell is most exacting," Irene said with fond regret, "as I have cause to remember. But the good doctor arrives within the hour. Perhaps, Nell, you should set your pince-nez aside and tidy up."

I looked down. India-ink archipelagoes spotted my hands. I knew that two red depressions from the spectacles bracketed my nose. And no doubt ink smudged my face so I resembled an overdevout churchwoman on Ash Wednesday.

"I am busy," said I, "and I do not intend wasting precious time preening for the advent of some . . . scandalous physician."

"I said nothing of preening."

"Primping, then."

"Primping! Certainly not." Irene sounded shocked. "I would never advocate primping. It sounds so schoolgirlish."

"Exactly." I bit my lower lip as my pen point wound around a small peninsula that curved suspiciously like the left descender of the tattooed "E."

And so I was situated when the doctor arrived, hat in hand and looking most distracted.

"So delighted to find you . . . all . . . at home," said he, with a glance to myself.

I nodded and continued my work. Possibly I should have stopped to take notes, but Irene's assumption that the doctor's visit was personal had irritated me. I dare not abandon my project; it would look as if I had hopes in a direction to which I never intended to turn.

She invited him to sit down and Godfrey offered him a brandy. They were as cordial as two parents receiving a suitor for an ugly-duckling daughter.

"Alice tells me that you are lightning with a fencing foil," he said to Irene.

Godfrey's eyebrows raised. He had heard nothing of our earlier exploits, as far as I knew.

Irene's head tilted modestly. "I enjoyed testing myself at Alice's class."

The doctor nodded nervously, as if pleasantries were over. "Any clue to the blackmailer?" he blurted.

"Our efforts have been distracted in other directions. Have you heard more?"

"No." Dr. Hoffman turned his brandy glass around and around by its narrow stem, a gesture that seemed unlike a precise man of medicine. "Look here. I think—I *know*—someone is following me."

Irene came to attention. "For how long?"

"The past day or two. Or three." Dr. Hoffman rubbed the bridge of his nose, leaving it as ruddy as mine. "Rough-looking sort. One-armed and a limp. Why would anyone want to follow me?" he demanded.

"For good reason," Godfrey told him. "You are the link between the blackmailer and his object. The blackmailer might wish to make sure that you are still in contact with the duchess, and thus a useful tool."

Dr. Hoffman looked unconvinced.

"The day of the prince's departure draws near," Irene said. "The blackmailer may be uneasy; it is a nerveracking business, blackmail; not for the faint of heart. A victim may suddenly become an avenger; promised cooperation may mask an attempt to expose the blackmailer. One should never attempt even the most innocuous blackmail unless one is willing to pay the consequences, Doctor."

"But what if it is *not* the blackmailer?" He raked his hand through his beard. "Can't you tell me how your investigation is progressing, so I may judge who the devil is hounding me?" He coughed self-consciously, then murmured, "Beg pardon, ladies," for his forceful expression.

"Truly, Doctor," Irene said with compassion, "there is nothing solid to report. We cast our nets in many directions, any of which may prove fruitful or not. Nell is painstakingly studying the geography of the island. Godfrey reads his eyes red in the newspapers and the law offices. I thrash in many directions. Perhaps if you described your pursuer in more detail?"

"Around sixty. A long nose, or longer than average. Seaman's clothing, you know the sort. Limps. For heaven's sake, I have not turned and stared at the man! How many one-armed men can there be in Monte Carlo?"

"Many," Godfrey observed with the wisdom of the bistros. "We sit on the selvage of a vast, inland sea. Sailors have lost life and limb since Jonah. One-armed men abound near the water."

The doctor made a sound of disgust, then gulped down his brandy.

"We can be especially watchful," Godfrey said, "now that we know one of us has drawn untoward attention."

Dr. Hoffman glanced at me, or rather at the maps spread before me. He cleared his throat. "I would feel more secure if one of you could observe the man. If Miss Huxleigh would care to walk out with me tomorrow, surely no one would suspect her of . . . of being an inquiry agent. She could either confirm my suspicion or dismiss it."

"Me?" Words failed me beyond that opening squeak.

Irene bounded to her feet. "An excellent notion, Doctor! You could ask for a no more acute judge of human nature than Miss Huxleigh, besides which you will find her company most engaging. And Nell desperately requires a respite from her labors. Say no more; she shall be assigned to you for the day. I am intrigued by this one-armed man with a limp. The infirmities seem most excessive."

"Then you agree that there is something sinister in this man's presence?" the doctor asked.

Irene's tented fingers tapped thoughtfully. "Too soon to say, my dear Doctor. We must rely upon Nell's keen powers of observation and discrimination. And you must make early targets of yourselves—shall we say at ten o'clock? You may call for her here; what you do with the rest of the day is up to you two. We will gather here at five in the evening to report on the day's doings." Irene shrugged happily. "Ah, there is nothing so gratifying as a pot that is bubbling, and I do believe that these events are coming to full boil."

She smiled happily from Dr. Hoffman to myself to Godfrey.

When Irene and I were alone later that evening, my pleas to be excused on the morrow went unheeded. We were on the balcony, where I sometimes let Oscar slither among the vines to collect what prey he could. I had found that if I left his basket open, he would return to it after such a sojourn as meekly as a mouse retreating to its hole.

"I am no judge of limping, one-armed men," I protested as I followed my ward's sinuous progress.

"You have seen me and Godfrey in disguise; surely that has given you some insight."

"But what if the fellow simply is that way? That does not prove or disprove that he follows Dr. Hoffman."

"And why, why should he follow Dr. Hoffman?" Irene mused. "After all, the blackmailer already has the doctor's address. A most interesting development."

"Besides, Irene, you have saddled Dr. Hoffman with me for the whole day. Surely such a long commitment is not required."

"The odd-armed limper may not appear until afternoon. And I did not saddle Dr. Hoffman with you; he requested you."

"That's just it. Why?"

Irene smiled almost imperceptibly. "Perhaps he craves your company."

"I am not vain, Irene. No, there is more to all this. Something is afoot."

"Indeed it is. The Indian tattoo artist is dead; Jerseyman is likely to be so if we do not discover who is eliminating the Quarter members; and now another sinister seaman is lurking about. You must determine if he is to be reckoned with."

"What of Godfrey?"

"He is scouring the records for likely shipwrecks and a list of the passengers and crew on the doomed vessels. He is in no danger. And neither shall you be, Nell, with Dr. Hoffman. I really think it a good idea at this juncture that our party be in pairs, in public places."

Her words gave me pause. While I indulged in it, Irene leaped in for another foray.

"What will you wear tomorrow? Lilac is a most flattering color. You may borrow my lilac lace parasol. It is excellent for viewing bounders without seeming to stare. Remember, it is not important where you go with Dr. Hoffman, merely that you are seen publicly."

"Mayn't Alice become angry?" It was my last argument.

"Alice has far bigger fish to fry now than Dr. Hoffman. She will be grateful to you for taking him off her hands."

So I went to bed, my head spinning at the turn events had taken. It was no wonder that my dreams were filled with lilac parasols; or that I spied a dark-clad, limping man scurrying like a rat through the shady mazes of Monte Carlo, while Dr. Hoffman, suddenly shrunken and sprouting white hair and beard, handed me a yellow rose; or that the sea around us pounded angrily and a great golden man with the head of a bull walked stiffly from the waves.

We broke fast early, Godfrey absorbed in the local paper and bound again for the Office of Maritime Records. Irene chirped like a linnet despite the early hour, a mood of hers that always aroused my suspicions. Godfrey left with a kiss to her hand, a bow and a smile to me.

"I will help you dress," Irene told me as we left the breakfast room.

"I am not a child," I began.

We were crossing the cavernous lobby. Abruptly we became aware of a commotion near the entrance. A long-haired hound came racing toward us on delicate, spidery legs, trailing a golden lamé lead. Immediately after came a hotel porter, calling "*Arretez! Arretez!*"

Irene frowned. "That is no way to gain obedience from a Russian wolfhound."

A figure followed dog and porter, trailing a cyclone of scarves and foaming red-blonde hair.

"Irene!" this vision rumbled in an arresting voice. "My delightful Miss Uxleigh!"

We were engulfed in clouds of heavy perfume as the brocaded figure embraced us in turn.

"Sarah!" Irene sounded delighted.

"You stay in this hotel, yes? How wonderful! I am ready for amusement." Sarah Bernhardt turned impatiently as the porter approached, panting, the wolfhound in hand. "Take him to my suite; he has been naughty and shall have no caviar tonight." She turned to us again, her pale face floating above a maroon marabou muffler. She resembled Ophelia after her death scene, if looking decadent implies perishing. "You must come to my suite and tell me all your doings."

"I'd be delighted," said Irene, "but Nell has an engagement with a gentleman today."

"A gentleman?" The actress turned on me like a wolf upon fresh meat. "Rich?"

"No," said I.

"Handsome?"

"Not really," said I.

Sarah Bernhardt frowned, then her face lit up again. "Scandalous?"

"Long ago," said I.

She was silent for a minute. "Perhaps you can do something about that, my dear Nell. It will make the gentleman so much more interesting—but then, you do not want to make him *too* interesting when I am on the premises. Speaking of which, Irene, how is that adorable Godfrey of yours?"

"Adorably busy and far from the premises," Irene replied.

Sarah sighed, a long and exquisitely shaded process that ended in a small smile that became a pout. "I shall have to content myself with very dull fellows, I see. I could not even bring my darling Panache with me. He is such an awkward size for train travel. You do remember my darling Panache, Miss Uxleigh?"

A daring solution to one minor problem I had encountered in Monaco had suddenly occurred to me. I nodded my remembrance of the odious python as the actress's monologue babbled on.

"Save for the casino, there is so little to do here, except to create scandal of course, but I have been busy with that in Paris."

"Oh, I think not, Sarah," Irene said. "There may be something very amusing to do, if we put our minds to it. Your arrival has given me the solution to a vexing difficulty."

Irene smiled at Sarah and Sarah smiled back, slowly at first and then more brightly, until the soberly elegant lobby seemed lit by twin chandeliers. The last thing I heard as I went to my room to prepare for a day with Dr. Hoffman and his unknown lurker was the sound of their laughter rising up to the high, ornate ceiling and sparkling like crystal.

Chapter Thirty-two

NO "Z" FOR ZORRO

"**A most** uneventful day," I repeated.

"*Nothing* happened?" Irene demanded with disappointed incredulity.

"We walked upon the promenade. We lunched at the Ritz. We visited the casino, where Dr. Hoffman bet a few francs on the roulette wheel and promptly lost them. Gambling is a most fleeting entertainment."

"But the one-eyed limping man?"

"The one-*armed* limping man. Yes, I saw him."

"And?"

I shrugged. "It is possible that he was following us, and it is possible that he was not. Have you ever noticed, Irene, how many sinister-looking men prowl the streets of an infamous resort such as this? If there had not been the limping man to worry about, I could have pointed out a half-score more whom I judged to be of questionable character."

"You were ever able to see the villainous among us," she commented. "How did the day go with Dr. Hoffman?"

"Most cordially," said I. "He was ever so polite; I was ever so polite. We both nearly swooned from a surfeit of courtesy."

"Do you think he is truly worried?"

"That, yes. If it is for the reasons he gave us."

"Why do you say that?"

"Oh, Irene, I spent the day with him; I could not help but draw some conclusions. Despite your attempts to have it otherwise, he harbors no personal interest in me whatsoever, although he politely feigned intense interest in my geographical investigations. From his carefully phrased questions, however, I gather that he is highly curious about the progress of your investigation."

"Natural enough," she said. "He is the odd-man-out in this affair, both romantically and vis-à-vis the puzzle."

"So my day was wasted."

"Not necessarily. You at least confirmed that the man he described is hanging about."

"And your day, Irene?"

"Sadly frivolous, I fear. Sarah and Alice and I, giddy girls all, amused ourselves at the palace. Now Sarah and I are ordered back by royal command tomorrow. I am most vexed that my social life is distracting me from the case, but there it is. I cannot snub the future Serene Highness of Monaco, nor the queen of the international stage."

"Of course not," said I. "Where is Godfrey?"

"Still engaged in fruitless search. He went to Marseilles. Perhaps the records will be clearer there."

"So." I glanced to the tabletop, where my map work lay abandoned. "We have all made no progress at the same time. I will concentrate on the tracing tomorrow. Perhaps that avenue will point to the solution that eludes us."

"Would you, Nell? I would feel so much less guilty to be on holiday at the palace if I knew you were glued to the parlor table here. But don't come to the room until midmorning. Godfrey will be tired when he finally returns tonight and may sleep late, and I must be off . . . earlier."

"As you wish," said I, as agreeable as country cream.

Of course I did not for a moment believe a word of it. More was afoot than I was deemed worthy of knowing, but two can play at that game, which was why I felt no compunction to tell Irene that I had spied not one, but *two* unsavory fellows following Dr. Hoffman. Neither one seemed inclined to confront the physician, so I judged the threat negligible.

As for Godfrey's extended absence, I suspected another cause: as once before, Irene was assigning him a side task that would prevent him from examining her own course too closely. That meant that she was up to something shocking. And if she had merely wasted the day at the palace giggling with her lady friends, then I was Eleanora Duse!

In the solitude of my small suite, I pondered the sort of escapade that Irene would desire to conceal from the two persons closest to her. I concluded that desperate questions require desperate measures.

Hence, long past midnight, when the late revelers had all reeled and stumbled to their rooms, I left mine. I wore mouse brown, which Irene would say is not becoming, but which is especially unnoticeable. After the debacle with Dr. Hoffman, I no longer felt I need stoop to female fripperies. I established myself in a linen closet, settling upon stored pillows and bolsters as comfortably as I could and leaving the door just ajar. Through the crack I could see the gleam of the gaslight sconces and view the entrance to the Norton suite.

The maids would be up and rustling at the crack of dawn, but when Irene said "early," she was a woman of her word. I hoped to observe some developments before being discovered by a hysterical chambermaid.

I had not taken a candle, for its light might betray me. Yet it was cozy there in the dark. As a child, I had often retreated to the parsonage linen closet to eat a forbidden fruit before teatime. Now that same childlike sense of hidden power thrilled my soul. No one would suspect my presence, a heady feeling indeed.

Hours passed, but still the gaslight burned with the same

steady glow. I found myself fighting sleep and sneezes; feather pillows en masse were an unexpected hazard.

Long hours in wait were at last rewarded. The door to Irene and Godfrey's suite opened. A man stepped out, his figure against the gaslight as sharp as a framed silhouette. And Godfrey was supposed to be sleeping late!

He looked up and down the passage, then went softly toward the stairs. I rose, finding my knees uncooperative after hours of crouching. I ignored their creaks—and those of the door as I opened it—to scurry down the hall after him.

This was real detective work! My heart pounded; my every step resonated to thunderclap proportions in my ears. I felt impelled to keep Godfrey in sight, yet feared that my eagerness might pull me too far too fast and he would see me.

The turnings of the stair were a torture. What if he had heard me and schemed to take me unawares? I celebrated rounding each turn with a pause to listen to my thumping heart. Then I feared that my caution might give him too much ground, so I hurried down the next flight. Finally, faintly, I heard footsteps on the grand staircase leading to the lobby. Even as I congratulated myself on keeping him within earshot, I realized that I would have to tread those unforgiving marble steps myself.

For this I was prepared; I had slipped a set of knee-warmers over the soles of my shoes.

The lobby lay dark and deserted. My prey was near the door when I rounded the last turning of the stair. Godfrey left the building as without incident I pattered down the stairs in my makeshift muffled shoes.

I skittered across the vast floor like a timid church mouse in an empty mausoleum. When my muffled feet slipped, I nearly fell, save for the lucky coincidence that I was near the great equestrian bronze statue of Louis XIV. While inveterate gamblers ritually rub the horse's left fetlock for luck, I seized it to prevent a nasty spill, and I was able to reach the outside with a great sigh of relief.

The waning night was strangely beautiful. The sea shone like beaten silver in the soft light of a quarter-moon; a ribbon of daylight trimmed the horizon, and a few last stars salted the heavens.

No one seemed about, save for a figure diminishing down the promenade. I followed, grateful for the thick-trunked palms, for the florid bushes of oleander, for the muffling lawn under my muffled feet.

Godfrey did not pause at the promenade's end, but plunged down the leafy embankment. I rushed to reach the spot before the leaves' last tremble.

The slope grew steep amid unclipped growth. Favoring wayward, natural foliage, gardeners in the south of France are far less tidy than our English sort. Scanty soil gave way to shifting sand; then tiny pebbles pressed my tender soles. The stones clicked as I passed, tsking at my every step.

The bushes ended. I paused, then parted the last branches to peer out at a bizarre party assembled on the beach. Mist draped the shoreline water and wrapped the persons before me in mystery, but I could see two men—no, three—and a woman! Irene! And Godfrey was joining them.

They met as conspirators, their demeanor hushed and restrained.

A man wearing only shirt and trousers in the predawn chill moved forward, moonlight painting his white shirt the pallid color of quicksilver.

"We will speak in English," he said, "since all present know it." The voice of the Viscount D'Enrique gave me a shock so intense I felt as if the Mediterranean had doused me with a wave of saltwater.

"Some know some English," corrected a tall, thin man whose accent was sliced as thick as Italian sausage.

"Signor," the viscount said, "for our purpose here this dawn, few words are required. Deeds will speak for us."

The man behind him brought forward the kind of case that might house a long, thin musical instrument in its velvet-lined interior. Indeed, as the man opened it, moonshine glittered on the metal within.

Then the viscount stepped back and the tall Italian bent to inspect the contents.

"Very old," the viscount commented. "In my family for generations." While the other man eyed the interior of the case, the viscount turned to the woman's cloaked figure. "Madame," said he, "if you choose not to take offense at such a trifling matter, this need not take place. He is foolishly young, your son, and unskilled. I am neither."

"Ne-vair!" came the ringing reply. The voice was as golden as the seam of sunlight now annealing horizon to sea.

I gasped, but who would hear me in the bushes when *she,* whose voice was known world over, was speaking?

"Monsieur," she went on, "my honor requires vengeance. Your attentions last night were highly unwelcome. Alas, I am only a woman and cannot defend myself, but I stand not alone in the world so long as my dearest and only son is willing to—nay, insists upon—defending my honor."

The viscount bowed stiffly. "I am too much of a gentleman to point out that *you* approached me, Madame."

The sea wind whipped a white silk scarf around the woman's features. Anyone not blind or deaf would have recognized Sarah Bernhardt in that signature drapery, even if the Voice had not first betrayed her.

Godfrey remained strangely silent. Perhaps he was acting as second to Madame Sarah's son, a courtesy he could hardly refuse, however foolish the cause.

The Italian had lifted a rapier to salute the warming light as reverently as a Roman priest might elevate a chalice. "Tole-do," he breathed. "It will do."

While watching him admire the rapier, I missed another arrival upon the scene—or seemed to—for a second white-shirted figure suddenly stood among them.

"I warn you, Monsieur," Sarah's voice rang out again. "My son fought a duel for my honor when he was only sixteen, and won. He has since fought three."

"Madame." The Viscount's voice came through clenched teeth. The growing light showed that his features were taut. "The matter over which he—and you—took offense is of your own illusion. You imagine me a fool if you think that I will retreat from any impudent youth, even your son. I will fight him as I would my worst enemy."

"At this moment, Monsieur," came a light, husky voice, "I *am* your worst enemy."

As the white-shirted youth bowed, pale sunlight glanced from the hair caught in a queue at the back of his neck. I knew that unmistakable shade of chestnut warmed by glints like Russian cherry-amber or the finest French brandy. . . . "Godfrey" had always been Irene, and now she had removed her hat and coat.

I rushed through the bushes toward the knot of people on the beach even as the noncombatants drew back. Two white-shirted arms lifted, gripping gleaming wires of unblunted steel.

The scene seemed miles away. I recall thudding over the pebbled beach like a runaway cannon, impelled forward but mindless. The sound of blade sharpening blade sliced the torpid morning air. Something reached out and snared me, a manacle of flesh around my wrist.

"Miss Uxleigh," that Voice purred near my ear, "I am delighted that you share my taste for early morning adventure, but, please, stay here, lest you inadvertently serve as a pincushion."

"Your son! It is Irene!"

"Shhh. Yes, of course, but we do not wish the viscount to

know. He might turn gentlemanly at this late date and refuse the contest."

"But he will hurt her!"

"We will hope not."

"We will do more than hope. I will stop them!"

Slight as the actress was, her grip was like steel. "No, Miss Uxleigh. We have gone to great trouble to arrange this adventure. The viscount deserves a . . . a come-up-with-it, as you say."

"A comeuppance, and what makes you think that Irene can outduel a practiced swordsman?"

"Because she wishes to, very much, and when she and I wish for something that much, we make it so."

"You are not . . . supernatural!"

"No, but we know what we are about." The blue eyes, so much deeper and darker than Alice's, bored into mine. "I have no idea of why Irene wishes to humiliate this rather unpleasant little viscount, but there must be reason. I have suffered my own humiliations and I will help her, even if it means preventing you from helping her. Besides, the Italian is her second. No one dies in duels anymore. He will see to it that no unseemly injuries occur."

"Unseemly? And what injuries are seemly in a duel, pray?"

Sarah Bernhardt raised a narrow finger to her lips. "Shhh. You are missing all the fun."

I turned to the field of combat. The duelists danced back and forth across the shifting pebbles. I could not imagine a more treacherous footing, but I guessed that dueling was forbidden in Monaco, as everywhere, and so the combatants had required a discreet site.

Now I saw that Irene's form was slighter than the other men's. Her features were unobscured by false whiskers. Yet she could pass for a young, rather theatrical boy, the son of the famous actress. It struck me that it would be politic for the viscount to treat such a challenger lightly, but he fought as intensely as when he had pummeled the unfortunate equerry. No quarter given anyone; he was that kind of man.

Irene darted back and forth with a sort of agile glee; I perceived that she had danced the viscount around to face the rising sun.

A lock of hair had fallen across her forehead. In the ruddy light it looked like a wound. I flinched each time the viscount's rapier point lifted to her face, but each time her own foil engaged it.

"Have you had enough, boy?" the viscount finally bellowed, winded.

"Not nearly," said he . . . she.

It dawned on me (perhaps my enlightenment paralleled the action of the rising sun) that this must be more than a game for Irene. Even she was not so depraved that she would do this for a mere lark, although, of course, the Divine Sarah would, and had.

The viscount was tiring. Perspiration pebbled his face. His sword arm did not lift as high or respond as fast as at first. His eyes squinted against the fattening sun. Too late he tried to force Irene into its glare. She had chosen her ground and held it, and now . . . now she lunged as if for the kill. The viscount leaped back, stung, his shirt rent open over his heart.

I saw no blood, but a strike such as that on a practice floor would have finished the contest.

The Italian barked one word; "*Basta?*" Even I knew that meant "enough?"

The viscount frowned. Irene's sleek head shook violently. She did not waste energy on words but lunged again, forcing her opponent to raise his blade and retreat. Again her stinger bloodlessly sliced through his shirt fabric. The garment gaped open, revealing the viscount's chest—revealing what had been concealed: the site of the tattoo!

Now I saw the point of Irene's madness. I leaned forward to spy what her rapier had disclosed.

They both moved too quickly. Had I glimpsed coils of dark hair . . . or a sinuous letter of the late Singh's design?

I found myself tightly gripping the Divine Sarah's hand, as she was squeezing mine,.not in custody, but in suspense. My concern was no longer for Irene's safety; I awaited the successful unveiling of the viscount's chest. If anyone had told me that I would someday stand on a beach at dawn hoping that a man's shirt would be sliced to shreds upon his body, I would have called that person insane.

Irene lunged again. This time a long, diagonal slash nearly halved the fabric. But still it hung from the viscount's shoulders. He hunched over, as if to keep the tatters upon his back. I began to detect a suspicious pattern beneath the flying shreds, began to discern an "S", or was it an "N"?

Irene lunged again, slipped on the stones and went down.

Another's fingernails bit into my palm. My own grip pressed a thin hand. Beside me, Sarah, her face aflame with dread and excitement, whispered encouragement in French.

The viscount grinned horribly and thrust his rapier at the prone figure on the ground.

Irene rolled away like a kitten and catapulted to her feet. The viscount's thin blade buckled as it struck stones. He turned, or attempted to, but Irene's rapier—behind him—plucked the shirt from his back in one fluid gesture and sent it flying into the sky like a torn white flag of surrender.

He pivoted, his face red with fury and defeat, his bare chest heaving, his slack stomach revealed in all its hirsute glory.

We stared at him, we three supposed ladies. I don't know why Sarah Bernhardt would ogle the viscount's bare chest, but I knew why Irene and I found it so riveting.

For it was bare indeed . . . of any trace of a tattoo.

Chapter Thirty-three

NELL LOSES AN OSCAR

❧

The viscount's second rushed forward to swathe him in a cloak. Without a word, the viscount turned and stalked down the strand, his second accepting the rapier from Irene and reboxing it with its mate. Then he, too, left, following along the shore.

No one had noticed me.

Irene was accepting the hearty congratulations of the Italian second, whom the daylight revealed to be a lean, rather homely man with thinning steel-gray hair and rakish eyes.

Sarah released my hand to rush forward and shake Irene's. "My adorable Maurice could have done no better. You must tell me your secret."

Irene pushed the errant lock of hair off her forehead and smiled. "Let me introduce Signor Genturini, swordmaster for the La Scala Opera House in Milan. He is my secret weapon, and my once and present tutor. I telegraphed him, and he came instantly to refresh my languishing fencing skills."

Genturini bowed far more fluidly than his age would have suggested.

"I must study with you!" Sarah insisted, gazing intently into his eyes.

"My honor," said he, bowing as he took his leave.

"Yes," Irene said, "you could never play Hamlet convincingly without mastering a few intricacies of swordplay."

"I should make a most dashing Hamlet," Sarah responded, assuming a pose. "I see that, now that I have witnessed you in Hamlet guise, my dear Irene."

Irene turned to gather her hat and jacket, which lay on the pebbles, then noticed me. Little shocked my friend, but the sight of me did that morning.

"Nell? How on earth—?"

"I suspected some deviltry, so I followed you."

"Before dawn? From the hotel? Perhaps I underestimate your resourcefulness. Yet I cannot commend your actions, however well-meaning. The viscount could have recognized you. That would have ruined all . . . as your impetuosity did before."

"My impetuosity! Now that is the kettle—and a very large kettle—calling the little pot black! Besides, the viscount has never noticed my existence in any situation, nor did he here."

"My friends—" Sarah took each of our arms, thus inserting her slender person between us. "You debate suppositions. It is true that the mediocre man did not recognize my so amusing Miss Uxleigh. His loss. Nor did he recognize you or your true sex, Irene, so you have no reason to belabor poor little Nell."

I outdid Sarah Bernhardt by at least three inches. How had I acquired that inaccurate sobriquet?

"And," I went on to Irene, "before I am taken to task, I must inquire how you expected a dab of stage swordsmanship to see you through a duel."

"After I saw the viscount pummel his miserable equerry, I knew I could duel the cowardly bully with a knitting needle and prevail!"

"Ladies, ladies," Sarah remonstrated sweetly, as if her temper were never displayed. "All this is past and done. We have had a most piquant escapade. What else is there to do but go to the Ritz and indulge in a most lavish breakfast?"

And so we all three did. But first Irene and I returned to the Hotel de Paris. No one glanced at us twice in the lobby, a sign, perhaps, that Irene was most effective as nature intended her: in the female form.

While she dressed, I fetched Oscar's basket from its place by the parlor windows. Irene did not notice my new burden until we were ready to depart for the Ritz.

"Why, Nell, what are you doing with Oscar?"

"I am conveying him to Madame Sarah, as a gift."

And so I did. The actress was most gratifyingly thrilled with my presentation, and for once, Irene was a silent witness to *my* exploits.

"My dear Miss Uxleigh! How delightful! You know, many of my so-called friends are absolutely silly about my pets. They regard the lovely serpent as a low and vile creature. Some even express a horror at the sight of one, at sharing the same chamber with one!"

"No!" I murmured in a tone of shock that passed muster with Madame Sarah.

"Sooo, I am pleased that you are brave enough to offer me this little gift. Let us see the scamp better . . . oh! the darling." She had pulled the snake from the basket as easily I would withdraw a ribbon—an incredibly thin length of scaled green. Despite the creature's fragile appearance, it speedily settled several times around its new mistress's neck like a jade choker. "Has it a name?" Sarah inquired fondly, her voice vibrant despite the living necklace at her throat. I thought the serpent a great improvement over garlands of human eyes.

"I have chosen Oscar."

"Oscar!?" The Divine One looked startled, then laughed. "Why not? It goes well with 'Otto,' and I shall have a wicked glee when I introduce it to our mutual friend, Mr. Oscar Wilde!"

Sarah threw the willow basket to the floor, unwound her new pet and lifted the snake high above her head. It flicked a long tongue at her. Then she wrapped it around her head like a turban and there it happily stayed, its lithe green body forming an exotic diadem in her fountaining hair.

Even I could see some beauty in the small serpent at that moment, and I felt assured that the late Mr. Singh certainly would rest easy to know that his former pet had a congenial home. I was also sure that Mr. Oscar Wilde could not fail to admire his new namesake.

Irene and I returned, sans snake, to the Hotel de Paris before noon. She retired for a nap and I adjourned to the maps and tracings in the parlor. Oddly, I was aware of the absence of the snake's little basket by the window. Despite my certainty that Sarah would provide the serpent with a freedom, a suitability of diet, and an appreciation that I never could offer, I realized that its presence had exerted a subtle influence upon me to which I had been totally blind. The thought turned my mind to the absent Casanova and then to the quieter, yet equally dominant, presence of Lucifer.

I recalled the parrot's scabrous but somehow cheerful yellow beak, its scaled yet agile legs, its round eyes so like a snake's staring expression. I conjured the cat's pointed ears, black and furred on the exterior and deep pink within, its emerald eyes and jet-black nose and whiskers . . .

And then, while engaged in such idle remembrance of these dumb (in Casanova's case, not sufficiently dumb) beasts, I made such a stunning discovery that when I leaped to my feet, I knocked my chair over.

My weary eyes regarded a certain portion of the map of the Cretan coast, then the configuration of the conjoined compass letters. I wrenched off my pince-nez, as if doing so would allow me to see the incredible truth more plainly.

I blinked. I pinched the bridge of my nose, which ached from the press of the spectacles. I clapped my hands over my mouth and danced around the table. In short, I behaved as if possessed by a monkey god. It remains one of my sincerest gratitudes to this day that not even an Indian snake was present to observe me.

Then I gathered my papers and slipped back to my rooms, awaiting the proper moment for revelation and glory.

Chapter Thirty-four

A NOVEL CLIENT FOR ·HOLMES

''I do not wish, Nell," Irene said, "to contemplate Vis-. count D'Enrique's chest over dinner."

"It is not my desire to contemplate the subject at any time, but surely the absence of a tattoo must alter your theories."

"Trial and error, Nell, trial and error. To that process all theories must be subjected. I admit that the fact that the viscount is apparently as innocent of tattoos as Mary's little lamb forces my speculations in another direction. Although—" she balanced a dainty furl of the Hotel de Paris's famed mandarin ice on her dessert spoon "—speaking of other directions, I suppose it is possible that Viscount D'Enrique's tattoo is in an untraditional place."

"Next you will be invading the man's bath! Surely the point of the scheme was that the tattoos be located in the same spot on each conspirator."

Irene let the ice melt on her tongue while she considered. "Quite true," she said at last. I must discover another thread to lead us through this labyrinth."

I cleared my throat.

"Yes, Nell? You have a suggestion?"

"I may have found a new . . . filament. But where is Godfrey? You seem remarkably resigned to his absence."

"I am not resigned to his absence, but satisfied of his need to be absent. There is a difference. As for his return, I expect him hourly."

"Well, then, perhaps you can finish that extremely dilatory dessert and we can return to your rooms, where I will show you a most intriguing thing."

Irene never displayed curiosity when one wished her to; it was one of her more annoying traits. Still, eventually we repaired to her rooms, where I was compelled to reveal my grand discovery to an audience of one.

"You will notice that I have meshed the four letters of the compass sufficiently that their lavish scrollwork intertwines."

She studied my arrangement like the most docile of pupils.

"You will notice also that I have marked off on this map a portion of the Cretan coast."

Irene went so far as to extend a hand for my pince-nez. Then she leaned over the table and examined the indicated elements with satisfying intensity and a number of noncommittal murmurs.

"You may have noticed, too, the small, decorative lozenges that appear near the O and the N."

"No doubt some eccentricity of Singh's, whose letters are otherwise admirably Western, if a bit rococo."

"These are *not* lozenges, Irene! These are not slips of the needle. These . . . flyspecks, these mere flecks in the larger design of the letters, are equally recognizable, if we will but see it."

"Excellent, Nell! And . . . they are?"

I leaned back. "Islands. Or, I should say, islets. I believe them to be very small, not worth recording on most maps, in fact. They may even vanish and reappear with the tides. We are lucky that one of Godfrey's maps indicated their presence. Yet these islets are the key to the entire cipher."

"Wonderful! And how is that?"

Her air of enthusiasm did not deceive me; I must prove my case or it would hold no water.

"I now ask you to examine the compass letters as I have arranged them."

"You have drawn them so close together that they almost resemble a tangle of ribbons."

"Exactly, and most people would see only the tangle. But what does the tangle enclose? More, of what shape does the enclosed space remind you?"

Irene pursed her lips and tilted her head. She twisted the drawing sideways, then angled her head again.

"The lower tail of the N descends between the O and the E, and the S nests under the E. It makes a rather pleasing design, but—"

"I will give you a clue."

"Can't you simply tell me?"

"Do *you* ever simply tell me?"

Irene smiled. "You obviously wish me to see a shape. Is it animal, vegetable or mineral water?"

I ignored her teasing. "Animal."

"Animal. Then I would say a snake; certainly the letters are serpentine. Too obvious? Well, then, what animals would cross your mind? Ah—a parrot! Or a cat!"

I must have blinked, for she suddenly returned her gaze to the paper. "And the lozenges are eyes! Or the islets are eyes, rather. Yes, I see it. But it looks more like a fox than a cat, Nell."

I spun a map tracing to her side of the table. "To the stranded party, it looked like a fox from the overlook above. And see on this map, the French cartographer has written Bai de Oeil-de-Reynard. Eye-of-Fox Bay! If you turn the map—so

—the topography matches the inner area of the conjoined letters. I even think that here, where the line of the fox's nose nestles into the tail of the S, is where the treasure cave lay before its collapse."

"You astound me, Nell! What clever work. Now we know as well as any survivor of the wreck where the treasure is to be found. All we lack to a solution is the identity of the Quarter members and their director, the knowledge of who pursued the sailors in Jerseyman's Quarter to their deaths, and how—and who was responsible for filching the palace sealing wax all those years ago."

Her list quite deflated me. "But now we know—"

"Exactly where the blackmailer will direct the prince's expedition, which we had only to discover by joining it. Oh, those deciphered tattoos will make recovery of the treasure surer, but as for identifying the villain . . ."

"You still believe that one controlling hand has directed all these events?"

"One person has at least set many of them in motion, yes. This was such an untidy scheme at the outset—a happenstance alliance of high- and low-born, a treasure lost beyond any one member's ability to claim it, and the wait of years for the means to raise it; the folderol of the tattoos, clearly devised by a subtle intellect to pacify the party and send its members off thinking the plan safeguarded by their very own skins; the special sealing wax; the drama of the severed fingers, the sailors' special method of identity.

"None of this was necessary, Nell, save to disperse the party with a false sense of security amid the trappings of a melodrama. The problem has not been Quarters and tattoos, but method and opportunity. Until the prince's oceanic expeditions developed methods of deep-sea exploration to rival the fictional exploits of Jules Verne's Captain Nemo, our mastermind has had to forestall the others and plan his own extraction of the treasure."

"But the viscount has no tattoo! Surely he would not be exempt."

"No, he would not be exempt. For the plan to work, its author would have to subscribe to all particulars—and publicly. Our man bears the mark of Singh upon his flesh, and also the burden of Singh's death upon his head; for why was the Indian killed except to ensure that no more Quarter members' relatives, such as Louise, could be brought into the equation? The loyal Jerseyman's crude approach alerted Louise's uncle to the treasure, stirred our interest, possibly drew the inestimable Sherlock Holmes into the Montpensier affair, and has nearly overturned the entire conspiracy."

At that instant the door to the suite flew open. On the threshold paused a great bear of a man with a mottled face. My heart nearly leaped from my throat. It was the second man I had spied following Dr. Hoffman.

"Quickly, Irene! The revolver!"

The intruder was undismayed. He took a giant step toward us, then laughed. "Don't tell me you don't recognize me?" he demanded, looking directly at me.

"Of course I do! You are the individual who followed Dr. Hoffman and myself the other day."

He laughed again. "For what purpose, do you think?" he asked with a leer.

"Who knows? Irene, the revolver! This man may be dangerous. He did follow Dr. Hoffman, as he boasts."

She remained by the table. "Why on earth would you neglect to mention him to me, Nell?"

"You neglected to mention a great deal more to me," I countered.

"My omissions did not come clattering into our rooms uninvited, like this ungainly fellow."

"For heaven's sake, do not debate it, Irene! Get the revolver! This may be the sinister intelligence you sense at the heart of the web."

At that the visitor laughed again, and Irene joined him.

I grasped the top rail of my chair, thinking to have it handy for defense.

"What I have come to report"—the brute in the doorway stepped closer—"is that Sherlock Holmes has led me to the maker of the palace sealing wax."

"How wonderful!" Irene clasped her hands like the rescued soprano in an opera before rushing into the villain's arms.

"Godfrey!" I complained as the light dawned. "You quite terrified me. I thought you were peacefully poking about in moldy records in search of shipwrecks."

He released Irene long enough to turn his hideous face in my direction. "I've found the wreck as well, in between shuffling behind the one-armed limping man who is scuttling after Dr. Hoffman. Or rather"—he turned to Irene—"I've found an obituary for Claude Montpensier, which says that he survived the wreck of the yacht *Solace* in eighteen sixty-nine. So at least we know the ship's name, if we are no wiser to the other passengers."

"What of Sherlock Holmes and the sealing wax?" Irene asked impatiently. "Are you sure it is Holmes?"

"The follower's a subtle prey to hunt, but of a size to be Holmes. I recognized a certain kinship in our common eccentricities. We smell of unlikeliness. Whoever he is, was, or will be, he has led me to one . . ."—Godfrey patted his well-padded person until he had extracted a grimy scrap of paper—"one Hyppolyte Cremieux, proprietor of a tiny chemist and stationer's shop near the base of the city."

To demonstrate his success, Godfrey reached into his torn pocket and extracted waxy shavings in the distinctive black-and-crimson swirling pattern.

"How did you acquire these?" Irene asked admiringly.

He lifted a worn and oversized boot to display its wax-impressed sole. "By accident. The floor was strewn with it. Once I realized this must be the source or a waystation for the palace wax, I set M. Cremieux—a frail old fellow—on a hunt for a nonexistent English herb among his dusty shelves. In a workroom behind the shop, I found the wax we seek, cut into cakes, wrapped in paper like soap, and closed with the palace seal."

"We have neglected the pursuit of the sealing wax between marrying off our young lovers and the shock of poor Singh's death. How on earth did Sherlock Holmes manage to find such an obscure place?" Irene studied the shoe, then frowned delicately. "Perhaps you could shed your disguise and tell us the rest in person."

Godfrey obliged by shutting the door to the hall at last and heading for the bedchamber in the rolling gait that I had observed on the street.

"Irene, if what Godfrey implies—"

"That Sherlock Holmes is the one-armed, limping man of whom Dr. Hoffman complained? If true, it is disturbing news. Most disturbing."

"I know you fear discovery—"

She whirled to face me, her dark eyes afire with suspicion. "But does he *not* fear discovery? Why does he invite it? A one-armed man with a limp, indeed! I suspected that description the instant I heard it. You saw Mr. Holmes play the humble cleric in St. John's Wood; it was the merest chance that his trick with the smoke bomb alerted me to his real identity. If Sherlock Holmes did not wish to be known when in disguise, I believe it would be so."

"You are saying the disguise is too blatant?"

Irene snorted as delicately as a fawn, although as disparagingly as a hod carrier. "A child could see through it!" She conveniently ignored the fact that I had not, nor had I seen through Godfrey's newest likeness. Her eyes narrowed further. "Why did Dr. Hoffman not penetrate it? Or was he meant to, and did?"

"I don't understand, Irene. You make this sound like a game within a game."

"Exactly. A game within a game, just as the compass letters must nest within each other to attain their greatest meaning." She gave me one of her extraordinarily luminous smiles. "You must tell Godfrey about your clever discovery, when he is himself again."

"He is," said the subject of our conversation, returning with his cuffs still rolled up from washing the last of the impersonation from his hands and face. "Do you mean to say that my astounding discovery has been eclipsed by Nell's detective work with the maps?"

"I would not go so far as to say 'eclipsed'," said I.

"Nonsense." Irene would have none of my modesty. "You must explain it to Godfrey."

Which I did, much enjoying his initial confusion and dawning delight as the linking of the map with the conjoined tattoos became clear.

"Splendidly done, Nell! You have solved the cipher at the heart of this matter." Godfrey leaned over the table to study the map, his handsome self again. "You know, Irene, we could overleap the whole tedious process of avoiding Mr. Holmes and of finding the conspirators and dash over to Crete to claim the treasure for ourselves. It is, after all, fair game."

"And still difficult to put one's hands on, or why would the blackmailer need to divert the prince's oceanic equipment to the site? Besides, consider the cataclysm that buried the hoard twenty years ago, and the deaths that have followed. Perhaps it is cursed."

"No!" said I. "I will not have a curse mixed in with all this stew. Tattoos and sealing wax and Sherlock Holmes provide enough nonsense at once."

Irene suddenly sat down at the table. "Nell is right. We must focus on the central knot. The question remains; why has Sherlock Holmes been drawn into this farrago? Why is he seeking sealing wax, and how did he find the manufacturer?"

"He followed Dr. Hoffman to the chemist's shop," Godfrey said. "This elderly Cremieux has been a patient of the doctor's since Hoffman began practice twenty-some years ago. An arthritic affliction runs in the Cremieux family, and this Hyppolyte has long been too frail to leave the premises."

"Why did Dr. Hoffman not say he knew the source of the wax?"

"It is secretly manufactured. I searched the workrooms for some time before I found the bricks of wax under a cloth. Luckily, old Cremieux is quite deaf, or he would have heard the extent of my search. Dr. Hoffman, besides, treats the man in his adjacent rooms, not in the shop. It is a process involving hand and foot baths, noxious herbs and manipulation."

"Or—!" Irene slapped her open hand to the tabletop. "Perhaps Sherlock Holmes did not follow Dr. Hoffman *to* the chemist's, but *from* it. That must be it! He is working backward to our muddle of blackmail, murder and sunken treasure—and maps. We must press on before he discovers the real problem underlying the Montpensier matter!"

Irene's amber eyes grew dark and dreamy as she gazed at the window. "An unknown blackmailer is part of the scheme; the loose end of the Viscount D'Enrique, who is close to the situation but barren of tattoos, or at least of the right tattoo in the proper spot; the dead sailors, two of whom died as if fleeing a demon, yet no obvious source of demons has appeared—except Singh's snake, and Sarah has that now."

Godfrey frowned, his agile legal mind balking at the apparent non sequiturs of her musings. Irene went on.

"Louise Montpensier and her uncle also came to this site. We have no knowledge of the state of Edouard Montpensier's skin, but it seems unlikely that he joined the tattooed brotherhood when his brother died, or Jerseyman would not have so forcefully inducted Louise."

I shrugged at Godfrey, who shrugged in turn at me.

"We have on the fringes, embroidering this motley group, as it were, the wealthy Alice, Duchesse de Richelieu, and her Grimaldi prince. And we may have undiscovered Quarter members lurking nearby." Irene sat suddenly straighter. "Or have we? Ah, there is no hope for it. I must consult Sherlock Holmes."

I turned to Godfrey, mouth gaping, to find that he had turned to me with the same mute but unlatched expression.

Chapter Thirty-five

IN ANOTHER'S GUISE

❧

Sarah Bernhardt swept into the Norton suite the following afternoon with her rice-powder pallor, her flaming golden hair swathed in scarves, and her painted crimson lips pouting, or—as the French more elegantly put it—pursed into *une petite moue.*

"Such an insufferable man, my dear Miss Uxleigh," she complained, sitting on the green brocade sofa, which clashed wonderfully with her cerulean silk gown. "I am amazed that he is civilized enough to speak French."

The Divine Sarah wielded her gold-headed walking stick like a scepter, an expression of frozen hauteur making her usually mobile face resemble that of a disheveled corpse.

"These English—pardon me, *cherie*—are so stiff. Your Mr. Olmes as good as told me that I was a bored prima donna and had no problem worth consulting him upon."

"What did you say?" I breathed.

"That I am a dramatic actress and not an operatic prima donna. That I do not sing publicly, that I have never sung, that I never intend to sing, although I may play Hamlet."

"What did he say?"

"That Ophelia may be more . . . up my alley?" She dispensed with the scarves in a series of gestures as airy as they. "I told him that I have played this part in Paris already. I then asked him if he had been in Paris and he said, 'Briefly, Madame'." The Divine Sarah leaned closer, her golden-brown eyes twinkling wickedly. "'Recently, Monsieur Olmes?' said I. 'Recently enough,' said he, clamping his teeth down very hard. A difficult man to seduce, I think."

I looked around for Godfrey, but he had gone out on another of his mysterious errands.

Madame Sarah laughed, that rich, unbridled laugh that was so recognizably hers. It was odd to hear it issue from Irene, who now stripped two or three gaudy rings from her fingers and deposited them in a sweetmeat dish by the sofa.

Still laughing softly, Irene collapsed deeper into the cushions, looking more like Sarah Bernhardt than ever, except for her citrine-colored eyes. She had even augmented her perfectly straight nose to the autocratic sweep of the Divine One's.

"Did you not tremble, Irene, masquerading as Sarah Bernhardt before the foremost detective in Europe?"

"No. A woman of such an exaggerated theatrical type does not appeal to Mr. Holmes on any level, moral or personal. His own dramatic instincts are cleaner, more surgical. He is a master of the understatement, while Sarah is always her own larger-than-life poster. Another's disdain is one's best disguise. Mr. Holmes considered me a silly, self-indulgent female not worth worrying about, beyond showing me the door."

"But what did you learn from this masquerade?"

"One, that he has come here from Paris. Two, that he is aware of the Montpensier case, as I suspected."

"How did you learn that?"

Sarah surfaced in an instant. "I plan to produce a play, Monsieur Olmes. A great *tragédie*. I have heard of so sad a case, a beautiful young girl killed by her wicked uncle, drowned in the Seine. I wonder if you could solve it for me so I have an ending for my drama."

"And?"

"He grew most stern and informed me that while the newspapers may profit from private tragedy, it behooves the rest of us to respect it. Perhaps I should search the classical sources for my plots, as did the Bard of Avon. Had I ever considered playing. Lady Macbeth? I seemed to share her bloodthirstiness."

"Then?"

"I rose to leave, carelessly dropping the invitation from Alice to my palace concert—sealing-wax side up. Well, my dear Nell, he had it in a flash and returned it to me, only glancing at the sealing wax, so eager was he to show me to the door. Perhaps it was my perfume." Irene fanned herself with a languid hand, wafting some tiger-lily scent toward my undefended nostrils.

"Perhaps he smelled a rat," I replied.

"*Touché*, Nell!" Irene always admired a well-delivered insult. "But you see what I have learned?"

"No, I do not, other than that Mr. Holmes is a sensible and upright gentleman, one not to be swayed by the wiles of a Scarlet Woman of the Stage."

Irene smiled tolerantly. "Don't you see? He *knows* that the wax belongs to the palace. Yet he has not the least notion of the wider reaches of this web. He is following a single filament—Louise Montpensier's death and her uncle's disappearance—from Paris. Somehow he has obtained the letters sent to her uncle and has had the good fortune—or the brilliance—to find the sealing wax first."

Irene rubbed her hands together in a most lusty Lady Macbeth manner. "Now Sherlock Holmes is working his way to our part of the puzzle, and he does not yet suspect any of it! It is not delicious?"

"It does not sound at all edible, Irene, but most dangerous and dishonest. What did you think of him?"

"Mr. Holmes?"

"You did not call on Mr. Gladstone, the prime minister!"

She leaned back, coiled into her gorgeous Byzantine robes like a girlish Sarah. "He is not handsome."

"No."

"Arresting, rather. When I first glimpsed him, years ago, I said that he had a busy, interesting face."

"I would have to consult my diaries on the precise phrasing."

"No matter. His mind is like a clockworks, always ticking and whirring. I fear that in the presence of an ultra-feminine woman it ticks in yawning, four-four time. I was as bland to his detective constitution as camomile tea. I bored him! I presented a nigh perfect impersonation of the most alluring actress of our age, and I bored the man silly!" She laughed rapturously. "He is remarkable. We must hurry or he will anticipate us all, as he almost did in London."

"Hurry at what, Irene? What is there for us to prove?"

She sat up and spoke in her normal tones. "We must see that Louise and Jerseyman have claim to whatever treasure is discovered. We must ensure Louise and Mr. Winter's desires for independence and foil Louise's uncle permanently. We must absolve her aunt of all complicity in the illusion of her niece's murder. We must protect Alice from the revelations of the blackmailer by unveiling him—or her—and then alert the prince to the ulterior purpose for his expedition."

She frowned. "And I really do think that we must find out how Sherlock Holmes discovered the manufacturer of the sealing wax, for therein lies the key to the whole problem. Oh, poor, prescient Mr. Holmes, you begin innocently at the exact point where all my efforts are leading me!"

Chapter Thirty-six

A NORTON TOO MANY

I **a m** suffocating from fine weather.

This unrelenting sunlight is clouding my faculties of reason. Perhaps some perfume still lingers from the overbearing presence of Madame Sarah Bernhardt, who, I suspect, visited me yesterday to exercise her colossal vanity, for she had no discernibly legitimate reason to call.

Of course, such women are often oblique, but something nags at my memory of that encounter. If I were in Baker Street, I would turn to my violin—or to the hypodermic needle Watson so dislikes.

However, the air cleared when Le Villard arrived today. His telegram came this morning and the man himself followed on the heels of it, such is the wonder of modern rail travel.

"My dear Holmes!" He grasped my hand. "You look pale. Can it be that the charms of what the poet Liegeard has recently christened 'the Blue Coast' have not pleased you?"

"Charms are in the eye of the beholder, Le Villard. I am not here to stroll. In fact, I have hardly shown my own face since I arrived."

"You must evolve a monograph on the art of disguise," the detective said.

"My dear fellow, monographs occupy my idle moments.

This is not one of them. I may shortly find it necessary to leave this place of coastal dalliance, however heavenly its color."

"Then you will have to drop the Montpensier murder?"

"On the contrary. I have one or two theories that require proving. I have telegraphed to various points of travel in Europe, England and America."

"America?"

I smiled at Le Villard's incredulity. That same naive, albeit flattering, air of surprise pervaded the tone of his frequent footnotes to my translated monographs, all of his explications singing the praises of the author's brilliant methodology.

Despite his Celtic quickness, Le Villard was as easy to confuse as Inspector Lestrade. "When I have assembled the necessary facts, I will reveal them. As for writing a monograph on disguise, I am not interested in arming the criminal element more than it already is. However, since my stay in Monaco, I have learned a good deal about sealing wax. There may be a new monograph in that."

"Sealing wax? Oh, you mean the strange stuff on the letters sent to Edouard Montpensier?"

"Strange stuff indeed, Le Villard! Did you know that there are three hundred and sixty-eight varieties of sealing wax in Europe alone? In this case, the sandalwood scent put me on the proper trail. Such a scent is not favored in northern Europe, so I was pointed to the Mediterranean. From there it was simply a matter of making the proper inquiries. Also, Edouard Montpensier has been seen about Monte Carlo, making his own inquiries."

"Montpensier! Here? You amaze me, my friend."

I could not help smiling wearily. "Have you ever viewed a piece of embroidery from the wrong side, Le Villard? All one sees is an untidy pattern of knots, and colors scattered randomly.

"So an investigative puzzle offers first the underside of

mystifying knots. Yet there is always a pattern. The missing Montpensier girl's father died in Monte Carlo. The distinctive sealing wax upon the strange letters sent to her uncle is made in Monte Carlo. It is not amazing at all that Edouard Montpensier should hurry here; he is but one knot in a scheme of many that will make perfect sense once the matter is turned right side up."

"You say 'missing.' You suspect that Louise lives?"

"I suspect that it is possible. And then there is another knot whose presence nags at me—these English Nortons who briefly entered the affair in Paris."

"I admit that Mr. Norton piqued my suspicions of Louise's possible survival, but this pair's involvement has been purely peripheral."

"They are still knotted into the fabric. The name 'Norton' is exceedingly common in England, but I have reason to remember it from a case not long past. I first dismissed a connection; I do not believe in coincidence. Now I am not so sure. I have been visited by a very commanding woman, an actress; she has put me in mind of—what was this Mr. Norton's first name, Monsieur Le Villard?"

"I . . . I do not recall. Of course my notes in Paris . . ." Le Villard's hands slapped his sides in self-disgust. "What foolishness I have shown."

"You have no recall of the Christian name?"

"Ah, Gervaise, Guy—?"

"Godfrey?"

Le Villard's dark eyes squinted. "Perhaps. I confess that Madame Norton was so distracting that I did not much notice the husband, or the woman who resides with them."

"Ah. In what way distracting?"

"Monsieur Holmes, as you know, we French are connoisseurs of female beauty. Madame Norton is one to make any man who meets her regret that she—or he—is married. Her form is very perfection; her hair, her eyes—a medley of the shades of the sweetest honey, gold and brown, glossy and rich. Her voice rivals that of the Divine Sarah herself. Beyond this, she is intelligent and charming. A woman of great quality. She could have been a queen."

"So she would have been—pardon, Le Villard. I compliment your descriptive powers, although you must concentrate more on detail rather than on the overall effect if you wish to apply your observations to police work. In this case, it has sufficed; I believe I have met the lady."

"Then the Norton involvement is not innocent?"

"I cannot say. Nor can I yet say what the full implications of this affair are. Certainly Madame Montpensier is innocent."

"You relieve me, my dear Holmes. At least I was not unwise to heed Monsieur Norton's warning."

"The unfortunate Mr. Norton."

"Why do you say that?"

I smiled again. "It is an unfortunate man who stands in the shadow of a beautiful wife; then, again, it would be a great advantage in detective work. I myself often wish for invisibility."

"But Holmes, you accomplish it superbly through the art of disguise."

I nodded in acknowledgement. "I must consider these matters, Le Villard, and then we will act."

"You see a quick end to the Montpensier affair, then?"

"Oh, to the Montpensier matter, certainly."

"There is another?"

"There is always another, my dear Le Villard."

Chapter Thirty-seven

AN UNPRECEDENTED ENCOUNTER

❧

What came to Irene was Sherlock Holmes.

"Godfrey!" she said at breakfast the next day, shooing the birds from her chair with the lace-flounced sleeve of her pearl-colored velvet morning gown. "We must pursue the avenue that Sherlock Holmes has opened for us."

"The chemist who makes the sealing wax, you mean?"

"I do."

"But, Irene," I objected over my morning cup of tea, "the sealing wax is surely a side issue now. The viscount has nothing to do with it; the prince's yacht sails within the week. We have a great deal more to worry about than a mere means when the end itself is in sight."

"If it is worth the attention of other investigators, it is worth ours."

"Ours?" Godfrey inquired.

"Yours, then." Irene smiled bewitchingly. "Perhaps you should revisit this—" She glanced at me. I riffled my current diary for the name, then showed it to her. "—this Hyppolyte Cremieux and discover what Mr. Sherlock Holmes found so fascinating about the man and his sealing wax. You no longer need lurk about in disguise, but may go as your own dashing self."

"How refreshing." Godfrey rose from the table. "Have you any idea of what I should look for beyond the obvious?"

"None," Irene admitted blithely. "Of course I would be most interested in knowing the direction that Mr. Holmes's inquiries took."

"Of course." Godfrey was off with a last significant glance to me.

"What shall *we* do today, Irene?" I queried.

"I have not decided." Irene began stirring her coffee, although her customary cream and sugar were well blended already.

Then she looked up, and her features sharpened with interest and alarm, changing from idleness to utter attention within the instant. She grasped my wrist as if she would break it.

"Nell, you have seen Sherlock Holmes in person."

"I have seen him. We were both of us 'in person' at that first occasion at Godfrey's chambers. Irene—!"

"You would recognize the gentleman again?"

"I should assume so; a year and a half does not ordinarily work great changes on most people."

"Would he recognize you?"

"Possibly not. I was of no great significance to him, although he—"

"Nell, do stop chattering and listen. Look slowly, but quickly; that is, don't be too tardy about it or we shall lose our chance. Behind you. Tell me that is not he!"

I turned. That is the only way to look behind one, although Irene's hiss indicated that my turn was not sufficiently discreet to satisfy her. There on the terrace many people were lounging at tables, talking, laughing, and walking toward the promenade.

One tall, top-hatted figure drew my eye. It was weaving between the tables, drawing nearer—but then, so were other gentlemen. The terrace of the Hotel de Paris attracted almost as many pedestrians as did the promenade.

"I cannot be certain, Irene. He had removed his hat when I saw him before, for one thing. For another, I have not on my pince-nez, and for yet a third thing, it was his voice that I most remember, so crisp and remote in its way."

"Oh, *do* be still!" Irene's hand throttled my abused wrist. "And look back at me! Of course it's he, and he's coming this very way. He shall pass right by us. Try to steal a glimpse of him then."

I did as instructed, my heart beginning to beat as rapidly as a rabbit's, thanks to Irene's air of urgency. She had languorously obscured her face by putting a hand to her temple, but her eyes glowed brighter than tiger's-eye gemstones. I could almost see her figurative tail twitch.

I prepared to snatch a look as the presence passed, save that it paused instead.

"Good day, ladies," said a voice I shall never forget. "I understand from the porter that I have the honor to address Madame Norton and Miss Huxleigh."

"You also have the advantage of us," Irene said, looking up. Only I would have detected that she was slightly breathless.

A small smile stretched those thin lips. "I am already known to you: Sherlock Holmes of Baker Street, London. I believe that you are more than sufficiently familiar with the exact address, Madame."

In the ensuing pause, I attempted to glance casually at the gentleman looming behind me. It could not be done without cricking my neck, so I continued watching his reflection as mirrored in Irene's expression.

Sheer shock had given way to a wary kind of amusement. "Pray be seated, sir," she said. "We have just finished breakfast."

He took Godfrey's vacated chair and removed his hat,

revealing a head of black hair that matched his strong eyebrows. I was able to observe him as minutely as he no doubt dissected others in the course of his cases. His eyes were gray, but not the open, amiable, silver-gray of Godfrey's. They viewed the world closely, as if looking through a microscope.

His long, thin fingers moved idly over the brim of his beaver hat and his walking-stick handle. All of his senses seemed restless, as if eager to be put to use. Certainly his eyes were gathering in every detail of our tabletop, of Irene, of myself, in glances that struck like summer lightning. Then he spoke again in that light, slightly high voice that barely veiled an almost chronic impatience.

"When I said that I had the honor to address Madame Norton, I might have been more explicit. I have the honor to address Madame Godfrey Norton, *née* Irene Adler."

Irene's hands fanned eloquently. "Is that so remarkable a thing, my dear Mr. Holmes?"

A smile tightened the corners of his mouth. "It is, when the newspapers would have you and your husband dead, Madame."

"The newspapers report many fictions as fact." Irene's honey-brown eyes grew ingenuous. "Is there some matter in which you wish to consult me?"

His laughter startled the pigeons into abandoning their posts on the nearby vacant-chair rails. "Indeed there is, Madame. There are many matters involving yourself that I would inquire into, but circumstances and civilized behavior allow me to pursue only one."

"How unfortunate."

"For myself, or for you?"

She shrugged, a slight, French shrug, and allowed her eyelids to drop for a moment. "For both of us perhaps, Mr. Holmes."

He looked away, then spoke, the brisk detective. "I wish to know all concerning the disappearance of Louise Montpensier of Paris."

"A rather sweeping request, Mr. Holmes."

"I never ask for crumbs when I can have the whole cake. Come, come, Madame, you are too clever to deny the obvious. You and your husband returned Mademoiselle Louise to the family home after a day's absence. Her disappearance came on the heels of that incident. You must tell me what you know."

"Why?"

He considered. "Most people, when confronted, would prefer to make a clean breast of a rather messy matter. I suspect that Louise Montpensier is not dead; at the least, you could speak to spare her aunt further suspicion. The woman is utterly innocent, though I cannot say the same for the uncle."

"Madame Montpensier will be cleared very shortly, I promise you."

"Perhaps, but in the meantime, where is Louise? I believe that you know, Madame, and that you have always known."

"Not always, Mr. Holmes. But I know that she is safe and happy now, as she was not before."

"And her adventurous absence?"

Irene's face dropped its mask of taut amusement. "The girl attempted to drown herself in the Seine, sir. Godfrey, my husband"—Mr. Holmes made a swift, dismissive gesture to indicate he knew that—"saved her. Then we returned her to her home, hoping that her family would not need to know of a young woman's temporarily overwrought feelings."

"Why did she attempt to take her life?"

"A young man whose attentions were not welcome to her uncle. At Louise's age, such impasses can seem insurmountable."

Irene had carefully adhered to the truth, as far as it went.

"And now she is—?"

"Where she wishes to be. She will notify her family as soon as possible. Or I can have her notify you, so you will not be defrauded of your solution."

The thin lips pursed, then an arctic twinkle lit those icy-gray eyes. "I detect another romantic elopement here, Madame. You grow overfond of the device."

Irene smiled. "It *is* a bit melodramatic, Mr. Holmes, yet I do have that weakness."

The walking stick lightly tapped the terrace flagstones. "There's more to it than the resolution of Louise Montpensier's romantic escapades. I have seen the so-called mysterious letters, which are as plain as child's play. Laughable as the scheme is, there is great gain in it—for someone. I do not imply yourself. I would imagine you to be quite nicely fixed now."

"Retirement has been kind to me."

"You must chafe," he said suddenly, leaning forward intently, "at the pseudonymous life. I myself find extended idleness an . . . agony. You cannot perform on the concert stage as long as you allow that fiction about the train wreck to persist unchallenged. What else remains for you, but to meddle in other people's affairs?"

"You do not call your own efforts meddling."

"I am a professional."

"As am I."

"No, Madame. You *were* a professional, a professional opera singer. Now you are barred from your vocation. It is no wonder that you have taken up an avocation."

"And that is?"

"You heard me: meddling."

"I think, Mr. Holmes, that it is you who meddles in my affairs, rather than the other way around."

"Then you admit that you are embroiled in something!"

"I admit that I have pursuits I follow, that is all."

"Hmm." Sherlock Holmes gazed morosely at his amber-headed stick. "You have been indiscreet in Monte Carlo. You have drawn attention to yourself by consorting with palace hangers-on. You have even sung in semi-public circumstances."

"What business is it of yours what I do, and where?"

His smile came quickly. "None, save that I would have attended your concert. I am a music lover, did you know?"

This time Irene blinked. "No, I did not. I must notify you of my next performance."

"Your next *musical* performance. I believe you have others, less meant for public consumption," he said obliquely. "So you will keep your knowledge to yourself. All the better! I do not like too easy a trail to follow." Sherlock Holmes rose to his full, imposing height. "I would remind you that if I have discovered your former identity, it is on the tongue-tips of all Monte Carlo."

"We will be leaving soon," she said, surprising me.

"I trust your cabinet photograph of a certain royal Bohemian personage and yourself rests safely."

"I have destroyed it."

Mr. Holmes frowned. "Can you trust the king to forget you?"

"It is not necessary. I have forgotten him."

He smiled to himself. "He has not forgotten you. Only recently he sent me a gold snuffbox in token of his undying gratitude. For nothing."

"In place of the ring you would not accept?"

"How did you know that?" Mr. Holmes regarded me for an instant, then turned back to Irene. "Your accomplices need tutoring. I perceived that I was followed to the chemist's."

"I was not able to do it myself. But then, you wished to attract our attention."

"True. I wanted to be led somewhere, and I found you at

the bottom of it. I hoped to learn more of your real purpose in being here."

"And have you?"

"Time will tell, although I do not have much of it to waste on a tangle of the sort I suspect you are following. More urgent matters call. However, if you persist in crossing my path, it will not be to your ultimate advantage, I assure you. Prior acquaintance will not sway me from my duty."

"Nor will it me." Irene rose on that avowal.

Mr. Holmes studied her face as he might a Gainsborough portrait in a gallery. There was much of the character reader in his scrutiny, but something also of the connoisseur admiring an elusive treasure.

Irene smiled slowly, her beauty and her certainty radiating like sunlight. It was the power of the performer that she unleashed on the famous detective. If he was not totally immune, neither was he susceptible.

He bowed to take his leave, first nodding at me. "I bid you good morning, Madame Irene."

"I have already found it so," said she.

Then he was gone, his footsteps fading into the general hubbub around us.

"Irene! You heard him. We must meddle no more!"

"Nonsense, Nell. Even Sherlock Holmes could not make swift sense of the many threads we investigate. When Louise sends a cablegram from America to her aunt, his interest in the affair will be satisfied."

"He will not take crumbs when he can have the whole cake; you heard him yourself. He strikes me as a man of his word."

"Of course he is, but I am too far ahead of him. He works from the narrow tip of the iceberg downward; I have plumbed the depths and need only to crown my achievement with the final peak of revelation."

Irene paused to let her features reflect her triumphal apex of emotion. "And now I am at last ready to orchestrate a climax to our diffuse drama that will amaze and baffle one and all, thanks to Mr. Sherlock Holmes."

Chapter Thirty-eight

THROUGH A DUCHESS'S WINDOW GLASS

❦

Madame Sarah Bernhardt held a most atypical soiree two nights later in the salon of her friend Alice, Duchesse de Richelieu, at the instigation of another friend, Madame Irene Norton.

Only a carefully chosen few were invited: the hostess, Godfrey and Irene, myself, the odious Viscount D'Enrique, Dr. Hoffman, the captain of the prince's yacht (one Jules Rousseau), Jerseyman—and Oscar, the ingratiating serpent.

Not every guest's appearance was voluntary. Viscount D'Enrique, I understood, had been loath to have anything to do with the woman whose "son" had bested him in a duel until Alice made clear that his future good graces with the ruling family of Monte Carlo depended upon his attendance.

Jerseyman also was reluctant, having been dredged by Godfrey from some musty bistro, where he still mourned his dead companion with a wine bottle. He looked rather the worse for it, despite the clean suit jacket that had been forced upon his spare form. A wrinkled red kerchief substituted for a tie and collar at his stringy throat, making him more than ever resemble an organ-grinder's over-attired monkey.

Outside the villa, the heavy sapphire-velvet curtain of the Monte Carlo night was ruffled by the winds that can buffet the Blue Coast. The shutters rattled, while heavy foliage scratched at the walls for entrance.

Whether by accident or by Irene's native sense of drama, the ladies' attire was a study in somber tones. The three other than myself wore shades of mourning, although gentlemen would hardly note thât. Alice was in a becoming lavender, Sarah in a changeable purple silk, and Irene in a rich black-and-heliotrope watered tafetta. They resembled a youthful convening of the Three Fates, if those mythical hags could be imagined in the prime of life.

Perhaps it was my imagination—my presentiment that at this artificial social occasion, old puzzles would be solved and a new culprit revealed as by a magician's agile hand—but the scene seemed painted in the jaded hues of the decadent bistro artists. The ample candlelight hardened Alice's pastel features and sharpened Sarah Bernhardt's white-powdered, feral face to a skull-like mask. Irene, among them the darkest of hair and dress, seemed as solemn as a heavily robed judge.

I, of course, wore my old mouse-gray India silk figured with yellow blossoms; since the comedy of Irene's assumptions concerning Dr. Hoffman's purported romantic interest in me, I had renounced female fripperies . . . and was not much noticed.

By the time we assembled in Alice's parlor, evening candlelight had dimmed its sunny color to a sad jaundice. I no longer wondered that yellow was sometimes considered a decadent color.

Alice served saffron champagne in crystal flutes, which was sipped with a kind of nervous temperance.

No servant entered the room, adding to the sense of conspiracy. Dr. Hoffman took the champagne tray from the butler at the double doors and brought it around to the guests himself.

Jerseyman squinted his disgust at this effete liquor, but wrapped a grimy hand around a glass stem anyway. The viscount clutched his flute as if wishing for a weapon to replace it. Captain Rousseau, the only newcomer to this cast of characters, about whose inclusion Irene had been extremely sphinx-like, sat stiffly on a fragile Directorre sofa, the foot of his glass balanced upon his knee.

Oscar contented himself with decorating Sarah's shoulders and disconcerting the guests by raising his head every so often to hiss mournfully.

"I confess, gentlemen," the Divine Sarah began in a throbbing tone, "to having lured you here under false pretenses. This evening's amusement will not be the usual melange of frivolous chatter and gaiety, but rather a demonstration conducted by my esteemed friend and sister of the stage, Madame Irene Norton."

Irene bowed her head modestly. "Captain Rousseau, I present this portion of a map. Does it mean anything to you?"

She handed him my sketch of that portion of the Cretan shoreline I had matched to the compass rose.

The captain, a stout man in his fifties with old-fashioned grizzled mutton chops, extracted a pair of spectacles and frowned at the paper Irene offered.

"'Tis a map, all right. This coastline could be anywhere on the seven seas, Madame."

"It belongs to this one."

The captain's head shook somberly. "A mere patch of a map tells me nothing. Have you any notion of how many jagged coastal miles of North Africa, not to mention the boot of Italy and the nose of Greece, skirt the Mediterranean?"

"No," Irene admitted sweetly. She took back my sketch of the pertinent coastline and offered it to Jerseyman.

The sailor precariously set down his champagne flute and smoothed the paper over his sailcloth-trousered knee. He reversed the map, then tilted it left and right, after which he looked up with a grin.

"Aye, that's the spot, Madame. Fox-Eye Bay. I've spent

half me lifetime staring at the image of that curlicue of coast on me shut eyelids. That's where I was swept ashore when we floundered in sixty-nine."

"I don't doubt it." Irene turned to the captain. "I wished to demonstrate, sir, that while general seamanship does not qualify one to recognize every bit of coast roundabout, even a simple sailor can commit a particular spot to memory if he has reason to."

"There's no mystery in it, Madame," the captain said gruffly, pulling a pipe from his frock-coat pocket. "Seamanship's a matter of memory at bottom, as well as a nose for the weather."

"Oh, but there is a mystery in it, an old and rather dangerous one. My husband, Godfrey, shall continue."

Handsome in his evening dress, Godfrey stood like a robed barrister at the bar, a paper of notations in his hand. "We have," said he, "heard a tale of treasure from this, er, thirsty seafaring gentleman before us." He indicated Jerseyman, who was in the process of draining his glass.

"He told of a pleasure boat that sank nearly twenty years ago, drowning many of the passengers and crew. The survivors, cast ashore, discovered, purely by the accident of their marooning, a massive golden hoard."

Sarah Bernhardt came suddenly upright on the sofa onto which she had subsided.

The duchess was also shocked. "Irene said nothing of this!"

"That is why it is a mystery," my friend herself answered them, "and why we meet here to solve it."

"But you said you would settle the matter of my . . . private affairs possibly becoming public."

"And I will, dear Alice, but first things first." Irene leaned back in her chair with a lighted cigarette and composed herself to listen once more to Godfrey.

He strode to the fireplace to rest a hand upon the carved white-marble mantel. "Whether these artifacts were a Mogul hoard sunk in the fifteenth century, or plunder from ancient Carthage, it was obvious to all the survivors that they were beyond price.

"They also shortly went beyond reach, for an after-gale from the same tremendous storm that had capsized the survivors' vessel, inundated the cavern in which they'd uncovered the treasure. A wave as high as a mast washed the cave and its secrets down the coast's hidden underwater slopes to a burial as sudden and capricious as its exhumation after all these centuries."

"What a tale, my dear Godfrey! I must have a play written from it."

"Alas, my dear Sarah," he rejoined with a bow, "there were no women survivors."

"It does not matter! I will play the heroic part, whatever the gender."

"There are no heroes, only survivors and schemers."

"Then I shall play the blackest villain among them!"

"Is there such a one?" Alice wondered.

"Certainly," Irene said. "You are being blackmailed; that alone is a villainous act. It is but the latest of such committed by the one who has directed this scheme since its inception nearly twenty years ago."

At this announcement we regarded each other in suspicion, for clearly this person must be among us, or there would be no point to the evening.

Then Irene nodded to me. "Nell, if you would be so kind as to pass the example of your handiwork among the party . . ." I produced my drawing of the compass rose pieced together from the tattooed letters. Then she took up the tale: "So there were almost twenty men, of high and low birth, cast shoeless together on an unknown coast with a treasure they had glimpsed but seen vanish from their grasp.

"It was not many years later that the first of the clues to the group's existence surfaced—or sank, rather. For that twilight evening in the early eighties, when Bram Stoker attempted to save an apparent suicide from the Thames, was the beginning of my acquaintance with the . . . ah, case, shall we call it?"

Irene smiled as she stood and began to walk around the circle of listeners, always the actress and, as such, careful to address each one in turn. She paused before Jerseyman.

"There were some irregularities in the death, for Bram was unable to revive the man. First was the matter of his missing finger—the middle one on the left hand, commonly called the second finger, since the thumb is disregarded. The finger was completely severed to the first knuckle, which struck me even at the time as deliberate, for no accident is so neat.

"Then there was the tattoo I discovered upon the dead man's chest. Nell, will you pass around the first illustration? Even then my reliable companion recorded the anomalies we encountered.

"Strangest of all was the man's behavior. Mr. Stoker saw him hurtle over the railing and into the water. He resisted all efforts to save him—and Bram is well over six feet in height and brawny besides. The man acted as if fleeing what Bram described as some 'devilish pursuer.' No one came forward to claim the victim or to edify the authorities as to his identity.

"It was not until Miss Huxleigh and I discovered a second body in the same condition being removed from the Seine several years later that I suspected that the two deaths were linked. We have little testimony as to the second man's state of mind at the time of death, although the body bore bruises, but his left-hand middle finger had been similarly cut off and his chest was tattooed—with a different letter. Nell."

I passed around the second initial, pleased by the polite mystification on their faces. One was feigning. Could it be the ever-on-stage actress, Sarah? The oily Viscount? The well-schooled but socially ambitious duchess? The loyal doctor and lover? The captain? The humble sailor we knew as Jerseyman? This was becoming more instructive than a melodrama. I redoubled my efforts to take exhaustive notes.

"But let us set dead sailors aside for a moment," Irene said so judiciously that I felt I had only to turn my head to see the two corpses neatly laid out on the perimeter of the chamber.

"Miss Huxleigh's recording hand was set to work again only recently in Paris, when a young woman of fine family was abducted from the Bois de Boulogne, rendered senseless and tattooed with yet a third letter of the alphabet, 'E'. When we found the pair who had assaulted her, we found a fourth and last tattooed letter. Together, they made the French compass points—*Nord, Sud, Est* and *Oest.*''

"This is ridiculous!" the viscount interrupted, his face white against its hirsute adornments. "This is a children's parlor game—compass letters and tattoos. I have better things to do."

"No doubt," said Alice in firm accents. "One of them may be explaining to the prince how bricks of palace sealing wax have played a role in this conspiracy for nearly twenty years. I believe your induction as secretary precedes that by some time."

The viscount sat back, but not comfortably.

"I agree that it is a sad tangle, gentleman," Irene resumed, "but bear with me. It took many years for these events to occur; their tracing has taken weeks; their telling will require only minutes. And the finding of the guilty party behind them all will occupy only seconds."

"You claim," the captain said, "that all of these circumstances are linked to the shipwreck and the treasure?"

"And to murder, sir." Irene smiled tightly at the sudden silence that smothered the room. Not even a shoe creaked. "It happens that the tattooed young lady—who is absent because she is no longer relevant to the case—is the daughter of a man who purportedly committed suicide in Monte Carlo in eighteen seventy-three, a man who bore a tattoo. Claude Montpensier."

"And despite his death and disgrace," Godfrey said, still standing by the fireplace, "Claude Montpensier proved to be the ultimate clue to our puzzle, for his was the only name that we knew for certain would be listed among the passengers on the doomed yacht."

"What of the crew?" Jerseyman asked truculently. "Don't we poor deck-swabbers count?"

"Crew listings are carelessly kept and subject to last-minute change," Godfrey said, reasonably enough.

Jerseyman lifted his empty flute with a scowl. The doctor went to fill it.

Captain Rousseau fidgeted on the delicate sofa, too dainty to contain his bulk. "A passenger could come aboard at the last minute in another's place, too."

Dr. Hoffman moved discreetly among us, refilling glasses all around, except mine, for I needed no champagne when I was taking notes.

"The point, Captain," Godfrey said, "is not who might have come aboard unofficially; the point is that I found at the Office of Marine Records a ship's passenger list that included the name of the late Claude Montpensier."

All of us sat forward intently, even the women, who were presumed to be innocent. The viscount stroked his mustaches and affected a disinterested look. The captain sat back heavily, as if shocked. Could he have commanded the doomed ship himself? Why else was he present this evening?

"Our sole known survivor," Godfrey went on, eyeing the increasingly inebriated Jerseyman, "cannot recall the name of the vessel. I reveal now that it was the three-masted schooner *Solace*, out of Monte Carlo. It was struck by a gigantic storm and sank on April twenty-third, eighteen sixty-nine, off the north coast of Crete. We had already determined that the fragment of coast depicted in the conjoined tattoos drawn by Miss Huxleigh had to be Crete."

"Why? Why must it be Crete?" the captain demanded, his voice hoarse with some emotion.

"Because," said Irene, "that is where the *Solace* was headed and where her survivors washed ashore. It also is where the duchess has been pressured of late to direct Prince Albert's oceanographic expedition. Obviously, at least one survivor of this wreck deeply wishes to return to the site. With the drownings of the sailors and the recent slaughter of the Indian sailor who had tattooed the men originally—and with the passage of time and the scattering of the conspirators—few remain to claim the prize. Now that the means—the prince's innovative exploration equipment—exists to raise the treasure, you, Captain, as master of the prince's yacht, are conveniently placed for such a scheme."

Captain Rousseau sputtered for a moment, then began coughing. Dr. Hoffman succored him at once with a glass of mineral water.

"He is not a young man, Madame Norton," the physician said, standing beside the coughing man, "and he has received a shock. I would not press him too hard."

The captain had taken a few swallows from the glass and now shook his head as if to clear it. "No, no. I am disturbed, that is all, because only today the prince told me that he wished to go to Crete instead of to Corsica."

"Excuse me if I doubt you. Perhaps, Captain," Irene said with silky indifference, "you would not object to two of these gentlemen inspecting your person for a tattoo. We already know that the viscount was not on the ill-fated voyage."

"How?" that gentleman demanded, as if angry to be left out of so devious a plot.

The Divine Sarah broke her silence with great style. "Because, my silly goose, you were foolish enough to duel 'my son' and let yourself be bared from throat to navel. And quite a circuitous trip it was; you should eat with more moderation, my friend. Then you would not require a corset for court affairs."

The viscount stood, his face as red as a Blue Coast peach. "The duel . . . your son? It was all a ruse to disrobe me?"

"Yes," replied Sarah with devastating brevity. "And my son was not my son, but my friend Irene."

The viscount glanced at Irene, then back to the actress. "This is outrageous. You mean to say that a *woman* bested me in a duel? Ridiculous!"

"Like many ridiculous things, it is also true," Irene said. "You forget I am . . . was . . . an actress also."

"You cannot 'act' swordsmanship, Madame."

"I did not need to. I have had some instruction in the art, and your skills are sadly spoiled for want of worthy opponents. But the duel was never the point, if you will; the point was whether or not you bore a tattoo. And you do not. Hence, you are innocent . . . of this, at least."

While we had enjoyed witnessing the viscount's discomfiture—like all bullies, he had a legion of victims eager to see him fall—no one's attention had been on the captain.

That changed in an instant. We heard a horrible cry and turned. The captain was lurching from his seat, his eyes nearly rolled back into his head, a ghastly look of dread upon his florid features. He twisted like a wounded whale, then stalked forward stiff-legged.

Dr. Hoffman and Godfrey moved toward him, both at once. Alice and I were frozen in horror, but Irene and Sarah were rushing toward the stricken man like Florence Nightingales.

His flailing arms repulsed the men and gave the women pause. In the next awful seconds, we watched him put his hands to his throat and begin to strangle himself!

"Stop, sir!" Godfrey ordered, rushing in to drag the madman's hands down.

The captain's strength was phenomenal. He pushed Godfrey back as if he had been a straw in the wind, then turned and bolted for the closed window.

"My God!" came the viscount's strangled voice.

At full tilt, the captain hurtled through latched panes of glass and the fastened shutters beyond. Night erupted into the candlelit chamber as if a giant fist had punched into our gathering.

A tinkling and splintering sound ran ragged up my nerves. Irene and Godfrey, with the viscount and the doctor close behind them, ran into the hall and then outside.

Alice had swooned, and Sarah tended her. Jerseyman sagged on the sofa, three sheets to the wind on the finest French champagne. I loosened my hands from the fists they had made and lowered them from my cheeks. Curious—or brave—I treaded over the few shards of glass that had fallen inside and reached the window.

The captain lay in the garden a half-story below, Irene and Godfrey kneeling beside his unconscious form, the doctor and the viscount standing behind them.

Irene looked up, illuminated with a kind of unholy radiance by the muted candlelight spilling from the window.

"Nell," she said, "will you fetch a candelabra to the window so we may see? I must know whether he bears a tattoo before he awakens and becomes quite unmanageable again."

Chapter Thirty-nine

ULTIMATE REVELATIONS

❧

A l i c e   H e i n e had begun to recover from her swoon and lay upon her brocaded sofa, attended by Dr. Hoffman and Sarah Bernhardt, while Jerseyman enjoyed a swoon of a different nature on the other sofa.

Upon regaining consciousness, the captain had been carried upstairs. Although two housemen were restraining him, hoarse shouts and muffled thumps indicated that he still was quite mad, if no longer able to damage himself or the house.

"Well, Irene, that ends it," Godfrey said gloomily, standing at the shattered French window, his hands in his pockets. "Never has a matter been so resistant to unraveling. I was certain the captain was our man, but you saw Rousseau's chest for yourself, bare of a tattoo. Apparently, the questions drove away his reason. I know I fear for my own. What is this nonsense I hear about a duel with the viscount?"

Irene glanced at that individual, who sat impassively in a corner chair.

"Nothing vital," she said vaguely.

Crossing the room, she gazed down in turn at the comatose Jerseyman and the reviving Alice. Then she strode to the fireplace, extracted a cigarette from her case and lit it with a taper.

"I am glad that the captain's injuries are only superficial. I think, my friends, that we have just observed an application of the potion that drove at least two sailors to drown themselves, one in the Thames, the other in the Seine. Singh sampled it also; otherwise, he would not have been an easy target for stabbing. Tonight Captain Rousseau came too close to exposing the culprit who hopes to claim all the treasure for himself. Thus he was rewarded."

"Why attack Captain Rousseau?" I asked.

"He'd agreed to aid the master conspirator, of course. That's why it was only necessary to divert the prince's yacht to Crete. The captain already had been bribed to help recover the treasure."

"But, Irene, who is left to suspect?" Godfrey asked. "You admit the viscount is innocent—"

She smiled. "I said he was innocent of tattoos and innocent of blame in this scheme. I did not say he was innocent. That would be going too far."

"Oh, speak sense," I said in turn. "You have run out of suspects, unless you claim that Louise's uncle—"

"No, of course not. Why do you think I sent him home to Paris?"

"—or that Alice blackmailed herself."

"Devious, but impossible. There were no women survivors. She could not have been a passenger on that voyage, anyway, being only eleven years of age and in New Orleans then. I sent a cable."

"Irene!" Alice sat up, her blue eyes batting vaguely in the candlelight. "You sent a cable to determine my whereabouts?"

"One never knows. Even Sarah may be suspect."

"How delightful!" cried the actress. "A murderess! My supreme role."

Irene merely laughed.

"What exactly injured the captain?" I thought to ask.

Irene smiled her approval. "I had not anticipated that we

would be treated to a demonstration. A natural poison, not fatal, though the madness it induces can produce lethal results. I suspect mandrake root, whose strong taste could be veiled in strong drink. Obviously, the captain paid scant attention to the liquid the doctor gave him; he would expect something medicinal to taste unpleasant. We must ask Monsieur Cremieux, the chemist, about mandrake tomorrow."

"And tonight?" Godfrey queried. "Where do we stand tonight?"

"At the apex of this long-standing accumulation of crimes. Only Mr. Sherlock Holmes is accustomed to stand on such an Olympian height, where he alone knows all, reveals all. I now claim that shadowy eminence for myself, and I wish to savor it."

"Irene! You can't keep us in the dark any longer!" I had not meant to sound so injured. "Surely we deserve to know everything."

"You do. You all do. First, I was not disappointed to see that Captain Rousseau was untattooed, although I had to confirm it. You see, I know at last who has instigated every turning of this plot."

Irene turned to Dr. Hoffman, who still knelt by the recovering Alice. "She will be quite all right, Doctor? Another shock should not harm her health?"

He nodded soberly, his intelligent dark eyes anxious at the implication of Irene's question. Was he tending a murderess?

I stared at the fragile Alice. My mind struggled to concoct a plot that made her the mastermind, one who directed even the clever ruse of blackmailing herself. Perhaps monetary gain was not the aim of this scheme; certainly Alice would wish the prince to make a prestigious archeological discovery. Had she learned of the treasure years ago from some conspirator? Had she begun lately to collude with her blackmailer?

"Alice," Irene said in a grim voice, "you will not like what you hear, but I have no choice. The murderer of sailors, the survivor of the *Solace* who has always intended that he and he alone reap the treasure's benefits, your blackmailer—" only I noted Irene's glance to Godfrey and saw his hand tense upon something in his pocket "—is none other than one most dear to you and trusted—"

Good Lord! The prince! He was old enough, powerful enough, perfectly placed to . . .

"—your advisor, your lover, your good friend—"

Alice's eyes fluttered wildly behind closed lids as Dr. Hoffman grasped her wrist.

"—Emile Hoffman," Irene finished, lowering her eyes to the kneeling man.

"Emile?" Alice's voice quavered with disbelief, but the doctor had loosed her hand to turn and stare at Irene.

"You are mad, Madame!"

"Am I? Would you care to remove your coat and shirt?"

"Ridiculous. I need not expose myself. The facts show—"

"The facts show that you were on Madiera in the early eighties, Doctor, which is where you met Alice. But why were you there if not to observe modern sea-exploration techniques? Those limpid waters are world-renowned for their diving opportunities. The love affair was unexpected. How it must have maddened you, then, when Alice's father compelled your love to leave a man too poor for her—when an emperor's ransom awaited you! Had you killed Claude Montpensier years earlier? No matter, it was then that you determined to have all to yourself, to become as rich as a Heine frere.

"You were helpless to raise the hoard then, although the years allowed you to eliminate any rivals who crossed your path. Then came the worst blow, Alice's liaison with the Crown Prince of Monaco. Long before, you'd evolved the plan of using the palace sealing wax, having treated the

Cremieux family's inherited arthritis since you were first a physician, and thus having ready, if clandestine, access to this rare substance. Do not deny it; Godfrey has interrogated Monsieur Cremieux, who was unaware of your secret purposes. Yet fate provided a final irony: Alice's new love, met on Madiera of all places, would become the means of wedding you to your long-lost treasure. You blackmailed your old love, using her one-time liaison with *yourself*, to win what has become your only love—the riches you glimpsed so long ago. Now do you care to reveal your chest?"

"No!" Alice rose defiantly, clinging to the sofa arm. "It cannot be Emile. He is a physician, not a murderer."

The viscount speedily stepped over, pulling Dr. Hoffman to his feet. "I had my shirt sliced off my back in a duel with a woman, Doctor. The least you can do is to oblige the lady with a look. I cannot guarantee what she will do if she has to resort to a rapier with you, but I can testify that she is capable of slicing you to ribbons."

Godfrey had joined the viscount in pinioning the man, staring piercingly at Irene at further mention of the duel. (Irene's explanations of the evening, I suspected, would not end until my friends returned to the privacy of their suite.) Even Jerseyman, roused from his stupor, stumbled over to Dr. Hoffman.

It was a dreadful scene: the candlelit salon so civilized, the group force pressing on the lone man so brutal.

Dr. Hoffman shook off their arms. He stared at Alice's distraught face, then lowered his gaze to his shirtfront and began undoing the buttons.

The only sound in the chamber was the pop of mother-of-pearl disks snapping free of starched linen. I could not bear to watch, not least because Dr. Hoffman had once been held up to me as a potential beau—surely long before Irene suspected his connection to the case.

I was torn between hoping she was wrong and berating myself for wishing my friend to fail.

When the shirt hung open, Dr. Hoffman lost his appetite for further revelation. The viscount did not hesitate, pushing the flimsy singlet aside to bare the man's chest while Godfrey held him.

Alice had turned her head away, but Sarah had drawn closer. I could not look, and then I could not bear *not* to look.

Irene sighed, and it was not in relief.

I looked at the man in our midst, suddenly sure that he, too, had proven as innocent as a lamb. Then—like an oriental dragon ambushing my eyes from a vase I had assumed to be unadorned—a massive, serpentine tattoo came into view: the ornate compass rose we had pieced together so laboriously from the marked flesh of three dead men and an abducted girl. The hand-sized insignia covered the man's skin above his heart with a grasping, painted fist of greed and guilt.

We all stared, unspeaking, at this unspeakable evidence.

"Not Singh's work." Jerseyman pushed closer, squinting. "'Cept for the 'E.' Singh never blurred his lines like that."

Dr. Hoffman looked up at last, his face angry. "None of you fools were capable of recovering my treasure! Why should I share it, when the plan was mine, when the means finally became mine? Fate! All fate, from the moment Alice's father wrested her from me. I swore not to die a poor man. No, this tattoo is not the work of some scurvy sea rat, save for the first letter. A discreet Marseilles tattooer added the letters as the number of the surviving Quarter members dwindled. This entire tattooed design is my invention, as this entire scheme is mine. As the treasure is mine."

Alice covered her face with white, beringed hands. "Dear God, I'd noticed a tattoo years ago. Emile was strangely secretive about it, never allowing me to see it clearly. I thought him embarrassed by a youthful stupidity, but the youthful stupidity was all mine, *is* all mine."

"Alice, no!" Irene eyed the captive. "You mustn't dwell on the past. You have a dreadful choice to make in the present."

"I? How is that?"

Irene nodded to Dr. Hoffman. He stood staring at Irene as if hoping to brand her face with his searing disdain. "If we charge him, these murders will be difficult to prove. And it will give him ample opportunity to reveal your former relationship."

Alice regarded the doctor for a long moment. His glance dropped without meeting hers. "I suppose it will," she said in a cool, rational tone. "And the alternative, dear Irene? I am sure that you have thought of an alternative."

"He will be free to leave here, to leave the Riviera," Irene declared. "No one will charge him or pursue him. The captain, when he recovers, will 'discover' the trove during the expedition, and the prince will ensure that the discovery is discreetly announced to historians and scholars. The treasure will grace the museums of the countries involved, as the find will enhance the prince's oceanographic reputation. His success will speed your marriage, for he will earn the people's incontestable favor for such an exploit. All surviving members of the compact who come forward, such as Louise Montpensier and Jerseyman, shall be 'rewarded' from the coffers of the Duchess of Richelieu for their long travail."

"I imagine," Alice said slowly, "that number does not include Dr. Hoffman."

"I imagine," Irene answered, "that such a decision will be up to the Duchess of Richelieu."

Dr. Hoffman shuddered and turned his face into his bared shoulder. "In reaching for all, I have lost all; I have even aided Alice's marriage to another." He looked for the first—and last—time directly at her. "I swear to you, I never would have revealed our former relationship to the prince.

You had money, some ten millions, they say. Why begrudge me mine? The blackmail was a means to an end, a threat I never meant to use."

"And now, Emile? If making good on that threat could gain you the treasure?"

"To defend my freedom, my fortune, my life—"

Alice turned away. "A pity that you did not consider the lives, freedom and fortune of those around you. A pity that you did not consider *me*."

"All this—the shipwreck, the discovery, the compact— had happened before we met."

"The first murder had not. Irene is right; meeting me brought you only dishonor. Please do not compound it by trying to justify your actions. May he go, Irene? I really would like him to go."

Irene nodded.

We watched Emile Hoffman compose himself; the neat hands I had observed closed his shirt, smoothed his disordered hair and beard, straightened his jacket. He was the competent doctor again, a far cry from the man who had slipped poison into a glass before our eyes but an hour ago.

As he began to leave the room, the viscount barred his way.

"Monsieur, your actions have threatened the well-being of a prince to whom I owe my allegiance. I doubt that these English and Americans have the stomach to enforce their wishes that you decamp quietly, but I assure you that I do. You will never again trouble the principality of Monaco or any of its royal house. Forget your treasure; it is a state secret now, and too dangerous to meddle in."

After a moment's silence, the doctor passed into the hall and out of the house. Through the broken window we heard the sound of his departing footsteps.

Jerseyman snored gently from the sofa that he had reclaimed.

Irene cocked her head at the viscount. "*Touché*, sir. I thought, given an opportunity, that you would snatch the prize for yourself."

"I would have," he replied with a worldly smile, "but you have given me no opportunity. Good evening, ladies, sir."

He, too, withdrew, and I found myself actually liking him.

Godfrey's hand left his pocket. He flexed the fingers to remove a cramp. "What a peaceful ending to such a long and bloody trail."

"All is well that ends well, my dear Godfrey." Sarah, with Oscar still snuggled on her shoulder, embraced Irene. She kissed Irene's cheeks—hesitated as a wicked gleam sparked her aquamarine eyes—then kissed both of Godfrey's cheeks also.

"My congratulations, dear friends, on the most entertaining evening I have spent offstage. I much dislike ruining another's climax, but I have a vital announcement. I will debut my Hamlet in Monte Carlo, privately, before my friends at the casino theater, in celebration of the discovery of this formidable treasure. Irene may play Ophelia, although the part does not suit her. So, Alice, I shall launch your Monte Carlo into a shining center of all that is cultured!"

At that moment, Oscar, in a fit of joy at his mistress's news, no doubt, wound himself firmly around her forehead.

The Divine Sarah frowned beneath her impressive tiara. "Or should I debut here in 'Cleopatra'? Oscar takes direction so well. He would make a divine asp."

Chapter Forty

A BAKER STREET
CONVERSATION

❧

"**It was** an uneventful journey, Holmes?"

"Quite. I have hopes of discovering the missing and so-called murdered girl living happily with her new husband in America, but first I will have to send some cablegrams. In the meantime, I have spoken to Le Villard—the best of his debased profession, a reasonable policeman—and Madame Montpensier is free of all suspicion, if not of a rather unfortunate husband."

"And Le Villard is satisfied?"

"He could not be otherwise. A promising detective, Watson, although possessing no very inspired methods. He has requested a new monograph of me, one on the varieties of sealing wax."

"Sealing wax? Ah, well, it will occupy you between cases."

"Indeed it will."

"Quite some fairy tale, isn't it, Holmes, this treasure just discovered on Crete?" I rattled my newspaper. "On an oceanographic expedition, so it says. A prince of Monaco was involved. You heard nothing about it while you were in Monte Carlo? That seems odd."

"No, Watson, it was found shortly after my departure. I took a rather circuitous route back to England. I must beg you not to question me further. The matter may never be made public, although I can say the world is now safe from the depravity of a demonic botanist. As for this Mediterranean find, I'm not surprised to learn of rich treasure thereabouts. Those waters have always attracted pirates."

"This goes back much further, Holmes. To the glory that was Greece, or Minos, anyway."

"That's as may be, but I am sure that such a hoard was the object of far more recent glory and greed. A pity that my schedule did not permit me to lounge about the neighborhood; undoubtedly I would have gotten wind of this most conveniently unearthed treasure. But that is sheer speculation, Watson, and I prefer facts for mental company. How did you occupy your idle hours while I was away?"

"Oh, messed about. Tidying my papers, that sort of thing."

"Working on the narratives of my cases, were you?"

"I imagine you noticed that the ink bottle had sprung a leak."

"Nothing so obvious."

"I thought I'd work up the matter of the King of Bohemia and the American adventuress."

"I doubt that *the* woman would care to be remembered in a story in the *Strand* magazine, Watson."

"Irene Adler, being dead, has nothing to say about it, Holmes."

"I would be careful in my statement of facts if I were you, Watson. It is best not to make assumptions."

"The papers reported the deaths of a Mr. and Mrs. Godfrey Norton in a train wreck in the Alps—on the St. Gothard line—shortly after Irene Adler married and fled London last spring. I am perfectly convinced that I may say anything I like about the lady, as long as the facts support me."

"Well, Watson, the quill is mightier than the sword and will leap in where angels fear to tread."

"I fear you have mixed your metaphors, Holmes."

"Still, I suggest caution. If one aspires to print, one can never know when a careless word or phrase may come back to haunt one."

"Irene Adler will haunt nothing now but some Alpine meadow. A pity. A greater pity that you and she never met face-to-face, undisguised. She was a most . . . perspicacious and appealing woman, despite her dubious memory, was she not?"

"That she was, Watson, that she was. Now, where have you put my shag while I was gone? I am used to a certain inspired disorder in my possessions that serves to counter the impeccably logical order in my mind . . ."

AFTERWORD

❧

The foregoing narrative is a collation of the recently discovered diaries of Penelope Huxleigh, an obscure Shropshire parson's daughter, with fragments of previously unknown writings attributed to John H. Watson, M.D.

Readers will be intrigued by the light this work sheds on personalities of an earlier day and a farther place, particularly on that vexing figure that many ordinarily intelligent scholars attempt to dismiss as a mere figment of the collective—or even the literary—imagination; Sherlock Holmes, the English consulting detective.

As companion to Irene Adler, the enterprising opera singer turned problem solver, Penelope Huxleigh was as closely situated as Holmes's biographer, Dr. Watson, to record for posterity the events surrounding this equally charismatic figure.

The current compilation touches on some obscure points in the Holmes "canon" as recorded by Dr. Watson and further proves the historicity of all involved, despite benighted opinions to the contrary, masquerading as literary scholarship.

"My practice has extended recently to the Continent," Holmes tells his biographer over his old brierroot pipe in the adventure published as "The Sign of the Four" in 1890.

Sherlock Holmes was indeed involved in the matter of a "French will" (now known to have been referred to him by Godfrey Norton), and did permit the French detective, Le Villard, to translate his monographs into the French language. The full collection may be viewed today at the Vielle Bibliotheque in Paris (where also may be found that formidable volume, the *Necronomicon*), and it is a remarkable series of documents. The English versions, alas, have vanished and would be worth a pretty penny if found.

It should be noted that Penelope Huxleigh's disdain of the French is a reaction to the day's Gallic chauvinism. These diaries are presented unexpurgated.

Holmes himself was highly complimentary to François Le Villard of the French detective service, a courtesy he did not extend to his compatriots at Scotland Yard.

Dr. Watson does not record that Holmes assisted Le Villard on the Montpensier case, but briefly alludes to Holmes's locating a girl in America after a female relative had been suspected of murdering her; the account can be found at the end of that famous tale, "The Hound of the Baskervilles."

This citation raises more questions than it settles, vis-à-vis the Huxleigh diaries. Dr. Watson claims that Madame Montpensier was suspected of murdering her step-daughter, a Mlle. Carere, not a step-niece. He also says that the young lady was found alive and married in New York City some six months later (which one assumes is better than being found dead and married).

This is not the first—nor will it be the last—time that two separate historical sources provide contrary material for speculation. My research proves one fact undeniable: "Carere" was Honoria Montpensier's maiden name!

Could the good doctor have been trifling with factual details again, in order to avoid embarrassment for the principals, or for himself? That seems likely; the Huxleigh material agrees impeccably with the historical facts (including Bram Stoker's rescue attempt of a drowned man missing one finger, who was never identified) and was never submitted for publication while the principals lived, unlike the Watson accounts.

It seems even likelier that Sherlock Holmes kept far more information than previously suspected from his Boswell.

This intriguing speculation sets the hackles to rising on the literary hound. Imagine what amazing exploits Holmes may have engaged in unknown to history, especially his adventures on the Continent, which are scantily recorded—by Dr. Watson, at least! Further study of the voluminous Huxleigh diaries could prove enlightening.

Other points in the Huxleigh narrative coincide scrupulously with the historical facts.

On Oct. 30, 1889, Alice, Duchess of Richelieu, *née* Heine, did marry Prince Albert Grimaldi of Monaco a month after the death of his father, Prince Charles—and almost a year after the events of this narrative. The nuptials took place in Paris, where both a civil and a religious ceremony were necessary. The Nortons and Penelope Huxleigh attended the latter, as did Sarah Bernhardt. Newspaper accounts cite the "angelic" singing of one Madame Norton, a friend of the bride.

The newlyweds' triumphal return to Monte Carlo was made in the following January, to Monégasque cheers. Thus Alice Heine became the first beautiful, blond American Princess of Monaco. Film star Grace Kelly would repeat this role sixty-seven years later, when she married Prince Rainier, Prince Albert's great-grandson by his brief first marriage to the "Scottish" Lady Hamilton.

As Her Serene Highness, Princess Alice won the people's hearts for requiring the casino to contribute five million francs to local charities. By 1892, the Monte Carlo Opera House was completed. It was renowned for mounting exquisite and ground-breaking works well into the twentieth century.

Such endurance was not granted to the royal couple. Although Prince Albert named two yachts after her, Alice ultimately proved to be a poor sailor. The prince became engrossed in his sea-going expeditions and in establishing his world-renowned oceanographic museum at Monte Carlo. His and his wife's paths diverged; there were rumors that Princess Alice took lovers, which would not surprise readers of the foregoing narrative. Blind Prince Charles proved not to have been so blind after all: the fairy-tale couple separated in 1902, never to reconcile, although neither did they divorce.

Prince Albert's "mothballed" attitudes toward women, as Alice described them to Penelope Huxleigh, may have hastened the estrangement. Shortly before the separation, the prince told the dancer Loie Fuller: "You American women are too new. You leave too little room for the lords of creation. How can we hold our own if you make inroads upon the intellectual domain which has always been sacred to us? Your women are cold sepulchers; they have too much head power. They may be statuesque, but masterful women are an abomination."

It is fortunate that the prince did not have more dealings with Irene Adler Norton than he did.

As for the Divine Sarah, she continued to live on her usual lavish scale, both financially and emotionally, and publicly debuted as Hamlet in 1899, becoming renowned in her later years for her portrayals of male roles.

No documentation exists on the longevity or final disposition of the Indian green snake known as Oscar.

Fiona Witherspoon, Ph.D., A.I.A.*

November 5, 1990

*Advocates of Irene Adler